THE THEFT OF SUNLIGHT

THE THEFT OF SUNLIGHT

INTISAR KHANANI

HARPER TEEN
An Imprint of HarperCollinsPublishers

HarperTeen is an imprint of HarperCollins Publishers.

The Theft of Sunlight
Copyright © 2021 by Intisar Khanani
Map art © 2021 by Diana Sousa
All rights reserved. Printed in the United States of America.
No part of this book may be used or reproduced in any manner whatsoever without
written permission except in the case of brief quotations embodied in critical articles
and reviews. For information address HarperCollins Children's Books, a division of
HarperCollins Publishers, 195 Broadway, New York, NY 10007.
www.epicreads.com

Library of Congress Cataloging-in-Publication Data
Names: Khanani, Intisar, author.
Title: The theft of sunlight / Intisar Khanani.
Description: First edition. | New York, NY : HarperTeen, [2021] | Series: [Dauntless
    path ; 2] | Summary: Disabled country girl Rae reluctantly becomes an attendant
    to Princess Alyrra, navigating palace life while helping investigate the child
    snatchers who stole the sister of Rae's best friend.
Identifiers: LCCN 2020023422 | ISBN 978-0-06-283574-1 (hardcover)
Subjects: CYAC: Courts and courtiers—Fiction. | People with disabilities—Fiction. |
    Princesses—Fiction. | Missing children—Fiction. | Magic—Fiction. | Fantasy.
Classification: LCC PZ7.K526524 The 2021 | DDC [Fic]—dc23
LC record available at https://lccn.loc.gov/2020023422

Typography by Corina Lupp
21 22 23 24 25   PC/LSCH   10 9 8 7 6 5 4 3 2 1

❖

First Edition

For every girl who chooses the hard road
and uses the fire in her heart to light the way.

THE THEFT OF SUNLIGHT

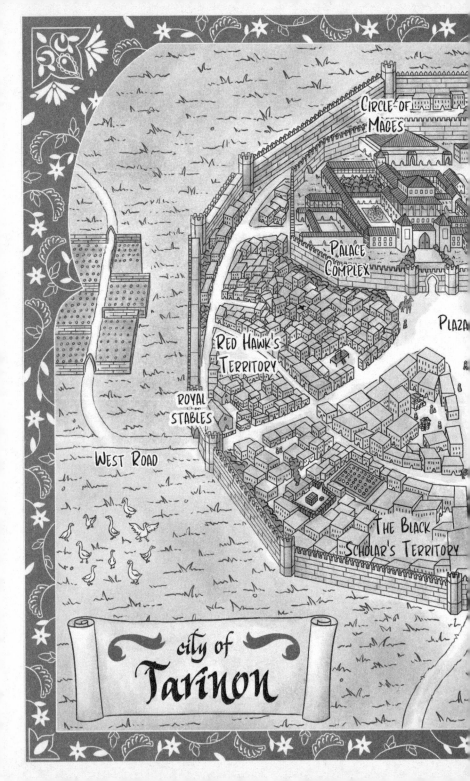

CIRCLE OF
MAGES

PALACE
COMPLEX

PLAZA

RED HAWK'S
TERRITORY

ROYAL
STABLES

WEST ROAD

THE BLACK
SCHOLAR'S TERRITORY

city of
Tarinon

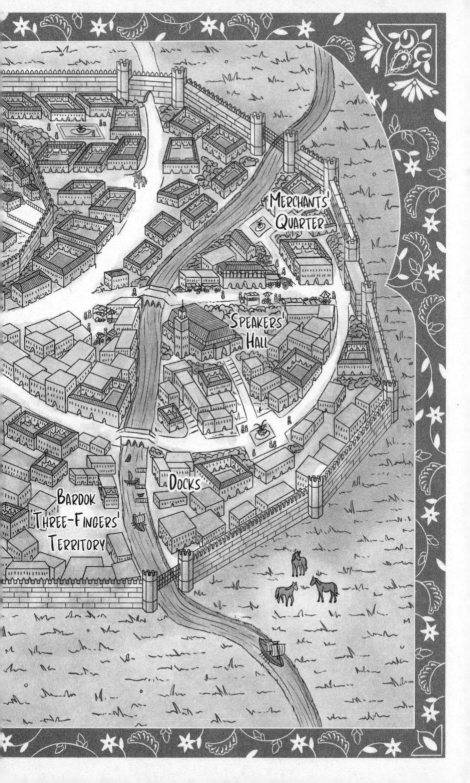

CHAPTER

1

T here's a mangy dog crouched beneath the second-to-last vegetable cart. As a rule, I avoid mangy dogs. Especially ones with bloodshot eyes and a clearly infected paw. But this is a sad-looking creature, its narrow face streaked with mud and its coat thinned to almost nothing over its ribs, skin scaly and pink beneath the grime.

"Something wrong?" Ani asks as she switches her brightly woven market basket to her other arm. At her side, her little sister, Seri, dips a booted toe into a puddle left from this morning's spring rains. The crowd around us shifts and moves, a sea of brown faces and bright clothing filling the wide town square to brimming. For a moment I lose sight of the dog as a group of older women push past, skirts flapping around sturdy boots.

"No," I say, turning to my friend. "I'm just wondering where Bean is. Have you seen her, Seri?"

Seri looks up, twin black braids swinging. "Oh yes! She's

across by the horses. Should I go get her?"

"Yes, please."

Seri grins and scampers away after my own little sister.

"Seri! Watch where you're going!" Ani calls helplessly.

"She's quick," I assure her. There's not much harm a six-year-old can come to at Sheltershorn's market day; for all the crowd of shoppers, almost everyone knows one another, and no one would be so stupid as to come galloping through on a horse. In truth, the biggest danger here would be the mucky puddles, and I'm pretty sure Seri loves running through those.

"Do you need anything else?" Ani asks, glancing into her basket. "Mama wanted me to find radishes, but I haven't seen any."

"Might still be too early," I observe. "They should have them next week. Ours are only just starting to mature."

Our home may be a horse farm, but Mama and my middle sister, Niya, make sure we have a few beds of greens and vegetables, and our early spring greens are growing strong this year. Really, the only reason we're here at the first big market day of the spring is to catch up with our friends.

Ani and I are still chatting by the cart when Seri comes racing back, dragging the much taller Bean by the hand. "I found her!"

"I was busy," Bean protests, nearly tripping as she jerks to a stop before us. At fourteen, she's like a young colt unused to the way of her limbs, still awkward and liable to knock things over, including herself. "Couldn't it have waited, Rae?"

I pretend to consider this. "But there's someone under the cart there I thought you might be able to help."

"Someone—?" Bean echoes at the same time that Ani swivels

around to look under the cart.

"That thing is—it's *diseased*!" Ani exclaims, reaching to grab Seri before she can dart closer for a look. "You can't mean for Bean to approach it?"

"Bean has a way with animals," I say serenely. Even mangy, red-eyed creatures that could scare away grown men.

"Oh, you poor baby," Bean croons, squatting beside us. The dog looks over and wags its scruffy tail once, proving my point.

"Come on out, sweet baby." Bean holds out an inviting hand. "We'll get you cleaned up and then *no one*"—she spares Ani a hard look—"can call you mean names. And maybe my sister Niya can take care of your paw. She's very good with cuts. And I know a thing or two about them as well."

The dog, lured by Bean's innate kindness, creeps out from under the cart and sits at her feet, earning a series of exclamations from the adults around us.

"Eh, Rae-girl!" the vegetable woman cries, her long silver earrings swinging. She's known us since we were born, and isn't the least surprised to see Bean with a bedraggled stray. "Take that creature away now. I can't have it by my food."

"Of course, auntie," I say, dipping my chin in respect. "Bean, do you think the dog can make it to our cart? You know where Mama left it."

"Sure she can," Bean says, one hand buried in the patchy bit of fur about the dog's neck, scratching vigorously. I wince. "Just . . . make sure to wash your hands afterward, all right?"

Bean casts me a disgusted look and rises to her feet. "Come on, little lady. You can ride in our cart, and we'll get you all cleaned up at home."

"You aren't actually taking that creature home?" Ani breathes. Even she doesn't dare say such a thing loud enough for Bean to hear.

"Of course she is," Seri asserts, her eyes shining with adoration.

"Someone has to take care of it," I say as the dog limps off beside my sister. "She'll fit right in with all of Bean's other reclamation projects. You'll see, Mama won't even say a word."

But Ani's not listening anymore. Seri's run ahead to catch up with Bean and the dog. Ani calls after her, "Seri—you may watch only! No touching! Bean, see that she doesn't!"

I suppress a grin and walk on, knowing that Bean will make sure Seri stays safe around the dog. When Ani quits yelling, I point out the final cart in the marketplace. "Good news! I've found your radishes."

Ani's face lights up, and she happily sets to bargaining for them. I wander a little farther on, coming to a stop where the road leaves the square. It's a bright beautiful day, the tall adobe buildings bathed in sunlight, the great wood timbers that strengthen each floor throwing shadows where they extrude from the walls. Above the noise of the market, I can hear birds chittering, and I can still smell the fresh scent of green things blowing in from the plains.

"Now there's a girl who'll end up alone," a voice says somewhere behind me.

I freeze up, my shoulders stiff as old wood. I can't even make myself turn around, or look to see who they might be talking about. I don't have to, anyhow. I know it's me.

"No surprise there," another voice says. "Shame her parents'll have to keep her. No one else will."

I make myself turn to the side and stump away, back toward Ani, because I don't need to see who's talking to know which boys they are. And anyway, I won't end up alone. I've got my sister Niya, same as she's got me.

"What is it?" Ani asks as I reach her. She glances past me. "Were those boys bothering you?"

"No." My voice is hard and flat. I try to ease it a bit. "They didn't say a word to me."

"Yeah, well, that's Finyar's son; he's always full of ugly things. Want me to punch him for you?"

I laugh, taken back to that day Ani and I became friends a good dozen years ago, when she punched a boy who was heckling me and then proceeded to play with Bean. Anyone who would take on bullies and then befriend a toddler couldn't possibly be someone I didn't want to know. Even if I prefer to fight my own battles.

She flexes her fingers now. "You know, you haven't let me punch anyone in *ages*. How are they going to learn their manners if someone doesn't set them straight?"

"They're not worth it," I say easily. That much, at least, is true. They aren't even worth acknowledging. "And it would ruin a lovely day. Let their mothers deal with them."

Ani snorts but lets the subject drop. I loop my arm through hers, and together we make our way back through the market. We spend a half hour catching up with mutual friends before parting ways, Seri pattering off to visit her grandmother and Ani calling admonishments to watch her step.

Ani and I get along wonderfully, Mama once told me,

because at heart we were both cut from the same stubborn cloth, tight-woven and sheltering. Ani would go to war for her friends, and for her sister. And I've learned to do whatever it takes to protect my own sisters: Bean from her hotheadedness, and Niya because of the secret she keeps.

Still, Sheltershorn is a quiet town. There are few dangers, even fewer strangers, and little that threatens us beyond inclement weather and the occasional accident. So, when Ani comes up to our cart over an hour later, as we ready ourselves for the ride back home, it doesn't occur to me that anything can be too wrong. The market is slowly emptying out, the remaining shoppers lingering over their purchases as they catch up with friends. There's nothing apparent to worry about.

"Rae," Ani says, glancing from me to Bean and back again. "Have you seen Seri? I can't find her anywhere. It's been an hour at least."

"What?" Mama asks, coming around the cart.

Inside the cart, seated as far from the dog as possible, my middle sister, Niya, looks up, gray eyes worried.

"It's my sister," Ani says, the gentle brown of her face faintly sallow. "I can't find her."

CHAPTER

2

"Could she have gone off with a friend?" Mama asks, calm as always.

Ani hesitates. "She said she was going to our grandmother's, but when I went to fetch her, Nani said she'd never come. No one's seen her along the way, either. I know she's not at home. I was hoping she'd come back to check on the dog."

Bean frowns. "She only helped me settle it in, and then she went back to you."

"You haven't seen her since?" Ani asks.

We shake our heads.

"We'll help you look," Mama says. "Bean and I will ask the market sellers with you. Rae and Niya, you head to Ani's home and ask everyone along the way. Niya ... you don't mind helping?"

It's not the question it seems to be. In that moment, I know Mama believes something bad has happened to Seri, because she's asking Niya to look for Seri in the way only she can, using the magic that she's kept hidden her whole life. Mama would never ask such a thing unnecessarily.

It's a risk—it always is, when Niya uses her magic—because by this point, we've broken every law there is about harboring a secret talent. She *should* have been taken from us when her powers first manifested, to be trained as a mage in service to the king, but Mama and Baba had met a mage or two by then. They didn't want their child taken away and raised to be a stranger. So they kept her, and hid her, and Niya has trained herself, working small magics around the ranch, and then teaching herself healing to help the animals, and eventually to subtly aid Mama's midwifery patients when nothing else can. Only a handful of people know Niya's secret, and for Mama to ask her to use her gifts now? She's very worried.

"Of course I'll help," Niya says. She grabs the small bag that holds her sewing and hops down from the wagon. "Come on, Rae."

"Were there any strangers here today?" I hear Bean ask as Niya and I start walking. I cock my head, listening, and catch Mama's answer: of course there were a few, but we can't assume it was strangers.

We also can't assume that it wasn't.

"Do you think she could have been . . ." Niya hesitates, and I hear the word she won't say, the one I don't want to speak either.

"That hasn't happened in years," I say, my voice short.

"But it has happened."

I look away. "That's why you need to track her."

It's still possible Seri only popped into a friend's house and is happily eating honey cakes, blissfully unaware of our worry.

But Ani's already been asking about her all over town; someone would have said if they'd seen her.

"Hurry," I say, walking as fast as my uneven gait can take me. Niya keeps pace easily. We call out to the people we see, all of them familiar, and by the time we've arrived at the blacksmith's home, right beside the smithy, there are a dozen more people out looking for Seri. All the children have been sent home, though.

"Rae?" Ani's mother, Shimai, calls out to us as we hurry to her. She stands with two other women just outside her house, one of them holding a bread basket. It's a normal scene. Too normal. It hadn't occurred to me until this moment that Ani's mother wouldn't know about Seri's disappearance. But then she says, sharply, "Seri's not at my mother's, is she?"

I shake my head. "She never went there. Do you know where she could be? Ani and my family are searching the market, and we've asked all along the way here. No one's seen her in the last hour or so."

Beneath the brown of her skin, Shimai's face pales, her lips bloodless. "She has to be here."

"We should mount a proper search," one of her friends says. "Before it gets any later. There's no time to lose."

"I'll check her friends' houses," the other says. "Shimai, where should I—?"

Shimai gives herself a shake and starts forward with a jerk, her expression shifting from panic to determination. She rattles off a short list of friends' names for her friend to check, directs the other to inform her husband, who is absent from the smithy today of all days, and sets off down the street toward the market to rally a proper search. As she hurries past, she says, "Rae, you get your sister somewhere safe. Both of your sisters, just in case. They can stay in my house, if needed."

"Yes, auntie," I say, thankful for the excuse to send Niya into the house.

I stand in the doorway, watching Shimai as she races down the street, her legs flashing beneath her skirts. Behind me, Niya runs upstairs. This is why Mama sent us here: if we can recover a hair or two, or possibly even a ribbon or scrap of cloth that Seri has worn, then Niya might be able to use it to track her.

"Got it," Niya calls from upstairs, and I sag against the doorframe with relief. "Took a hair from her comb."

"Good. What else do you need?"

"Water. I've got everything else."

There's the kitchen, which has the decided advantage of keeping us hidden from sight. "Will a bowl do?"

Niya nods. "Just fine."

"This way." I lead the way through a house I know as well as my own. The adobe walls are smooth and cool, the kitchen shutters pushed open to light the room with its fire grate to one side and its low worktable to the other. I fill a bowl with water from a pitcher while Niya hurries outside, returning a moment later with a leaf in her hand. She pulls the door shut behind her.

I set the bowl before her as she drops onto a cushion before the table. "Do you know how to do it?"

She shrugs, delving into her bag. "I've never tried tracking before, but I know how to make a compass. If I can get the compass to point toward her, rather than north, then we'll have a direction."

"Brilliant." I sometimes wonder if Niya wishes our parents

hadn't hidden her. Wishes she could have learned these things properly instead of fighting her way to each new success, all in secret.

"Not my idea," she mutters. "Heard about it once. It has to do with flow."

I nod and close the connecting door to the kitchen, as well as the shutters. I light a lamp to take the place of the sunlight. When I turn back, Niya has set a leaf on the water, and on top of that, her prized silver needle. She snips a small length of the hair she took from Ani and Seri's room and sets it beside the needle.

There are two ways mages have for working with the latent magic around us—what is often referred to as the current. One can work with the flow of magic, directing it into new uses and directions, or one can work with the patterns that exist already, replicating those with slight shifts to achieve one's aim. Flow tends to be the preferred method taught in Menaiya, because, quite simply, it is easier to master. Niya discovered a long time ago that a fever might be understood as a flow of heat and healing through the body, which her magic could mimic and more efficiently complete without harming the body.

Now she holds one hand over the leaf with its double burden, her head bent so low I can barely see past it. If she starts with the attraction of a magnetized needle toward the North Pole and redirects its flow—from the pole to Seri—we'll have a way to focus our search.

I wait, listening for the sound of someone entering the house. Anything to indicate I need to hide what Niya's doing. I can hear a woman calling to her children somewhere in the distance, and the general sounds of the town: a wagon creaking its way down the road, chickens clucking in someone's backyard, and, faintly, people calling Seri's name.

I swallow and glance back at Niya.

She looks up. "It's not working. I don't know if it's me or . . ."

"Here," I say, catching the end of one of my braids. "Try my hair. See if that works."

Niya takes the bit of hair I snap off and bends over her bowl again. I grip my skirt with my fists and hope, *hope* that it's Niya's magic that isn't working, and not . . . not that Seri is truly beyond our reach.

"It's working," Niya says, her voice flat. I look down to see the leaf has turned, the silver needle glinting brighter than it should as it points straight toward me.

I raise my eyes to Niya's. Seri isn't just missing. She's somewhere even magic can't find her.

She's been snatched.

CHAPTER

3

Mama sends me home with Bean and Niya. While they shut up the house, closing the shutters and bolting the doors, Baba and I take a dozen horses with us to town as mounts for the search parties. By dusk, Sheltershorn feels like a different place, the square deserted and the streets empty. Not a child can be seen anywhere, all of them kept indoors for fear that the snatchers might strike again while everyone is searching for Seri.

We search through the dark, hour after hour. But night edges into dawn, and the search parties have scoured every hidden vale and winding road, and there is still no sign of Seri. Mama and I return home to rest for a few precious hours as dawn burgeons into day. Baba will lie down at a friend's house in town, that he might rejoin the search efforts that much quicker.

"Any news?" Niya asks as she and Bean join us to help untack the horses.

Mama shakes her head.

"We're not giving up," I tell my sister. "We just need a rest. Is there anything else you can do to help?"

Niya shakes her head. "I've tried a dozen different things. Nothing works."

"It's not your fault," Mama says, her voice rough. "Even the Circle of Mages hasn't figured out how to track the snatched."

"Do you think they've tried?"

I glance at her, steadying myself against the wooden stall, exhaustion dragging at me. "They're the highest group of mages in the realm. Why wouldn't they?"

She drops her gaze to my feet. "They'd have to care."

I grunt in agreement, and leave Bean to finish looking after my horse.

Mama and I rejoin the search again near mid-morning, having slept away the intervening hours, only to find it is over.

"It's no use," one of the organizers says, her eyes so darkly shadowed they look bruised. "Wherever Seri is, she isn't *here* anymore. We've sent search parties down all the major roads. We'll have to put our hope in them."

I follow Mama to Ani's house, unable to quite come to grips with this. When we arrive, I slide out of my saddle and lean against Muddle's solid mass. She turns her head to regard me, one ear permanently crooked, and then leans down to take a taste of my skirt.

Mama calls to me. I free my skirt and trudge toward the door.

"They *can't* give up." Ani's voice is like a slap in the face. I jerk to a stop as she storms out of the house. She glares at Mama and me, and then strides away.

"Ani!" her mother calls. "Anisela!" She casts a helpless

glance at me. I'm already moving as she says, "Don't let her go off alone, Rae."

I catch up with Ani at the first crossroad. She stands there looking one way and then the other, as if lost. As if her sister might suddenly show up once more, a smile lighting her bright, chubby six-year-old face, the wind whipping her hair out of the twin braids she always wears, same as my sisters.

"This way?" I suggest, taking a single step in the direction that will lead us out of town. No need to parade her grief before everyone.

After a long moment, Ani dips her head and we fall into step together. She doesn't say anything, though she adjusts her stride so that I can keep up. We pause when my own house finally comes into view, the red-brown adobe walls rising tall. The house is bounded by a low stone wall, and past it is visible our goat pen, and then the long, low bulk of the stable. Beyond that are the practice rings, with horse fences made of wood carted in from the distant mountains, and then the pastures where most of our herd grazes.

The house lies quiet, Bean and Niya closed up indoors, waiting for news.

"I didn't believe it could happen to us," Ani says abruptly. "To my own sister. Did you ever—well, *you* would never be snatched. But your sisters, do you worry about them?"

I tamp down on the hurt. She is angry and grieving and oblivious to how her words might sound to me, true as they might be. I was never at risk because snatchers take only the able-bodied. I answer quietly, "I worry a great deal." Especially about Bean. Niya, with her magic, might be able to keep herself safe and win an escape, but Bean has no such advantage.

Ani nods.

It's hard not to fear for every child in Sheltershorn, though the snatchers come so rarely. The last time it happened, three years ago, two children disappeared altogether, went out to play and never returned home. And as with Seri's disappearance, no amount of searching, not even by the best of our trackers, returned a child to us.

"They found that boy who disappeared once, a few years ago."

That was ten years ago, when Ani and I were only eight. I remember it well, for none of us were allowed out of our houses for nearly two weeks, until the threat of more children being snatched had waned. The boy escaped of his own accord and was rushed away to stay with relatives far out in the plains. His family followed after him within a week, leaving behind the life they had built here in order to keep their family together.

"He even escaped the Darkness," Ani says. "He might be able to tell us something."

The Darkness. A poison the snatchers plant in the blood of those who are snatched. If they manage to escape, it blossoms in their veins and eats away at their minds until they are left a husk of themselves. Our religious scholars have found a treatment, and while it's effective in destroying the Darkness before it can take a child's mind, it's devastating in its own way, for the Blessing washes away the child's most recent memories.

Most folk find the Blessing worth the resultant loss—what are a few weeks or months of your life compared to your whole mind? But some, like the parents of the boy who escaped, prefer to take the risk to keep their child whole, and instead flee deep into the plains. And sometimes, if they go far enough, fast enough, the Darkness does not touch their child.

"If he could tell us anything helpful, surely we would have heard by now," I tell Ani, not wanting to give her false hope.

"I can't give up," Ani says desperately. "I *can't.*"

If only there were some lead, some small clue to grasp at, but we've turned up nothing: no one remembers anything unusual, every stranger has been accounted for, every wagon searched. There is not a track out of place, nothing.

"Baba is riding east with two other men, following the road to Lirelei," she says. "Everyone's heard that . . . that the children might be sent on from the eastern ports."

"It's good that he's going," I say. It's only scraps of rumor and fireside theories that suggest the snatched end up as slaves in other lands. Who sends them, how they are to be discovered—no one knows. But it's worth the journey if Seri can be found.

Ani turns to me, her face tight with fury. "Children disappear every *day.* Have you thought about that? Perhaps only every few years for us, but in the cities? Across the whole of this kingdom? It must be a few every day. How can it go on? How is it that no one manages to stop it?"

I shake my head. It had been easy enough, these past years, to pretend the snatchers were not so constant or near a threat—because they rarely strike here, in so small a town as this. But now little Seri is gone, with her laughing eyes and impish sense of humor. Niya asked if the Circle of Mages really has tried to track the snatched, and I wonder if they have. If they care, or the royal court cares, or if anyone at all knows how the snatchers are able to hide every last trace of our children.

Ani takes a deep breath. "What use are the taxes we pay? What use is our king and all his soldiers, if they can't stop our brothers and sisters from being stolen on the streets?"

"Not much," I admit. It might be treason to say so, but there is no one to hear us on this empty road. I run my hands over my head, tug at my braids, hating this helplessness. "What can we do, though?"

"I don't know," Ani says, and for the first time since she came to our cart asking after Seri, she begins to cry.

I fold her into my arms, holding her tight as she sobs into my shoulder, and promise myself I'll keep trying. And I won't give up either.

CHAPTER
4

That night, we sit around the kitchen table, looking in silence at the potatoes Bean has cooked, seasoned with salt, cumin, and a little garlic left from last fall's harvest.

"I didn't burn them," she says tentatively as everyone remains still.

"No, love," Mama says. "We're just tired."

Baba nods. "And tomorrow will be a long day caring for the horses. We've ignored them enough already, and ridden half of them harder than we should."

He's right, of course. I barely wiped Muddle down, let alone curried her. I know Bean made sure to pick out all the horses' hooves as they were brought back in, and everyone's been watered and fed and put out to graze, but we've over forty horses. I *know* the horses need more than we've given them. But I can't help asking, "Isn't there something more we can do for Seri?"

"Pray," Mama says.

"Everyone's praying," I say tightly. "You're the one who always says that as much as we ask for help, we have to help ourselves."

"I know, Rae. But we've done everything we can. It's out of our hands now."

I hate that I don't know how to argue with her. But Seri *can't* be tracked. By tonight, her father will have reached the nearest small city where a mage might be found. I have no doubt that their attempt to track Seri will end as Niya's did: with nothing.

Bean reaches over and slides her hand into mine, squeezing tightly. I look across the table at our parents. "What about the snatchers themselves? Can't we find some way to stop them?"

"What can we do?" Baba asks. "We're horse ranchers."

I have no answer. I don't want to believe there's nothing we can do. I can't. But I still have no answer.

The meal finishes in the same silence it began. I push away my plate, glad to be done. The potatoes may not have been burned, but they still tasted like ash on my tongue.

"I wasn't going to mention this quite yet, Rae," Mama says before I can rise, "but a letter came for you yesterday—well, for us. It's from your cousin Ramella."

"Melly wrote?" It's not unusual; we keep up a regular correspondence, and I look forward to her yearly visits with her husband, Filadon. He's an actual lord with a small holding, and they spend most of their time at court in Tarinon. "To both of us?" I clarify, because that is the odd part.

"To us," Mama says, indicating herself and Baba.

"What about?" Bean demands. "Are they coming to visit?"

"It's an invitation for Rae to join them at court."

My sisters and I stare at her, and then I shake myself once. "Well, she asks that every year. I've no interest in the court." The prospect of visiting the king's court, being surrounded by the wealthiest families of our land and all the vaunted beauties of their lines . . . me, with neither a title nor riches nor beauty to my name? No, thank you.

Mama slips a fold of paper from her pocket and slides it across the table to me. "Why not read Melly's letter first?"

Niya takes the letter and spreads it open for us both to read, Bean crowding over my shoulder to see as well. Ramella has learned recently that she is with child. The other night—wait, what?

"Melly's pregnant?" Bean sputters at the same time that I go back to reread that sentence. "Oh, Rae, you *have* to go!"

"She'll have friends to be with her," I say almost absently, reading on: it occurred to my cousin that she would enjoy my company in the city over the next few months.

"Friends?" Bean nearly screeches. "Rae! This is Melly! We're her *family*."

I nod, still reading. Filadon is greatly occupied helping with the preparations for the prince's wedding, as well as other affairs of state, and they would appreciate my presence. Could my parents possibly spare their dear cousin Amraeya through the summer?

"Rae?" Mama asks when I finally look up. "Would you like to go?"

"I don't know how you can expect me to go now," I say, disbelief tingeing my words. "I cannot possibly leave Ani, and we've the horses to take care of as well."

"We are Melly's only family, though," Mama says. "Think about it."

"The royal wedding's coming up," Bean adds.

"That's true," Baba says. "If you leave in the next couple of weeks, you should make it in good time for that."

"And," Bean says with growing excitement, "maybe you'll even meet someone for yourself."

My laugh comes out as a derisive huff. "Bean. My prospects of marriage are as good here as they are there."

"How do you know? You've never been there. Maybe you'll meet someone."

"I'll meet many people," I agree. "None of whom would marry me. And none of whom I would wish to marry."

"But . . . ," she begins.

"I'm a cripple."

The cold simplicity of my words brings Bean up short.

"It's just a slight limp," Niya offers timidly.

"All right. I'm a turnfoot." It is the same name the village children threw my way when we were young. The same name over which Ani threw her first punch in my defense. The hurt has long gone out of the word, but it doesn't change the fact that that is how people see me. And the royal palace—where Ramella and Filadon live—is unlikely to be filled with people who appreciate limping peasant girls.

My family has nothing to say in return.

"I can't leave Ani right now," I say. If I can't find Seri, the least I can do is stay by Ani while she grieves. When Mama parts her lips to argue, I add, "And anyhow, there's Spring Fair to plan for. I always help Baba with that."

"The fair?" Bean repeats in disbelief. "How can you compare the *fair* to court?"

"I'm sure there are a good number of pigs in both places," Baba points out thoughtfully.

"Oh, Baba." Niya half moans.

"Ani does need you," Mama says, meeting my gaze. "But let's not make any decisions quite yet, shall we? Just think about it."

"All right," I say, my mind already made up.

CHAPTER
5

I ride over to see Ani again the following afternoon. Shelters-horn is busy again, though there are still no children visible. But the work of living must go on, and those who dropped everything to help with the search have once more picked up where they left off. Wagons move ponderously through the street again, and a few women have gathered on the corners to share whatever bit of news they've come by.

Ani meets me at the door of her house and nearly drags me away. "I need to get out," she says. "I can't stand any more aunties right now. Even with all their news."

"News?"

"It's strange," Ani says absently. She sets a pace I can easily match. "Are you all right with a walk?"

"Just fine." We head down a side street, taking the most direct route out of town possible. When we reach the edge of the plains, I say, "What's the strange news, then?"

"You know our prince was betrothed to that foreign princess from across the mountains? Turns out the girl that's been staying in the palace all winter long was an impostor—some noblewoman who didn't like the true princess and betrayed her along the journey. The story is she used magic to switch places and silence the true princess, and sent her off to work as a goose girl once they arrived in Tarinon. The king only just figured it out."

"That's . . . strange." It sounds like something out of a fireside tale, believable only by the light of the flickering flames. "You're sure the story hasn't been blown out of proportion?"

Ani shakes her head. "The king's couriers brought the news with the mail. They said the impostor's to be closed into a barrel pounded through with nails and dragged behind a brace of horses till dead."

"*What?*" Since when has our king meted out such horrific punishments? He's known to be proud, certainly, but not cruel.

Ani grimaces. "That's the punishment the impostor chose for herself, thinking it would be done to the true princess."

It all sounds very elaborate, and absolutely horrifying. Betrayal and cruelty cloaked as justice, and at the heart of it, magic used as a weapon against the royal family. I hope—oh, how I hope!—they won't start searching for other hidden magic. At least this impostor came from another land, and not Menaiya itself.

"It's all the aunties have been talking about today," Ani says.

"I'm sorry," I say. How must it feel that Seri's loss has already been overshadowed by other news?

Ani sighs. "Anyhow, I'm sure you'll get better details than us. Isn't your cousin staying at the palace right now?"

I nod. "She is. She's even invited me to spend the summer

there." Baba had suggested I could make it to the wedding, but I don't think I want to see a girl who was forced into servitude now be forced into marriage. Unless, I suppose, she wants that future.

"Will you go?"

I look at Ani, but she's very carefully gazing out over the plains. We've left the town behind us once more. "I doubt it. I'd rather stay here."

Ani snorts. "Any other girl in this town would be jumping at such an opportunity."

Any other girl in this town would have less chance of being ridiculed by a court obsessed with beauty and fine manners. "Not enough horses there," I grouse. "And not enough work to do."

"You are such a stick in the mud," Ani says, smiling faintly.

I'm so glad to see that smile, I shrug and say, "Mud is very comfortable."

"There's more to life than horses, you know."

"True. There are smithies too."

Ani shakes her head, the smile dropping away. "When would you go?"

I sigh. "Soon. And I'd rather not go just yet."

We keep walking, following the path around past the road I came in on.

"I dreamed about her last night," Ani says abruptly. "About Seri. I dreamed I was walking with her, and we were laughing about something, and then I turned around and she was gone. I couldn't—I could barely breathe when I woke up. I couldn't sleep again. I can't not think about her, Rae."

I nod, because I don't know what to say.

"Mama says it isn't my fault. That, if they were watching her, it would have happened anyhow. That I did well realizing she was missing so quickly, and getting help, but *she was my responsibility*. I let her go off instead of walking her there . . ."

I stop and wrap my arms around Ani and let her cry again, wishing I had a way to stop her pain, to undo what has been done.

Eventually, Ani steps away and wipes her nose on her sleeve, her eyes red and puffy. "Sorry," she says.

I shake my head. There's nothing to apologize for.

She threads her arm through mine and we turn back to town. "So," she says roughly, and for a moment I think she will start crying again. But then she clears her throat and asks, "Why don't you want to go to Tarinon?"

I shrug, my uneven gait all the more obvious beside her steady step.

"I think you should go," Ani says.

"Why? There's no real need for it." I eye her askance. "I didn't think you would want me to leave."

"I don't," she admits. "But can you tell me, truly, why you don't want to go?"

What is it that's holding me back? I hesitate, thinking of all I've heard of the court, and admit, "I don't want anyone's pity."

A silence.

Ani's arm tightens around mine. "People are stupid wherever you go. That doesn't mean you should never leave home."

"I know," I concede. Yet I don't see any reason to expose myself to more than I must.

"Good," Ani says as we near her home. "So when do you leave?"

I let out my breath in a helpless laugh. "Are you all trying to get rid of me? And here I thought we were friends and my family loved me."

"All true," Ani says. "Which is why you had better tell me when you expect to leave next time we meet."

As if it were as easy as that. I shake my head, look up at Ani's house, the darkened window of the room she used to share with her sister. The room that is hers alone now.

"I don't want to leave," I say, and Ani hears the change in my tone. She pauses beside me. "I don't want to leave you alone with your grief and go off to the palace, even if Melly would like my company."

For a long moment, Ani stands with her head bent, her eyes on the hard-packed earth underfoot. "Perhaps you could ask someone there," she says, the words so soft and unexpected I don't know what to make of them. She turns her head, and her eyes are as deep and dark with grief as they were yesterday, as if there were no light left in her at all. "Tarinon is a big city. Someone there might know more about the snatchers—have an idea where the children are taken. They *must* know more."

"It's possible," I allow. For the chance to learn what's happened to Seri, I could easily put up with being snubbed. Melly might be able to help me find out what the guards have learned about the snatchers, what the king thinks. Though I don't think she could influence anyone—she and Filadon are not especially high in rank.

Still, it might be worth it to simply ask the questions. To do *something*.

"I'll still be here when you get back," Ani says. "And it will be easier knowing you're doing what I can't."

I nod. But will it make a difference? Couldn't I learn the same just by writing to Melly? It's not like I'm going to take on the snatchers myself.

"Think about it," Ani says, and squeezes my hand.

"I will," I say, and walk with her back into a house that will always feel a little emptier than it was.

Sometime in the middle of the night I jerk awake from a deep, heavy sleep. I sit up, muzzy headed and afraid, and realize with a sickening lurch that Niya isn't sleeping beside me anymore. She's gone.

No. She can't be. She's slipped downstairs for something. Anything. I wait, but there's no sound of movement in the house. After a few increasingly shaky breaths, I rise and let myself out of the room. By the time I reach the stairs, I'm hobbling as fast as I can. Only about halfway down do I catch a hint of lamplight coming from the kitchen.

I make myself take a slow, deep breath. It was foolish of me, I know, that irrational, unspeakable fear. There was no reason whatsoever for Niya to leave our room and then somehow get snatched. I've just let myself get carried away by my own fears. I give myself a slight shake and pad down the stairs slowly and steadily, as I would normally.

In the kitchen, Niya sits on a stained old blanket, kept for dirty work, one hand resting on the stray dog's back. If it weren't for the utter focus of her gaze, and that a ruby pendant glitters faintly in her other hand, there'd be no indication whatsoever that she is working.

But she is. I've seen her work this sort of magic on our sick animals before. If her compass used the concept of flow, healing magic is primarily about patterns. Such magic is never easy, and only the best of our mages become healers, if they so wish. Niya might never have attempted it had a faerie visitor not mentioned pattern magic as his parting word of advice to her.

A healer-mage might remind a body of the pattern of unruptured flesh, using their magic to return wounded flesh as close to that pattern as possible. Or, as Niya found while accompanying my mother to our community's local births, the body knows the pattern for a healthy birth, even if it cannot achieve it. Magic gently introduced and carefully woven can turn a child from breech to anterior facing, can remind vessels to close, muscles to squeeze tight a rupture before a woman might bleed out. I remember the brightness in Niya's eyes the first time she came home, knowing that the secret application of her magic saved the life of the woman she and Mama had gone to help, that one more family would remain together, one more child would keep her mother.

I settle across from her on the blanket, and watch as the dog's skin slowly—so slowly—eases toward a healthier color beneath a dried, scaly layer of old skin. Niya is reminding the skin how to fight infection, how to push out what is unwanted, and while it will take days and possibly weeks for the dog to fully heal, eventually she will.

"There," Niya says finally, setting aside the pendant. "That should help her. And Mama can have her pendant back, now that I've drained it."

I smile. "She'll be happy to hear it."

A gemstone can be used to hold a reserve of magic, but the act of draining the magic alters its structure somehow, so it can only be used as an amulet once. Niya has slowly worked her way through our jewelry, storing what magic she doesn't manage to use in her daily little spells around the house—kneading birdsong and a warm spring breeze into her bread, or spilling a bit of sunshine into the laundry. Every now and then she's able to perform a big enough working that she uses the magic at her disposal and drains an amulet as well, and then we get our jewelry back. True mages, of course, have much larger gems than we do, and their amulets can become a source of great power. I don't think Niya particularly cares about that, though. A small gem holds more than enough for her needs.

"Couldn't sleep?" I ask her.

"I can't stop thinking about Seri. I can help this dog—and I'm glad of it!—but I wish I could do something for her too." She turns to me, gray eyes intent. "There has to be something we're missing. Children can't just disappear. Even dead bodies can be traced."

"I know."

"So what do we do?"

Nothing. If Niya does something to uncover the snatchers, not only does she risk being abducted herself, but her talent could be discovered and that would destroy her in a different way. She'd be made an amulet bearer, her magic constantly drained to an amulet to be used by the mage who becomes her master. I won't let that happen.

"I don't know," I say. "But I might just go to the palace to see what I can learn. The king must be doing something; perhaps there's someone among his staff who knows more."

Niya stares at me. The dog wiggles her shoulders beneath Niya's hand, asking for a petting, and she automatically starts scratching. "You'd do that?" Niya asks.

"Yes. And if no one's doing anything, as you say, I'll call you in and you can knock over some snatchers for me. Put your pattern and flow to good use."

Niya laughs. "You'd never send for me. Just . . . if you really plan to learn about the snatchers, be careful, all right?"

I reach out to touch her arm. There is one truth, one future we have always promised each other: when Bean is married and leaves, and our parents are grown old, we will still always be there for each other. Niya because she can never dare to marry, given her secret, and me because I will never find anyone.

"Always," I promise. "You're not getting rid of me that easily."

CHAPTER
6

I bring up my decision to my parents the following morning after breakfast. "I don't know that Melly really needs my company," I admit. Far more likely, she's happy to have an excuse to finally make me visit her. "But it would be nice to see her. And . . . I intend to ask her what's being done about the snatchers, if something more can't be done."

Mama considers my words. "There's no harm in that. Just be careful about who you speak to. And Rae, bear in mind that if it were easy, it would already be done."

"I know." I don't expect it to be easy. But Niya's counting on me to do what she can't, and, like Ani, I can't give up. I know I won't find Seri in Tarinon, but this is still part of fighting for her.

"Is there anything else?" Mama asks as I continue to sit there.

Of course there is. If I go, I'll be leaving my whole life behind. And that means my sisters as well. "I'm worried about Bean and Niya," I confess. "About not being here for them. If anything should happen." Unspoken but not unheard are the last of my fears: that if the snatchers should return, I might lose a sister while away at court. Or that Niya might be found out and taken from us, my parents punished for hiding her.

"Suppose I promise to watch them?" Mama says lightly.

I laugh.

"I could bar Bean from accompanying me to Spring Fair in your place," Baba says doubtfully. "But she may never forgive you."

"She wouldn't," I agree. "And you're both right: they don't need me as long as they have you. But I still worry."

"I'm glad you do," Mama says. "That makes you a good sister. But they should be all right through the summer, and they will want to hear all your stories when you return."

"Excellent," Baba says, as if it were settled. "You'll be ready to leave next week, then?"

"Next week?"

"Our own Veria Sanlyn is traveling to Tarinon for the wedding," Baba says, naming a local noblewoman. "Her head hostler came by to see if he could cajole me into selling her a brace of horses for her carriage—as if we breed carriage horses! At any rate, I mentioned you might be traveling there. The hostler informed the housekeeper, who spoke with the lady herself, and she sent an invitation for you to ride along with her." Baba smiles, well pleased with himself. And even I have to admit it is rather perfect.

I frown. "I suppose Sanlyn will be expecting to see those horses, then."

"Oh, no," Baba says. "I've been very clear that we have a

lovely riding horse that might suit her perfectly instead. I was thinking of Lemon, really—their dispositions are of a kind."

"Baba!" I say, amused despite myself. Mama just shakes her head.

I spend the day with the horses, glad to return to the steadying routine of cleaning, training, and—to be honest—visiting with the horses. As with the day before, I take some time in the afternoon to ride into town to check in on Ani, who is pleased to hear that I do in fact have a day of departure to report.

In the evening, as we settle on cushions in the sitting room, Niya brings out her work basket. Mama and Baba are lingering in the kitchen, voices lowered, though Mama's muffled laugh tells me that, whatever their conversation, it isn't a grim one. Bean sprawls on a cushion, utterly uninterested in the horse blanket she's supposed to mend.

"I've been working on something for you," Niya says. "For your birthday, but I think I can get it done for you before you leave. Shall I show you?"

"Oh yes," I say.

She removes the topmost items in her mending basket and delves into the bottom to lift out a new sash. It is tradition to wear an embroidered sash about one's waist, and Niya has embroidered more than a few designs for us over the years, but this is something different altogether.

"It's a story sash," Bean gasps, delighted. "What story did you do? Oh! Will you make me one too?"

Niya laughs. "Of course, but first I have to finish Rae's." She offers it to me, and I carefully unfold it. The fabric itself is a simple cream, but the sash almost shimmers with Niya's mul-tihued embroidery, so elaborate it takes my breath away. Story sashes contain the symbols and colors of a story so that it can be carried with you and passed down to those you love. They are rare nowadays, with paper being available and the embroidery itself so time-intensive. Which makes it all that much more spe-cial a gift.

The first few bands of embroidery are purely decoration, but then the story begins—a twist of blue around a black center: *There was and there was not.*

"A princess!" Bean says, happily jumping ahead to the styl-ized image of a girl with long braids.

Niya laughs. "Not yet. You see how the leaves wrap around her? She's a girl who lives in the forest."

"Yes, but *there*"—Bean points to the other end of the sash—"she's getting married and that yellow twist around them is a crown."

"That's how most stories end," I agree, amused. "It's Riha of the Woods, isn't it?"

"Mama said that was your favorite tale growing up. You always used to tell it to us too," Niya says.

"I still love it. Thank you, Niya."

"You should stitch in something useful too," Bean reproves her. "Stories are all very well and good, but suppose she needs something?"

One of Niya's favorite magical skills involves hiding things in her stitches, things which can only be regained when the stitches are undone. She learned this, as she has learned much of her magic, the hard way: in this case, by accidentally stitching Baba's prize nanny goat into a whorl of embroidery. At a harvest fair livestock competition. Right behind the judges' backs.

Niya nods. "I was planning to hide some coins, in case you ever lose your purse."

"Could you stitch up my bone knife too?" I ask. A gift from that same faerie visitor who suggested pattern magic to Niya a year ago, it looks like an old chipped kitchen knife to most. I am the only one who can see its shining ivory blade and onyx-and-mother-of-pearl handle. But more than that, it's sharp and useful, and while I hope I won't need it, it can't hurt to have it handy.

"Of course," Niya says. "I've put a backing on to protect the knots, see?" She turns the sash over, and sure enough the other side is plain cream, only the ends, where they would hang free, embroidered on both sides. "Anything I add for you, I'll bring the knots through the backing so you can easily break them and release what I've hidden."

"Sounds perfect."

Niya hesitates. "I also—I've been experimenting with protections. See this border here? That's where they're sewn."

"You can stitch *wards*?" Bean asks, properly impressed.

Niya shrugs. "Maybe. I don't know how a real mage would do it."

"Who cares what a 'real' mage would do?" Bean demands. "That's amazing!"

Niya smiles shyly. "I can add some to your sashes too, Bean, once I'm done with Rae's."

"Oh *yes*," Bean says. "Will it stop horses from stepping on my boots?"

Niya frowns. "Right now they mostly work against other

magics, but I can experiment with physical force."

"Just don't hurt yourself while you're at it," Bean says cheerfully.

Niya laughs. She will likely do a much better job of keeping herself and Bean safe than I ever could. But I'm still going to miss them and worry about them, anyhow. I claim big sister prerogative on that.

"You'll watch their horses," Bean says, now that my magical packing list is settled. "I want to know what kinds of horses the prince and all ride. I suppose they must be better than ours."

"Maybe," I concede. "But their hostlers have bought from us at Spring Fair before."

"Which horses did they buy?" Bean asks, intrigued.

From there, we quickly descend into a discussion of which dam's offspring was sold when to the royal hostlers, a topic our father takes up with great spirit when he and Mama finally join us. Niya and Mama exchange a commiserating glance and focus on their sewing.

CHAPTER

7

A week and a half later, I watch avidly from my carriage window as we trundle up a great, wide city avenue. This is West Road, the road off of which the true princess lived as a goose girl in the royal stables, and it passes through the poorest part of the city. The yellow-brick buildings rise up to two or three stories, not unlike the somewhat shorter buildings that make up our village. But there the similarity ends, for these adobe walls are stained, the plaster cracked and broken here and there, revealing the bricks underneath. The people are thin and poorly dressed, but it's the children who shock me: squatting in the dirt to play, barefoot and dirty-faced, their figures painfully thin, and even a few, here and there, who wear nothing but a long tunic, as if the cost of pants were too much for their family.

Only as we reach the center of the city do the buildings seem to gain in wealth, fresh coats of paint on the walls, the streets wider. And the children are clean and well dressed. Finally, we enter the wide plaza before the palace gates. Beyond the impressive walls, the palace rises in a multitude of rooftops, all of them cloaked in dark green clay shingles. The walls are white stone, carved intricately, and the doorways arched. If I have never seen poverty the likes of which exists on West Road, I have likewise never seen such wealth as this palace. I just manage to close my mouth as we roll through the main gates and turn down a side road, skirting the palace itself.

A few minutes later, the carriage comes to a stop in a small courtyard allowing entrance into a series of apartments, including, as I am informed, my cousin's. A footman opens the carriage door for me, and I step down as Veria Sanlyn bids me a brisk adieu.

The journey to Tarinon took four days, and each of them cemented further in my mind how little I want anything to do with the nobles of the court. To be sure, Sanlyn was not rude. She merely provided a space for a local horse rancher's daughter to sit in between the cloth-bound packages of fancy dresses and uncut fabrics awaiting their final fate at a city tailor's hands. After a kind greeting and a nod of her head, Sanlyn had no more interest in addressing me than she did my trunk, set at my feet.

But I did not come here to pretend to be a noble. In my last week at home, I visited Ani daily, holding her when she cried and trying to ease her anger and despair as the days passed and even her most sturdy hopes gave way to grief. Sitting with Ani, I promised myself I wouldn't stop trying to learn more about the snatchers. I don't imagine I can stop them myself, but if I can ask the right questions in the right places, if I can just get someone at court to care, perhaps they can still be revealed and destroyed as they deserve.

"Through the doorway there, kelari," the footman says now. "I'll bring your trunk at once."

I nod and cross to a wooden door, carved and inlaid with a bronze floral design. A maid answers my knock, smiling brightly. "If you'll follow me, Veria Ramella is expecting you."

She ushers me past the ornate chair she must have been waiting in and along a short hallway rich with mosaic-tiled walls and carved ceiling timbers, to a set of elegant marble stairs. We proceed up these, the maid pausing at the top to allow me to catch up, and continue on through the first door on the right, into what must be my cousin's apartments. They are not overly ornate, but I am taken aback by the richness of them, from the deep hue of the brocade sofas to the silver trays and crystal decorations. And there are actual luminae stones set in lamps, lending their steady magical light to the room. *Luminae stones.* If only Niya could be here to study them. Or I could take one home to her.

"This way, kelari," the maid says, a faint note of amusement in her voice.

I tear my awed gaze away from the room to focus on her. "Thank you."

She ushers me through a connecting door to an inner sitting room. I step in with a sense of absolute relief: here is a room that feels just like those at home, wool carpet underfoot and cushions against the wall, and only half the room furnished with the fancier low sofas and wooden side tables the rich prefer. The room is an exact depiction of my cousin's marriage, she from a merchant's family, used to simpler living, and he very much a noble, however small his holding.

They are seated together on the sofas, deep in conversation, Melly facing me. She looks up, her face brightening at the sight of me. Her belly is just beginning to fill out her tunic. Filadon perks up and twists to see me. He is handsome, his features bordering on pretty: well-shaped eyes, sculpted lips, dark hair curling around his ears. I have sometimes wondered how Ramella, whose beauty is of a simpler, gentler demeanor, managed to get past his facades, and how he, in turn, could have won her trust.

"Kelari Amraeya has arrived," the maid says, completely unnecessarily at this point.

"Cousin Rae!" Filadon cries cheerfully, jumping to his feet.

I grin and dip an awkward curtsy as the maid lets herself out. "Verin, veria."

"Oh hush," Melly says with obvious amusement. "Don't you go around bobbing at us like that."

"Well, I *am* at court now, aren't I?"

Melly just shakes her head and crosses the room to embrace me. She looks hale and hearty, her eyes clear and her skin glowing with health. "It's been a long time—I'm so glad you accepted our invitation."

"Bean would have tied me up and delivered me herself if I'd refused." And I couldn't forgo the chance to learn more about the snatchers—though that's a conversation for another time, after I've settled in.

Melly pulls back from her hug with a laugh. "Bean is quite a force to be reckoned with, isn't she?"

"Always has been," I agree. "So what will we be doing while Filadon is off being noble?"

"Unfair!" Filadon cries. "I demand company. Surely you don't intend to ignore me for your whole stay?"

"I'm here for Melly, not you," I inform him equably.

Melly, ignoring Filadon, says, "I am hoping to introduce you to my circles before the wedding, and of course you'll meet the royal family at some point in the festivities. As such, our first order of business will be to expand your wardrobe."

No doubt because courtiers don't usually take care of their own horses, or wear the clothes to do so. I muster up a smile and nod. "I thought you might say that."

Melly raises her brows. "Oh, well done, Rae! Not even a grumble!"

I raise my brows in return and say earnestly, "I believe going to court is rather like going to war: one must wear the appropriate armor, or expect to be stabbed through and trampled underfoot."

Filadon huffs with laughter. "Well, Melly, I don't think we have anything to worry about. Rae is clearly prepared for politics."

Melly just *hmm*s softly and offers me a cup of mint tea.

The next two days pass in a whirl of cloth and confusion. I must get used to small things I've never thought about before—having a bed that I might fall off, rather than a mat I can roll away each morning; having a bathing room attached to our apartments with flowing water rather than a bucket and washcloth. "We can visit the palace bathhouse if you prefer," Melly tells me, and though we have a communal bathhouse back home too, I don't take her up on it.

But the majority of my time is spent shopping. Melly takes me out into the city to search for all the fabric and trimmings we'll need. "We'll use my palace seamstress," she tells me. "But there's no reason you shouldn't see a bit more of Tarinon."

The more I see, though, the more I wonder about the division between the palace and the people. In Sheltershorn, no one is truly poor. Not in the way I see here, half-clothed children, all sinew and bone, running past the door of a shop selling imported silks. It feels . . . wrong, somehow, to be buying such extravagant fabrics, ordering beadwork and embroidery done, when the moment we step outside, we cross paths with laborers in ragged clothing, their faces tight with exhaustion.

Still, I can't go to noble gatherings in just the clothes I've brought with me—however nice the three new outfits Mama and Niya made for me may be, they won't last me the whole of my stay.

On our second afternoon, as we step out from a shop where we have just purchased an abundance of lace, I spot a sidewalk vendor selling fried flatbreads from his cart.

"Come on." I grab Melly's hand and tug her along. "I need to eat."

Her eyes light up. "I haven't had street food in *forever*." She casts a wary glance back to the main road, where we left the carriage.

"Why?"

"Nobles don't eat off the street," she says.

"What?" At her somber nod, I drag her forward with renewed determination. "Who's going to tell? Come on, I think he even has spiced potato ones."

Melly follows along more than willingly, happily buying two for herself. We meander down the alley, for the first time all day not actually shopping.

"Is it hard?" I ask, breaking the silence.

Melly sends me a curious glance.

"Being noble, I mean? Not having grown up that way?"

She shrugs. "I don't know if I would have chosen it, if I'd understood," she says. "We all have ideas about how wonderful it must be to wed a lord, or live at court, or whatever. It isn't all pretty dresses and gold."

"I don't believe you ever thought it would be."

She finishes her flatbread, wiping the grease from her fingers onto a handkerchief. "No," she says. "But I still didn't truly know how my life would change. Lucky for Filadon, hmm?"

"Does he know how you feel?"

"In part." She grins. "Why do you think we visit you all in the country every year?"

"Must be to curry favor with the high-ups," I say wryly.

Melly's laugh is a short, halfhearted one, quickly gone. "I miss little things," she admits. She gestures vaguely to the alley. "Filadon and I discussed whether I should call in the merchants I order from, or whether you might enjoy going out into the city more. We both agreed on this. Once I've introduced you to the other ladies and we start accepting invitations, you likely won't get much chance to go out."

"What do you mean I won't go out?" I demand, bewildered.

"Not like this. Seeing all the shops, wandering the city? It isn't done."

"You can't be serious."

"I am," Melly insists, gesturing to the muddy patches in the unevenly cobbled road. "Can you imagine a court lady walking through this muck?"

"How do they buy what they want, then?"

"We all have our preferred tailors or jewelers or what-have-you who come up to the palace and take our orders from the comfort of our own sitting rooms."

It takes me a moment to process her words. "You mean, they never leave the palace?"

"Not to shop. And not to just browse and wander. There are a few parks, a river walk, that noble parties will frequent. They drive there and back, though."

"But how do they know they're really getting what they want if they haven't seen what's available?" And how do they know what's really happening with the common people if they live their lives shut up in their gilded rooms? No wonder neither the king nor the nobles have done anything to stop the snatchers. They've nothing to do with the world around them.

"All the best things come to the palace," Melly says.

I raise my brows in disbelief.

Melly smirks. "Fine, then. We'll never know if some merchant who isn't among the favored few has something amazing, because we'll never see it."

"That's absurd." To think they believe themselves the best, when they're shuttered away like ailing nanny goats.

Melly shrugs. We turn back toward the main road, nodding to the shopkeepers whose merchandise we've already looked at. My eyes alight on a young man sitting on a stool at the front corner of a shop. He has a small bowl on his lap with a heap of early peas to shell, but his fingers have gone still, a single pea pod hanging from his fingertips. His eyes are dim, unfocused. As I watch, the shopkeeper crosses to him and gently lays her hand on his shoulder, calling his name. He doesn't respond.

"Rae?"

I glance to Melly, find her watching me. "That boy," I whisper. "Is he all right?"

She follows my gaze to the boy and we watch as the shopkeeper takes the bowl and sets it aside, then helps the boy up and guides him to the back of the shop.

"Come," Melly says, threading her fingers through mine and leading me toward the carriage.

"Melly?" I ask as we cross the pavers.

"He's as well as he'll ever be, Rae. He has the look of someone who's been touched by the Darkness. There's nothing anyone can do for him but treat him gently and help him through his days."

I twist to look over my shoulder, but I can no longer see into the shop from here, and anyhow, the boy is gone. And I shouldn't be staring.

"The Darkness," I echo, turning back to the carriage.

"You've never seen what it does," Melly says, the words not quite a question.

"No." We only ever lost a few children to the snatchers, and only one of them returned—and he fled into the plains to escape the Darkness. I never saw anything like the look of this boy, whole and handsome and utterly hollow. This is why the Blessing is necessary—to protect children who escape the snatchers from losing the very light of their minds and spirits.

We clamber up into the carriage. I sit quietly, my thoughts caught on the memory of the boy, his hands gone still around the peas, his eyes unseeing. This is the other side of what the snatchers do, and the sight of it both sickens and enrages me. How *dare* the snatchers destroy our youth even after they have escaped? How can our only answer be a blessing that steals our children's memory—instead of a way to finally stop the snatchers themselves?

I've allowed the last two days to slip by without thinking too much about the snatchers, about the questions I promised myself I'd ask. It seemed wise to settle in first and then broach the subject. But I cannot shake the image of the boy. Tonight, when Filadon joins us for dinner, I'll ask.

CHAPTER

8

Filadon arrives just barely in time for dinner, sliding into his seat at the table—no low table with cushions to rest upon here!—just as the maid brings out the meal.

"How was your day, my love?" he asks, leaning over to brush a kiss on Melly's cheek.

She blushes, the brown of her skin warming with a faint rose undertone. "You do see that Rae is here, don't you?"

Filadon turns to me with exaggerated surprise. "Rae! Wherever did *you* come from?"

"The country," I say helpfully.

"Oh hush, you," Melly says, swatting his arm. "Rae and I had a lovely day, thank you for asking. We spent the morning shopping and the afternoon with the seamstress, and by tomorrow the first of her new outfits should be arriving."

"I am impressed," Filadon says. "With the first of the wedding festivities less than a week away, you must have been very persuasive to manage to order a whole wardrobe. *Everyone* must be ordering clothes."

"You know she's always had a soft spot for me," Melly says. "Now she likes Rae too."

"She was very kind," I chime in. Melly's promise to pay extra for a rush delivery did not go amiss either.

"And how did you find the city today?" Filadon asks, as he did yesterday.

"Lovely and chaotic and busier than Spring Fair," I say. "But I saw one thing—a boy, actually."

"Ah," Melly says at the same moment Filadon says, "Oh?"

"Melly says he was touched by the Darkness."

Filadon looks at me, his gaze oddly intent. "I see. You've never met such a child before?"

"No."

"It's a tragedy," he says with a slight tilt of his head, as if waiting for me to go on.

"I wondered," I say carefully, "what the soldiers here do to stop the snatchers—if anyone is investigating them. I thought you might know."

"Would I?"

I shrug. "If anyone could stop them, I assume it would be the high marshal, or the royal family themselves. Do they—are they aware of the snatchers?"

Filadon smiles, a quick, sharp grin that is bright teeth and brighter eyes. His words are strangely at odds with that look. "An excellent question, Rae. By and large, the court believes the snatchers to be a figment of the commoners' imagination—a sort of bogeyman to scare children into behaving, and explain away the fate of runaways."

"That's ridiculous."

"And yet, it is what the court believes."

"How do they explain the Darkness, then?"

"The natural result of a sudden illness, or a blow to the head. Or"—he shrugs—"a purportedly magical bogeyman to complement the snatchers. If one doesn't frighten you, the other will."

"Someone has to do something," I say, desperation warring with disbelief. How can the nobles discount this reality so completely? "We lost another girl in Sheltershorn. She didn't run away. She was stolen and couldn't be traced—her father tried a mage in one of the cities he rode to. *Niya* tried within an hour of the girl's disappearance. The snatchers aren't some collective delusion. They're *real*."

"We know," Melly says quietly.

I turn to her, trying to tamp down my emotions, but that fierce anger at Seri's loss, that grief is still there, its claws buried beneath my skin along with the memory of Ani's pain. "Then why does no one believe you? At least enough to look into it? If they investigate, they can't help but find the truth of it."

Filadon weaves his fingers together and rests his chin upon them. "Melly can't," he says conversationally. "The court only listens to what they want to hear from whom they want to hear it. If she brings it up, it's her common background speaking, not her intelligence or knowledge or ability."

Melly nods, her expression hard. I wonder how often her perspective is discounted because of her background. I haven't even met the court and I'm already livid with them.

Filadon sighs. "And I . . . don't have quite as much power as you might think."

"You're a lord," I say, but it's almost a question.

Filadon smiles briefly. "I am, and I have a friendship with the prince many are jealous of, but in return I gain very little. He does not shower me with gifts and rewards, nor do I expect them. Which means, in the court, that my worth is improved only so much. I am still just a lord with a small holding of little interest to anyone but myself."

"The prince won't listen to you?"

"He might," Filadon concedes. "But until now, he's been far too wrapped up in greater concerns—dangers he dared not turn his back on."

It's probably too soon to ask if the true princess has any thoughts on the subject, given her time living in the city. She's only been at court for a week or two now.

"I'll think about this," Filadon says, turning back to his meal. "Perhaps we can discuss it again in a few days."

"I'd appreciate that," I say, aware that I am asking a lot of him. Melly shoots me a grateful smile and turns the conversation to Filadon's day, spent in company with the prince and his betrothed.

After dinner, I retire to my room only to be called back a few minutes later by Melly, who gently reminds me of the cobbler's impending visit, coming to measure me for slippers to match all my outfits.

"Oh," I manage, and force a smile.

I commission shoes once a year and I hate it. Baba and I ride two days east to the nearest large town on the Kharite Road. There, a cobbler measures my feet, taking into account the turn of my left ankle and heel such that I walk on the outside of my foot rather than the sole. This affects the way the sole of the shoe itself must be shaped, as well as the overall shoe. After much muttering and grumbling, the cobbler provides us with a pair of riding boots, a pair of daily use slippers, and one set of fancy embroidered slippers, all at a relatively outrageous price. He's the only cobbler who has been able to make shoes that don't hurt me.

"Does this cobbler—has he worked with any other customers like me?" I ask as I follow Melly to the outer sitting room.

Her eyes darken with understanding. "I can't say, but I'm sure he'll do a good job. He serves a number of noble families. His reputation will be on the line if he doesn't do well by you."

I wish I could rest as comfortably in this knowledge as Melly does.

She reaches out to pat my shoulder. "It will be fine," she says, as if she can see the future.

The cobbler is a middle-aged man with a too-wide smile and well-manicured hands. He wears a pair of simple leather slippers, embroidered in dark colors—understated and elegant, meant to show off his skill without being pretentious.

"I understand," he says as he waves me to the sofa, "that you will require special shoes. I am quite looking forward to the challenge."

My smile, stiff before, feels like it is carved upon my face. I seat myself silently.

"Now then, let's have a look—"

"These are the slippers I have been wearing at home," I say in an effort to prepare him so that he won't say something I'll hate him for. "They fit me perfectly, so you should be able to use them as a template for my new shoes."

"Do they?" he asks, taking them from me. He sets the right slipper down and focuses on the left, turning it this way and that. "Very interesting construction. I don't see why such a turn of the sole is necessary."

Because I would rather not have seams beneath the side of my foot?

"As I mentioned," Melly says, "the construction must suit my cousin's needs."

"Quite, quite, veria. If I can take a look at her foot, we'll see what I can do to make an even better slipper."

I bow to the inevitable with what grace I can muster and extend my foot.

"Hardly what I am used to," he tells Melly as if I were not attached to the foot he is inspecting. As if I had chosen to be born with a deformed foot merely to aggravate him. "But of course I can work with it."

He sits back without having made a single tracing, and after a quick conversation regarding colors and beads, the passing over of various swatches of fabric, and the promise given of new slippers to be delivered in the next two days, he departs.

"That wasn't too bad," Melly says, watching me carefully.

I shrug, well aware it won't be so easy. "Depends on what he delivers."

The following morning I walk into the dining room to find Filadon and Melly deep in discussion.

"Rae," Melly says, catching sight of me, but there's no warmth in her voice. She gives herself a slight shake and says, somewhat more like her usual self, "Come join us."

"Is something wrong?" I ask, crossing to her.

"Not at all," Filadon says, looking like a cat that has got into the milk. "Things have come right, and with your help, I think we may have an answer to a rather difficult question Kestrin has put me."

"Do let her sit down, Filadon," Melly says. "She hasn't yet had a bite to eat."

"The *prince*?" I demand, wondering what I could possibly have to do with him.

"Yes, yes, Zayyid Kestrin. *Do* sit down or Ramella will have my head."

"Among other things," Melly mutters in my ear as I bend to give her a quick hug. I swallow a laugh and slip into the seat beside her. "Don't let him bully you. He's got one of his harebrained ideas."

"Those are typically such fun," I say, starting to grin.

"Sometimes," she agrees. "Harebrained ideas at court are a bit different."

"Now, Melly," Filadon says, taking her hand with a mischievous smile. "Don't prejudice our dear cousin."

She says with mock severity, "Rae is here to visit and keep me company. *Not* anything else." She eyes Filadon darkly. "And she's my cousin, not yours."

"Details," he replies, waving a hand. "Let's put the question to her, why don't we?"

"Please do," I say. "Before I die of curiosity."

Filadon sobers as he turns to me. "I assume you heard all the news about the impostor and the true princess. You haven't asked a word."

"It wasn't my concern," I say. "I only heard that the true princess has been found, and the impostor executed. Rather terribly."

"She was hanged," Melly says. "Though I doubt that got out as far as the tale of what she would have done to the true princess."

"The princess prevailed upon Kestrin and the king to change the sentence," Filadon explains.

I'm glad to hear that, at least. The initial sentence involving barrels and nails still makes my skin crawl. "But what does any of that have to do with me?"

Filadon studies me in silence.

"Go on and tell her," Melly says.

He sighs. "To put it plainly, the new princess has asked Kestrin's aid in finding someone trustworthy to help her. Someone who will not divulge her secrets or betray her."

"Help?" I ask mildly.

"Not *help*," Filadon says quickly. "She's maids and servants aplenty. This is different."

"He means a royal attendant," Melly explains.

Me? A royal attendant? I haven't even *seen* the court yet, let alone developed any concept of dress or propriety or anything, really. How could I possibly attend the princess? A small chuckle breaks from my lips. "That's *absurd*."

"Rae, let me explain," Filadon says, sitting forward.

"Please do," I say. "And while you're at it, tell me why the princess would want a clubfooted country girl with no clue about

the court, or fixing her hair, or doing whatever else it is attendants do."

"She has a maid for her hair, and three other attendants who
can see to the rest," Filadon replies. "You don't have to know the
court; in fact, she needs someone who doesn't have previous alliances. You just have to do whatever it is you think she needs."

"Such as?"

He glances to Melly, who answers. "Make sure she knows
about our customs so she doesn't offend anyone by mistake. Listen for gossip and intrigues and tell her what she needs to know.
Keep her confidences, I suppose. And do what she asks you to do
without betraying her trust."

"Exactly," Filadon says. "You'd be part of Alyrra's entourage,
if you will, staying by her side and giving good counsel."

Good counsel? "I can tell her about horses," I say dryly. "Not
much else."

Filadon shakes his head. "You might be surprised."

"I suppose that's possible." Though vanishingly unlikely.

Filadon nods as if that has decided it. "Good, then. We ought
to be able to meet Kestrin after breakfast."

"What?" I blink at him and then look down at my still-empty
plate.

"She hasn't agreed to it yet," Melly interrupts sharply.

"Let her think about it," Filadon says, stealing her argument.
"I'm sure Kestrin will want to discuss it with her, and they can
both see what they think. After all, Kestrin can't decide whether
or not to recommend her if he hasn't met her."

"I don't know," Melly says, reaching over to spoon spiced liver
onto my plate. "The royal attendants are all from the nobility

themselves, Rae. Younger daughters of families with smaller holdings, women who won't inherit much and so must make a good match. It's a bit of a stretch for Filadon to propose you because you've never lived here and aren't his direct relation."

As Melly's cousin, my standing will be negligible. Her lack of lineage and title might be overlooked through her marriage, but I'm just a poor relation brought in from the country. The other attendants will resent that and the court will hardly respect me for it. I have only to look at my four days of traveling, feeling more like an extra bundle stashed in the carriage than a person, to know that. Just as telling, Filadon doesn't argue this particular point. But . . . attending the princess also means I'll be able to talk to her—she must have already heard about the snatchers, living on the outside as she has. She might listen.

"I understand," I say slowly. Melly purses her lips, still worried, so I add, "Anyway, can you imagine what Bean would say if she found out I refused to meet the prince on my third day in town? She'd never forgive me."

Melly laughs. "True enough."

CHAPTER

9

"Don't forget to address the prince as 'zayyid.'"

I shoot Filadon a glare. "I do know some things, even if I am from the country."

He just gives a little *hmm*. I wipe my hands nervously on my skirt as we wait for Kestrin to join us. Of course I'm to call him "zayyid," but then what? Curtsy and . . . say what? I bite my lip. Perhaps I shouldn't have cut off Filadon quite so harshly. "Anything else?"

"Be yourself."

"I thought that was the last thing you're supposed to do at court."

"True," Filadon says. "I suppose you could try being Melly."

I thump his arm. "You're useless. How does the prince put up with you?"

He grins, glancing away. We sit together in a small salon

of sorts, low-backed sofas running along the wall, a few small hexagonal tables bearing silver trays set here and there, ready to hold drinks or food as the need may arise. I clear my throat, look around again at the understated wealth of what appears to be a rarely used room. Chatting about being an attendant over breakfast and waiting in a well-appointed room to meet a prince are two very different things, it turns out. "I'm not so sure about this, Filadon," I say unhappily.

"I didn't think you'd have second thoughts so soon," he says, frowning.

I haven't had time to have first thoughts. "I don't really know anything about the princess," I say, which is neither here nor there.

"You'll meet her soon, if all goes well. She's a bit more like you than she is like me, which is why she needs an attendant she can trust."

She certainly does after her last companion betrayed her so thoroughly, though what Filadon means by comparing me to himself, I'm not sure. "Why would she trust me?"

More than that, why would she trust a relative of Filadon's if she's looking for someone without prior political allegiances? Unless, I suppose, it's essentially impossible to find someone without any allegiances at all, and this is one that she doesn't distrust.

"You'll have to earn her trust," Filadon allows. "But you'll still be a sight better than her other attendants."

"What do you mean?"

Filadon sighs. "Mina isn't too bad, but the other two—Jasmine and Zaria—have not quite realized they should respect her."

"She's a *princess*. Why would anyone think it acceptable to insult her?"

"They see a girl who was tricked out of her rank and title, which they blame on her perceived foolishness, rather than the impostor's treachery."

"Tricked?" I echo in disbelief.

He turns a level gaze on me. "Trickery is just another word for betrayal."

It's a truth I've known half my life, the little tricks played on me by the town children because I could not keep up with them—because I was clumsy and slow and different—tasting of betrayal. Still, calling what was done to the princess nothing more than trickery seems a bit much.

"You must consider that the princess spent the whole of the winter happily working as a goose girl," Filadon goes on. "There is no one here, except perhaps you and Melly, who can understand that. As far as her attendants and half the court are concerned, that stands witness to her stupidity."

"I think I'd go back to the geese if I were her," I say with some asperity.

"Which is why you would make her an excellent attendant," Filadon says.

"I don't know. It doesn't sound like she's had much power or choice in all the things that have been done to her. Sure, I can understand her preferring hard work to court politics—at least on the surface. But . . ." I shake my head. "I don't think I want to get involved in power at that level. I don't understand it, and

I won't be able to help her."

Filadon leans back, watching me. "Let me tell you a little story," he says quietly. "One that stays between us. Once upon a time, a prince learned that his betrothed had been betrayed and replaced. So he went to the true princess and offered her a chance to return. She refused."

I stare.

"She is only here because, in the end, she chose to return in order to serve our people better and stand by Kestrin when he most needed it. Do not be confused by what else you might hear."

"You're saying she has more power than the stories grant her."

"A great deal more," Filadon says. "The court will come to see that eventually, and she can manage the politics. In the meantime, she needs someone she can lean on without having to wonder if she can trust them to be there."

"I see." It's got to be hard to have gone through what she did, and end up someplace where everything is political and her attendants . . . aren't what she needs. I suppose I could stand in for her for a little while, if she wants me, as unlikely as that seems.

"So now that you understand the princess," Filadon says, "tell me what you hope to gain from being an attendant."

"Gain?" I echo. It's true I want to speak to the princess about the snatchers, but I'm not aiming to be her attendant in order to use her, at least no more than she intends to use me.

"Why else would you agree?"

"Because you bullied me into it?"

He smirks. "Hardly. You would have said no if you didn't want to be here."

"Told you already, Bean would have my head if I passed up

a chance to meet the prince. I'm just keeping myself safe from future sisterly assault."

"Could be. Could be you think it will take you up in the world."

I stare at him. "Up? The farthest up I want to get is riding my horse. And maybe having a good view of the wedding."

Filadon's eyes flicker with amusement, but his expression remains serious. "Some attendants are made rich through the rewards they're given for pleasing the royal family."

"And some country girls are perfectly happy with their horses and goats as is. I'm not interested in, well, having your life. No offense meant."

He laughs, but I catch the flash of surprise in his eyes. "I'm heartbroken."

"It'll mend."

"So why would you do this? Seriously, now, Rae."

I consider the snatchers, and the truth of a princess who has no one to lean on, and the stories Filadon has told me. "I suppose I like that she wanted the impostor hanged rather than tortured."

Filadon raises his eyebrows, but I can't tell his thoughts past that affectation. "Interesting."

I cross my arms, watching him. "You've changed. Or maybe you were always this way, I just didn't see it when you visited." Filadon was always cheerful and genuine and—*open* in a way that he isn't here. He's still deeply himself, but there are more layers to him now, and I can't quite parse his motivations.

He sighs. "A horse ranch is a little different from a court."

"Wouldn't have guessed," I say, waving a hand at the richness of the room. "Must be the lack of manure."

"Oh, there's plenty of that here."

I let out a bark of laughter. His eyes laugh back at me, and I find myself saying, "I don't like that sometimes I can't tell what you're about."

"I wouldn't be much of a politician if you could."

"Maybe, but whose *gain* were you thinking of when you suggested me for this post?"

He doesn't even blink. "The only trouble with you, Rae, is you're a little too straightforward."

"It's the country girl in me. You didn't answer my question."

"I'd rather not play word games with you."

"So you try to distract me?"

He chuckles. "Not much likelihood of that, is there? Once you get your teeth in something, you don't let go."

"Why thank you," I say with mock coldness. "I don't know when I was last complimented so nicely."

"I have a way with words," he agrees. "I think it's why Melly chose me."

I look at him, and warmth fills my heart for this man, however hard he may be to read. He clearly loves my cousin well, and isn't afraid to speak of their love, acknowledge it time and again. He might make light of himself, but never her. "I'm glad she has you," I say quietly.

That wasn't the rejoinder he was expecting, and he goes still, looking at me. Really looking, as if there were some subtext he should have read into my words. But then he responds, just as quietly, "I'm grateful for her every day of my life."

Beautiful man. I smile, and lean back against the sofa, and

look toward the door. What would it be like to be loved like that?

Now, there's a foolish thought. I shift, one foot flat against the ground and the other turned, and keep my gaze on the door.

"The prince should be here shortly," Filadon says after a moment.

I nod, and even though he never did answer my question, I say nothing else.

The door opens a few minutes later. The prince enters, dressed for the morning in formal attire, a brocade knee-length sea-green coat over a cream tunic, his pants loose and flowing. He wears embroidered leather slippers with such long curling toes that I have an urge to tell Filadon that no, they are not suited to manure at all. But I refrain, rising to face the prince in silence.

"Filadon," Kestrin says with a nod. His features are sharp, aristocratic, with high cheekbones and a defined jaw. He would look exceptionally handsome but for a grayish tinge to his features. Perhaps he's been unwell.

Filadon bows. "Zayyid, may I present my wife's cousin, Kelari Amraeya ni Ansarim," he says, naming me as the daughter of my father.

"A pleasure." Kestrin inclines his head to my curtsy.

I smile, unsure whether his words require a response. *Mine too? Good to meet you?* Better to keep quiet.

"Will you be staying with us long?"

"A few months, zayyid," I reply, meeting his gaze. I had thought Filadon's look inscrutable, but this man appears to have all the emotion of a stone. "Through summer's end."

"Very good. Filadon has spoken to you, I surmise."

I dart a glance at Filadon, who merely watches us, unperturbed. Surely the prince should want to know more? "Yes, zayyid."

"Your service will be appreciated. You will, of course, be recompensed. Most attendants receive ample reward over the course of their service, but, since you will be leaving so soon, we will make arrangements for you."

For all that Filadon has just suggested this to me, I am disconcerted by his words, the directness of them. "I don't require payment."

"A reward, then," he says, his eyes warming fractionally. "I would not have it said that we did not value you."

I flush, ready to argue, but Filadon shifts, stepping on my good foot.

The corner of Kestrin's mouth quirks down. "Though I honor you for your sentiment."

He turns back to Filadon. "My betrothed is in her apartments just now. If you escort Kelari Amraeya there, they may meet."

"As you wish, zayyid," Filadon says, bowing. He takes my arm, pinching me gently to remind me to curtsy.

Kestrin nods and a moment later he is gone, the door closing behind him.

"That's it?" I ask, turning to Filadon.

He shrugs, showing not the least sign of curiosity at the strangeness of Kestrin's interview, or the quickness of his decision. "I expect Zayyida Alyrra will make the final decision."

"I thought the decision was also mine to make." I should at

least write to my parents before deciding.

Filadon glances at me from the corner of his eye. "You committed to it when you discussed payment with him."

"Oh."

"Never mind." He pats my arm in a brotherly fashion. "I'll speak with Kestrin and make sure this 'reward' will suit you and your family."

There's not much my family needs. I follow Filadon into the hallway, pondering the possibilities. "My father's been wanting a new stallion for our stables."

"A new stal—" Filadon blinks at me. "You want a *horse?*"

"A stallion, preferably. We've got good breeding mares, but—"

"Shh." Filadon darts a glance over his shoulder, but the hallway lies empty. "Someone might hear you."

"I can't imagine why that would be a problem."

"Rae," Filadon says, with great patience. "It's best not to speak about breeding animals while in the palace."

I eye him askance. "I'm quite certain half the gossip in this place has to do with marriage. Not to mention rumors about illicit affairs. I can't believe discussing horses is somehow worse."

His mouth compresses into a half-amused grimace. "You are correct, but you'll still have to trust me on this one, Rae."

"Fine," I say, heaving a sigh. "Baba will be disappointed."

Filadon exhales with a laugh. "I'm glad you're so positive about taking the post now."

"I'm not," I say with perfect honesty. "However, I can always do something abysmally stupid when I meet the princess and then she won't have me."

Filadon pauses mid-stride, his mouth half open.

"There's always a way out if you look hard enough," I observe. "You're a bit too rule-bound in this court of yours."

"We're something," Filadon agrees. "What, exactly, I leave to you to figure out."

CHAPTER

10

Filadon guides me up a back stair and through a guard room to the royal wing. There, he knocks at one of several exquisitely carved and inlaid doors. A beautifully dressed young woman answers. She curtsies and then looks past Filadon to me, brown eyes sharp.

"My relation, Kelari Amraeya, here to see the princess," Filadon says.

"Of course. You are expected." The woman steps aside to allow me entry. I watch her face as I step in, and feel the old irritation as her features jump in surprise before she recovers herself, cool amusement showing instead. "Have you twisted your ankle?" she asks lightly.

"No," I assure her. "This is how I walk."

"Ah." She glances toward Filadon, expression bland. "Verin?"

"Kelari Amraeya is still learning her way around the palace.

I would appreciate it if you would call a page to escort her back to my apartments."

"I'm sure it won't be long," she says, which doesn't strike me as a particularly nice thing to say.

Filadon's eyes darken, but he merely dips his head and departs. I follow the lady—an attendant, I would guess—through a wide welcoming hall, low sofas lining the wall interspersed with exquisitely carved tables bearing the ubiquitous silver trays, as well as painted vases and various other gold and silver knick-knacks. I suppose we might sell our herd of horses and buy the contents of this room, but that would leave us without enough to afford the rest of our house.

The princess sits at a dressing table in her chamber, her embroidered skirts spread around her, watching as a tall young woman proffers various jewels for her consideration. Alyrra is young, younger than I am, but the intelligence of her eyes and solemnity of her expression suggest a maturity well beyond her years. I study her covertly, keeping my head slightly bent. Being from the western kingdoms, she has the pale skin and lighter-colored hair of those peoples, though not terribly so: her cheeks have a faint natural blush that grants her some color, and her hair is a deep brown.

She waves her hand to dismiss the jewelry before her and turns toward me with a polite smile. I sink into a somewhat jerky curtsy.

"May I present Kelari Amraeya," the first attendant says briskly.

"Welcome to Tarinon, kelari," the princess says, her tone neutral.

"Thank you, zayyida." I rise from my curtsy, silently cursing my clumsiness, aware of the disbelieving look the tall attendant bestows on me, as if I were accentuating my clubfoot on purpose.

"How long will you be staying with us?"

"Till summer's end," I say, resolving to ignore the attendants. At least for now.

Alyrra tilts her head. "How have you found the city so far?"

I hesitate, unsure what she means by her question. "It seems a great and varied place, zayyida, but I've really only seen a little of the city. It's still all very new."

"I see." She turns to her attendants. "Where might we be able to see the city from the palace?"

The taller attendant gives an elegant little shrug. "We rarely have occasion to look at the city from here. Perhaps you might try the palace walls."

Zayyida Alyrra looks at her, waiting, but no further answer is forthcoming. "There is nowhere else you might suggest?"

"Not that I know of," the woman says. Her companion who escorted me here makes no response at all, her head bent. Surely the princess shouldn't be climbing the walls to look at the city? I cannot make out if they want Alyrra to go or not—are they setting her up for a social fall, or do they really think this appropriate?

"The palace walls it is," Alyrra says cheerfully, rising from her seat.

The tall one's lip curls with amusement. My hands tighten into fists, hidden among my skirts, and have to consciously relax them as I step aside for the princess to pass. I no longer have any doubt that princesses are not supposed to climb the palace walls;

if nothing else, her attendants should have suggested a different sort of outing. Surely the princess realizes that?

"But you haven't finished dressing, zayyida," the lady who met me at the door says belatedly. Perhaps she does care.

"The jewelry can wait."

"Your visit with Veria Dinari?"

Alyrra spreads her hands. "If there's one thing I've learned here, Zaria, it's that no one is ever on time. I might as well be fashionable for once."

A faint smile curves Zaria's lips, but she wipes it away at once. If she's Zaria, I'd stake my favorite saddle on the taller woman being Jasmine. No wonder Alyrra's looking for another attendant.

"Walk beside me," Alyrra says to me, starting forward. "We can talk along the way."

I hurry to catch up, but she says nothing more until we have left her apartment and descended the great sweeping staircase that serves as the main entrance to the royal wing. "Jasmine, Zaria, would you lead the way?"

"Oh, we have barely ever visited the walls," Jasmine says, spreading her hands wide, as if this wasn't her idea in the first place.

"Of course," the princess says. "I can't imagine you would have. Come, Amraeya, I'm sure we shall find them well enough ourselves."

Jasmine and Zaria tag along behind us, letting forth the occasional barely audible remark or stifled laugh. Remembering the princess's face when I entered the room, I can't believe her oblivious to the snubs of her attendants. But for whatever reason, she's chosen not to respond to them. Now she asks me about my family, the town where I grew up, even the various roles I fill on our ranch.

"I worked a little with horses," she remarks as we emerge from a side door onto the paved road that circles the palace. The walls loom above us. Alyrra seems to know her way out perfectly well. "It was one of the more difficult choices I have been faced with: to take the position of hostler, or return to being princess."

I glance at her quizzically, but she seems perfectly serious. "Are you happy with your decision?" I ask, because this I do need to know about her, if I am to be her attendant.

"It depends on the company and the time of day." She smiles. "Horses are a great deal easier to get along with."

"Most horses," I agree.

"Most days," she returns.

I grin and glance up at the walls, looming ever bigger before us. "Zayyida?"

"Yes?" she asks, slowing slightly.

I gather my courage, aware that Jasmine and Zaria are not all that far behind us, and say, "I am not sure that it is done for royalty to visit the walls."

She takes my arm and says, her voice strangely cheerful, "I appreciate your concern, kelari. Come along."

We come to a stop before the gates. The guards have snapped to attention, but their eyes keep running over our little group as if they can't quite comprehend what we are doing here. "I am looking for the stairway up," the princess says to them. "I am hoping for a view of the city, and my attendants think you will know better than they how to find it."

One of the soldiers steps forward, a silver ring through his ear proclaiming his status as captain. "Zayyida wishes a view from the walls?"

"If it can be arranged."

He bows. "Of course. Is there a particular part of the city you wish to see?"

"The west side."

"If you will follow me." He leads us farther down the wall. At intervals we pass doors built into the wall, until, reaching a particular one, the captain opens the door to reveal a tight staircase, each flight built above the previous.

"Oh!" Jasmine cranes her head to look up. "I don't think I can handle such a height."

"Then stay below," Alyrra suggests gently. "I would not want you to overexert yourself. You may both wait here. We shall be down shortly."

She turns back to me, hesitates. "Will the stairs be all right for you?"

"Just fine," I assure her.

"I should have asked sooner," she murmurs, so quietly I'm not sure if she's speaking to me or herself. Still, I like her very much for it.

Three long flights up, we step onto the ramparts. A cool spring breeze blows, tugging at our hair and rippling our skirts around us. The princess walks forward to lean against the edge of the wall, gazing out over the city. I wait a step behind her.

"What do you see?" she asks.

I move forward, my hands reaching out to touch the white stone. The city spreads out before me: the same road that I drove in from, filled with buildings crammed together, laundry flapping on rooftops, and below, tight alleys disappearing into shadow. Down the great road that runs here, I spot children playing, though they are too small and far away to see clearly. Still, I remember what I saw from my drive up the road well enough. But what does the princess want me to say? Surely it would be rude to raise issues with her in our very first meeting?

"I see a city far greater than the town I live near," I hedge. She waits. I look out. The people below move quickly, appearing and disappearing from view. I can make out a few run-down shops, though what they sell, I cannot be sure. What else should I say?

She lets out her breath and steps back from the wall.

"There is a great deal of want," I say, the words a little too fast. She pauses, turning toward me. I go on. It's not like I'll have this chance again. "More than I've seen in Sheltershorn. The children are not well clothed; the people do not—I can't say what it is, but they don't look well. The buildings are old; they haven't been repaired in a long time." I point out over the nearest rooftops. "There is one that has fallen in on itself."

"What do you think of it all?" she asks.

I turn my head to meet her gaze. She watches me keenly, her features schooled into pleasant curiosity but her eyes sparking with eagerness. "It's a pity," I say finally. "But perhaps if you see it as well, then something might be done."

"Shall I fix the building that has fallen in on itself?" she asks.

"Not the building," I say, trying not to sound like Bean when someone asks something utterly ridiculous. I'm relatively certain the princess is testing me, but it's hard not to laugh at such a question. "You might look to the children."

She gazes out over the wall. "I might," she agrees. "I have heard," she goes on slowly, "that some children are snatched and never found again."

Hope spikes through me, and I press my lips together firmly to keep from grinning at her, or blurting something overeager.

She looks at me when I don't answer.

"Yes," I say softly.

"What happens to them?"

I take a breath, my thoughts flying to Ani and her grieving family. "In our town, we believe they are sold into slavery."

"Where?"

I shake my head. "Away somewhere. In other lands."

"It seems strange that so little should be known. Do the children never escape?"

She meets my gaze, and I realize in that moment that she knows. That this conversation is to find out about me, rather than the snatchers. "They do sometimes," I say quietly. "They are taken to the Speakers for a blessing to prevent the Darkness—a sort of illness in the blood that can destroy their minds if left unchecked. The Blessing leaves them their minds, but takes a portion of their memories."

"Interesting."

I blink. "Zayyida?" I ask uncertainly.

"Interesting how people are too terrified to ask their children what happened to them before the Blessing, and how little good it does to ask such questions afterward. Don't you think?"

I hesitate. "No one knows when the Darkness might strike.

There are rumors that it can take a child while they tell their story; I don't know if such tales are true, but I doubt a family would be willing to risk it. But you're right. It does no good to ask afterward."

"Indeed." Alyrra leans against the wall, half-turned toward me.

Although the Darkness does not always take our children. Not if they leave the villages and towns, traveling deep into the plains, or even into the mountains. Why that should help, I don't know, but it does. I always assumed everyone knew this, but perhaps it is known more in the country than the city. I open my mouth to say as much, but Alyrra speaks first. "I suppose a princess who knows nothing of such things can hardly hope to change them."

No. She's supposed to care, as are Zayyid Kestrin and the king. They're *supposed* to do something about this. Why bring up the snatchers if only to assert her own perceived helplessness?

The thought brings me up short. Why did Alyrra bring up the snatchers at all, let alone as the first serious question she has posed me? I remember Filadon's sharp grin, the brightness of his eyes when I first pushed him about the snatchers last night. Filadon must have known Alyrra cares about this, which means surely, if she has brought it up, she doesn't intend to give it up after a single conversation.

Alyrra waits, her head tilted toward me. I get the feeling she listens, so I may as well speak.

"I don't know much of the palace or court, zayyida," I say into the quiet. "But perhaps, if you cared to find out more, we could at least better understand . . ." What? The Darkness? How the snatchers work? I'm not sure exactly what I mean, other than that I want the snatchers stopped. "What's happening," I finish vaguely.

"There is that. Still, the people have other needs, do they not?"

Disappointment flares through me. Perhaps I was wrong about her, about what Filadon may have shared. But she is right—there are children going hungry on the streets here, families who spend every waking moment working to earn a meal or money enough to guard themselves from the weather. After a moment, I say, "Of course, zayyida."

"Hmm." She looks back out over the wall, then at me. "I have convinced Zayyid Kestrin to open a house of healing in the city to mark the royal wedding."

"A house—of *healers?*"

"Yes. A place for people to be seen by healers, as well as a healer-mage to attend the more difficult cases." There is a tightness to her features, her eyes suddenly shadowed. "It would be free to those who could not afford it, and a nominal cost for those who can. What do you think?"

A healer-mage . . . I look out over the walls and hold that thought for a moment. When I was born, my parents took me to a healer to see if anything might be done to help my foot, but there was nothing she could do. What we needed, she told my parents, was a healer-mage who could help guide the bones to straighten. When Baba finally found one, he would not entertain their request for even a single consultation. We were peasants to him, and he wished nothing to do with us. My parents rarely speak of it, but I wonder sometimes if that is why, years later, they chose to keep Niya with them, hiding her talent so she would not grow into such a person.

I clear my throat. My own history aside, the princess's idea sounds a little too good to be true. "Where would it be located?"

She smiles, a quick sharp twitch of her lips that makes me think she is inordinately pleased with my question. "We've spoken with a number of guilds, as well as local community leaders, and identified a building in the southwest part of the city. The west side is perhaps the least affluent, but the south side is not much better. So we would strive to serve both. The project is already begun, and the first floor of the house should open the day after the wedding. I would like to have someone check in on the progress daily and report any issues that arise to me. I do not believe my other attendants are quite suited to such a role. Would you like it?"

I hesitate.

"Yes?" In that moment she looks young, hopeful. She reminds me of Niya; they might even be the same age. Only the princess has no older sister, no friend, not even a dependable attendant. And she is trying to remain aware of the needs of the people, and that is a wonderful thing.

"Yes," I agree.

The princess smiles, her whole face warming. The line of her shoulders eases; I had not realized how tense she was till now. "Good. I've been waiting for you."

I find myself smiling back at her, and I am suddenly, deeply grateful that Ani pushed me to come, because that brought me here, to this woman who wants to make a change in the world and thinks I am the one to help her. And perhaps, once the wedding is past, she will bring up the snatchers again, or else I will.

"I suppose there is one more thing we should discuss," Alyrra says.

"Yes, zayyida?" I ask, unsure what else she might ask.

She eyes me with amusement. "What do you think of our little trip to the wall?"

"Zayyida?" She already knows I was concerned about it.

"Why do you think we came here?"

Is that a trick question? "To see the west side?"

"Look behind you," Alyrra instructs. I turn to see the roofs of the palace rising before me. Covered in dark green clay shingles, the nearest roof is of a height with us; beyond it the roofs rise and fall. I can see elevated balconies and unshuttered windows, all more than high enough to see beyond the walls. I turn back to the outer view, trying to make sense of this. If Alyrra *knew* there were places within the palace to see past the wall, why did she allow her attendants to play such a trick on her? Unless she saw through it and used it to her own ends.

"I believe," Alyrra muses, "though I cannot be sure, that this is the safest place in all the palace to have a conversation." She allows herself a faint smile at my stare. I had not considered that even the royal family would have to watch their words. I glance to the side. The captain stands beside the stairwell. We are just far enough, and the breeze steady enough, that our conversation should have escaped him.

"Many of the halls and rooms in the palace have secret passageways running beside them. Conversations are easily overheard. It is something you will have to be aware of as well—both those who will listen in on you, and those who will manipulate you to learn what they wish."

"I understand."

She nods. "When I asked my attendants for a recommendation on where to see the city from, I had hoped you and I might converse in the hallways on our way there, far enough ahead of them that they would not catch our words. Instead, they provided us with the perfect location for such a conversation."

She used *them*? Oh, now this I like about her!

"What I will ask you to do"—Alyrra flicks her fingers toward the city—"will stay between you and me until I am ready to share it with whom I choose, as I choose. So, I ask of you two things: your confidence, and your discretion."

"You have them."

"You are sure you wish to be my attendant, Amraeya?"

"Yes," I say without hesitation.

Alyrra smiles that same warm, open smile. "Then let us go back to my rooms and discuss how all this will work."

CHAPTER

11

Melly and Filadon show their pleasure in the news I share with them in predictably different ways: Filadon bright and sharp and very self-satisfied, and Melly fairly glowing with pride. She makes certain only that the decision was truly mine, and then happily leads me off to a storage room to go through her trunks and find more fabric to have sewn up for the *very many* additional outfits I will apparently require in my new role.

"You'll have an abundance of functions to attend, morning and evening," she tells me when I express my disbelief that I will need any more than the dozen outfits we already ordered. "You'll need more jewelry as well."

Which will all take money. Mama and Baba gave me quite a bit, but I've used a chunk of it ordering clothes and jewelry the last few days. Perhaps I should have told the prince to just give me a new wardrobe as his "reward."

"What I don't understand is how the prince decided so

quickly if it was such an important issue for him to vet me," I tell Melly as we step into the storage room. Alyrra at least had taken the time to chat with me; Kestrin and I barely exchanged a dozen sentences.

"Don't you? Did you ask Filadon?"

"Not really."

She doesn't answer immediately. Instead, she hefts open a trunk and lifts out a stack of fabric. "I expect the prince watched you for some time before approaching. He no doubt heard your conversation while you waited with Filadon."

I stare at her. "But how——?"

"There are a hundred secret listening places in this palace." A fact Alyrra already shared with me. "What did you discuss before he arrived?"

With a sinking feeling in my stomach, I admit, "Why I was willing to take the post and what I expected to get out of it."

"He was listening," Melly says flatly.

"But that would mean Filadon knew."

"Yes." Melly holds a sea-green silk, her finger tracing a swirl of lilac and white embroidery. "Filadon is—he will look out for you, Rae, but his first loyalty is to the royal family." She hesitates. "He's different here from who he is in the country. That's part of why I've always loved visiting you."

I look down, not sure I want to watch Melly's face, the worry line that appears between her brows. "He *is* different," I agree. "But he still loves you very much. That much even I can see."

She sets the blue silk aside abruptly, her expression unreadable. "This is a good one, but I want a few more colors for you. Do you have jewelry to match?"

"I've got my grandmother's ring," I say, holding out my hand to show off the thin band set with a ruby, the setting itself made of two simple curves meeting on either side of the stone. If she doesn't want to talk about her husband's politicking, the least I can do is change the subject.

Melly snorts. "That's a pinky ring."

"Attendants don't wear pinky rings? What is *wrong* with people here?"

She swats her hand at me. "Rae, half the time I can't tell when you're teasing me."

"I do know that rubies won't match sea-green silk," I tell her. "But we ordered that zircon set yesterday with rubies and sapphires both. Won't that do?"

"Ordinarily, yes, but from now on everything you wear should perfectly complement the rest of your appearance. For this, white gold with sapphires."

"Do I look like I have five horses to spare to buy such trinkets?"

"Oh, Filadon will pay," Melly says firmly. "This was his idea, after all."

A very appealing offer, but . . . "It was my choice to become an attendant, and I'll pay the price, thank you very much. Though," I add grudgingly, "if you'd warned me just *how much* these women wear, I probably would have made a different decision."

She laughs. "Filadon and I both knew. And we agreed that we didn't want you to worry about the cost. The princess needs a dependable attendant; if you can do that for her, you'll gain in the end, and so will we. That's how politics works. Filadon would much rather cover the cost of a few dresses and earrings than pull back now, or not have served the family by introducing you to them. This is as much about the princess and you as it is about Filadon and the prince. So let Filadon manage it."

I hesitate. "But—"

"No buts, Rae. We're getting you a full wardrobe worthy of an attendant, jewelry included, and you are not going to argue with me. Now, what about this orange?"

Having seen the princess's attendants, I know I need to dress the part. But that isn't my concern; the cost is. Still, I've a rather strong suspicion that Filadon is playing a long game, and if he wants to pay the price of it, I should probably allow it. Especially given that my family *can't* pay much more without selling off horses earlier than we'd like. So I settle myself beside Melly without further argument and consider the benefits of wearing orange.

My first morning as an attendant passes tolerably well. With the help of a pair of footmen, I shift my belongings to the attendants' quarters where I will be rooming with Mina, the third of the princess's attendants. It is she whom Alyrra assigns to show me around and acquaint me with my duties.

Veria Mina is of average height with a pleasant demeanor, her brown eyes steady. She isn't striking, her very manner retiring, as if she's learned to survive by not drawing attention to herself. Considering Jasmine's hard beauty and cutting mannerisms, that might not be too far from the truth.

She waits patiently as I unpack my belongings, her hands busy with a bit of embroidery. Our room is exquisitely appointed, with gorgeous mosaics upon the wall, carved ceiling beams, plush carpets, and embroidered silk bedcovers upon the low beds. It takes me only half an hour to transfer my belongings to the remaining wardrobe and set out my writing box on the desk. I sent a long letter to my family last night, following up on the short note I sent upon arrival. But with the three to four days it takes for a letter to reach home, it will still be a little while before I hear back from them about my new position.

"Ready?" Mina asks as I turn away from the writing desk.

When I nod, she sets aside her embroidery and ushers me into the princess's apartments. She reviews our duties as we go over the rooms. As Filadon assured me, we don't clean—there is a pair of maids for that—but we do make sure the rooms are sparkling, help the princess select jewelry and outfits for her daily wear, and generally make sure she's comfortable.

"But our true duty revolves around attending the princess when she goes out," Mina explains. "She has asked that you attend her this afternoon. She'll be going out for a drive with Zayyid Kestrin. It will be relatively private, and a good way for you to learn your role. Just follow Zayyid Kestrin's attendant's lead if you are unsure what to do."

Follow *his* lead? "But won't one of you come along?" I ask. I hadn't thought I'd have to attend Alyrra at once, without either training or another of her attendants present to ease the way.

"I'm afraid not," Mina says with a politely kind smile. "I believe the princess thinks this will be an easier start for you. We'll go over all the possible scenarios you may need to respond to beforehand."

"Thank you," I say, since there's nothing else I can do.

By early afternoon a blanket of clouds has blown in, thick but gentle in its grayness, offering the promise of a light spring rain. I meet the princess together with Mina in the inner sitting room. Alyrra inquires after my day and then leads me away, bidding Mina to take the afternoon off.

We join the prince in an outer courtyard, his own attendant three steps behind him. Kestrin greets Alyrra with unaffected pleasure, his features mobile with emotion, utterly unlike the detached, shrewd young man I met only yesterday. She smiles in response, her whole face warming. If Filadon hadn't told me they'd known each other longer than the brief week or two since the princess returned to the palace, I wouldn't know what to make of such a meeting.

"You have met my newest attendant, of course," Alyrra says, turning slightly to nod toward me.

I dip into a deep curtsy, aware of the jerkiness of it as I reach its lowest point. Oh well. It's not as if the prince didn't notice when last we met. If he doesn't mind, why should I care what his attendant thinks?

"Kelari Amraeya," the prince says.

As I rise, he introduces his attendant, an impeccably dressed and distantly polite young man. The princess and I are then ushered into the waiting carriage, the interior all gilt edges and shining velvet.

Kestrin sits opposite Alyrra. They discuss first the project Alyrra mentioned to me yesterday—her house of healing for the poor folk of the city—and then the various preparations for the wedding. I take my cue from Kestrin's attendant, sitting quietly and watching the buildings through the window. As the carriage rolls past the city gates, I glance about once, uncertainly, for I had not thought we would leave the city proper. But no one else takes notice, and since I have no idea of our destination, I keep my silence.

The carriage turns and the fields give way to a graveyard larger than I have ever seen. Great plots of land, lined with low stone boundary walls and filled with row upon row of graves, each marked by a few stones laid at the head. This must be where all the dead of the city are buried. The carriage rattles along, the first drops of rain spattering against the glass windows.

"We're almost there," Kestrin says, and the carriage falls silent.

We come to a stop by a plot with a slightly higher wall, the stones nearly black, unlike the more typical gray stones used to build the other walls. I clamber down after the prince and princess, pulling my cloak's hood up to shield myself from the gentle rain. Of all the places I'd imagined we were going, a graveyard was not among them.

Kestrin and Alyrra proceed through a wrought-iron gate held open by a footman. I glance uncertainly toward the other attendant. He nods his chin toward the gate and then steps forward himself. Right, then, to the graves we go.

We remain a good distance behind the royals, coming to a stop when they do. They stand before yet another seemingly anonymous grave, their voices nearly inaudible. It takes me a moment to realize it is the most recent of all the graves here, for there are no more after it, nor is there another row behind us. It is the last grave in a smaller yard, whose wall is more carefully crafted than all the rest. We have a tradition of burying all of our dead in this manner: a few stones at the head, no marks of distinction. But the graveyard itself creates a subtle distinction, one that must mean something. Just as the way that Alyrra and Kestrin face the final grave here means something.

"Is that the queen's grave?" I ask softly, my eyes flicking to where the royal couple stands.

Kestrin's attendant gives a single silent nod.

Here lie generations of kings and queens, princes and princesses. One day, the king and Kestrin and even Alyrra will be buried here. Today, Alyrra has come to pay her respects to her betrothed's late mother.

I stand patiently, keeping most of my weight on my good foot. My newly made slipper is tight on my turned foot, its shape not quite right, and already I can feel where it's rubbed away a layer of skin along the top of my foot. I'll no doubt have blisters as well, along the side of my foot that rests against the ground. If only we'd chosen to ride through the rain, I could have at least worn my old riding boots, polished to a shine and a perfect fit. Never mind. There's nothing to be done now but try not to limp more than usual.

Eventually, Kestrin and Alyrra turn and start back to the gate. But when they reach the carriage, they pass it, crossing the road to the opposite graveyard and following the wall to an opening: no gate here.

Kestrin waves away the guards who rode out with us, now standing watch around the carriage and the edges of the graveyard, then glances back at us. "Kelari Amraeya, you will accompany us?"

I nod, for all that his tone makes it clear it's a command and not a question. Kestrin's attendant takes the prince's cue and falls back to wait beside the carriage.

I walk on, my leather slippers with their embroidery slowly picking up mud and the hem of my skirt growing heavy with dampness as it brushes over the low grasses here. I've never minded getting wet before, but I've never worn such fine clothes in the rain either. I can only hope they withstand the outing. If I have to get a new outfit each time it rains, I might just need to drop a pitcher of juice on Alyrra and get myself dismissed.

Ahead of me, Kestrin and Alyrra come to a stop before an open grave. I stare, but there's no mistaking it: not the mound of soil beside the hole, not the shovel left upon the ground, and certainly not the hole itself, gaping wide.

I swallow, glancing over my shoulder. Kestrin's attendant remains by the gate, waiting patiently. The soldiers—three quads for a total of twelve men—remain alert, some of them watching the road, and no fewer than four of them watching the royals from afar. This was planned, right? Clearly it was. But the idea of leaving a body unburied for hours just so someone could come look at it seems horribly wrong.

I stop a short distance away and keep my eyes on the ground at my feet. I don't want to catch even an accidental glance of what lies inside the grave. It will just be a shrouded body, I tell myself. It's not as if I would know who they were.

"He was a good friend," Alyrra says, her voice uneven. "I thank you for allowing this."

"Would that I could have protected him," Kestrin says. He stands near her, but there is an awkwardness to his stance. He wants to comfort her, but it is not his place—not until they are married.

Alyrra lifts a hand, wipes at her face. She's crying; a quiet, steady sort of weeping. I plunge my hand into my skirt pocket and pull out a kerchief. Hobbling forward, I offer it to Alyrra.

She takes it with a watery smile. I drop my gaze and find myself looking into the grave, at a horse's head. A tingle of shock runs through me as I stare at the thing, for it is only the head and a portion of the neck nailed to a wooden plaque. The eyes and lips are sewn shut with dark thread, the mane stringy and tinged with black, the cheeks stained gray with damp. It is a ghastly sight.

I take a quick step back, looking away so Alyrra won't see my revulsion. It's not the horse's fault. Or the princess's—at least, I doubt it, given that she clearly mourns what's been done to the creature.

"Farewell, Falada," the princess says, and I'm grateful she didn't notice my reaction.

Princess. The word drifts up from the grave, soft as a spring breeze. My gaze jerks back to the horse's head, only now its eyes are open and seeing, the stitching gone. Its lips, however, do not move, even as its voice murmurs, *Farewell.*

I don't know what magic this is, what could possibly cause a *horse's head* to open its eyes and send words up from its grave. Nothing comes back from the dead, or so I've always been taught.

"Farewell," Alyrra says again, as if there were nothing strange here whatsoever. Kestrin stoops and lifts a sheet from where it lies folded at the foot of the grave. At Alyrra's nod, he shakes it out and bends, letting it go as it flutters down to cover the head. With a soft sigh, Alyrra turns and moves past me, toward the carriage.

Kestrin falls into step with her. I stare at him, and he flicks his fingers toward the carriage, reminding me to move, before returning his gaze to the princess.

Right. Move. Because I did not just see some grisly horror within the grave, nor then see it transform and hear it speak.

The ride back passes quietly. Alyrra does not seem given to conversation, and Kestrin, after a few quiet words, lets her be. I am grateful for the silence, grateful that I do not have to listen or respond to anything, for my mind is too busy wrestling with the reality of what I've seen.

By the time we arrive at the palace, I have made up half a story to explain the inexplicable: the impostor had the princess's horse killed, its head nailed to a plaque as a reminder to the princess to keep her silence, or distance, or whatever it was the impostor wished. It seems possible, but does not even begin to explain how a disembodied horse's head opened its eyes and spoke.

Perhaps Filadon knows. But no. I might ask after a gray or white horse the princess once had, but I sincerely doubt the princess wants me spreading rumors about, or even confidentially inquiring after, horses that speak from the grave. Literally. If I want direct answers, I will need to ask her, or not ask at all.

I grip my hands together in my lap, keep my gaze lowered, and remind myself that the creature at least did not seem evil. There was nothing dark or malicious in its look. In truth, when it opened its eyes, it was a sight less grim than when it slept with its eyes stitched shut. And it is clearly being buried. Whatever secrets it carries, whatever truths the princess wishes kept silent, they will end there, at that grave.

At the palace, Kestrin escorts the princess up to her rooms, bidding her adieu at her door. I follow her in. She pauses a moment, her gaze going to the bell pulls along the wall, the green one to call her attendants, the blue to raise the alarm in the guard room, the cream for the servants. Then she turns to me, evidently deciding I am better than a bell pull, and holds out my kerchief.

"Thank you, Amraeya," she says. "You will want to change into something dry, I'm sure. I am going into my room. Send Jasmine and Zaria in to me, would you?"

"Of course, zayyida," I say, taking the kerchief. It is damp in my hand, a testament to her tears. Her eyes are faintly pink even now.

I curtsy and let myself out, grateful to leave the princess and her secret grief.

CHAPTER

12

I raise my hand to knock on the doorframe to Jasmine and Zaria's room. The door is cracked open, but I don't feel so friendly with the women within that I might just swing it open.

"What was the prince thinking?" Zaria demands. I pause despite myself—surely they don't know about the horse's head too? But she goes on, "A cripple? To wait on the princess after all she's been through? *I* would have been insulted."

"She doesn't know enough to be," Jasmine says lightly. "Imagine, an attendant who can't even curtsy properly!"

I let my hand drop, my cheeks burning with mortification. But I *can't* curtsy any better; my foot won't allow it.

Jasmine says, "But then, perhaps it merely requires a different perspective. Our barnyard princess, lover of animals that she is, has taken in a little lame mongrel. Why should any of us be surprised?"

My hands curl into fists at my side as Zaria titters in response.

Barnyard princess? Lame mongrel? How *dare* they?

"Oh, but Jasmine, think on it! This peasant knows nothing! And she'll be an embarrassment to the princess wherever they go, hobbling about like a—well, like a lame dog. Why would the princess do such a thing?"

"Why would the prince? Really, the girl grew up on a *horse* farm. As if dressing and attending a princess were akin to saddling a horse! I tried, Zaria. Truly, I did."

"Did you?" Zaria says, her questioning tone echoing my sentiments. What does Jasmine think she did other than mock the princess?

"The *walls*! And I was so obvious about it! A peasant has no place in the palace proper. The only way to show such a creature the city from the palace is up on the walls with the common soldiers. And what does the princess do? Go running up there with her pet in tow. You would think she had more sense!"

"Oh," Zaria says uncertainly. "Is that what you meant?"

No, it wasn't. I remember clearly Jasmine's snide amusement as we started off for the walls. That wasn't what she meant at all; this is just the story she wants spread so that the princess will look a fool rather than Jasmine herself appear malicious. Trickery is just another word for betrayal, Filadon said. And here it is, on the other side of the door from me.

"What else could I have possibly intended?" Jasmine inquires lightly. "Well, there is no help for it. We shall have to put up with the cripple until a replacement is found."

"But didn't your cousin—"

"I am *well* aware that my cousin was passed over, Zaria. There is no need to bring that up. I am quite sure you would have been passed over as well, had you not already been established as an attendant. Then again, if the princess is looking for *peasants*, none of us should have been selected." Jasmine heaves a sigh, and I hear a rustle of cloth as she moves across the room, toward the door.

With a quick inhale, I raise my fist and rap on the doorframe, hard and loud, because retreat is not an option.

"Yes?" Jasmine swings open the door.

"You're wanted," I say briefly. "Both of you, in the princess's rooms."

"Veria," Jasmine says, voice sharp.

I smile and dip my head, as if she were addressing me rather than schooling me in how to address her. Then I turn my back on her and start toward the room I share with Mina.

"You will address me as veria," Jasmine says, her voice pitched to carry.

I turn back to her with a false smile plastered across my face. "Of course, just as you will address me as kelari," I say. "What else would we call each other?"

She blinks at me, taken aback, and I seize the opportunity to slip into my room before she manages to snap a reply. Mina looks up from her desk, a letter half-written before her. "Are you back, then?"

I nod, though the answer is perfectly apparent. I can hear Jasmine muttering in the hallway, Zaria's voice responding.

Whatever they're saying, I don't want to hear it. I start across the room toward my own desk.

"Amraeya? Are you all right? You seem to be . . ."

Haunted by an undead horse's head? Paying the price of

listening at doorways? I look toward Mina tiredly. "Yes?"

She watches me , eyes narrowed. "Is your foot hurting you?"

I grimace and sink into the chair. "A bit." I cross my leg over my knee, slip off the still slightly muddy slipper, and inspect my foot. The skin is an angry red where the top of the shoe rubbed, and there are blisters already forming along the side of my foot.

Mina's breath hisses between her teeth.

"Do you know where I can get some bandages?" I ask lightly. "I don't think the cobbler quite made these shoes right."

"You should, perhaps, see a healer," she says, her voice that same detached polite tone she uses with the princess. But a faint line has appeared between her brows. Does she not allow herself to worry about others? Or rather, to show her concern?

"Is there—where would I find one?" I ask.

Mina smiles faintly. "We're in a palace. There's even a healer-mage, though she won't see everyone. Do you wish to ask the princess to refer you?"

"No, they're just blisters." As long as they don't get infected, I can manage. Mina nods and gives me directions to where I can find one of the resident healers, and then shoos me off.

I start back to the royal wing sometime later, my foot wrapped in bandages and my ears full of admonishments for wearing such shoes—in the pursuit of beauty! As if, the healer's look said, I could attain such heights. I was more than happy to leave her care and hobble my way toward the royal wing. I take the back way there, up the stairs to the guard room so that I don't cross paths with Jasmine if I can help it.

There's only one group of four guards in the room—a standard quad. They are all steadily watching the doorway as I step through, as if they heard the uneven sound of my ascent, however quiet it seemed to me.

I offer a smile that is more grimace than anything, and head for the connecting doorway. One of them rises and moves to intercept me. I nod as the man reaches the doorway at the same time I do. He looks vaguely familiar. Did I see him this morning at the graveyard?

"Kelari Amraeya," he says, dark eyes flicking over me. "Is all well?"

"Yes, kel," I say uncertainly. "Is it not allowed to use the stairs?"

I specifically remember Mina recommending them as a less visible approach to the royal wing. I'd rather not think she misinformed me. Unless it was a different set of stairs she pointed out. . . .

The soldier gestures me through the door and steps out after me. "Not at all. It is only that the stairs are designed to amplify the sound of anyone coming up, that we may not be taken by surprise. We are not used to the sound of your step."

"I see," I say dryly.

The guard continues to walk with me. He wears the light armor of the royal guard, leather and studded velvet. He is easily a head taller than I am, with deep brown eyes and a generally pleasant face, though now the skin around his eyes is tight, and his jaw is set. The look of him puts me on edge. At least the door to the attendants' quarters is right here.

"The princess seems pleased with you," he says, turning his head to catch my gaze. The silver ring through his left ear glints in the light of the luminae lamps, the inset sapphire glittering blue. A highly placed captain, then, and not just a guard.

"Thank you," I say, unsure what response he expects from me.

He comes to a stop before me, just blocking the door.

"There is something I hoped you could tell us. The second grave the princess visited this morning; what was in it?"

I look up at him, taken aback, the memory of the horse's head flashing before my eyes.

"Yes, that expression," he says. "You wore it at the graveyard as well, after you looked into the grave. What did you see there?"

I swallow. "It was a grave, kel. I am not used to looking in one. That is all."

"That isn't an answer," he says quietly.

The princess's secrets aren't mine to share. If the royals didn't tell their guards what was within the graves, then, arguably, they don't need to know.

I make to step around him, one hand reaching for the door-knob. "I don't see that it's your concern."

He turns with me, his hand closing over it first. "It is, actually. It's our job to keep the royal family safe. We cannot do that if we do not know whether she buried a friend or enemy, or something else altogether—and how they came to be there."

"They came to be there because they were dead," I say, keeping my voice even despite the anger roaring through me. Is he actually trying to intimidate me? "Considering the prince was there as well, I suspect the princess will be protected. In fact, I suggest you bring up your concerns on how to keep the princess safe to *her*—I'm sure she'll hear you out."

"There's no need for that when you can answer us just as well," he says, his voice low. "What was in that grave?"

"Ask her yourself. I'm going in," I say through clenched teeth, reaching to push his hand away from the doorknob. Instead, he releases the knob, his fingers closing on my wrist. I try to pull back, but his grip is too tight. He steps toward me, shoving my other shoulder so that I am pressed up against the door. His chest walls me in, one hand pinning my wrist to the door, the other resting beside my head. I fight back a surge of panic that overwhelms my anger.

"Not yet," he says, his voice deceptively mild. Behind him, I hear no sound of movement, no voice. My breath rattles in my chest. Either his whole quad planned this, or they haven't yet noticed what their captain is doing. I'm not sure they'd stop him regardless.

He tilts his face down, looking me straight in the eye. "It's a simple question, my girl. I'd like to think we can trust you. What did you see?"

My girl? Oh no. I'm not his girl, or the princess's lame mongrel, or a fool whose mind is apparently as useless as her foot. I answer him, but not in the way he expects. I snap my knee up into his groin, wrenching my hand free at the same time. He yelps a curse, reaching for me even as he hunches over, but I slam both hands against his chest and shove.

I may be a royal attendant, but it wasn't all that long ago I was working with horses, lifting saddles, and carrying bags of oats and barley. I send him backpedaling halfway across the hall, his eyes wide with surprise.

I yank the door open and step through. "Stay out," I snarl, and slam the door with all my strength.

CHAPTER
13

The princess returns before dinner, bringing Jasmine and Zaria with her. Thankfully, I am not expected to attend her tonight. The graveyard was enough of a first day for me, and I am still slightly unbalanced after my hallway encounter with the captain. At least the salve the healer gave me has numbed the ache of my blisters.

Alyrra seems pensive, having little to say about Mina's selection of clothes for the evening. She only nods and thanks her, and asks us to select the jewelry as well. As she turns away, she pauses, her gaze catching on me—or rather, my wrists. I shift, pulling my hands up into my sleeves, but Alyrra reaches out uncertainly.

"Amraeya—?"

"Zayyida?" I ask, keeping my voice light and unworried.

She looks up, her brows furrowed and her eyes wide and sickened.

"Is there something wrong?" I ask, careful not to glance down to my wrists. *Why* did the seamstress insist on cutting the sleeves just short of my wrists to show off the gold bangles that haven't yet been delivered? I don't even *like* wearing bangles.

Alyrra jerks her attention away, to Mina. "Mina, would you wait in the outer room for me a moment?"

Mina casts me a worried glance. I shrug uncertainly. She dips her head and departs, closing the door behind her.

"Amraeya . . . is your wrist bruised?"

I hesitate.

"Please, will you show it to me?"

Alyrra looks unwell, her face decidedly pale and her brown eyes shadowed. Looking at her, I don't know what to do. What are the ramifications of reporting what happened to me?

She closes the distance between us and her hand wraps around mine, her fingers cool. "Let me see, Amraeya."

She lifts my hand, and I let her slide back the sleeve to show the ring of bruises just above my wrist. For a long moment she looks at it, her expression hidden from me by the tilt of her face.

"Who did this?"

I don't know what will happen if I tell her, but at the same time, she ought to know that the royal guards are more than capable of bullying others. So I say, finally, "A soldier. He wanted to know . . . about the grave. About what was in the second grave. I didn't tell him."

Alyrra lets go of my hand and steps back. I tug down the sleeve again.

"I see." Her voice is soft and shaky. "I am sorry, Amraeya. It won't happen again."

How can she be sure of that?

"Come, let's go out to Mina."

When we reach the outer sitting room, Mina rises to greet us once more.

"Please check at the guard room and ask Captain Matsin to wait on me," Alyrra says. "You may go to your own quarters after that, and take a rest. I'll ring for you when I'm ready to go to dinner."

"As you wish." Mina hurries from the room. I watch her go with a sinking sensation.

"Come sit," Alyrra says, and seats herself stiffly on a sofa. I sit down as well, wondering how this can possibly come right with Alyrra as upset as she is. Or perhaps as princess she can demand things of captains and expect to be fully obeyed.

A confident *tap-tap* sounds on the door. I rise, knowing it is my duty to open the door and hoping against hope it will not be the captain from this afternoon. If it's another captain—or his superior—this whole conversation will go much easier.

"Stay," Alyrra says. I turn with a sense of relief, only to find Alyrra watching me sharply.

As I sit down once more, the knock comes again. This time, Alyrra calls out, "Enter."

It is him. He steps in, closing the door behind him and then bowing to Alyrra. He flicks a single glance at me, an acknowledgment that merely places me as present in the room. I can't read his emotions at all. My stomach tightens into a knot, though I know he can't possibly pose the princess any danger. And if she establishes he's to leave me alone, he will, won't he?

"Captain Matsin," she says. "I asked a favor of you this morning."

I look at her sharply. What?

"Zayyida."

"I trusted you to see to it in an honorable manner."

He stiffens, and so do I, a dreadful realization creeping over me. Surely not—I must be mistaken.

"Why does my attendant have a bruise around her wrist?"

He pales slightly beneath the brown of his skin. His gaze flicks to me again. "Forgive me, zayyida. I did not intend to cause harm. I did not think I was that rough."

"You—" I glance between them, trying desperately to understand.

"I am sorry, Kelari Amraeya," Alyrra says with careful formality. "Zayyid Kestrin and I requested Captain Matsin to test your trustworthiness. As my attendant, you will be privy to a great many things that must not be shared. I needed to be certain that you would keep my confidence regardless of who approached you, or how. I did not intend for you to see into the grave this morning, but once you did, it seemed as good a test as any."

I stare at her, willing her words back into her mouth. Willing them unspoken, unheard. She *asked* Matsin to corner me? I shake my head, as if I could undo this whole day by refusing it.

"Kelari Amraeya," Matsin says quietly, "I beg your forgiveness. I meant to frighten you, and then only in order to test your honor. I did not mean to harm you."

"I see," I say, and have to swallow to wet my throat. "Well, I am not sorry that I kneed you and shoved you."

His lips twitch. "It was well done, kelari. You protected yourself, and kept the princess's confidence."

Oh, indeed. I don't need his praise to know that.

I push myself to my feet, anger and a sickening sense of betrayal warring for dominance in my breast. "Zayyida, I have had a long day. Permission to retire."

Alyrra winces. "I am sorry this played out as it did, Amraeya."

"I understand," I say, although I don't, really.

"You will attend me in the morning?"

It's a question rather than an order, and in it I hear Alyrra's concern that she has pushed me too far. Perhaps she has. I don't know—I did not think this day could get any more unsettling. Now I don't know what to think.

"With your permission, zayyida, I require some time to reflect." I move past Captain Matsin toward the door, careful not to meet the princess's gaze.

She nods. I let myself out at once. Unfortunately, Captain Matsin follows me, closing the door behind us.

"Kelari," he says as I walk quickly down the hall to the attendants' access door, my uneven gait loud in my ears.

I turn. "What do you want?"

"I—I asked your forgiveness," he says, coming to a stop a few paces away. "Will you grant it?"

For a long moment, I consider him. He claimed he didn't mean to harm me, and I can believe that—the bruise is no doubt because of how forcefully I yanked my hand out of his grip. But he did mean to frighten me, to bully me, depending on Alyrra to explain his actions away. All to assure themselves I would be loyal to her. It is a strange thing to realize, as I meet his gaze, that I can forgive what he has done, but I won't forget it. "Yes," I tell him.

He dips his head, but his eyes still watch me. Perhaps he's as aware as I am that forgiveness does not mean everything. "And the princess? You will continue to serve her?"

"That is no concern of yours," I say, and turn on my heel. He watches me in silence as I hobble to the attendants' door, his gaze like a burr against my skin.

Halfway down the inner hallway toward my bedroom, I come to a halt. Mina will be there, and she'll want to know what just transpired. I don't want to talk to her. I don't want to talk to anyone, really.

I turn around and stump back to the hall door. When I peek out, Captain Matsin is no longer in sight. No doubt he's returned to the guard room. Well, then, I'll just have to leave via the grand staircase and hope no one is standing at the bottom to watch me limp my way down.

My hopes are sadly unfounded, for when I am halfway down, a group of young noblemen appear, proceeding toward me from the hall below. Of course.

I keep my head bent and they pause at the bottom of the stair to allow me passage. It's only as I reach the bottom that I realize the party contains Zayyid Kestrin, his attendants, and what appears to be another nobleman or two.

I step aside and curtsy, my cheeks burning.

"Is all well, Kelari Amraeya?" the prince asks, no doubt because I *shouldn't* be using this stair without the princess. Or maybe because I look as upset as I feel.

I dip my head further. "Zayyid."

He gestures to the man beside him as I rise. "Allow me to

introduce my cousin, Verin Garrin of Cenatil. Garrin, this is Kelari Amraeya, attendant to my betrothed."

"Honored," the man says, bowing. Garrin is handsome in a damning sort of way, his midnight hair falling just past his shoulders, his high cheekbones accenting the shape of his eyes and the length of dark lashes that are, no doubt, the envy of half the young women at court.

"And my remaining attendants, whom you have not met," Kestrin goes on, and introduces them one by one.

I smile and nod and dip small curtsies, and find the prince watching me narrowly, his smile pleasant and his eyes sharp as onyx. He knows. He knows what Captain Matsin was ordered to do—he was part of the whole plan to test me—even if he doesn't know about the bruises as yet, and he must see in my face that I don't want to be here. He's trying to show me some favor now, assure me of my place and establish it in the court, so that I would neither want to leave my position nor dare risk the embarrassment of walking away from it now.

Except I don't *care* about the court. I would much rather have my horses and forget all this—this ugliness, and the otherworldly reality of undead horses, and the indisputable truth that even those one means to serve can betray, whether intentionally or not.

I dip a last wooden curtsy to the prince. As they start up the stairs, I turn to finally make my escape.

"She doesn't seem pleased to be here." Garrin's voice floats down toward me.

"Let us hope we can convince her yet," Kestrin returns.

I clench my jaw and keep walking. So many games. I can't even tell whether I was meant to overhear that or not, but it seems likely. Why did I ever think such a position would be a good idea for me?

No reason, but that I felt sorry for the princess, to have attendants who would misguide her, to have come through such a harrowing experience and find herself alone yet again. It didn't occur to me she might play her own games.

But that's not altogether true. I had some strange, irrational idea that I might be able to influence things here in the palace, bring attention to the snatchers. And the princess *did* mention them up on the palace walls. But what do I actually know about palace life? How did I think for even a moment I could navigate a place like this *and* influence people so far above me? And not get caught up in games and manipulations and—and the outright ghastliness of the dead horse's head. Though I don't suppose anyone could have expected that. But I don't want anything to do with it, not with the horse's head, or the clever princess, or her scheming attendants.

I wend my way out of the palace, pausing only to ask a servant for directions, and keep going until I'm facing the wide cobbled space outside the palace walls. I turn slowly, unsure what I'm doing. There is West Road leading down to the stables where the princess once worked, the cobbles still damp from the rain earlier today. And in the opposite direction is East Road heading toward the merchant center, where Melly and I went shopping. Where I saw the boy with the Darkness.

I stand a long moment looking toward the road, and then I

start walking. I don't understand how politics work, or the palace, and I'm not sure I want anything to do with either. But at least I can ask questions here. The people of the city are bound to know more than we do in Sheltershorn. If I can learn anything at all, perhaps there might be some hope of tracking down Seri. Or keeping the snatchers from visiting Sheltershorn again.

CHAPTER

14

It takes me three-quarters of an hour to reach familiar streets, and another quarter of an hour after that to find the shop where the boy sat, the bowl of peas before him. Today he sits at the back of the shop, lost in the early evening shadows, a cat on his lap and a faint, gentle smile on his face.

"Can I help you?" the shopkeeper asks. She is a small woman, her bearing confident, her hair braided back to reveal attractive features and an intelligent gaze.

I should buy something. I look around uncertainly as she waits. Her store is filled with lace and beaded trim, tassels and corded knots pre-fashioned into buttons. My fingers brush my pockets, but I don't have my purse with me. No, I walked out of the palace in my attendants' clothing, looking rich and without a coin to spare.

"Is something wrong?"

I look up with some embarrassment. "I seem to have left my purse at home. I'm sorry."

She laughs, a kind sound that makes the boy look up, the smile on his face growing wider. "I've done the same before."

"Do you mind if I sit down a moment before I go back? I didn't think I'd be walking so much today." I didn't think at all, or I would have realized that my foot only felt so good because of that salve the healer gave me. With its numbing effect long since dissipated, I can tell my skin is not happy beneath the bandages.

"Of course," she says, and offers me a seat on a small, round cushioned stool. "Have you been in before? I don't know that we've met."

"We haven't," I agree. "I passed your store the other day and decided I wanted to come back and see it."

"But you're not from the city? You have a bit of an accent."

My cheeks warm. No doubt everyone I've met in the palace has noted it. "I'm from Sheltershorn. I'm visiting my cousin for the summer."

"Ah! You've come for the royal wedding."

We pass a comfortable few minutes chatting about the upcoming wedding and how business has been good for her given how a good half of the city's population is dedicated to having new clothes for the celebrations. She sits by her counter, winding up reels of lace and sorting them into the appropriate baskets.

"Will there be celebrating in your town as well?"

It's the opportunity I've been looking for. "There were some festivities planned," I say slowly. "But no one's thought about it the last week or two."

"Whyever not?"

"We lost another child," I say quietly.

She sits back slowly, the lace forgotten before her. "The snatchers."

I nod. "We don't lose children very often—we're a small town. Does it happen more here?"

"Every day."

"Surely someone is trying to stop them," I say, as if my wishing it would make it so.

"The snatchers are brutal. They kill or take those who discover them. And those who escape—you see what happened to my Andril."

My eyes flick to her son. He is watching the cat again, but even now, as present as he is, there is an absence to his gaze.

"I—I'm sorry."

"It is no fault of yours. He escaped them but didn't make it to the Speakers in time. Eventually, word reached me of a boy who had been found and was being kept at a temple a day's ride downriver. So my prayers were answered, and I had my son back." She clears her throat. "I am grateful every day that he is with me, but I wish—I wish it had not cost him so much."

"Did you ever learn how he escaped?"

She shakes her head.

I take a slow breath. "Are there others who have escaped? Whose families might have some idea how the snatchers work, or how they might be stopped?"

"Oh, child. These are dangerous questions. No one speaks of the answers. To do so is to invite the snatchers' attention, and that is death, or worse."

"Death?" I echo.

"You are perhaps protected from such realities in your town, but here . . . if the snatchers get word that someone is trying to bring attention to them—perhaps that they have some small detail gleaned from a child before their Blessing—the reprisals are quick and brutal. I have a friend whose daughter escaped. It was after those terrible days following the queen's death."

That had been bad news, certainly, but it hadn't felt so terrible to us. "She was a good queen," I say rather lamely.

The shopkeeper shakes her head. "She was, but I meant the spate of disappearances that happened over the course of the days of mourning. We must have lost near two dozen children in those three days."

Two dozen children? That's—I realize the city could easily hold ten thousand people and still have space for more—but over twenty children lost in a handful of days is almost beyond comprehension.

"My friend's daughter was the only one who got away," the shopkeeper continues. "She told the whole of her story before being blessed, and my friend's husband went to every guardhouse he could find with her story. Somewhere between one and the other, he was set upon and beaten to death."

I stare at her, horrified. "But—but how could they have known?"

"He was not quiet about what he intended. If they knew from the rumors spreading through his neighborhood, they could have easily tracked him."

"Did the guards do nothing?"

"What were they to do with a dead body?"

That's not what I meant, but it's answer enough. They took no action with the girl's story either. I rub my arms, chilled. Here is all the answer I need: acting on my own, seeking the truth on the streets, I will be able to stop the snatchers no more effectively than this man. And might lose my life in the attempt as well.

"So you see that you must be careful too," the woman says, her voice kind. "I understand why you spoke to me, but do not ask anyone else lest you become a target yourself."

I dip my head, but I can't help asking, "Do you remember the girl's story?"

"Whether I do or not, I won't be sharing it. Didn't you hear me, child? The telling of it could spell your death, or mine."

"I understand," I say, although I don't. Surely she doesn't think I'm allied with the snatchers? She's trying to protect both herself and me, but that leaves all the rest of the children of our land at risk. Still, I doubt I can press any more answers from her.

Outside, the streets have dimmed, evening settling in, and I have a long walk ahead of me to the palace. My feet hurt, and I've no doubt the blisters along the bottom of my turned foot have burst. They will be a mess beneath the healer's bandages. Well, there's no need to go back to her. I know what to do with blisters. I'll just go to Melly's apartment and take care of them myself.

I bid farewell to the shopkeeper and start the trek back to the palace. The streets are just as busy as earlier despite the lengthening evening; apparently the city doesn't go to sleep with the sun as Sheltershorn does. I'm grateful for the bustle; with so many folk around it feels safe enough to walk the main streets. But, unlike home, no one pauses to ask if I am all right, and those who note my limp look away almost immediately.

A man barrels around the corner not three paces from me, his shoulder slamming into mine. "Watch it," he growls as I stumble to the side, arms pinwheeling out—and then my foot slides in a patch of mud and I come down hard on my knee.

I bend over, my breath hissing between my teeth, aware that the man has already hurried off. In Sheltershorn, everyone on the street would have hollered at him, told him to go back and make amends. My skirts are splattered with mud, but at least that was a softer landing than the cobbles that start up not twenty paces on.

"Are you all right?" a voice asks. I look up to find a young woman beside me. She's slightly older than I, dressed in a simple but well-made outfit of green and cream, hair done up in a businesslike bun.

"I'm fine," I say, expecting the woman to walk on like everyone else. I push myself to my feet. The palace is still a quarter of an hour's walk. My foot will likely be a bloody mess by then, and I've no one to blame but myself. I knew these shoes were no good—knew it before they were ever made—and I shouldn't have left the royal wing in them regardless of whom I wanted to avoid.

The woman, still lingering beside me, says, "That was rude of him, wasn't it? He should have at least helped you up." She shakes her head. "Perhaps he was raised in a barn."

"Animals are kinder," I say, which is not precisely true. I've been knocked over by our horses more than once, and not by accident either. "Or at least, people ought to know better."

Her right eye creases with amusement. The other is hidden beneath a patch of honey-colored leather, prettily edged with an embossed pattern of vines. "True. I think that's why I prefer books. Where are you headed? I'd be happy to send someone to fetch your carriage."

She must think me a wealthy noblewoman from my clothes. "I'm going to the palace," I admit. "But I'd prefer to walk. Thank you."

I start forward, limping rather more than usual. I just want to curl up in my bed and forget this day.

"Veria?" she asks uncertainly.

I turn back, embarrassed by my lack of manners. "No, it's just kelari. And I'm sorry. I've been having a difficult day."

"I don't mean to intrude, but did you know the palace has a side entrance? It's closer than the main one. I work at the tax offices. I can show you the way, if you'd like."

I pause, aware of the city folk still walking by, the fact that this woman has been kind twice over. "My name's Amraeya," I say. "And I'd be very grateful to you if you could shorten the way for me."

She dips me a friendly curtsy, a smile spreading across her face. "I'm Kirrana. And it's really not far from here."

"I didn't realize the tax office was on palace grounds," I say as she falls into step with me.

"There's a *lot* on palace grounds," she informs me. "But the main income for the kingdom? There's no other place for it. There's also the Circle of Mages' complex, though you likely won't have any need to go there. And a good number of other administrative buildings. The front is all palace—that's all you've seen, isn't it? The back is everything else." She tilts her head. "Have you seen much of the city?"

"Not very much. I've been shopping a bit."

"Oh, but there's so much to explore," she says, and happily launches into an overview of the various things to see in the city, from Speakers' Hall—the great temple on the river where the highest Speakers make their home and young Speakers are educated—to the docks themselves, to the best teahouses, bathhouses, the glassworker's shop, and, at my request, purveyors of street food.

We reach the side entrance a few minutes later, and she vouches for me to the guards, though I don't doubt my clothes help, even if they are spattered with mud.

"You'll be all right from here?" she asks, having delivered me to a path that leads, in one direction, toward the tax offices and, beyond them, the women's residence, and in the other direction, the palace proper.

"Just fine," I assure her. "Thank you, again."

"Of course. Evening, kelari." She dips me a curtsy and hurries away before I can attempt one of my own. I like her, I realize. It would have been nice to get to know her, to plan to meet her again. But her quick departure tells me what I should have already guessed: that palace folk don't socialize with tax clerks. Still, now that I know about the side entrance, perhaps I'll run into her again.

I turn back to the palace and manage to collar a page as I

limp through the third hallway I reach, and he guides me to Melly's apartments.

"Rae?" Melly says, poking her head in from the inner sitting room as I close the door behind me. Her face lights up. "Oh, you've come to visit!"

"Hallo, Melly," I say, amused despite myself. "I'm afraid I have a reason."

"That's—Rae, why are you limping?"

"That would be it," I say, and slip my turned foot out of its slipper, lifting it to show off the soiled bandages. It looks much worse now that the blisters have burst, splotches of faintly red-yellow wetness discoloring the bottom. "What," I say brightly, "do you think of the cobbler's improvements?"

"I think we are sending for him right now," Melly says with an edge of steel to her voice.

"It's already night," I point out, slipping my foot back into my shoe and limping my way to where she waits.

"Precisely why he will need to get to work at once if you are to have something better to wear tomorrow."

Tomorrow. Assuming I go back to the princess. "I need to talk to you about that too."

"Of course," Melly says, "after we've sent for the cobbler."

"But—"

"Sella!" she calls, and raises her brows at me. I subside, making for the carpets on one side of the room with the utterly welcoming cushions set out upon them. I don't want sofas right now; I want the comfort of home.

After the maid departs with orders for both the cobbler and tea, Melly offers to fetch my regular-wear slippers that I left behind in their guest room. "You rest your feet," she says crossly when I make to go with her.

I ease off the offending slippers, tuck my feet beneath my skirt, and let myself rest.

I miss home. It's a startling realization to have, for I've only really been here for a few days. But after today's events, I want my family around me: Mama and my sisters, and Baba's gruff care. I even want Muddle with her mixed-up manners and her simple horsey self. What I *don't* want is to see the palace cobbler again, or Captain Matsin, or even the princess, really.

Melly returns, shoes in hand, and sets them aside to pour me a cup of tea. "I'm listening," she says, sitting back. "You can tell me now."

I stare down at the cup of tea, seeing again the damp, matted visage of the dead horse's head within the grave. But no, that's not the worst of it. I take a breath and say, "She tested me, to see if I would tell her secrets."

"I see."

"I didn't, of course, but I'd rather not work for someone who would do that to me." The faint purple edge of a bruise just shows below the hem of my sleeve. My fault, certainly, in aggressively defending myself, but I shouldn't have had to feel the need to defend myself at all.

Melly worries at her lip with her teeth. "She probably needed to know, early on, if you would betray her."

"So she betrays me instead?"

"Was it a betrayal?"

It felt like one. The words rest on my tongue, but I don't want to speak them. Perhaps I'm overreacting. Perhaps I'm just not cut out for this.

"You called it a test," Melly observes when I don't answer.

"Yes. And it made me see that I don't know how politics works, Melly. I don't understand it, and I don't want any part of it. Because if that's how things *begin*, I can't assume they'll get any better."

Melly shakes her head. "Now that she knows she can trust you, there's no need for her to try you again. The royal family values loyalty. You've proven yourself already, on your first day. It will only get better from here."

Will it? And better in what way? I'll be following the princess around, privy to secrets I can't even comprehend, to what purpose? None that I can see. She doesn't really need me for her house of healing project; it's already being overseen by others. They can send her whatever updates she might need.

"I should have just stayed home," I say, looking down at my tea. "The princess can find someone else to keep her secrets. I don't want them."

Melly frowns. "It's not like you to walk away from a responsibility. Whatever happened, and whatever secret you *are* privy to, are not small things, are they? Don't answer—I know you can't. I wish Filadon were here to discuss this all."

"What sort of advice would he give?" I ask.

Melly shrugs. "The political sort. Whether to extract yourself or not, and how. But I imagine he wouldn't want you to leave yet."

No, not after he introduced me. My performance—and

loyalty—will reflect on him. What would it cost me to stay just through the wedding and then bow out? Would that be enough to keep from injuring Filadon's relationship with the royals? "I could stay through the wedding, but I don't want to stay with the princess all summer. I don't think I can handle it much longer than the wedding—if I can manage that at all. Horses don't politick like this."

Melly looks toward the door, and I can almost see the thoughts ticking through her mind. "Let me consult with Filadon. Tomorrow we can come up with a plan for you."

Which means I will have to get back on my feet and limp my way to the royal wing for the night, though at least not quite yet. I still have to finish my tea.

"There is the cobbler," Melly says at the sound of a knock on the outer room's door.

I grimace.

"I'll handle him," Melly says with a warrior's ferocity in her eyes.

Better her than me.

The cobbler appears quite pleased to be shown into the inner sitting room, despite being called here so late in the evening. But the moment Melly meets his gaze, he realizes it is not because we wished to show him honor or beg his aid.

"Kel Herra," she says with biting politeness. "I am afraid the shoes you have provided my cousin will not do."

He straightens his shoulders. "I improved their design, veria. It may require a tweak or two, but . . ."

"Cousin," Melly says, nodding at me. "Would you be so good

as to show Kel Herra what one day in his 'improved' shoes has cost you?"

I don't *want* to. Once he looks at my turned foot, he'll blame my deformity for the damage his shoes have done me, but I grit my teeth and extend my foot, baring the discolored bandages.

He frowns. "I don't see how that could happen, veria. Are you—"

"Indeed," Melly says, cutting him off, "and yet it has. My cousin's feet do not just develop blisters of their own accord; it is the shoes that are at fault. We require a new set of shoes tomorrow, made on the old pattern, if you are able." Her tone makes it clear she has her doubts.

"Of course I can follow a pattern," he says haughtily. "*Anyone* can follow a pattern, even a bad one. But that will hardly produce a shoe I would be proud of."

"Are you proud of these?" I demand, holding up the slippers I've worn all day. The inner leather is stained with blood and fluid.

"The *workmanship* is perfectly fine," he says.

Oh yes, because my foot is to blame, nothing else.

"A well-made shoe will not harm the wearer," Melly says coldly. "That is the most basic definition of well made. We put our trust in you, kel, and I expect you to make this right."

Herra flushes and dips his head. I let Melly complete the conversation. By the time he leaves, he's promised to deliver a new set of slippers by morning, and will wait to hear from me before starting the next pair. I only hope I'll be able to tell how well the new shoes fit despite my blisters. Though I may not need the next pair at all.

Melly sighs as the door closes behind him. "I'm sorry, Rae. I didn't fully appreciate how difficult this would be for you."

"It's all right," I tell her. "I'm just grateful you handled that."

Besides, the shoes are the least of my concerns.

CHAPTER

15

When I walk into Alyrra's bedchamber the following morning, she smiles somewhat hesitantly. I curtsy in my new set of slippers—delivered at dawn and carefully padded with bandages—and gather myself to make the speech I have spent the early morning hours composing.

The princess is quicker. "I am so glad to see you this morning, Amraeya. Let us go for a walk together before breakfast. Jasmine, will you come with us?"

"Zayyida," I begin, fairly certain I want to walk as little as possible today.

"I know we have things to discuss," she says earnestly. "But let us discuss them on our walk."

Jasmine and I follow her out and through the quiet halls to a courtyard the likes of which I've never seen before: it is a small forest growing hale and strong in the heart of the palace.

Catching my astonished gaze, Alyrra says, "It is a wedding

present. Zayyid Kestrin knew I would miss the woods of my home."

But this little glade is well-established, the work of many years. Wasn't the wedding only just arranged last fall? Perhaps Alyrra does not realize how old it is. Or perhaps, much more likely, there are more secrets at play here than I have been given to understand.

"Jasmine, why don't you rest here on the bench?" Alyrra says. "You have a long day ahead of you."

Jasmine obeys, shooting a derisive glance my way. Mina had been terse yesterday evening, saying very little other than to inform me the princess had asked after me, and that I cannot abandon my duties without notice. No doubt Jasmine and Zaria enjoyed the fact that I'd disappeared without a word, to all appearances proving myself unfit for my position. Jasmine probably expects I'm about to be chastised—or relieved of my duties. I can't bring myself to care.

Alyrra leads me along a winding gravel path into the trees. The uneven footing does not help my aching feet at all.

"You intend to leave," Alyrra says as the woods hide Jasmine from sight. I can still see a flash of her yellow skirt through the trees, but Alyrra's voice is low enough that it will not reach her.

I focus on the princess, on the way she watches me, her expression grim. Well, that's not my fault either. "Forgive me, zayyida, but I do not think I am suited to the politics of such a position. I can stay through the wedding if you wish it, but no longer."

"I am sorry for how—for what happened yesterday."

"The horse's head?" I ask bluntly. "Or the guard who cornered me about it? Or the fact that I actually feared what he might do?"

"Falada—the horse. He was a friend of mine," Alyrra begins. "I do not understand the magic at work through him, but I wished him laid to rest."

"I understand." But I'm not interested in remaining here, and she's wise enough to hear what I don't say.

She grimaces and looks away, through the trees toward Jasmine. "I didn't think things would go as they did. Please don't leave, Amraeya." She takes a breath as if bracing herself and turns to me. "I would like you to learn more about the snatchers."

I stiffen. Filadon must surely have reported my questions about the snatchers to Kestrin, and so Alyrra knows. Unless she read me so easily from our conversation on the walls. Either way, she knows this is the one thing that would keep me. I swallow and say, "I thought you didn't intend to look into them." But that's not right either. "No, you just wished to test me first, didn't you?"

She nods. "They are not to be trifled with. You must be both brave and able to keep your work secret in order to help me with them."

I fist my fingers into the fabric of my skirts. But there is no investigating the snatchers, is there? At least not according to the shopkeeper. I wouldn't even know where to start without getting myself killed. In truth, investigating the snatchers myself wasn't my plan in coming here—I just meant to find out what *was* being done. But can I really walk away if I'm the one who can do something?

Alyrra tilts her head, watching me. "I have a contact in the city who may be able to shed some light on who they are, how they operate. One of my friends in the stable will be able to take you to meet him. If you will go."

"I take it," I venture, "that your contact is not entirely on the right side of the law." If he were, she wouldn't need me to parley with him. She could invite him in and chat with him here.

Alyrra offers me a crooked smile, unexpectedly endearing in its wryness. "No," she says. "Not entirely."

I don't want to suddenly find that I like her, that she reminds me a bit of Niya, even down to the secrets she has allowed me to hold for her. This woman ordered a man to corner me, to intimidate me, to stop just short of assaulting me. Admittedly, I don't know what her exact orders *were*, and I do know she apologized for the bruises I gained in escaping Captain Matsin. And he apologized as well. Light and shadow! I don't want to be reasonable about this. I'm not even sure what reasonable is.

"I have to be able to trust you," I blurt. "I can't wonder if—if something that happens to me is because you ordered it."

"You have my word," Alyrra says, meeting my gaze steadily. "I will not test you again, nor ever order any harm to you."

Is that enough? Are there other things I should ask to protect myself?

Alyrra goes on, her voice almost pleading. "If you take this on, the discretion you must practice will protect you as much as any of the people you come into contact with. The snatchers will not abide someone learning about them."

She's still asking my forgiveness, still trying to explain. Looking at her, I remember Seri's laughter, and her family's sorrow. I remember every child who has been lost from our village over the years, and I understand completely. The snatchers *are* ruthless. And I will do everything in my power to stop them.

"I understand," I say quietly. "How do I meet your contact?"

Alyrra grins at me, looking both young and so much older at the same time. "A ride and a walk. I'll arrange it for you."

"I look forward to it," I say. Especially the ride, though I don't admit that aloud.

As if to prove to all concerned that I am, in truth, her attendant, Alyrra invites me to attend her at lunch. She has arranged for me to meet her contact in the afternoon; attending her in the meantime allows her to begin my introduction to the court. It's a gentle start for which I'm grateful, considering her family will arrive later today and her attendants then will no doubt be under careful scrutiny.

"She's getting you out of the way so you won't be limping around her family," Jasmine tells me in a rare moment of communication. "Don't think too much of it, *kelari*."

I don't think the princess gives a rat's claw about my limp, but Jasmine certainly can't see past it. "I'm not really sure why you're so concerned about me," I tell her with a smile that masks my fury, "but I do appreciate it. *Veria*."

Jasmine slides her eyes to the side in a look of utter contempt—as close as she gets, I suspect, to rolling her eyes—and turns her back on me.

Thankfully, it is Mina whom Alyrra brings with us to lunch. We enter a gathering room, lined with sofas and filled with nobles and honored guests, most of them milling about the room in small groups. Across from us, the great double doors that will open into the dining room remain closed for the time being.

"Veriana," Kestrin says, moving at once to intercept Alyrra.

He flicks a glance at me, his head dipping slightly, and then refocuses on the princess. Mina motions me back, and we step aside to stand by an empty sofa while the two converse together.

"In a gathering like this," Mina explains, "we leave Alyrra to mingle as she wishes. If she's ever alone, or she motions for us, we join her. Otherwise, we are here as members of the court, and can meet those we know."

Unfortunately, neither Filadon nor Melly appear to be in attendance, which puts to rest the possibility of my meeting anyone. Across the room a woman stands quietly, tall and slim, her hair gleaming black with a faint sheen of blue, a matching iridescent pattern curving down over the brown of her neck and disappearing beneath the long, layered dress she wears. Two young men stand behind her, dressed in similar robes, with that same pattern upon their skin. It looks almost like fish scales.

"Don't stare," Mina says sharply. "That's the princess of the water people who live off the shore of Lirelei. She's come for the wedding. You'll do well not to insult her."

I swallow hard and drop my gaze. Water people? I've *heard* of them, but they always seemed more myth than reality. "My apologies," I murmur.

Mina sighs. "I must greet Veria Dinari. I'll see if I can convince her to meet you. She is Verin Melkior's wife."

I nod, recollecting that Melkior is the lord high marshal of the realm, which means his wife will have a high ranking as well. Mina departs, drifting over to chat with a pair of women who might be about my mother's age.

"Kelari Amraeya?" someone asks from beside me. The voice is velvety smooth, deep and sweet with a lilting accent. It's the sort of voice that immediately puts me on edge. I turn to find myself facing a faerie, tall and elegant, with eyes so dark they appear fathomless. I blink. The faerie remains.

It wouldn't be that strange ordinarily. The so-called Fair Folk live across the Winter Seas, and after seeing the merfolk here, I would expect the family to maintain diplomatic relations with Fae lands as well. It isn't the presence of a faerie that startles me; it's the presence of *this* faerie with his night-dark hair cascading over his shoulders, setting off the almost luminescent paleness of his skin and the obsidian depths of his eyes. His beauty is as dangerous as a blade, and as familiar as an ally once met.

"Verin Stonemane?" I say, my voice soft with disbelief. "I didn't expect to meet you here!"

"Nor I, you," he replies, bowing with exquisite grace.

I remember, belatedly, that I should have curtsied first and dip into a jerky return, my cheeks warming. Desperate to distract him, I ask the first thing that comes to mind. "How is Storm treating you?"

His lips twitch with amusement—because *of course* one does not inquire after horses before all else, at least not at court. "She's a fine mare. I haven't regretted my visit to your farm. But what brings you to the king's city?"

Slavers. Stupidity. Or, to be perfectly honest but less precise: "My cousin lives at court and invited me to visit, and now I have somehow become attendant to the princess."

"I have no doubt you will serve her well," Stonemane says steadily. He is one of the few who have uncovered Niya's magical ability, and so he knows very well what lengths I would go to, to protect my own. In helping him leave our home unnoticed by a crowd of suspicious townspeople, I was ensuring his silence about my sister's secret as much as I was aiding him. In return, he granted each of my sisters and me a gift. Mine was the bone knife now sewn into my story sash.

"Thank you," I say, and give in to my own curiosity. After all, if he can ask what I'm doing here, I can ask the same of him. Politely, as one does in court. "Are you staying here in Tarinon very long, then?"

"For the time being: I serve as permanent ambassador from Chariksen."

I make a thoughtful sound. "Do permanent ambassadors normally walk around the countryside looking for horses?"

"Sometimes," he says, his eyes brightening with amusement until it seems that starlight dances over them. It's utterly unnerving. "When the fancy takes us." He nods his head toward Mina. "I believe you are being called. I look forward to meeting you again."

I take my leave of him with some relief and join Mina where she hovers behind the princess. Alyrra is chatting with Kestrin as well as his cousin Garrin and a middle-aged man who bears such a striking resemblance to the prince he can only be the king. The noblewoman Mina greeted earlier remains at a distance, clearly having decided she does not yet need to meet me.

"Ah," the middle-aged man says, shifting to look at me. "This must be your newest attendant."

At least this time I remember to curtsy. Filadon would be relieved.

"Tarin," Alyrra says, confirming my suspicions, "allow me to introduce Kelari Amraeya ni Ansarim, cousin by marriage to

Verin Filadon. She does me the honor of attending me."

"Indeed," the king says, dipping his head in acknowledgment. "We have long been pleased with Verin Filadon's service, and welcome you to the palace, kelari. In a court as renowned as ours for hospitality, I have no doubt you will be made welcome."

"Thank you, tarin," I manage, well aware that the whole of the room is listening now, and the king has just commanded their support of me.

The king, thankfully, seems to consider our conversation done, and turns to lead the way into the dining room.

I spend the meal seated toward the end of the table, Mina across from me and a few seats farther up. Those nearest me do no more than smile and bid me welcome. They are none of them rude, and for that, I suppose, I must thank the king. But not one of them converses with me more than necessary.

I find my eyes drifting to Stonemane, seated across the table and halfway up. Across from him, barely visible to me, sit the merpeople. Stonemane is engaged in quiet conversation with the lord to his left, but as he turns back to his plate, his gaze catches mine. A faint, derisive smile plays over his lips, as if he knows better than to read anything into my study of him. Embarrassed, I drop my gaze to my plate of spiced, curried goat on its bed of fragrant rice.

"You know the foreign ambassador, kelari?" the lady at my right asks, her expression keen.

"We have met before," I say, grateful to have someone to speak with. "He came to stay at my family's home once."

In order to buy horses from us, but there's no reason to mention that.

"How curious! But you did not know who he was? You seemed quite surprised to meet him here."

"I did not know he was an ambassador, veria," I admit. "But certainly we knew he was a nobleman."

"Hmm. Country families must have little regard for propriety if you did not know that much."

Oh, the nerve of the woman! "We at least know how to give a guest their due," I say sweetly.

"You cannot do so if you don't concern yourself with learning the simplest things about your guest," she says, all gentle condescension. "At least you have found *one* friend here, though. That must be a relief for you."

"Quite," I say, and turn my attention to my meal. But her words settle into me. I cannot avoid the truth that I *wasn't* relieved to see Stonemane. I'm far too conscious of his beauty, no doubt in large part because of my own lack of grace or looks.

I glance back up the table at Stonemane, at his long, slender fingers wrapped around his meat knife, at the line of his jaw, and feel that same tightening within my chest, as if I were drawing in, hardening my heart. I look down, take a bite mechanically, the food tasteless in my mouth. Have I really grown so little? I thought I had made some peace with myself after his visit, some peace with how much anger I carried for how people see me. *You should on occasion be kinder to yourself,* he had told me when he gifted me my bone knife.

But here I am, reacting the same way again to his beauty, even if I might consider him now a friendly acquaintance, if not actually a friend. And who else have I thought less of, because of their beauty rather than their character? I don't want to do the same to others, regardless of whether they are as beautiful as the Fae, or as plain and different as I.

Seated beside Kestrin is his cousin Garrin, whom I've barely spoken to, who greeted me yesterday when he did not have to— no doubt to support his cousin's betrothed, but still. I had seen only a man who was too beautiful for his own good. Why had I let myself think such things?

How easy it was to sit among my family and promise myself I would change, that I would be kinder to myself, that I would not judge others harshly because of the hurts I've nursed. Cripple. Turnfoot. Words that have haunted me my whole life—I thought I would cut them out of me, allow myself to live without the certainty that I was somehow less: less beautiful, less deserving.

I had taken the bone knife Stonemane gave me and promised myself I would do better. And yet I have not changed at all.

CHAPTER

16

A lyrra seems pleased with my first court appearance. We return to her rooms, and after a few words she dismisses me for the afternoon. I change into one of my simpler riding outfits, trade out my slippers for my old riding boots, and head down to a small courtyard that grants access to the main gates via a side road.

My excuse for leaving the palace is the one Alyrra created for me during our first interview on the walls: I am to visit her house of healing project on a daily basis, to ensure it progresses well. Filadon has had a horse sent up from the stables for me, one that will be mine to use for the duration of my visit. It was a generous gesture, offered with the sort of sparkling smile I knew meant trouble. And indeed, Moonflower is a pretty little black mare with a splotch of white on her forehead and eyes that glitter with distrust. *Why* Melly allowed her husband to buy such a mean-tempered creature, I can't understand, but I am coming to think the ways of marriage are complex and generally unknowable.

Other than a few short struggles for control, which I manage to win mainly because I have dealt with ornery horses before, the ride to the house of healing goes well. The page who accompanies me to show the way departs almost at once, while I go in to meet the overseer and look through the building—a great, three-story affair, currently filled with the dust and debris of renovation.

Overall, the house of healing appears to be progressing well, the usual bumps and unexpected problems being dealt with competently enough. The overseer is happy to answer my few questions and send me on my way back toward West Road. My role in this endeavor truly is only an excuse to get me into the city.

When the street I travel meets West Road, I turn down it and continue on to the royal stables just before the city gates, as Alyrra directed me. I ride around the first stables to the second and tie Moonflower to a post. As I turn toward the building, a woman steps out.

"Kelari Amraeya?" she asks, her eyes moving from me to my horse. No doubt she knows exactly who it belongs to, and from that inferred my identity; she's a hostler, after all.

I dip my head. "And you are Kelari Sage?"

She nods. Sage stands slightly taller than I, her hair gone to gray and silver. Her face, though, seems younger than her hair would suggest.

"Rowan," she calls over her shoulder. "Will you see to Moon-flower?"

A male voice returns an affirmative from inside the stables.

"Come, then," she says, flashing a friendly smile. "We've a

short walk to make. You don't mind, do you?"

"Not at all," I assure her. To her credit, she only focuses on my feet for a moment as I turn and fall into step with her, and then she looks ahead. Someone must have mentioned my limp, or the rumors about the princess's newest attendant have already run through the stables.

"Do you know where we're going?" she asks.

"To meet a contact of yours who might be able to help with some information we need. Beyond that, I don't know much."

Sage nods. "His name's Artemian. I spoke with him this morning, when I heard from the princess, so he knows to expect us."

Us? It hadn't occurred to me that Sage might be a partner in this with me, but Alyrra did say that her friend would put me in contact and provide a way to keep in touch. Perhaps I should have expected it. "Do you know what this is about?" I ask carefully.

"What the princess wants? Yes. And I'll support her every way I know how." Her voice is hard, tight. There is some history here I don't know. She gives herself a slight shake and says, "Well, every way but one."

"What's that?"

"Thorn asked me if I'd like to join her up at the palace."

"Thorn?" I echo, confused.

"The princess. That was her name out here."

I nod; of course she could not have gone by her true name. "You aren't interested in leaving the stables?"

Sage raises her brows. "Even princesses can't have everything they want."

"No," I agree. "But she did call you her friend."

Sage's whole face warms with a smile. "I knew I'd like you. I'm glad to see you don't have any airs. You stand by the princess, or I'll come after you, hear?"

I laugh, delighted. "Glad to meet you too."

We've left West Road behind for smaller streets that wind between buildings. The streets are busy despite the slight spring chill, the cobbles damp from yesterday's rainfall. Women linger in doorways, young boys squat in front of shops, and children hunch over games of marbles, or run pattering past us playing catch-me and other childhood favorites.

Sage slows before a building where a young boy plays on the step. He looks up, his gaze assessing, and then says, "The Tattered Crow," pointing down the alleyway.

"Aye," Sage says.

Grinning, the boy hops to his feet and races off in the opposite direction.

Sage continues on as if it were perfectly normal to have urchins redirect you.

"Are you sure we can trust the boy?" I ask uncertainly.

"It's fine," she says. "They pay the street children to help them—keep watch, run small errands, the like."

I thought we were just talking about the one man, Artemian. "Who, precisely, are 'they'?"

Sage glances around to make sure no one's listening. "Thieves."

Well, that would certainly qualify as "not entirely on the right side of the law." I cast my mind back over what I know of the city. "Are they part of a ring? I've heard of the Black Scholar and Bardok Three-Fingers." Neither of whom have particularly pleasant reputations, but then, to be the head of a ring of street thieves, you'd have to be ruthless.

"You've heard of Red Hawk as well, I presume. Artemian is one of his men."

I frown. "Red Hawk? He's ... newer, isn't he?" There've been a few stories—whenever one of the thieving rings does something particularly brash, the rumors reach us. The name, as unusual as it is, sounds vaguely familiar.

"Relatively. The Scholar came into power near on fifteen years ago. Red Hawk's only got two or three years. But he's a step better."

"How?"

She shrugs. "He doesn't kill indiscriminately. He pays the street children well enough to keep them. He stands by his honor."

"Thieves' honor?"

She nods, as if that should explain everything. Maybe it would if I were city bred, but it doesn't mean a thing to me. Which means it's best to just ask. "The rings don't have anything to do with the snatchers, do they?"

"No," Sage says sharply. "At least, not this one. They helped when—a young woman went missing."

Sage's voice ends on a rough note. That's it, then: the history I don't know. She's lost someone as well. I almost tell her about Seri, but she's not asking for empathy or acknowledgment, so I keep quiet. At least it's a good sign if the thieves were helping to search for a girl who disappeared.

We round the corner to the Tattered Crow, a mosaic depicting a disheveled crow decorating the wall beside the carved door. It's a distinctly grander building than those around it, though that merely means it's been kept up, with a few small prosperous touches. The surrounding buildings, in contrast, are dilapidated, the door altogether missing from the building across the road.

Inside, the innkeeper directs us to a staircase with a jerk of his chin and the words, "First door on your right."

I follow Sage up the stairs one step at a time, favoring my turned foot. Walking hurts, but stairs will be worse. It's better to go gently.

"Sorry," I mutter as I rejoin Sage at the top of the stairs.

She shakes her head and leads me to the door, rapping smartly upon its surface. A voice calls for us to enter. Sage pushes open the door to reveal a pair of men waiting for us. I don't like this. I don't like that our meeting location was changed, or that there are now two men where we only expected one. I touch Sage's arm, as if to keep her from entering.

"Kelari Sage," the elder of the two men says, rising to greet us. He must be about as old as Sage, his face weathered and his dark hair pulled back tightly. A scar traces its way down from the corner of his lip to his chin, giving him a perpetually grim look. His eyes are dark and sharp as two midnight jewels. I doubt he misses much.

"Kel Artemian." Sage steps forward, out from under my hand, and dips her head in greeting. "Allow me to introduce Kelari Amraeya."

I force a smile and nod, and make myself step as lightly as I can into the room. There's no need for them to know that I can't run even if I wanted to.

We seat ourselves in a pair of chairs across from the two thieves. Apparently, city folk emulate the palace folk; even here, in a humble inn on the west side, there are chairs instead of cushions on the floor. Just as well; I can hide my foot beneath the fall of my skirts and conceal my weakness that much longer.

Artemian sits up straight in his chair, but his companion lounges, one leg stretched out, long hair tied back, his seat set back just slightly from the circle. His face is young; he sports a smooth-shaved chin beneath a slender nose, his eyes deep set. His gaze flicks over us. He can't be much older than I am, but he lazes in his seat with the benign ambivalence of a lion observing cubs at play. Wonderful. Some kind of shady character for sure.

Or am I merely pushing back at him because he is handsome in his own way? No, it's there in the expression on his face, the way he sits: he considers himself powerful, and he's amused by the secrets he's keeping—including his identity, for Artemian makes no attempt to introduce this companion of his.

Instead, Artemian asks, "How is it we can help you?"

"The princess wishes to learn what she can of the snatchers," I say, turning my focus to him. "She hopes you might be able to help her."

Artemian nods. "How are you involved?"

"I am one of Zayyida Alyrra's attendants. I serve as a go-between for her."

He studies me. "You're new, though, yes?"

"I'm from the town of Sheltershorn," I say, meeting his gaze, "and will only be here through the summer."

A smile hovers at the corners of his mouth, making it quirk slightly as the scar continues to pull down. "You don't have the look of the city about you."

"I shall consider that a compliment."

He lets out his breath in a half laugh. "Of course. Now, why should we trust you?"

I blink, taken aback, and then realize he's perfectly right. "You shouldn't. You don't know me and I don't know you. But I've given the princess my word, and I will hold by it. I want the snatchers stopped. I've seen in my own town the sorrow of the families whose children have gone missing, and I'll do what I can to end such a tragedy. You can trust me in that, and trust that I won't bring you harm if you're helping us."

His lips are still smiling, but his eyes are shrewd as ever. It's hard to tell what he really thinks of me. "I see. What is it you need in particular?"

"To begin with, we need to understand how the snatchers operate."

Artemian shakes his head. "There is not much to share. They are careful of their secrets, and brutal in protecting themselves. Right now, we leave them alone, and they do the same for us. We've no interest in changing that balance."

Surely this isn't all they can tell us. I didn't agree to continue working for Alyrra just to be told, yet again, that the snatchers are dangerous. "Can you at least tell us who they are? How they're organized?" I demand. *Anything, really.*

"Or even how to catch one for questioning?" Sage adds.

Artemian hesitates. The second man, his hand resting on his knee, taps three fingers just once.

Artemian sighs. "It may be possible to catch one of the actual snatchers—but it will be like catching a pickpocket in place of a master thief: what he could tell us would be limited by the great amount he doesn't know. And we would have to dispose of him afterward."

"Dispose of him?" Sage echoes.

I cross my arms, holding myself in. No. That can't be right. The snatchers might be murderers, but that doesn't mean we should do the same. There *has* to be another way. I can't—this can't be the only choice there is. I look away from Artemian to find the younger man watching me steadily, but there is something faintly pleased about the way he regards me. Is he amused by my reaction?

"So you'd have to kill him," I say, just so no one can pretend we're talking about anything else right now.

"If he's a snatcher, he probably deserves it," Sage says, her voice hard.

"Are you asking us to kill for your princess?" Artemian eases back, studying Sage.

I feel a rush of relief that they aren't actually offering such an option quite so easily as it seemed. "I don't think we can decide that for her," I say quickly, afraid of what Sage might come out with next. "Why would you be willing to do it anyway?" I ask. "If you're worried about keeping this balance?"

Again, Artemian's eyes flick to his companion, just a subtle check as he tilts his head before saying, "We lose some of our street children to snatchers every year."

"With all the children you have," Sage says slowly, "all those extra eyes, you can't say how they operate? It seems a little strange."

"As I said, they are brutal. Witnesses either join them, are snatched themselves, or die."

That's consistent, at least, with what I've heard. "It doesn't seem as though catching a single snatcher will do us much good—not if, as you say, they know only a little of what they do." Nor do I want blood on my hands. There has to be another way. Surely, as thieves, they have some ideas that wouldn't occur to a country girl? "What approach would you counsel instead?"

"The princess needs support. And a change in the laws—one that sets harsher punishments for stealing children as well as for aiding and abetting the slave trade. She'll also need a number of quads who can officially arrest suspected snatchers for questioning. Or to whom we can pass a snatcher. Until she has that, there's nothing we can do."

Sage glances at me. "Her quads—?"

I shake my head. "She doesn't have her own men yet." Even Captain Matsin is, as I've learned, Kestrin's captain and not really the princess's. "And I don't know that she can change any laws quite yet either."

Artemian dips his head. "Perhaps within a few months of her wedding, she can look to the laws," he suggests. Which really means that I need to have Alyrra start looking into the laws and building support with the king now, in order to start effecting change then. "The snatchers will keep until she's ready to take them on."

"They'll also keep snatching," I point out. How many more girls like Seri will be lost in the meantime? Surely there is something that can be done—*now*.

"Then it will be that much more important for the princess to focus on strengthening her position quickly and effectively."

Sage sits back. "That's all."

"Yes."

Light and shadow, *no*. I have to consciously unclench my jaw, because there's nothing I can do here, no way to argue myself to a better option. These men won't help, not as things stand, and all my future holds is reading through the laws and preparing Alyrra to change policies once I'm gone. And attending meals where I am smiled at and treated with polite contempt. No, I decide. I'll just have to find another way.

Sage sighs and brushes out her skirts as she rises, almost businesslike in her resignation. "We thank you."

"You know where to find me, if you need to speak again," Artemian says.

I rise and follow Sage to the door. The other man watches us steadily, his expression inscrutable. He must be Artemian's superior, young though he may be. But just who he is, what his relation is to the infamous Red Hawk, I have no idea.

We head back toward West Road, Sage adjusting her stride to my slower-than-usual gait. My turned foot burns where the remaining blisters have burst, not even my trusty old riding boots able to cushion them enough through all this walking. But thinking on it only makes it worse. Instead, I turn the inn room conversation over in my mind again. "They're hiding something," I finally say.

"What do you mean?"

"They have to know more than they've said. The other man

with Artemian was controlling how much he told us. Did you notice?"

"I don't know about that," Sage says, unconvinced. "Why wouldn't they tell us more if they knew?"

"Maybe they don't want us to upset their balance."

She shakes her head. "It isn't a balance if they're losing children to the snatchers." She purses her lips. "You're suspicious of them, aren't you?"

"That the only solutions are to kill someone or call in guards? Yes, I am suspicious." I chew my lip, running through the conversation again. But I can't quite put my finger on what's missing, what we *can* do that they don't want to discuss. As Mama always says, "You don't know what you don't know."

We reach West Road in silence. We're almost halfway to the palace—I could walk down to the stables and then ride back up again, or I could just go straight home and take care of my feet. "You want to walk up from here?" Sage asks, reading my look easily enough.

"It would be faster," I admit. If there were any carriages for hire, it would be even quicker and much less painful, but, despite the fact that I've actually brought along my purse today, I don't see any carriages.

"No one should bother you on a main road. Just promise me not to leave the road."

"You're worried about snatchers?" I ask, taken aback. Almost, I tell her, *I'm a cripple. I've always been safe.* Snatchers only ever take able-bodied children. I can still remember the town mothers mentioning as much to my mother when I was small, a consolation for having such a child. I also remember Mama descending upon her would-be supporters with a blistering rage that left them careful of her—and me—for years.

"There's other trouble too," Sage says now, her voice hard and brittle.

"True enough," I agree carefully, watching her. "I'll keep to West Road."

"You'll discuss the laws, and the need for guards, with the princess?"

"Of course," I say. And somehow, I'll find another way forward as well.

CHAPTER

17

I make slow headway along West Road, my foot aching. The streets are quiet—not empty by any means, but there appears to be a slight lull now, in the midafternoon. It would be a pleasant walk if I were in less pain.

"I am curious about your foot," a voice says at my shoulder.

I nearly jump out of my skin. Artemian's companion reaches out a hand to steady me, laughing softly. Artemian himself, though, is nowhere to be seen. It takes a moment for my breath to return, and for the stab of pain through my foot to ease. But the man just raises his brows, awaiting my response.

"Good afternoon to you too," I say with a note of sarcasm. I wiggle my elbow in his grip.

"It is," he agrees, letting go. "Though there will be an even better one next week."

"What?" I ask, bewildered.

"The final wedding procession," he clarifies. "The nobles

will leave their handsome villas with only a skeleton guard. They'll need an escort to get through the streets, you see, and everyone among the staff who can escape for it will do so as well. *That* will be a lovely afternoon."

"You're going to rob them?" I ask despite myself, well aware that he's playing me, checking to see how much I know about him and his associates, and how much I'm willing to let pass.

"We must all be true to our callings," he says. "A thief must, on occasion, thieve, and a royal attendant must, on occasion, walk through the city streets in pain."

I stiffen.

"I know what pain looks like," he says quietly. "What I'm curious about is what happened, and why you haven't had your ankle looked at. Or is it your foot?"

He has *no right* to ask such a thing. "Whatever it is, it's not your concern."

"Perhaps. I can't agree if I don't know, can I?"

"You don't need to agree," I snap, and start forward.

He matches my pace, an easy enough feat when every other step feels like I am setting foot in scalding water. It's just a question of him walking slowly enough.

"When I told Artemian I was following after you, he didn't think you'd be easily impressed. Even if I used my best manners."

Oh, indeed. If these are his best manners, he must have grown up in a ditch. "Since Artemian didn't mention who you are, I don't see any reason to mention anything to you."

The man laughs and, catching my hand, tugs me to a stop and sketches a bow. "Bren, at your service."

I wriggle my hand free, immediately disliking this carefree, affable persona he's projecting. It seems far less genuine than the smug, observant young man from earlier today. "Bren, is it? And you're, what, one step above Artemian?"

"Not precisely."

"So why were you telling him how much to tell us?"

Bren grins appreciatively. "You're a sharp one."

"Why, thank you. I needed someone to tell me that." I start walking again. Once again, he falls into step with me. He's here for a reason, and it would behoove me to humor him. But I can't think why, if he had something to say, he wouldn't have done it at the inn.

"Come now, people will think I'm bothering you," Bren says. "Especially when you glower like that. We can trade questions and answers if you like."

Fine, then. "Why are you walking with me?"

"To learn why an attendant would choose to walk around in pain, and . . ." He pauses, waiting.

"And?" I finally prompt. I am doing this for the snatched, I remind myself. And Alyrra. If he does have something to share, I need to play along to get it out of him. Even if he's asking questions I don't want to answer.

He smirks. "Tell me what I want, and I'll tell you."

I stop and look at him. He is half a head taller than I, slim and handsome, with a thick tail of hair pulled back. More than anything, he is young. Quite possibly as young as I am, which makes it interesting indeed that Artemian would obey him. "Who are you really?"

He tsks sadly, shaking his head. "We'll never get to any answers if you keep asking questions."

My lips twitch upward involuntarily. His eyes glow in response. *No.* I'm not amused by him. I won't be taken in by this act of his, even if I have to play along. I take a breath. "Very well. I wore a pair of new shoes yesterday that didn't fit properly. I'm not going to let a few blisters stop me from my work."

"Blisters only?" he asks, confused. But then he can't see the shape of my foot beneath my skirt, the particular way my riding boot is made, and there is no reason I can think of that I need to explain myself to him.

I raise my chin. "I've answered your question; it's time you answered mine. Who are you really?"

"Just what you said," he replies, mischief lighting his eyes again. "And just as clever as you."

"Oh? Just that?" I echo dryly, utterly underwhelmed by the helpfulness of his answer. What I said? What? That he was Artemian's superior?

He grins. "Certainly. For instance, I can tell you have no interest in taking our advice to leave the snatchers to other people."

"None whatsoever." Though what exactly I can do to learn more I have no idea. Perhaps the princess will have another lead for me.

"In which case," Bren goes on, "you might want to consider a couple of things."

I latch onto this as if it were a rope. "Such as?"

"When a snatched child is recovered, necessity dictates that they're taken to a temple."

"For the Blessing," I agree. "But that removes all their memories."

"To find out anything real, then, you'd need to find a child before they are blessed."

"I've considered that," I say. I sent a letter home last night, to see if my parents would know how to track down the boy from our town who escaped the snatchers and whose family moved with him far into the plains. Given time, I might be able to find them. But perhaps Bren has a better option. "Is that something you can help us with?"

He pauses where an alley intersects with the road, turning to study me for a long moment. "Where do you think the snatchers take their slaves?"

My brow creases. "Away? I don't really know. I always assumed it was someplace where slavery is allowed."

Bren makes a noncommittal sound.

"Where are they sent?" I ask uncertainly.

"Come back in a few days and I'll show you one such 'away.'"

"Here?" I demand, my voice soft with shock. "You mean—"

"You'll have to wait and see."

He meets my gaze, and there is nothing of the cocky, arrogant young man in him now. He is still and serious, his eyes just dark enough to frighten me. They are eyes that have seen a great deal more than I can imagine.

"How will I know to meet you?" I ask. "I assume you've decided against involving Sage, or you wouldn't have waited until she and I parted ways."

"True," he agrees, that smile touching his lips again. "She's a little too quick to accept the need for murder. That's a road she'll regret walking, and it's not a path I tread lightly myself. So it had to be you. Is there anywhere you'll be going in the city on a regular basis?"

"The princess's house of healing. I'm to check in on it every afternoon, though not tomorrow."

"Because of the wedding ceremony," he says knowingly. "Tomorrow's too soon, anyhow. I'll find you there when I'm ready." He tilts his head. "The other thing you might want to consider?"

"Yes?"

He catches my hand and lifts it, as if he were going to bow over it again—only he doesn't. Instead, he gives my hand a slight shake and my sleeve falls back to reveal the ring of bruises there. His fingers tighten around mine as I try to pull away, a firm pressure, not hurtful but very much there.

"You ought to learn how to fight."

The words are quiet, surprisingly gentle. He drops my hand and, with a dip of his chin, departs. I stare after him, cradling my bruised wrist against my body even though it doesn't hurt. That was what he was asking about, at the beginning. Only he started by questioning my limp instead of my bruises. Well, I'm glad. I wouldn't have wanted to tell him the truth, or to have to lie.

It isn't until I reach the palace that I realize there was a third thing I should have considered: a thief is still, at heart, a thief. My coin purse is missing, and with it, a good quarter of the money I had left to me.

I doubt learning to fight will help defend against that.

CHAPTER
18

"It's outrageous," Mina says with quiet fury as she shimmies out of the tunic she wore this afternoon and into a far more heavily embroidered one for dinner. "The foreign queen brought along the impostor's *father*. The princess had to stand there and greet the man whose daughter *betrayed* her and stole her position."

I stand in the doorway, all thoughts of thieves and snatchers driven from my mind. "What?"

"You should have seen Zayyid Kestrin's face! Truly, if he could have put a sword through the man, I think he would have. But Alyrra didn't show a thing. Just smiled and nodded as if all were well, and then took Kestrin's arm and patted it to bring him back to himself."

"Did it work?"

"What?"

"Patting his arm?"

Mina pauses in pulling up her skirt. "Actually, yes. He went all still, and then he gave that Verin Daerilin a smile that"—she shudders—"I would never want aimed at me, and bid everyone welcome as well."

"Why did the impostor's father come?" I ask, moving to sit down on my bed and work off my boots. "That seems impolitic at best."

"At *best*," Mina agrees, and it occurs to me I have never seen her this animated before, this angry, even if her actions are still small and controlled. It's there in her voice, in the emphasis she places on words when her voice is usually so neutral. "Apparently it is a long enough journey that they had already departed their hall when the king's messenger reached them on the road. He claims he stayed with the party in order to make amends."

"Hmm."

Mina hurries over to her dressing table. "Can you check in on Alyrra? She wanted company. Zaria is with her right now."

"Of course," I say, looking down at my feet, hidden behind the side of the bed from Mina. Yet again, blood and the watery discharge from burst blisters stain the bandages. "Is it acceptable to go dressed as I am?"

"Your hair is fine," Mina says generously. "I would just pull on a quick change of clothes and go."

I nod and slide my feet into a pair of slippers before she sees them. I can pull a skirt off or on easily enough regardless. I discard my riding clothes in favor of a regular skirt and matching tunic, bind a fresh sash about my waist, and head over to Alyrra's rooms.

Alyrra seems drawn and quiet. I pour her a cup of tea while Zaria helps her decide which of the two outfits laid out for her inspection she should wear this evening.

"That's someone at the door," Zaria says suddenly, and I realize the faint tapping I'd heard was a knock on the door to the suite.

"I'll see who it is." I head through the inner sitting room to the outer, where someone raps on the door once more.

I open it to find a pair of pale-faced men with closed expressions.

"Fetch my sister," the first says in heavily accented Menay. He is tall and broadly built, with hair the color of darkened straw. Between the gold chains hung about his neck and his foreign clothing—a stiff, tightly cut tunic with puffed sleeves, and pants that appear sewn onto his legs—I've no doubt that this is the foreign prince I'm looking at.

"I said, fetch my sister," he repeats, his voice curt.

"Zayyid," I say. "If you will come in, I will let her know you are here."

He pushes his way in, barely waiting for me to get out of the way. I turn and hurry from the room.

"Who is it?" Alyrra asks, at the door to her bedroom. She glances toward the door to the outer room, but from this angle she can't see the men.

"I think it is your brother, zayyida. And another man with him."

"What does the second man look like?"

"Tall, of a larger girth, and somewhat older. His hair is reddish brown. More red, I think."

"Ah," she says as Zaria stiffens. "That will be Daerilin. I'll ask you both to stay with me. Let us go see what they want."

The men stand before the couches, silent and clearly displeased. As Alyrra steps out with the two of us behind her, the foreign prince greets her with a voice that drips contempt. It takes me a heartbeat to figure out why I can't untangle his words: he speaks their own western tongue, with all its sounds shoved to the front of the mouth. I glance toward Zaria. Her brow is furrowed, and her head is tilted, as if that might help her better understand.

The other man, Daerilin, says something and Alyrra's voice answers, soft with shock. And then I do understand, for Daerilin says the impostor's name: Valka.

I hear Zaria's quick intake of breath, but she makes no move. Alyrra's brother breaks in, his words harsh, contemptuous. Then the lord speaks again, demanding. They watch Alyrra with bristling anger, and even though Zaria and I stand to either side of her, just behind her shoulders, she bears the brunt of their wrath alone.

For a long moment, Alyrra remains silent. My hands curl into fists. They have come here demanding to know something about the impostor—and they very clearly don't care what Alyrra has been through. She says something slowly, quietly. Daerilin snaps back at her. *Snaps.*

I take a jerking step forward to stand shoulder to shoulder with Alyrra, and all three turn their regard to me.

"Amraeya," Alyrra says, her voice just slightly uneven. "Please summon a quad for me. Use the bell pull."

I dip my head and cross the room to the bell pulls, giving the blue one a single deft tug. Hardly more than a moment later, a quad shoves open the door, their swords drawn and their expressions grim. I recognize their faces, Captain Matsin's most of all.

"At ease," Alyrra says. "I did not mean to cause alarm. I merely require your services as an escort. My brother and Lord Daerilin wish to visit the impostor. Will you take them to her?"

The soldiers stare. Matsin clears his throat. "But, zayyida—"

"Where she is now," Alyrra says firmly, overriding his protest. "They wish to see her at once."

"Zayyida," Matsin agrees, his voice flat. But the impostor was already executed before I came, wasn't she? I thought she was hanged. And how could this—this despicable excuse for a brother come here with such a request?

"You call her 'impostor'?" the foreign prince demands in Menay.

"I call her what she is," Alyrra replies coolly. Then, to the soldiers: "Please stay with our guests through their visit and escort them home after. I would not want anything to happen on their way through the city. Report to me once you return."

"Where have you been keeping her?" the foreign prince demands.

"You will see," Alyrra says, gesturing toward the soldiers. Captain Matsin bows, and with a rustle of clothing the men leave, the prince swearing under his breath, loud enough for all to hear.

"Zaria?" Alyrra turns to us, her face paler than usual and two bright spots burning in her cheeks.

"Yes, zayyida," Zaria says, her eyes wide.

"Valka will have been buried by now, won't she?"

Zaria nods emphatically. "The king granted your request. I'm sure it was done at once."

"Then at least it won't be too gruesome. Let us finish dressing."

Zaria hesitates. "Zayyida, should we—is there anyone we should inform?"

Alyrra looks at her, her lips parted to refuse, and then she blinks. It is as if she has never before had anyone who would care to know before now. What sort of mother does she have—what family is this?

"I will write a short note for Kestrin. Amraeya, will you summon a page for me?"

By the time the boy arrives, the note is signed and sealed, and he departs with it at once. Not ten minutes later, Kestrin knocks at the door. Alyrra meets him in the inner sitting room. Zaria and I hover by the door, for it isn't quite proper for them to be alone.

"You are well?" Kestrin asks, crossing the room to Alyrra. He comes to a stop opposite her, his gaze running over her as if he might discover some harm done to her. Bruises, I think, remembering her reaction to my wrist. That is the sort of man her brother is. My stomach tightens into a knot.

"I am perfectly fine. Though I would prefer not to see my brother again tonight."

Kestrin nods sharply. "I'll see to it. I'm going to assign Matsin and his quad to you for the rest of your family's visit. The quads you have are all good men, but Matsin knows your family."

"He does," Alyrra agrees. "I would rather not hide, Kestrin."

"You won't." The words are fierce. "Should your brother be fool enough to try anything here, he will learn what Menaiya is made of."

I stiffen, startled by the restrained fury in his voice. Alyrra does not answer.

"Forgive me," Kestrin says after a brief silence. "I spoke in anger. But I will not allow such a man to trifle with you."

"I appreciate that," Alyrra says finally. "But this is my battle to fight."

"Then I will stand by you." Moving forward, he takes her hand and presses it between his own. "I am here for you."

"I know it, verayn," she says. *My lord*, a typical conjugation of "verin," but it feels like something more here, her voice heavy with emotion.

He squeezes her hand. "Kelari Amraeya?"

I blink, surprised to find the prince has turned his attention to me. I wasn't sure he even saw us here. He trains his gaze on me, regal and powerful and not the sort of man I might argue with. Zaria remains perfectly still beside me.

"You are the newest of our attendants, so I will just mention this: an attendant can be dismissed only by the person they serve. You understand?"

"Completely."

"Good. I shall be counting on you—on all of the attendants— to maintain your posts regardless of what may happen."

I can only hope that whatever it is Kestrin fears might truly be prevented by our presence.

CHAPTER

19

That evening and the following morning pass quietly, with no sign of the foreign prince or the impostor's father. Mina and Zaria attend Alyrra at breakfast. I watch Mina upon their return, but she glances at me only once, with a minute shake of her head. It tells me nothing at all, other than, I suppose, not to ask anything aloud, which I wouldn't have done regardless.

Alyrra sends Mina and Zaria out to dress, and drifts over to gaze at the silk tunic and skirt made specifically for the wedding ceremony this afternoon. The pale pink tunic and deeper rose skirt are exquisitely embroidered with gold thread and pearls. Her fingers brush over the embroidery, flip the hem of the tunic. She seems pensive.

Today's ceremony is the smallest of the celebrations to take place: the formal wedding itself, preceding the various banquets and festivities that celebrate it. She won't be considered actually married until the end of the week, when the final wedding processional and feast are held. After all, a wedding that only lasts a day is hardly a wedding at all.

Unless, perhaps, Alyrra is used to other traditions for a wedding, or a different sort of dress from what lies before her.

"Do you miss the type of clothes you used to wear in Adania?" I ask, remembering Mina's description from last night of the queen's strange long dress, with its tight bodice and many-layered skirts.

Alyrra shakes her head. "No. I prefer the dress of Menaiya."

"No one would fault you for occasionally wearing something from your own home. At least, I don't think so. . . ." Then again, what do I know? It would be wiser, perhaps, to ask Mina.

Alyrra just grins. "No, thank you. Your clothes are much more comfortable."

"Comfortable?" I repeat, taken aback. The outfit before her is so heavy and stiff with embroidery, I'd hardly call it that.

"They're easier to breathe in. I don't have to worry about being able to move. Admittedly, I often adapted my clothes after my mother had them made so that they gave me a little more space."

"That's . . . huh."

She chortles with laughter. "Amraeya, you must work on your ability to cover your disbelief."

"*Well*. You just told me your people care more about how a woman looks than if she can breathe. Pardon me if I don't know how to be polite about that."

"We are not *completely* backward."

"I did not say a word about being backward. But I think it's just as well you came here. And not only because now you can breathe."

"No, of course not," she agrees, and wipes her eyes. "But I do breathe easier here, and for that I'm grateful."

I have the distinct feeling we are no longer talking about Adanian dress.

I wait, but she doesn't say anything, and I take the chance to change the subject to the one thing I can't bring up around any of the other attendants. "Zayyida, I wanted to speak with you about another matter. We discussed it before, that other day in the wooded courtyard."

She nods, her smile giving way to a clear, focused look. "Excellent. Would you just close the door?"

I nod and do as she bids. She takes a seat on a carved arm-chair with a brocade seat and back, and gestures me to its twin. I ease myself down and launch into a description of my meeting with Artemian and Bren, their advice for her to develop her own quads and look to changing the laws.

"Who did the second man say he was?" Alyrra asks.

"He called himself Bren."

"That's . . . not particularly Menaiyan, is it?"

I shake my head. "No, it doesn't fit. It may just be an alias. Do you know . . ." I hesitate, try again, "Have you met Red Hawk himself? This man acted like Artemian's superior, but he wouldn't tell me anything when I asked."

"We've met," the princess says. "Red Hawk was . . . quiet and serious, and dangerously sharp. He was also unexpectedly kind."

"Someone different, then, I suppose." Bren had been more

abrasive than kind. And I wouldn't have called him quiet and serious by a long shot. "At any rate, he also intimated that some of the children who are snatched end up in the city."

"You mean they are enslaved *here?*"

I nod. "He will arrange to show me one such place in the next few days, I believe. I'll be able to tell you more then."

Alyrra nods, her face pale and her eyes bright with anger. "Well done, Amraeya. I'll look forward to hearing more from you. I am working with Kestrin to recruit the men I need for my own quads, but I suspect for something like this, a royal quad assigned as my bodyguards will not do. I'll speak to Kestrin about how it should be set up, though the actual work will have to wait until after the wedding." She pauses. "That goes for the laws as well. If word gets out that I am looking to change laws before I am even properly wed, that could make things difficult—regardless of my intentions."

"It's only a week," I point out. "And by then, I may have more information for you."

Alyrra smiles. "I look forward to it." She glances over to her wedding clothes, sighs. "I should like a few minutes of quiet before getting ready for the ceremony."

"Of course, zayyida."

I rise and dip a curtsy, my foot aching, and slip away to wait in the outer sitting room. I settle on the sofa, carefully wiggling my feet loose in their slippers. I don't want them *off* in case anyone enters, but I'll take a moment's respite.

I look up as the hall door swings open and find myself staring at the foreign prince. I blink, as if clearing my eyesight might take him away again. But no, he strides into the room, his teeth bared in a dangerous smile.

"Where is my sister?" he demands as I rise from my seat on the sofa, smashing my feet back into my slippers.

"Zayyida Alyrra is resting—"

"Good. Stay here." He pivots, making for the door.

"She doesn't wish to be disturbed," I say, my voice sharp. He can't go in there—not alone, not unannounced, and not with that look on his face.

He ignores me, stepping through the door and shutting it behind him. I break into a shambling run, remembering Kestrin's reminder not to let myself be dismissed. I wish, suddenly and desperately, that another attendant were here. Even Jasmine I would be grateful for. But the entrance to the attendants' suite is off the main hall as well, and it's only me here.

I push the connecting door open, but the inner sitting room lies empty.

"Zayyida," I gasp out as I hurry across to the wide-open door of the princess's bedchamber. Oh, why can't I run faster?

As I near, I hear the foreign prince spit a word that I don't need translated to guess the meaning of. The princess makes a small sound. She's afraid. I push myself forward till I gain the door to her room. Brother and sister face each other, Alyrra beside the bed, the foreign prince a couple of paces before her.

As I watch, he asks her something. She straightens her shoulders as she answers, looking more the princess—and he lunges for her.

She throws herself to the side, but she's not quite fast enough. His hand closes on her elbow, dragging her back viciously.

I cry out, fury and fear making my voice a sharp thing. How *dare* he attack her?

They freeze. Then, slowly, the prince turns to look at me, his pale eyes glistening with malice. I raise my chin, glaring at him. "Zayyida," I say, forcing my voice to come out clear and strong. "Can I be of service to you?"

"Amraeya," Alyrra says, her voice not quite steady. "Be so kind as to call—"

"Get out." Her brother drops her arm and starts toward me, striding across the room. "Now."

Alyrra takes the opportunity to slip around the side of the bed, heading toward the blue bell pull there.

"I cannot," I tell the prince, playing for time. "It is our duty to always be present with the princess. Zayyid." I tack the last word on as an intentional afterthought.

His expression, already ugly, grows meaner still.

"Perhaps," I say as he comes to a stop before me, his chest as broad as a wall, "you would prefer to have this conversation in the sitting room. Then I might sit out of the way and not be a hindrance to you."

"Your servants require schooling," the prince says to his sister. Alyrra has gained the other side of the room, her hand reaching for the bell pull. He starts to turn toward her.

"Incorrect," I snap, fear making me reckless. He can't see what she's doing—not if he's really capable of attacking her. "It is you who have no manners, but that is hardly a surprise."

"You little piece—"

"We have *heard*," I interrupt, stepping farther into the room so that he has to turn to follow me, his back still toward Alyrra as she tugs on the bell pull. "We have heard," I repeat, "that your people have little consideration for your women. Or perhaps it is just you. However, in Menaiya, a man cannot corner a woman in her bedroom, even if she is his sister. Or do you have so little honor that you are lost even to that?"

He lunges forward. I try to twist away, but I'm too slow—his fingers close on the front of my tunic and he shoves me back, slamming my shoulders into the wall.

"Brother, let her go," Alyrra cries. But her quad isn't here yet—even they cannot move that quickly—and the prince's face is twisted with fury.

I feel an answering rage in my breast. "Attacking a cripple?" I taunt him, my voice coming out with a slight wheeze. "Do you think *that* will impress the court?"

His lips lift in a snarl, and then his hand slams into my cheek in an openhanded slap. My face snaps to the side, and my other cheek hits the wall. Pain blinds me. I stumble as I try to clear my vision, sliding slightly, for he no longer holds my tunic.

"Stop!" Alyrra cries. "Stop!"

"Your maid must learn her place, just as you ought. I've no compunction in teaching you both," he says, turning to her.

He's going after her again. I realize it as he takes his first step, see the terror in Alyrra's eyes. *Where is that thrice-cursed quad?* I take a deep breath and launch myself at the prince's back, one arm hooking around his neck at an awkward enough angle that, between the sudden twist I force upon him and my weight slamming into his back, he staggers a step. Then he reaches around, grabs me by the arm, and tears me off him, sending me backpedaling onto the floor.

A quad bursts into the room, swords drawn. The prince pivots, and then steps back in surprise. They surround him in a moment, swords held high and steady. I sit on my backside on the carpets, staring at them, my breath coming in gasps. Captain Matsin glances from me to the princess.

"Take him out of here," Alyrra says, enunciating each word clearly, her voice finally gaining the sound of steel. "Post a guard at the foot of the stairs, and see that he never, *never* has access to this wing again. Am I understood?"

"Yes, zayyida," Matsin says, dipping his head. His sword does not waver.

"You are too dramatic, as always, little sister," the prince says, smirking. "What is a conversation between siblings? If your maid had behaved better, she wouldn't be where she is now."

I pull my legs beneath my skirt, try to get my feet beneath me. How *dare* he?

"Get out now," Alyrra says in a strangled voice.

The soldiers close around the prince, and I have the distinct feeling that if he doesn't start moving, they will use force. He must sense it as well, for he starts for the door. "Another time, then," he says as his foot crosses the threshold.

Captain Matsin reaches to close the door. "There will be no other time."

It is as much a threat as the prince's words.

CHAPTER

20

"Keep the cold compress applied a little longer to reduce the swelling," Berrila ni Cairlin, the palace's healer-mage, tells me. "Beyond that, there's not much to be done."

I grimace. Earlier, Berrila sent a wash of cool healing magic through me to slow the bruising across my cheek. As the ache of my swollen cheek eased, I felt the pain of the raw skin and healing blisters on my turned foot gentle as well. When I opened one eye in surprise, Berrila met my gaze as if daring me to say a word. I didn't, of course. There's no way I'm arguing with anyone helping my foot heal.

But even her magic could only do so much. Berrila was clear that my body would have to heal in its own time. Magic is good for stitching cuts together and stopping internal bleeding and any manner of things, but the body must still complete its own healing.

I sit in my desk chair and hold the compress to my cheek.

Mina sits across the room in her own chair, watching me grimly. She has said very little since I explained what happened, her expression shuttered. It's a stark contrast to her fury over the impostor's father presenting himself at court just yesterday.

Berrila bids us a brusque farewell and departs. I lean my head against the chair back, my mind replaying the incident with the foreign prince. I should never have allowed him through to the princess—I should have called out loudly for him to stop, effectively warning Alyrra of his arrival. Instead, I scampered after him like a fool, and put both Alyrra and myself at risk.

Footsteps approach, and I open my eyes to find Alyrra herself stepping into the room. I start to rise to curtsy, but she holds up a hand. "Please don't get up. How are you feeling?"

I set the compress aside. It seems rude to speak with it attached to my face, even if it means she'll see my cheek more clearly. "I am well, zayyida."

We stare at each other a moment, and I cannot tell what she is thinking. Then she turns to Mina. "Would you wait in the common room? I wish to speak with Amraeya in private." She turns back to me as Mina moves to the door. "In truth, Zayyid Kestrin wishes to speak with you as well. Will you see him?"

"Of course, zayyida," I say unhappily. I failed him, fell short in doing what he asked of me, and I can only hope he won't be too angry with me.

Mina slips out, curtsying again as she reaches the hall, and then Kestrin enters. His expression remains still as he catches sight of me, the bruise marring my face, but his eyes brighten with fury, the emotion sharpening his cheekbones.

I rise and dip into a curtsy, my foot aching as always. One

would think you could get used to the pain, but it is always shifting, putting my teeth on edge—which only makes me feel the stiff ache of my bruised cheek more. At least it distracts me from the fact that Kestrin is staring at me, his eyes brilliant with rage.

"Kelari Amraeya," he says finally.

"Zayyid," I say, easing out of my curtsy. "I ask your forgiveness—"

"We are very much in your debt."

I blink up at him, taken aback. He crosses the room to take my hand and bow over it, deeper than necessary.

I gape at him. Is he serious? What debt can he mean when I allowed the foreign prince to corner Alyrra? If I'd been faster, I could have warned the princess. If I'd been wiser, I'd have found a way to keep the foreign prince distracted without inciting him to violence. If I'd simply had more experience as an attendant, I likely would have known what to do from the outset.

Kestrin catches my expression and his own eases slightly. He steps back, releasing my hand. "You provided Zayyida Alyrra the opportunity to summon a quad. Unfortunately, that 'opportunity' came at a cost to yourself."

Relief floods through me: he doesn't blame me. And Alyrra must not either. I shrug and say easily, "I'll mend."

"Indeed," Kestrin says, his tone . . . bemused?

Was I supposed to wallow in misery before him? Does he think I've never dealt with pain before?

"I've spoken to Filadon. We—"

"You *what*?" I break in, horrified. This is certainly something I would have preferred to relate myself, if only to be able to assure my family at once that I was not that badly hurt.

Kestrin's mouth quirks. His anger is still there, in the sharpness of his cheekbones and the faint glitter of his eyes, but he's tamped it down. And it isn't directed at me. "I'm afraid it was necessary. The story is spreading through the court like wildfire. It seems the prince did not realize that our attendants are all from noble families, unlike the servants he brought with him."

"I'm not all that noble," I point out.

Kestrin raises an eyebrow. "You are Filadon's kin, and that is noble enough in our eyes."

I'm actually Melly's kin, to be accurate, but Alyrra is shaking her head at me from where she stands just behind Kestrin, so I keep my mouth shut.

"The prince has been placed under guard as a protection for our people. Only his own servants may enter his rooms. He has been invited to depart shortly after the wedding." Kestrin sighs. "Zayyida Alyrra and I have discussed with my father what further measures we wish to take."

I nod. The man is the crown prince to his own land. Just the fact that he's been asked to shorten his stay is significant.

"However that may play out, though, tempers are running high. You have become quite the heroine in the court's eyes, and the more they see of your injuries, the more furious your new self-proclaimed friends will be."

Self-proclaimed—? It isn't surprising that the court would rally around their prince and his betrothed against a foreign attack, especially when the attack came from her brother. It isn't even surprising that the people who wouldn't acknowledge me two days ago would defend me now, the honor of the court at stake. What's surprising is how very candidly Kestrin has acknowledged their hypocrisy.

He goes on, "That leaves us with the question of how to navigate the next week or so."

By which he means the wedding with all its festivities.

Alyrra takes a half step forward to join the conversation. "Verin Filadon has requested that you be allowed to stay with him until the foreign prince has departed. And, to be sure, that would certainly ease relations in the court."

That's how it will go then. Disappointment flickers through me, though I'm not sure why, or for whom I feel it. "As you wi—"

Kestrin coughs once, hand raised to his mouth in what can only be an affectation. I blink at him.

"We have discussed his request," Alyrra goes on, a slight tilt of her head to include Kestrin, "and with your permission will deny it."

"You would?" I say blankly.

Kestrin grins, looking suddenly and strangely boyish. "Zayyida Alyrra needs a full set of four attendants to match mine for the ceremony this afternoon. And all the evening celebrations. And the wedding processional. I suppose I could make do with three, but really, I am used to having my four."

I stare at him.

"You don't really mind, do you?"

Kestrin awaits my response. But I don't have an answer—not one they want to hear. Because staying at the forefront means that the whole of the court will be looking at me, pitying me for my bruised face and turned foot, and I don't want that. I've never wanted that.

Alyrra says, hesitantly, "Amraeya, if you prefer not to step forward, then we will support you in that. But I would not hide you unless you wished it."

"I understand. But"—I glance from her to Kestrin and back again, knowing I'm missing something—"what is your real purpose?" I can't forget that they are both politicians at heart. He has some purpose here, and no doubt Alyrra does as well.

They exchange a glance.

"What is yours?" Kestrin asks instead. "This is your decision, kelari. If you wish, you can stand before the nobles of the court and look that man in the eye, and show him that he has not won—because he will be there. We cannot keep him from the ceremonies, though I might wish it."

"And if I stay back, then he will think *he* won?"

"Yes," Alyrra says, her voice weary. "It is how he reasons."

Which means that keeping me beside her at the wedding is the only way Alyrra can make a clear statement of what she will and won't allow, and who has the real power between them.

"Well, we can't allow that to stand," I say firmly. I will simply have to deal with the looks. It will be worth it, to raise my chin to that despicable prince and let him know that he has not cowed me, nor beaten Alyrra. "The wedding ceremony is in another hour or two, isn't it?"

Alyrra smiles, but she still looks tired, wrung out. "We will be a little late, I expect. Fashionably so, I'm sure. I'll send in one of my maids to help you."

"And I've no doubt everyone will know exactly why we're late," Kestrin says with relish. "Thank you, kelari."

I dip my head. Whatever politics he's playing at by using me, I don't particularly mind right now.

He departs with a polite farewell. Alyrra follows him to the door, then pauses to look back at me, as if her words were caught on the tip of her tongue. Perhaps she wants to warn me about her brother again, though I already know what sort of man he is. Or perhaps it's regret in her eye and she doesn't know how to voice it.

"Zayyida?" I ask.

She hesitates. "You'll tell me if you decide you'd rather not be there? Or even if you come now but prefer not to attend me to later functions?"

"I will," I say slowly. My mind flicks back to that moment when he slammed me against the wall—and when I threw myself at him after that. And before that, to that obnoxious thief Bren, holding my hand in his, baring my bruises, and giving advice for which I had hardly spared two thoughts.

"Amraeya?"

"I wish I knew how to fight. How to defend myself and you. I think I'd feel better knowing that."

Alyrra stares at me, and then her lips curve in a faint smile. "As would I. That, at least, I should be able to do something about. Thank you, Amraeya."

And that's the other thing I would change. "Back home, everyone calls me Rae."

Her smile is brighter, truer, as she says, "Rae, then. Thank you."

CHAPTER

21

By the time I've dressed and the princess's maid has finished styling my hair and lining my eyes with kohl, I've no doubt we're running very late. As I rise to my feet, I glance at the mirror. The handprint upon my face has darkened to a deeper red with hints of blue. My cheek is swollen, the skin slightly shiny. My other cheek bears a much smaller, lighter bruise where my face connected with the wall. However lovely my hair and makeup, no one's going to be looking at it.

"Is it all right?" the maid asks uncertainly.

"Perfect," I say, and slide my feet into my new slippers, lined with velvet by Melly's request to cushion my latest set of blisters. The shoes are surprisingly comfortable.

I hurry through the common room on my way to the princess's rooms. No doubt I'm the last to be ready. As I reach the hall, Jasmine steps out of the princess's suite.

"Kelari Amraeya," she says quietly.

I pause, taken aback by her manner. "Veria?"

"I—" She comes to a stop before me, her gaze fixed on my cheek. Then she grimaces and looks me in the eye. "I'm sorry this happened to you. I'm not sure I agree with the princess's choice in making you an attendant, but even you don't deserve such treatment."

"Thank you?" I say, for there is as much kindness as insult in her words. In an attempt to change her focus, I ask, "Is the princess all right?"

Jasmine lifts a shoulder. "She seems fine. I think she's used to . . ." She hesitates.

"Used to hiding things like this?" I ask.

She swallows. "So it would seem."

"I suppose the court now has a better idea of why she might not have looked for help from the royal family after she was betrayed," I say slowly. "I think I would have stuck with the horses myself."

"Geese," Jasmine corrects me.

"Geese. Much safer than her brother."

She tilts her head, kohl-darkened eyes narrowed in consideration. Can a betrayal actually benefit a person, if it takes them away from what they fear? Was the princess protecting herself by embracing her new life as a goose girl? Was she, perhaps, not as much of a fool as the court believes?

Jasmine makes a faint, thoughtful sound, and turns toward the door. "Come along, or we'll be late. I told the princess I'd fetch you."

I fall into step with her and we make our way quietly to the princess's suite. Alyrra looks exquisite, the pale pink and deeper rose of her attire bringing out the natural color in her cheeks. She is steady and quiet, and asks me only once if I am well. We escort her down to the great receiving hall, and from there out the main doors to where a line of carriages waits to bear the royal party to Speakers' Hall.

I look out as we clatter through the city, past buildings strung with brightly colored flags, people of all ages lining the road. We come finally to a soaring bridge that spans the river runring past the hall. With the water glinting in the bright spring sunlight, the river seems somehow both eternal and ephemeral. Something that will long outlast me, and the palace, and all my worries, even as the water I look upon is continuously changing, being carried on to the sea in a cycle of flow and rainfall our scholars are still trying to understand. The river I see now, and the river I will pass over on our return, will be two different rivers, though they flow through the same place.

On the other side, we turn down a wide boulevard and roll to a stop before the hall. Built of shining white stone, with exquisitely carved arches, it is breathtaking in its beauty. The whole wide plaza before the building has been cleared by guards, spectators lining up on the other side of the wide avenue to catch a glimpse of the royal family.

Alyrra alights first, stepping aside to wait for us. I get down last, knowing it will take me the longest. Just as I lower myself down, the foreign queen sweeps up to join us, greeting Alyrra with a word and a nod. She is slightly taller than Alyrra, with dark chestnut hair and a cool demeanor. This is the first meeting between them since Alyrra's brother attacked her, and yet her mother gives no indication of concern. I would have expected at least a question as to her daughter's well-being. What I see instead in the woman's strange hazel eyes is a hardness that explains how the prince was allowed to grow into the man he is.

Once all the royals have gathered, they turn toward the hall. Waiting before the great doorway stand two men and a woman, all in the sky-blue open-fronted robes of Speakers, an indigo emblem on each breast. The man at the center steps forward, and together they bow to us. I take my cue from the other attendants, curtsying low while Alyrra offers a smaller obeisance.

Behind them stand a pair of men. One, a captain I have seen at least once in the royal wing's guard room, takes a step forward and nods to the king. The other, a tall, gaunt man draped in mage's robes, dips his head as well. They must have been trusted to assess the hall for dangers. I look past them, into the main interior courtyard of the building, but can make out little.

Speaker Adashay, the head Speaker and highest religious authority of Menaiya, leads us within, the other two Speakers flanking him. We proceed into a vast central open-air courtyard, complete with central reflecting pool. Standing to one side is a small table, elegant in its simplicity, set only with a single goblet, a golden cord, and a thin sheaf of papers. Beside the table rests an ornate couch with deep royal-blue cushions, the wood inlaid with mother-of-pearl and onyx.

It's a little surreal, the exquisite surroundings, the royal family, the greatest Speakers of our land gathered together. I *knew* they would all be here, of course; it is the royal wedding, after all. It's just strange to find myself here when two weeks ago I was caring for my family's horses and then searching the plains for Seri. This is a world away from that.

We walk Alyrra and her mother to the couch and help settle Alyrra upon it. Rows of court nobles are seated in small wooden chairs across from the sofa, here to witness the wedding and its blessing. At home, the wedding formalities are often witnessed only by the couple's closest relations, but I suppose a royal wedding is a different beast.

As we withdraw, Kestrin moves to sit alongside Alyrra, with the king and Garrin standing behind him, just as the foreign queen accompanied the princess. And there, having clearly arrived separately, is her brother. He steps up to Alyrra's side and stands there, chin raised and gaze moving slowly, arrogantly over the gathering.

I wait, knowing his gaze will come to me, and I'm not disappointed when he looks right at me and his lip curls in a faint smirk. My heart beats faster than normal, though I don't know if it's anger or a residual panic called up by the cold malevolence in his pale eyes. I lift my chin in return, and meet him glare for glare.

The ceremony begins, Speaker Adashay intoning a blessing in the Old Tongue, but the foreign prince is still looking at me, and I won't be the one to turn away first. Let him look. I have nothing to hide, *nothing* to apologize for, and I will not allow him any space for victory.

Vaguely, I'm aware that Kestrin and Alyrra have each sipped from the goblet, have bound themselves and their service to God, and Adashay has moved on to the actual wedding itself. But the foreign prince doesn't look away, and neither do I. I just blink slowly, and watch as his face grows redder and harder with each passing moment. I've spent a lifetime putting up with cruelty and

I'm not afraid to look his viciousness in the face.

"Together, you will learn mercy and forgiveness," Adashay says. "You will learn to build on one another's strengths and cover one another's weaknesses. Together, you will oversee the needs of your people. Will you so bind yourselves?"

I hear Kestrin and Alyrra assent, a mere murmur below the thud of my heart. There is a rustle of paper as the final marriage contracts are presented to the royal couple, and the foreign prince glances down, distracted. He looks up again at once, his face mottling and eyes full of fury. Even though it isn't really a fair victory, I grin at him and turn my gaze to the royal couple.

Kestrin and Alyrra each lift a hand and entwine their arms so that their palms press flat against each other, side by side, neither one above or below the other. The woman Speaker lifts the golden cord from the table and gently winds it around their arms, binding them together, a symbolic joining of strength and mutual support.

I've seen this ritual many times before, though the cords I know are made of bright thread rather than gold. The binding is the final rite of the wedding. The king steps forward to offer a drink of almond milk flavored with orange water to his new daughter, and the foreign queen does the same for Kestrin, and the families are sealed, the alliance established, the ceremony complete.

Now will come the festivities: a day at the baths first for the women, then for the men, followed by the sweetening, and then the actual wedding procession and feast.

As servants bring out trays set with dozens of fragile cups filled with the same drink offered to the royal couple, Mina murmurs, "Try not to look back at the foreign prince now."

I glance at her, surprised.

She shrugs. "You were not particularly subtle about it. You may have won that round; leave it at that."

"He started it," I say, as if I were a child.

Zaria huffs softly on the other side of me. Jasmine, on the far side of her, doesn't seem to have heard us.

"You mean everyone noticed?" I ask, my gaze darting from Zaria to Mina.

Mina eyes me with disbelief. "I can't imagine too many of the court missed it."

"Oh." My cheeks burn and I give thanks that at least my skin will not show my embarrassment half as much as the prince's revealed his.

"Have some almond milk," Mina says, and lifts a cup for me from the tray a servant offers us.

Almond milk and orange water is a delicious blend, one I've had at weddings at home as well, though somehow the taste is fuller, more sweet than I've had before. I sip it slowly and do my best not to look around, though now I can feel just how often people's faces turn toward me, the way their eyes slide over the bruises on my face.

I chose this, I remind myself. I chose to make a show of myself, and I'm not going to mind it now. Let the prince be ashamed, if he can feel such an emotion.

I glance toward the royal couple just as the foreign prince himself steps forward to congratulate them, one hand out toward his sister. Alyrra doesn't move, looking up at him from the couch. Instead, Kestrin rises, gripping the man's hand with his own, his other hand coming up to grasp his arm. He leans forward and murmurs something in the foreign prince's ear, smiles briefly, a cold, sharp look, and returns to his seat.

"I do wonder what he said," Zaria murmurs.

Mina nods.

"*Rae*," a voice says, and I turn to find Melly before me, moving so fast I nearly drop my drink as she wraps me in a hug.

"It's all right," I murmur, wrapping my free arm around her. Is she shaking? "I'm all right."

"It is most certainly *not* all right," Melly says, pulling back to glare at me. "How bad is it? It looks painful. Did he hurt you anywhere else?"

"No," I say, giving her shoulders a squeeze. "I'll be all right, Melly. Truly."

Melly lets out a slow breath, and her eyes glance about once as she becomes aware of the many, many eyes watching us. Then Filadon steps up beside her, bows to me, and says darkly, "I'll have further words with Zayyid Kestrin, cousin."

I expect I can't talk him out of that, so I thank him instead.

"I am—" He shakes his head, starts over. "I do not know what to tell your parents. At least the man is now under guard, and the princess will have an escort until he departs—which means you will too."

"I'll write my parents," I offer. "I'd prefer they hear the story from me."

Filadon nods. "Send your letter to me and I'll enclose it with mine. It's best if they hear from you, but they should also know that I will do my utmost to protect you."

I dip my head, and after a few more words, Melly and Filadon join the line to congratulate the royal couple.

I take a slow breath and turn my attention back to the gathering. A tiny, gray-haired woman who wears her clothes like battle armor and bears her cane as though it were both support and weaponry alike makes her way over to us. She greets Jasmine and Zaria, then Mina, and then she says, quite unexpectedly, "And you will, of course, introduce me to your newest companion."

I dip a hasty curtsy as Jasmine presents me to the woman, one Veria Havila.

"I, for one," she announces loudly, "am so very glad you have joined our court and were able to be here today. You've done our princess a service, and so honored us all."

She most certainly noticed my staring match, then. I duck my head, feeling my face warm again, my swollen cheek tingly and stiff. "I thank you, veria."

"I like the looks of you, child. I'm sure these girls will take good care of you."

"Of course, veria," Jasmine says brightly. "She *is* one of us."

Havila *hmm*s to herself, and I catch in her bright-eyed look an amused awareness that Jasmine would not have made such a claim yesterday. She steps away, and another noblewoman moves in to demand an introduction. It seems that almost every lady who approaches the royal couple stops by to make my acquaintance afterward, proof that the story of the prince's assault positively screamed through the court.

Finally, the stream slows and a servant comes by with a tray filled with an array of honey-dipped sesame cookies. I take one, grateful to eat something—I forgot altogether to eat lunch. Although just nibbling on the cookie tells me that chewing will be an uncomfortable experience for a day or two.

"That was well done of Veria Havila," Mina murmurs. At my questioning look, she goes on. "She's one of the pillars of court society. By demanding an introduction at once, she set the example for the remaining ladies. When Dinari came over after that—well, I knew everyone would be by shortly."

"Oh," I manage. Wasn't Dinari the woman Mina had hoped to introduce me to before—the one who had, apparently, refused that opportunity? "That was very kind."

Mina nods. "Strategic, I'm sure. It shows her support of the princess, which will be much appreciated by the royal family right now. But yes, also kind. Be sure not to lose her support."

With such a vote of confidence, it seems best to keep my silence. Instead, I turn my attention back to the nobles paying their respects to the royal couple. As I watch, Genno Stonemane approaches the couch, and beside him, another man. Or rather, Fae. Though he bears Stonemane company, they are nothing alike beyond the velvet darkness of their eyes. This Fae is dark as the richest of earth, his beauty as profound and gorgeous as the deep wood, so unlike Stonemane's colder, paler beauty, if just as dangerous. His hair is braided into long ropes that fall down his back, glinting here and there with jewels.

"Who is that beside the Fae ambassador?" I ask Mina softly.

"Adept Midael, the Cormorant. He rarely takes part in court gatherings, so you likely won't see much of him."

The Cormorant? What sort of title is that? I thought a cormorant was a seabird. I glance at Mina and make myself focus on the first part of his title. "Adept?"

"One of their more advanced mages, I think. It's curious to

have them both here now. We haven't had a nonhuman member of the court in years."

"No dragons?" I quip, remembering the creature I met with my sisters some time ago. She had been sentient and capable of her own magical brand of speech, but she had also been hunted by the king's soldiers. Dragons are distinctly not considered on par with the Fae or the merfolk.

Zaria laughs softly, having turned her attention back to us. "No. Even the merfolk are only here for the wedding. They arrived a few days ago, and will leave again a week or two after."

Jasmine nods. "Delegates come and go. It's rare to have an ambassador such as Verin Stonemane, let alone an adept in residence."

I hesitate. "Why would there be a Fae mage at court?"

Mina shrugs and Jasmine shakes her head. It is Zaria who says softly, "They say he's here to build relations with the royal family. But what I heard is that it really was a curse that took the queen, and he's come to see it doesn't take anyone else. When the prince went missing, it was the Cormorant who joined the search party. But then the prince came back of his own accord, so maybe the curse is just a rumor."

A chill sweeps up my spine. I do my best to stifle my shudder. Not that such a curse makes sense magically speaking—enchantments require power to continue. Curses usually feed off the person they are set upon, drawing from their natural reserves in a parasitical relationship. A curse dies with the person it is attached to, assuming it isn't stripped away by a mage first. A curse doesn't pass from one person to another, generation upon generation. Which I suppose means there are likely more mundane reasons for the royal family's dwindling numbers.

"I don't believe there's any sort of a curse at play," Jasmine says, her voice firm. "And it's best if you don't mention such things, Zaria. We don't need any more rumors causing trouble."

Jasmine defending the royal family from rumors rather than starting them? The foreign prince's attack really has had an impact on her.

Zaria looks away guiltily. "As you say."

CHAPTER

22

We return to the palace in the same carriage we arrived in. The Menaiyan royal party gathers in the main courtyard before continuing to the royal wing together.

"A word with you, verayn," Alyrra says as we come to her door.

Kestrin dips his head and motions one of his attendants to stay with him. Alyrra nods to me and steps into her rooms. I follow after her, leaving the rest of my fellow attendants looking slightly put off.

Kestrin's attendant takes a seat on one of the sofas, off to the side, so I do the same opposite him. Alyrra doesn't sit. Instead, she turns to her husband and says, "Will you tell me what you said to my brother, after the ceremony?"

Kestrin hesitates, watching her, and then admits, "I told him that if he ever touched you again, I would see his entire land gutted before he was ever made king."

I stiffen, glance desperately at Alyrra. Surely she won't allow such a threat to stand against her people? Even if it is meant to be against her brother?

Her jaw hardens, and she says, harshly, "You wouldn't. I know you wouldn't."

"No," Kestrin agrees. His smile verges on tender. "You know me better than that. But he doesn't."

"It's an empty threat?" Alyrra asks. "That doesn't seem like something you would do either."

I'd have to agree.

Kestrin shrugs. "It was the only threat he is likely to understand. I had to give him fair warning."

"What do you intend to do, then?" Alyrra asks, as if it's a certainty her brother will come after her again.

"I think you will agree that no one but he, himself, should pay the price of his decisions."

Alyrra considers him. "I believe that is so for most crimes. But you haven't answered my question. What will you do?"

Kestrin looks away, toward the window. "Whatever it takes."

"Verayn," she says. She's only said *my lord*, but it sounds like an order. "Did we not agree this is my battle to fight?"

His expression hardens, but after a moment he nods. "We did. I will not act without your blessing. You can trust me that much."

"I trust you a great deal more," Alyrra says, smiling wryly, the tension gone out of her. "And you know it. Now, I had best freshen up before dinner."

He blinks and then grins at her, amused to be dismissed so casually.

After he and his attendant depart, Alyrra turns to me. "This conversation . . ."

"What conversation?" I ask brightly. "Did someone say something?"

Alyrra laughs. "I'm glad I have you, Rae. You'll come to dinner?"

"Of course, zayyida."

"You can take tomorrow to check on the house of healing, and whatever else you might need to do. I'll need you again at dinner, but otherwise I should be fine."

"Thank you," I say, grateful for the reprieve she's offering me. Now that I've proven I'm not hiding, it will be a relief to step out of sight.

I wake sometime after dawn, light filtering in through the curtains. I stretch my arms and wiggle my toes, testing the muscles of my feet. My blisters are still a little raw.

I turn my head and spy Mina asleep, her hair spilling across her pillow. I ease myself out of bed, wrap a shawl about my shoulders to ward off the chill, gather my writing supplies, and slip out of the room. Whether or not I can sleep, there's no reason to wake her. In the common room, I pour myself a cup of tea and set to work on the letter I promised I would write my parents.

I've already sent them two—one upon my arrival in Tarinon, and a second upon my appointment as attendant, as well as a separate letter to Ani. With the distance and the fact that

Sheltershorn lies on one of the less ridden routes serviced by the royal couriers, I haven't received any reply from them. But I should hear something soon.

Finished, I send for Moonflower and then return to my room to change into a riding outfit from home. I add my story sash and a cloak to keep off the light spring rain, and slip out once more, looking forward to escaping the palace altogether.

My visit to the house of healing reveals only that the work continues, the overseer assuring me that all is progressing as promised. He shows me around the ground floor once more, and then ushers me out. The rain has left off for the moment. Still, there's no sign of any thieves skulking about outside.

I walk over to where Moonflower waits. The boy I left to watch her happily accepts the pair of copper coins I promised him and runs away. I stand a moment, watching after him, and wonder if I might ride through the city a bit before returning to the palace, get to know it better, perhaps find someone I can speak to about the snatchers who won't betray me to them. But Moonflower's mood this morning is especially foul, perhaps because she's a wet, finicky creature. And I'm not sure it's wise to trust my questions to a stranger; not after what the shopkeeper told me.

I reach to unwrap Moonflower's reins from the hitching post.

"That's a pretty little mare you have," a voice says from behind me.

I startle, which makes Moonflower throw her head back and snort.

"Really," I say, turning on Bren. "You didn't have to sneak up on me to say that."

He shrugs, setting the folds of his cloak swaying. "Where's the fun in that?"

I shake my head and murmur consolingly to Moonflower, who does not look at all willing to be assuaged. If only Bean were here; the animals always seem to find her voice calming.

"She's my cousin's mare," I tell Bren, which is more or less true. "Also, she bites."

He tilts his head to the side. "A good deterrent against horse thieves."

I give him a warning glare. "Don't touch my horse."

"I thought it was your cousin's."

"Consider it our horse," I say firmly. "And don't touch my purse either." Though this time I'm not actually carrying it. Instead, I've worn the story sash Niya made me, with its stash of coins and my bone knife magically hidden within it. I'd kept the coins for the boy loose in my pocket. Still, Bren ought to know I'm aware of his actions.

He laughs and sweeps me a bow. "I am but a thief at your service, veriana."

I feel my face heating. "It's just kelari." Which, thankfully, can't be conjugated to have a "my" attached.

"All right, Just Kelari, will you walk with me?"

I look at him sharply. "Where?"

"A ways, actually. Bring your horse and we'll see it stabled somewhere it won't bite passersby."

I can't help the twitch of my lips. He winks at me and then steps away, as if afraid I might kick him. I almost laugh, and am glad he's not looking to see. I don't think he needs any encouragement.

Bren strolls along beside me as we set off, and I try to ignore how handsome he looks with his hair tied back and his face for once neither smug nor smirking nor dangerously observant. I ought to be used to seeing handsome men by now, but the court nobles are all exquisitely groomed and far beyond me. Bren is well-groomed, but there's a slight roughness to him. He feels like someone I might have met back home. Except he's not. The way he controlled the conversation Sage and I had with Artemian . . . that's not something I should forget.

"You're taking me to see children who have been snatched," I say quietly.

"A few, yes."

"Is it safe?"

"For us? Certainly. If you want to keep these boys safe, you won't ask them any questions." His glance grazes the bruise on my cheek, a mottled purple, and it's a testament to how quickly that story spread through the city as well that he does not mention it. He goes on, "In fact, it's best if you appear somewhat . . . subservient. Meek. I'll be your pleasantly violent husband, and we are looking to build ourselves a new home beside my parents' house. Don't speak if you can help it."

There's a hard steadiness to his face that tells me he's considered these roles carefully, and chosen them to match what he expects to encounter. I dip my head. I'd rather not lie, but between the warnings I've heard of the snatchers' ruthlessness and the fact that Bren can't very well admit his own identity as a thief, there's not much choice. "Where is this place?"

"South side. Not our friend's territory, so best not to mention his name. It's not that long of a walk, though."

The south side would be the Black Scholar's territory, and not a place Red Hawk or his men would be welcome. Interesting, though, that Bren has to leave his own territory to show me what he's found. One would have thought he could more easily find something to show closer to home, and thereby avoid the risks inherent in trespassing.

I glance askance at him, and he raises his brows at me, eyes gleaming. I don't like that look—not the mocking amusement, nor the casual intimacy. I turn my gaze ahead again. Better not to encourage him with more questions.

We leave Moonflower at a stable attached to an inn a few blocks away. As we depart, Bren pulls up his hood and indicates I should do the same. "It's better if folk don't note our features in passing."

"Good thing it's been raining today," I observe as I tug my hood up. Even if it isn't raining right now, there are more than a few people who have left their hoods up. We won't stand out. "How long have you known about this place?"

"Just found it yesterday," Bren says.

I frown. "It wasn't raining yesterday. Did you not wear a hood?"

"I stopped by in the evening. It was cool enough to warrant a cloak. Why? Are you worried for me?"

What? "No," I say, and find myself flushing.

He grins and brushes his shoulder against mine, as if he were my brother. "If you say so."

I shake my head and keep my mouth shut. I'll only make it

worse if I speak. We complete the rest of our walk in silence.

We stop just outside a brickmaker's yard. Across from the central building where the kiln burns rises a wide wall of baked bricks many layers thick. Bren rattles the iron gate while I stare over the low boundary wall at the half dozen or so young boys carrying bricks, stacked into piles of six and balanced on their heads. They bring their loads to the wall of finished bricks, passing them up to a boy stationed there who adds them to the ever-growing wall, and then go to fetch more. The youngest boy can be no more than seven. They are thin, their worn tunics and pants hanging off their limbs and their feet crusted with mud—though they are certainly better clothed than many of the children I have seen on the streets. They work silently, uncomplainingly, but there's a hollowness to their gazes that unsettles me.

Bren rattles the iron gate again, calling out, and a man pokes his head out of the kiln building. He waves and hurries over to greet us. He is short and lean as a whip, his mustache thick and his hair threaded with gray.

"You've come back, kel! Welcome, welcome! And this is your lovely wife?"

"She wanted to see the bricks," Bren drawls. "Says she only wants the best for her house. Figured I'd humor her. You know women."

I feel my cheeks warm yet again. I keep my gaze focused on the man's chest.

He laughs genially. "No need to worry about old Téran's bricks! I fire them at the perfect temperature; that's the key." He turns to me, his eyes lingering on my bruised cheek. "My bricks will last a hundred years, easy."

I dip my head. "I'm glad to hear it, kel."

"What did I tell you about speaking out of turn?" Bren asks, leaning toward me, his voice silky smooth.

I keep my face downturned, my teeth gritted. These may be the roles he's chosen for us to play, but I don't like them one bit.

"Remember that," he says softly, and turns back to the brick-maker.

I keep my head ducked after that, following Bren and Téran through the yard to the open-air hall leading to the kiln, where they discuss the making of bricks. I pretend attentiveness but really, I am watching the boys. They are all of them still damp from the morning's rain, their hair flat against their skulls and hanging in rattails, their clothing clinging in wet folds. As they pass us in a never-ending round, I catch sight of scars on their legs, an oozing cut on one of their hands. Never once do I manage to catch their eyes.

I watch as a boy passes us to fetch a load of still hot bricks that have recently come out of the kiln. The kiln itself is housed in a single room reached by the hall we stand in. Above the kiln room's doorway hangs a bit of wood with a shape carved into it, or perhaps burned, though I can't tell what it's meant to be, over-lapping curves and then lines crossing over them.

Across the hall from the kiln is a small room. I glance within as another boy passes us to take his stack of bricks outside. The room is small and dark, with a bit of rubbish in the corner. No, not rubbish—blankets.

I shift, peering inside. Toward the top of the walls a series of bricks have been left out beneath the overhang of the roof, allowing for ventilation. Their absence allows just enough light for me to see that, beyond the small pile of worn blankets, the room contains only a single bucket. It doesn't take much imagination to guess what that's used for. This isn't an empty storeroom; it's where the boys sleep.

I ease back, assessing the door. It's solid wood, with a bar to close it—on the outside. I stare at it as if I could will the bar to the other side of the door, make it a protection for these children rather than a tool of imprisonment. But there's no arguing with it.

I turn back to the kiln room, the conversation between the men barely registering. My eyes wander over the kiln, the bricks cooling in racks. The room is sweltering hot, the air above the bricks wavering. No wonder the boys' hands are so rough. They must have been burned daily by the bricks until their hands built up enough scar tissue to protect them.

"You've some good helpers here," Bren observes, starting back out toward the gate.

"They do their job," Téran says as I trail after them.

"Do they live around here?"

Téran grins, but it's an unpleasant look on him. "You could say that. I give them food and board, and they work for me. No one else wants them, I can tell you that."

"Good of you to take care of them, then," Bren says, a slight edge to his voice. I glance at him. It's the first indication I've caught that the boys' labor bothers him. But his expression is only mildly curious as he says, "And what do they do with their time off? They have family around here to visit?"

"Nah, they're all of them orphans. We're our own family, see? There's nowhere else for them to go."

"They must be grateful to you indeed."

"They ought to be," Téran says. "Sometimes they need a little help with that. But you know how that is."

Bren reaches up and places a hand at the back of my neck. "Certainly do," he says, and I finally understand the reason for his act. This is how he has won the brickmaker's trust enough to have such an open conversation: parading my meekness and bruises to show that he too favors violence to maintain his power and authority. He must have taken his measure of the man when he visited yesterday evening.

"We'll be back," Bren says now, dropping his hand from my neck to my waist. "Unless, dear wife, you are not pleased?"

"No, no," I say quickly, as if afraid to countermand him. "It is as you wish."

Téran smiles broadly. "Let me know how many cartloads you'll need, and I'll have the order ready within a week."

Bren agrees, and a few minutes later the iron gate closes behind us.

I glance back as we walk up the street. "Why don't they run? The boundary wall isn't that high."

"Look around," Bren says, his voice hard and flat. "Do you see all these people? If they spot a boy on the run, they'll grab him and take him back."

"But *why*?"

"Because, as far as they are concerned, the boys owe that man a debt. He gives them food and board, and they work in return.

No doubt all of these people have been told that Téran paid for the boys' travel expenses to come here, and that debt must be paid off as well."

I shake my head. "But they're not actually in debt."

"He bought them from underground slavers," Bren says, and there is that edge again, razor sharp. "That is the debt he means, and they will never pay it off."

"Are they orphans?"

"Does it matter?"

"No," I admit. I glance toward him, then back to the road, thinking about the things he hasn't said, just how well he understands these boys' situation. The fact that he is doing this work, never asking for anything from the princess or me. There can only be one reason. "How did you come to be a thief, Bren?"

He casts me a look equal parts appreciative and pained. "You've figured it out, have you?"

That the first thing he ever stole was his own freedom? I shake my head.

He laughs, a harsh, empty sound. "Observant. I knew that from the start."

I keep my eyes on the ground so he won't see my pity. I've always hated the sight of it in other people's eyes, and I won't subject him to my own. Instead, I say, "Are there many others like these boys?"

"Oh, a great many. And girls too, though they often end up in brothels."

I look up, sickened. "But that means . . ."

"That they are raped daily by anywhere from five to eight

men who could, if they cared, actually free them? Yes."

I shake my head, as if I could deny the reality of Bren's words, the violence of them.

"You understand now why the princess needs a change in laws—laws that will prosecute men like the brickmaker and the brothel owners? And why she needs soldiers who will not turn a blind eye to those boys for the price of a few coins, who won't instead go in for a few minutes with the girls they're actually meant to protect? You understand?"

"Are they—are most of the children who disappear still here in Menaiya?" I ask. I cannot quite wrap my mind around the enormity of such a truth. The horror of it.

"Not likely," Bren says. "I only wanted you to see that it isn't all away from here. I suspect most of the slaves are trafficked to other lands. The ones here in the city? Their families are likely far out in the country and have no idea where to look for them."

"There was a girl taken from our town," I say slowly. "I didn't think she'd be brought north, but—"

"No, you're probably right. She'd have been taken to the nearest port. From Sheltershorn, that's straight east and down the river a bit to Lirelei, isn't it?"

I glance askance at Bren, but it shouldn't surprise me that he looked into where I'm from. He clearly pays attention to details. "You think she's in Lirelei?"

"She'll be gone by now," Bren says. "I'm sorry, Rae. I don't think you can find her."

I nod. But I'm not giving up on stopping the snatchers, and perhaps, somehow, we'll still recover her.

The stable is just ahead of us, which means the end of our conversation. Once I have Moonflower, I expect Bren will depart, and with him, any chance of answers for the rest of my questions.

"The boys back there," I say abruptly. "How do we help them?"

"We don't," Bren says coolly. "Talk to your princess; she'll have to see to it."

But she can't. Not yet, though I suppose if I can map out where the brickmaker's yard is—if I can find my way back, at least—I could lead a contingent of soldiers there when Alyrra's able to order it. But she isn't even fully married yet; she only has the soldiers Kestrin has put at her disposal. She can hardly order a raid on a brickyard on the south side, however small and irrelevant it might seem.

On the south side. I look straight at Bren and ask, "Why is it that we came to the south side to see this?"

"Because that's where the brickyard is?"

That's not it at all. "You mean there *aren't* such places on the west side. Does Red Hawk care as much as you do about slavers?"

"Too clever by far," Bren murmurs softly. And then, more loudly, "He lets me do as I please when it comes to them. In return, he has my loyalty. Any other questions, or am I free to go?"

I feel myself flushing. "You were always free to go."

"Then I take my leave of you." He catches my hand in his and sweeps me a mocking bow. "Just Kelari."

Halfway back to the palace on Moonflower, I realize my grandmother's ring is no longer on my little finger. I stare down at my bare pinky finger as if the curved band with its tiny ruby might spontaneously reappear. *That's* what comes of asking a thief questions he doesn't want to answer.

I should have worn my purse instead.

CHAPTER
23

Upon my return to the palace, I can't seem to sit still. The memory of the brickyard clings to me, the silent boys with their hollow eyes and thin bodies a reality I can't leave behind. Nor do I want to. Only there's nothing I can do about them right now—except pray, as Mama always says. I do say a prayer for them, but I want desperately to *do* something as well.

Without any requirements on my time before dinner, I stop into my room. Alyrra has just left for lunch, which means I cannot even tell her about what I've seen. I go to look for Melly, figuring a cup of tea might help. But she is, apparently, at lunch with the princess.

I stand a moment in the hallway outside her door, rubbing my arms, and then set off without direction, filled with nervous energy. At least I can walk right now, my foot aching but not actually hurting. The healer-mage's intervention has certainly helped, and the velvet-lined shoes, made to the shape of my old slippers, are cushioning my feet properly. I'll make myself stop before I get to the point of starting new blisters.

Eventually, I find my way out through a side door. I've left my cloak behind, but the sun has finally come out, and while it's cool and the ground is wet, it isn't too chilly. I follow a path and find myself intersecting another pathway I recognize: this is the way I came when Kirrana showed me the side entrance to the palace complex on my first, miserable day as attendant. Was it really only four or five days ago?

I follow the path away from the palace, past what I now recognize as practice fields for the soldiers—they had only looked like a dark expanse when I passed them that night—and around a curve to a series of buildings. Benches are set out across from them, right where the sun warms them. I sink down onto the nearest, stretch my legs out before me to rest my foot, and try to think about what I've learned today.

In the end, it isn't as much as I'd like: I want to know how the boys came to be where they are, what they know of the people who snatched them, how many other children are held helpless within the city and across our kingdom. I want to know who has knowingly kept them where they are, and who has been unintentionally complicit. I want to break them out of their prison, consequences be damned. If only I had the ability. Or my sisters with me.

Between Niya's quiet, steady focus and magical talent, and Bean's drive to right all wrongs, I would have the support I needed to do *something.* God knows we've helped others before. At least I might have had a chance of helping these boys with my sisters' aid. But it's just me here now, on my own in a strange city, and I don't know what I can accomplish alone.

"Kelari? Oh, it is you!"

I look up with a blink in time to realize it's Kirrana, a tiered metal container in her hands, before she plops down on the bench beside me and opens up her container. She separates the tiers to reveal a generous meal of spicy fried potatoes, a separate dish of chickpeas, and a cloth-wrapped set of flatbreads.

"Would you like some lunch?"

I look at Kirrana, and it occurs to me that she isn't looking at me at all. She's very carefully *not* looking up. Ah, the bruise on my cheek.

"It's all right," I say. "I don't mind if you stare."

She flicks me a glance, her gaze skimming over my cheek, and then she hands me a flatbread. "Eat."

"No questions?" I ask as I tear off a piece and scoop up a bite of chickpeas.

She shrugs. "I find that food usually helps when I'm feeling low. You can talk, though, if you want to. I'm pretty good at listening."

"Let me guess: You're an older sister?"

She grins. "No, I'm the youngest. You're the oldest, though, aren't you?"

"Well, yes."

"See, that's older sisters for you, not believing the young ones can listen."

"That's not true at all," I protest.

She grins and prepares an especially large bite for herself. "I'm listening right now," she says, and pops the bite into her mouth.

I can't help laughing, my bruised cheek aching, as she watches me patiently and chews. And chews. She raises her brows, her left brow arching over her eye patch.

"You've figured out who I am," I say.

She swallows. "It's not like you made it a secret. You did tell me your name. I'm sorry, you know. We all heard what happened."

I nod. "It's—that's not why I'm here."

"So why are you here?"

"I don't know." I look across at the buildings and find that I *do* want to talk. "Do you think the snatchers are a real threat?" I ask abruptly. "Or just a fiction?"

"They're real," she says, her voice low.

"How do you know?"

A pause. She sets her flatbread down, her expression still. "My brother was snatched when he was eight. I was three. We know he didn't run away." She swallows. "My mother still mourns him. We all do."

"I—I'm sorry." I hadn't meant to dredge up such pain for her.

"Not your fault," she says, and picks up her bread again, but she doesn't eat it, just sits with it in her hands. "Why do you ask?"

"A girl disappeared from our town just before I came here. And today, when I was out in the city, I saw some boys who . . ."

She looks at me sharply. "Who what?"

"Who might have been snatched. They were working, and the man who kept them said they owed him a debt, but the way he kept them—" I swallow hard. "They couldn't leave. And they weren't from the city, had no one here to protect them."

"They couldn't *leave?*"

I nod.

"Have you told anyone? Someone ought to be able to help them."

"I will. And that might help these particular children, but..."

"You think there are *more* in the city?" Kirrana demands.

"Perhaps. And there are certainly more who are smuggled away."

Kirrana looks down at her half-eaten flatbread, thinking. "You want to find the rest, help everyone."

I nod, even though it sounds absurd spoken aloud like that.

"The princess might listen to you."

"Yes, but to help anyone else, she'll need more information than I have. She can't launch an investigation without evidence, without proof that the snatchers even exist."

Kirrana looks across the way at the buildings, one of which must be the tax office. "I wish I knew how to help you."

So do I. I brush the crumbs off my skirts. "It's all right. I'll keep trying, and perhaps I'll find out something more."

She puts out a hand, just barely touching my arm as I rise. "I'm here. If I can help, I will."

I thank her, though I'm not sure what a tax clerk could do against slavers.

I update the princess on my visit to the brickyard in a quiet moment before the evening's banquet. She listens silently, her expression grim.

"If everyone around this brickyard is complicit in keeping them . . ." She shakes her head. "That's going to make it that much harder to find such people, because no one will report them."

I nod, steel myself for this next bit of news, for it still makes me sick. "My contact also said that there are brothels where snatched girls are kept by force. He said when guards go to investigate, they take—they visit the girls for their own pleasure, and leave the brothel owner alone."

"No." Alyrra's expression is livid. "*No.* I'll have every brothel in this city shut down!"

"Who will you send?"

That brings her up short, but not for long. "We'll need a force of soldiers dedicated to stopping the snatchers—men and women who volunteer to do so. I'll talk to Kestrin." She pauses. "It will have to wait until after the wedding. I can't make such a change yet. In fact, it will be better if Kestrin and I do it together, rather than me alone."

"Then he knows you're looking into the snatchers?"

She nods absently.

"Does anyone else?" At her look, I say, "I need to know whom I can trust with this. Who in the palace knows what you're trying to do?"

"Kestrin," Alyrra says at once. "I assume Filadon would be trustworthy, given how close he is to Kestrin, and that he recommended you specifically."

Did he? "You mean, because he knew I would care about stopping the snatchers?"

"Yes."

I *thought* so.

She laughs. "Such a bright, sharp look, Rae! I see he didn't tell you."

"He's very good at keeping secrets."

"That he is," she agrees. "As we navigate the palace side of things, I expect we will include Garrin. He has . . . indicated a wish to support us, which I don't mind taking advantage of. Kestrin says his cousin is unquestionably loyal."

I nod. Garrin is too far above me to be much of an ally, but it's good to know that Alyrra will be able to rely on more than just her husband.

"You've done well, Rae," Alyrra says. "This is a definite start."

"It's where some of the children end up," I point out. "We don't know how they get there, or who actually does the snatching. Nor do we know where the rest are sent."

"I know. But even this much is more than we had last week."

More, but not enough. And I don't have any further leads. If only I could have spoken to the boys in the brickyard. . . . "If we can rescue the boys I saw, they may be able to tell us how they were transported, who sold them to the brickmaker."

Alyrra nods. "If we have a mode of transport, you think we'll be able to start looking for that as well."

"At least more effectively than we have up until now."

"I'll speak to Kestrin. I know the royal guards have different roles from those of the river wardens, or the soldiers who patrol the city. If we could just send one of his quads to collect the boys, it would be an easy thing, but I suspect it will have to go through the proper channels or we'll risk alienating those we need on our side."

"I understand," I say, even though I cannot help thinking of the boys suffering days or weeks longer because of bureaucratic logistics.

In the next room, the connecting door opens and footsteps

sound softly on the carpet. Alyrra says, brightly, "Our self-defense lessons will begin in the morning, before breakfast. I've asked all my attendants to take part."

"Yes, zayyida," I say as Jasmine steps in, glancing toward me. Alyrra nods to her, and sends me off to get ready for the evening banquet.

The meal is a long one, but the nobles I am seated beside are pleasant, and kindly include me in their small talk about the weather, the festivities, and everyone's clothes. I smile and nod and do my best not to say anything to test their patience. The sheer opulence of this dinner seems a world away from the grim reality I glimpsed earlier today.

My sleep that night is plagued with haunting visions of the brickmaker's boys, their eyes filled with darkness and their hands scarred and weeping blood. I dream of a labyrinth constructed of yellow bricks that walls them in, rising up between us as I race toward them. Finally, I find a break in the wall, but when I reach it, the foreign prince turns toward me, a smile on his lips and his pale eyes glistening with violence.

I wake with a jerk to the stillness of my room, the faint sound of Mina's breathing. But there is no sleeping after such a dream. Dawn cannot be more than an hour or two off. At home, I would go out for a ride on Muddle, or just walk out into the plains and sit down to rest in the quiet. Neither is an option here. I lie in bed as long as I can, and then grab a shawl and slip out to the common room. And laugh at myself. Because here too I have nothing to do—no horses to check on, no mending, no cooking, not even a treasured book to read.

I make myself tea, hot water from the kettle kept upon a

mage-made warming stone, a scoop of leaves dropped into the pot, and think about the boys I saw, about Seri and if she will ever be found, and the way Ani wept as I held her, as if her sorrow might break her open. I think about how little I actually know and whether I will be able to do anything to stop the snatchers.

I don't have any answers. I lean my head against the sofa, and remember Bren's face when I guessed his past, the fact that as a thief he has shut down or driven out every slavery operation he could find in his own territory. I think of the old grief in Kirrana's eyes as she spoke of her stolen brother, her offer to help however she could.

The snatchers may be ruthless, but I have a wealth of secret allies, people with their own losses who will help me. I pull my feet up onto the sofa, resettle my shawl about my shoulders. They may be street thieves and tax clerks and shopkeepers rather than lords or guards, but that doesn't make them any less important. All I need to remember is that they are there; that I need only find them to be able to move forward.

The snatchers have been stealing people for about thirty years now—Mama once said that when she was a child, they never feared such a thing. I'm not going to be able to dismantle their operations in a week, or a month. But I know what I want.

I'll simply have to be patient in order to get there.

CHAPTER

24

"Your timing leaves something to be desired," Mina tells me as we ready ourselves for our first self-defense lesson. "It's the day of the baths! Could you not have kept such a helpful suggestion until after the wedding was completely finished? I mean . . ." She glances at my cheek with its purpling bruise and says with a hint of guilt, "It *is* important, but it is also a rather busy week."

"I know," I say apologetically, wishing I'd at least managed to sleep a little later.

"Well, there's no help for it, I suppose. You should have heard Jasmine when she learned we would be training with a quad." Mina smiles despite herself as she puts on an emerald-and-gold earring.

"Are you sure you want to wear jewelry?"

She grimaces. "Our instructions are to wear our usual clothes and jewelry so that we will know what we can or cannot manage in them."

"Ah." Well, I suppose I could put on a couple rings and a necklace. I rub my pinky, missing my grandmother's ring.

A half hour later, we convene in Alyrra's rooms. A royal quad escorts us down through the palace to a small courtyard I've never seen before. The distant sounds of clattering and the occasional *baa* tell me we're near the kitchens.

Zayyid Kestrin waits with Captain Matsin at the center of the courtyard. After the usual courtesies, Matsin has us line up before him. "The first thing to know about defending yourself from an attack is that you are not trying to hurt your opponent," he explains as we face him. "Your one and only goal is to escape. If your opponent loses their balance and falls, you run. If they are hurt enough to pause for even a moment, you run. If at any point you can run, you do so. Is that understood?"

We all nod, but I've already lost. All the women here can run, and with a little practice in their skirts, they'll have a chance. But me? Not likely.

"Excellent," Matsin says. "This morning, we will focus on how to punch effectively, and then how to block a blow."

He pairs each of the attendants with a soldier, Kestrin coming to stand opposite Alyrra. Matsin himself walks over to be my partner. He inspects my fists, critiques my form as I practice how to piston out my fists in what he calls a jab-cross—first one fist, then the other—and then in a softer voice asks, "How well can you run, kelari?"

I glance at him and find myself both amused and strangely

pleased that he did think of me. "About as fast as you can jog, I would assume," I say lightly.

He nods. "Then we focus on your fighting. It is imperative that you learn as quickly as possible."

"Is that why I have the best teacher?"

"Arguably, the prince is better than I," Matsin says, and taps my fist. "Straighten your wrist to remain in line with your arm; that will deliver the power of the strike. The impact should be on the first two knuckles of your hand."

We drill a jab-cross for half the session, then learn two different blocks that merge seamlessly into a punch or shove counterattack. We pair up to try them on each other as our teachers watch. Thankfully, I am matched with Mina, while Jasmine and Zaria break off together and the princess faces Kestrin. Mina seems to have a natural affinity for self-defense, earning a hard-won word of praise from Matsin as he watches us.

"Again tomorrow morning?" Matsin asks Alyrra, and she inclines her head, her face pink with exertion.

My body feels good for the first time in a while—I've missed that slightly achy feeling of having engaged in hard work. And, from the look on Alyrra's face, so has she.

Two hours later, we arrive at the baths. They are a place both familiar and utterly foreign. Set apart from the palace by an open courtyard of sorts, the bathhouse is a large, opulent building, all curved arches and carved pillars and brightly tiled designs. Within, the changing room is filled with bath attendants, a team waiting in preparation for Alyrra, while a smaller group behind them casts their eyes toward us. There is already a wide array of noblewomen here, many of whom I now recognize, and there is much hugging and cheek kissing and laughter among the crowd.

Only the foreign queen stands fully clothed, shifting uncomfortably beside the noblewoman who traveled with her. "Alyrra," the queen says as we approach her.

"Mother," Alyrra says brightly. "I'm so glad you've joined us."

"Am I supposed to *undress* in front of everyone?" Her voice, while low, cuts through the conversations around us.

"This is a tradition I'd like to honor," Alyrra says with a smile that doesn't reach her eyes. "It is certainly different from our own traditions, but I am hopeful it will be quite enjoyable." She turns to us, effectively cutting short the conversation. "Forgive me, Mina, but I cannot remember what we do from here."

Mina dips her head. "We change, zayyida, and then proceed into the bathing rooms." She glances once through the gathered women, and then adds, "Perhaps Veria Havila might serve as a better guide for your first experience in the baths? If she would so honor us?"

Havila steps forward from where she stands beside a bench, her cane tapping on the tiles. She's already undressed and wrapped in towels, the wrinkled skin of her arms sagging. The foreign queen stares with faintly restrained horror at the picture presented by this most formidable matriarch of the court.

Havila offers Alyrra a slight curtsy, made deeper by the dip of her head. "It would be my honor, zayyida, to accompany you and your mother through the day."

Relief courses through me. Havila may not equal the foreign

queen in rank, but she no doubt will know how to handle her. And, judging from the looks Mina is receiving, a good number of the women present approve of her inviting in an elder to create a buffer for the princess.

The bath attendants finally descend upon Alyrra and her mother as Havila explains to them what to expect. I retreat with Mina by my side, Jasmine and Zaria moving to a different bench. Our own bath attendants appear to accept our clothes and hand us towels in return. Mina steps out of her shoes and slides off her skirt, and Jasmine and Zaria do the same. I grip my skirt, as if I could take that off and leave my feet covered. I really *don't* want to take off my slippers. While I've gone to public baths a thousand times before, it was always with my family, among women who had known me my whole life. Exposing my foot here is different.

"Your slippers," my attendant says patiently.

Gritting my teeth, I slide out my feet, ignoring her hiss of shock, and pass the slippers to her. She takes them gingerly. I turn my back on her and finish undressing. My turned foot may feel better, but it's still pink and covered with the remains of blisters. There's nothing to be done but hope no one looks down. It's a stupid, pointless hope, but I find that I can occasionally be quite good at those.

But it isn't my foot that draws attention in the changing room; it is Alyrra—or her scars, to be exact. I knew she had a few, a pale curving scar over her knuckles, and another thin scar on her right arm, but as she undresses, three, four, five more come to light. These are not the small scars of nicks and scratches; each of these bears witness to a larger accident in its own right . . . or not an accident at all. I press one hand against my bruised cheek and look away. This is all wrong.

But no one says a word; whatever story is written on Alyrra's body, she is a princess and that is a question even Havila won't ask. Instead, the older noblewoman leads the party into the main room, where an actual pool of faintly mineral-scented water waits, steam rising from its surface. Our own bathhouse in Sheltershorn contains a room of benches with buckets to be filled with heated water, and drains in the floor to take away the water.

Melly finds me and, after a quick embrace, points out where a few older women are gathered to one side. "They can't manage the steps, so there are buckets there. You can use them as well, if you'd like."

Rather than plunge my foot in the near-scalding water of the pool? "Thank you," I say with undisguised gratitude, and go off to join the women. Havila remains by the large pool, a servant hurrying to bring her a stool, and there she sits while an attendant washes her down, chatting with the foreign queen who cannot quite bring herself to enter the pool and eventually calls for her own stool.

The rhythm of the bath, though more elaborate, is familiar to me: bathing, scrubbing our skin raw with goat-hair mitts and black soap, entering the steam room with its heated stones, and then a massage—though here, there are attendants to massage us, and no one trades massages with their friends, just as no one has to scrub themselves. But, like home, this is a social time, a time to catch up and reminisce and share stories.

And, like home, there are all different types of bodies here, tall and short, thick and thin, though palace folk tend toward more curves.

"You've such strong muscles!" my attendant tells me, drawing a couple of amused looks, but beyond that, I feel strangely comfortable here. After all, there is Havila with her cane, laughing and demanding joking tribute and ordering the court around her, Alyrra tucked safely beneath her wing, and the foreign queen beside them, her expression reserved but not contemptuous.

Yes, I realize with some surprise. That is what has put me at ease: Havila, strong and capable and granting no concession to those who might see her weak knee as a vulnerability. She owns her body even here, where all can see it, and I find myself in awe of her.

I close my eyes as my attendant applies a thin clay mask to my face, and try to imagine not caring what others think of me— to be so sure of my power and place that I can demand others' respect and ignore those who do not grant it. But I am not Havila. I will never be a noblewoman of her rank or stature. And my deformity came at birth, not with age.

"Try to relax," my attendant says, laying a hand on my shoulder.

I nod and rest my head against the warmed stone I lie upon. But my body tightens again, as if anger were a thing I am used to cradling within me. I can't seem to find a way to lay it down, to let go of the resentment within me. Why must I always be made aware of how others see me? I don't want to keep carrying this sense of being judged and found lacking. I don't want to be made to feel less just because my foot is turned one way instead of another. It still bears me forward every day of my life.

"Time to wash off," my attendant chirps.

I sit up and follow her to a rinsing station: a bench before a tap that offers a stream of hot water. Alyrra has already moved back to the room with its soaking pool. I rub away my clay mask and continue after her, pretending that somehow, before I leave the baths, I will be able to wash away the things I no longer wish to carry.

It is a nice dream.

CHAPTER

25

It is nearly evening when we finish at the bathhouse. After the final rinse in the pool, there were refreshments, mint tea, biscuits, and pastries. No one dared depart until the princess did.

Dinner tonight will be a private affair, and Alyrra has given both Jasmine and me the rest of the day off. We share a quiet meal in the common room before retiring to our respective bedrooms. I'm delighted to find a letter waiting on my desk: the first from home that I've received. I devour the cheerful missive from Mama, with interjections from my father duly noted, and little messages added at the bottom from my sisters.

I smile as I read. Bean is ever so glad I've left, as she is going to Spring Fair for the first time, departing in a few days, though a glance at the date on the letter tells me they must have left by now. The fair itself will be preceded by a celebration for the royal wedding on the day of the wedding processional. So she will have that pleasure as well, even if she did not make it to the king's city.

Mama and Niya are looking forward to a quiet couple of weeks at home; they have hired extra help for the horses, and Mama mentions the likelihood that they'll get the spring washing done so that they can put away all the heavy blankets and winter cloaks. Ani, my mother says, is doing as well as can be expected. Niya and Bean have made a point to visit her twice, and her other friends in town have also been keeping her company. Mama has encouraged her to write to me, so perhaps I will hear from her soon.

I begin a response at once. I have only just finished that and begun a letter to Ani when a knock comes at my door.

I open it to find a page. He glances once toward the empty common room, black hair flopping over his forehead, and whispers, "A friend of a friend wishes to see you at once."

"A—what?"

The boy flicks me a sharp look. "You know."

I don't.

He checks the common room once more, and mutters, "Red Hawk."

Oh. "Himself? Or—?"

"His men," the boy says, clearly peeved with my country stupidity. "You know the Tattered Crow?"

I nod. It's where Sage and I met Bren for the first time. Though how I'll find my way there alone, I can't say. However, I'm not about to admit that as well.

The page bows. "At once, kelari. If you can."

He departs, leaving me wondering just how accomplished Red Hawk is, that he has servants in the palace who carry his messages. Or Bren's messages, as the case may be.

Never mind. I need to go; it's already dark, and I do not want to be out on the streets alone late at night. Sheltershorn is safe enough, but I suspect the city is different. Perhaps I can hire someone to guide me; after all, the Tattered Crow is an established business and not itself a secret location.

I change quickly, slipping into a comfortable tunic and skirt set from home, and wrapping Niya's story sash about my waist. Coins and my knife, I remind myself. And whatever protections her magic might offer, though I have no intention of being cursed tonight. I take along a few spare coins in my pocket, in case I'm able to hire a guide.

Down the back stairs, I head toward the side exit of the palace so any nobles won't take note of my departure as they might in the main halls. As I turn down a quiet hall, though, I find that not all the nobles are congregated at dinner, for there, walking together, are Genno Stonemane and the Fae mage, Adept Midael. They are both dressed elegantly, their fashion more Fae than Menaiyan today, with long flowing robes trimmed in braid.

Stonemane catches sight of me at once, his brows rising, and then he turns and says something to his companion. Midael flashes me a single curious glance, dips his head, and departs in the other direction.

I admit to being curious myself. I continue down the hall, aware of my uneven gait as Stonemane glides toward me, his robes rippling around him.

"Kelari Amraeya," he says, dipping a bow.

"Verin," I say, making my own curtsy. "You are well tonight?"

"I am." He pauses, and I can feel his gaze resting on my cheek. I keep my eyes firmly on his chest, which is much less unnerving than the otherworldliness of his eyes. "I was glad to see you at the ceremony and dinner."

Ah. He's checking on me, as he hadn't been able to before the whole of the court. It's sweet in a wholly unexpected way. "Thank you," I tell him.

He nods, his gaze flicking over me and then—pausing. "Your sash is . . . intriguing."

Light and shadow! "Do you think so?" I say as lightly as I can. I was hoping Niya's work was subtler than that.

He lifts his hand, tapping his opposite arm once. For a heartbeat, the sounds around me dim, the distant murmur of the world falling away, and then the sensation passes and it's as if the hallway brightens once more.

"A guard against listening ears," Stonemane says to reassure me. And then, in answer to my question, "Unless someone sees them at work, you should be able to pass off your sister's wards as typical. Though they are certainly novel in their design. If the wards are activated, though, you would arguably have other, larger problems to deal with. I wouldn't worry about it."

"If you can see all that, then . . ."

"Fae, remember?" he says, well-deep eyes rising to meet my gaze.

As if I could forget. "Would it be better not to wear the sash at all?"

"After your most recent experiences at court? I would recommend wearing it at all times." Stonemane's voice is deceptively blithe for how the planes of his face have hardened, his eyes reflecting no light at all.

I swallow. "Is the foreign prince . . . he's not a mage, is he?"

"Not a drop of magic in his blood," Stonemane says. "And now I had best go, before I commit some sort of political blunder."

Such as warning me to ward myself against the foreign prince, because even if he doesn't have magic, he might still find a way to use it against me?

"Thank you, verin," I say, amused.

He dips his head, an answering smile upon his lips.

I continue on, managing to leave the palace without meeting anyone else I know. I slip out the side exit of the palace walls, nodding to the guards there, and make my way around to West Road. My turned foot aches a little, but it's well cushioned and should weather a little walking just fine. The streets are quieter now, though there are still women walking about, mostly in pairs and trios, but their presence is reassuring. Just as I am trying to decide how to hire a guide to get me to the inn, Artemian steps out of the shadow of a nearby building.

"Hallo, Rae," he says cheerfully.

"Oh, *good*," I say with desperate relief. "At least you'll know where we're going."

He laughs. "That I do."

"Which is not the Tattered Crow," I hazard.

"Not at all," he agrees. "This way."

We follow West Road another block before crossing over it to dive into the streets and alleys beyond.

As I accompany Artemian down a side street so old none of the pavers lie flat, I ask, "So what does it mean, precisely, to be the friend of a friend?"

Artemian glances at me, his mouth curved in a disbelieving smile pulled tight at one corner by his scar. "Tell me you've at least *heard* of Red Hawk."

"And the Black Scholar and Bardok Three-Fingers, yes."

"A friend of a friend means one of Red Hawk's men. Or women."

"He has women?" I'm not sure I like the sound of that.

"Certainly, but he treats them as he does his men. We're all thieves, Rae. Nothing more, and nothing less."

There is more to anyone than what they do to earn a living, but I don't argue it with Artemian—that isn't his point.

We turn down a street that looks vaguely familiar. "Are we— is this the way to the brickmaker's place?"

"It is. We'd have preferred to keep to the west side, but it seemed best, in this case, to stay as close to where we started as we could," he says, his voice all business now. "It's getting cool. Perhaps we should put up our hoods?"

He tugs up his own cloak hood, and I do the same. We're entering the Black Scholar's territory again, and I don't at all want to meet with a second thieving ring tonight.

We continue on a ways, turning a few more corners into unfamiliar streets. As we pass a pair of men chatting to one side, they nod to Artemian, then return to their conversation, but their eyes continuously scan the street. Lookouts.

"Why is it best for you to stay in someone else's territory?" I ask, unable to tamp down my unease.

He shrugs one shoulder. "Because if you must trespass, it's best to stay hidden and only move when you're sure no one is looking. In here."

Artemian knocks a quick pattern on a door, and a moment later it swings open to admit us. I stop on the threshold. There, gathered together in a knot to one side, are the brickmaker's boys. Every single one of them, from the frightened seven-year-old to the boy with the infected cut on his hand, now black around the edges. Seated cross-legged beside them is an old woman, her hair braided back and three items set beside her: a bucket of water, a silver cup, and a white opal. She wears the sky-blue robes of a Speaker, the hem frayed.

On the other side of them sits Bren, his head bent as he speaks quietly with the boys.

"Ready, then?" the Speaker asks, looking from Bren to Artemian and me.

Bren gestures toward me, eyes on the Speaker. "If you would allow the kelari a few minutes to chat with the boys?"

"Of course, though I do not like to wait. Until they are blessed, their safety is not assured."

I stare at Bren. "You—?"

He meets my gaze, and while his expression remains steady, his eyes glow with amusement. I no doubt look like a country idiot, staring at him in shock.

"We've spoken with the boys already, but I thought you might want to ask for yourself how each of them ended up here."

He returns his attention to the eldest boy, just beside him. "The kelari is trying to stop the snatchers. She's working for the royal family. Whatever you tell her, she'll use to help other children."

The boy and the others around him look up at me, and then away. They are waiting, and I realize in this moment that they do not yet believe they are free. They are still in someone else's power, still held captive, and they will not truly believe they have escaped until they have returned to their families—if their families can be found. And even then, they will take some part of their prison with them, a trauma they may struggle against the rest of their lives.

I kneel beside Bren. One by one, they admit their stories. One boy joined a pair of travelers who promised to help him find work in the city and then sold him to a middleman whom the brickmaker bought him from. But every one of the remaining five were snatched from the villages where they lived, hidden in false-bottom wagons and then moved to riverboats. All five lived north of the city, and were brought down the river to Tarinon.

Riverboats and false-bottom wagons. No people yet, no names, but a mode of transport is something.

"We should proceed," the Speaker says, one hand gripping the cup. She's filled it, droplets of water shining on its side.

Bren nods, glancing back at me. "Rae?"

"Yes, go ahead," I say.

I've never watched the Blessing to cleanse a child of the Darkness. It's curiously simple. The Speaker presses the opal to the youngest boy's forehead, murmuring a prayer, speaks another prayer over the cup, and passes it to him to drink from. What's far more disturbing is the shudder that runs through him around his third or fourth sip, the way his hand sags and the Speaker rescues the cup from his uncertain grip without letting a drop spill.

He looks around, his eyes huge and wary. "What's happening?" he asks in a high, wavering voice. "Where is my mama?"

"We'll send you home to her," Bren says, one hand reaching to rest on the boy's arm. "You'll be all right now."

I cannot quite place his tone, the timbre of his voice. There is an ache there that makes my own heart clench.

The Speaker moves on to the next boy, quickly dipping the cup into the bucket and beginning over again. He reacts with similar confusion, though he narrows his eyes as he looks at the other boys around him. Perhaps he has been with the brickmaker long enough that the Blessing does not reach as far back as the days when he was free.

On the third boy, something goes wrong. He grunts as he holds the cup to his lips, his whole body jerking. The Speaker leans forward, grabbing the cup and shoving it between his lips as his eyes roll back. And the other three unblessed boys are seizing up as well. I freeze as the men surge forward, each reaching for a different boy.

The Darkness. It's rising up in them, and the boys cannot drink now, cannot control their bodies at all.

Bren grabs the third, half-blessed boy, holding his head straight as the Speaker pours a sip of water in his mouth, one hand locking the boy's mouth shut so that, a moment later, he swallows. "Another," Bren says roughly, opening the boy's mouth. He's shuddering but not seizing up anymore, and he's able to take the next sip with only a little help.

But the other three boys are wheezing and crying out, their bodies jerking, their eyes rolling back. Artemian holds the eldest gently, allowing the boy's body to twist.

The Speaker starts on the fourth boy, her hand shaking as she pushes the opal against his forehead, her words tripping over themselves as she rattles out one Blessing and then the next, the cup in her hand, pouring water without concern now, because if he inhales the water that is less danger than if he does not drink at all. Finally, horribly, the boy's body relaxes and he coughs and coughs and *coughs*, but his eyes are his, and the Speaker turns to the fifth boy, Bren moving with her.

I glance between him and the eldest, the sixth. There is saliva dribbling from his mouth now, his eyes disappeared beneath slits. *Please, no.* Artemian huddles over him, and the boy's body seizes up again.

I grip my skirts, wishing there was something, *anything*, I could do. The tips of Niya's story sash brush my fingers. I look down. Her sash, with magical wards that she created, new and unusual and unknown. Enough so that Stonemane noted them. Maybe they can't do anything, but maybe they can. I look up to the boy, jerking on the floor, and past him to Bren, holding the fifth, his lips white and his eyes dark. They are thieves, their whole lives dependent on secrecy. And lies. They will never reveal the secret of my sash.

I tug it open as I scramble forward, using one hand to slide it under the boy's neck as he jerks, and twist the ends together around him.

Artemian looks up in surprise. "What are you—"

The boy takes a gasping breath, and then relaxes. Together we stare down at him. He gives a little shudder, but it isn't a seizure. His eyes look back up at us, afraid and very much still him, still knowing and focused and *there*. I let out my breath with a half laugh, tinged with hysteria, and tamp it down at once. "You're going to be all right," I say as the Speaker turns to us, her eyes wide.

I had forgotten to consider her.

No matter. I'll take Niya's sash and walk away from here, and she'll never see me again.

But she heard Bren, knows I'm connected to the princess. She'll figure it out—

"Give the Blessing," Artemian says sharply. The boy sits up, Artemian's arm around him, his other hand sliding over mine to hold the sash together. I release it and move back. Bren watches me from the other side of Artemian, his gaze sharp and thoughtful.

The Speaker goes through the Blessing quickly, and when Artemian hesitantly unwraps the sash a few breaths later, the boy remains sitting, his memories gone but his mind still his. Bren reaches out and takes the sash from Artemian.

Oh no. He is *not* taking that from me. I cross my arms and meet his gaze.

He dips his head, but when he speaks, it is not to me at all. "We thank you for coming here," he says.

"What is that sash?" the Speaker asks. "I have never heard of anything that could stop the Darkness. There is only the Blessing."

"Fae magic," I blurt, because I need some explanation that protects Niya. At least there isn't a mage here to gainsay me. "I wasn't sure it would work, but their magic is different from ours. It must have reached into the boy in a way that our wards can't."

She nods at once. "Can other such sashes be gotten? They could save so many children."

They could. They could, except I don't believe my own lie. Niya said specifically that the protections she had sewn into the sash were against magical attacks. Which means that the

Darkness *isn't* something that blooms from within a child's blood. It's sent against them. The Darkness is an attack.

In a land where magic is so rigidly controlled, there is only one group that could cast such a spell so regularly as to make the Darkness a threat. The answer is terrifying.

"Kelari?"

I blink at the Speaker. Shake my head. "I—I don't know." I don't know *anything*.

Bren rises and steps between the Speaker and me. "If more sashes can be got, I'll make sure you are the first to learn of it. I thank you, truly, for coming."

The Speaker nods and packs up quickly, sparing me a single glance as she moves to the door. But then she looks at Bren and doesn't say a word. I was right, at least, that thieves and secrets go hand in hand.

CHAPTER
26

Outside, Bren offers me my sash without a word. For a half moment, I'm so startled by his actions, I can only stare. I thought for certain I would have to fight for it. His lips twitch, and I snatch it from his hand before he changes his mind.

"It's not Fae magic, is it?" he asks as I wrap the sash about my waist.

I look up, my hands tightening the knot. "What else would it be?"

He considers me silently. I meet his gaze, and the moment draws out a little too long.

"There was something that stopped you back there, when you were answering the Speaker," he says.

I glance either way down the street, but there's no one here but the lookouts at the corner, too far to hear. "That's because, Fae or not, it's only a ward," I say. "It shouldn't have worked, not against something in the boy's blood."

Bren's eyes narrow. "Then how did it stop the Darkness?"

"It's simple," I say. "The Darkness isn't what we thought. If my wards only work against magical attacks, then the Darkness was never within those boys. It was sent."

"*Sent*," Bren repeats, the word sharp and sibilant. There's an instinctual readiness about him, a looseness to his stance, that speaks to just how deadly he thinks my words are. "Do you know what you're saying?"

"That there's only one group who could coordinate a kingdom-wide magical attack upon our children? Yes. It doesn't seem possible that the Circle of Mages, tasked with protecting all of Menaiya, could be allied with slavers, and yet there is no other explanation."

Bren rubs a hand across his mouth, glances toward the end of the alley. "If the snatchers are aligned with the mages, then we have a whole different level of trouble on our hands."

"I know."

"Do you?" he asks. "No, I don't think you do. Do you know what men are capable of doing to hide their actions? To keep themselves in power?"

I have an idea. "They're already selling our children into slavery. I suspect they could easily turn on . . ." On the princess, as well as me. And on my family.

"Very easily. They will destroy anyone who even attempts to uncover their actions. Your royals aren't going to be able to take out the mages. They're much more likely to lose the throne in a political coup and have a puppet put on it in their place."

"The Circle is that powerful?" I ask, my voice dry.

Bren tilts his head. "They were pushing for a spare heir to be named when the prince went missing for a handful of days just a month ago. They got quite close to succeeding, if the rumors are to be believed."

"Then . . . what do we do?"

We look at each other a moment, and then Bren takes my hand and threads it through his arm, as if we were at court, or sweethearts, and starts forward. "Let's walk."

I take a quick half step to catch up with him, and he adjusts his pace with a slight jerk, as if he'd forgotten himself for a moment. I glance at him, but he's looking ahead. "First, you'll have to prove this theory of yours. You'll need to let someone inspect that *Fae magic* of yours, and correct me if I'm wrong, but you're not going to allow that, are you?"

I stiffen and then curse myself, because of course he can feel my reaction through my arm. I tug my hand free at once. I should never have let him touch me so casually anyhow, and of course he did it so he could read my reactions better.

He breathes a soft laugh. "It's nice to know even country girls have secrets. Did a lover give it to you?"

"Oh, shut up," I say, and my irritation makes the lies I need to protect Niya come more easily. "That's absurd. I bought it at Spring Fair a year ago. I was told it was Fae magic, though I didn't quite believe it then. What kind of Fae would enchant a story sash? So no, I don't know where it came from. But I do know that if the mages are involved, there's no way I want them to see the one ward that does work against their spells. It has to be built differently. Once they know how, they'll change what they're doing to get past this as well."

"True," Bren says. "So what will you do?"

I don't know.

"I don't recommend destroying our royal family. I'm not a great fan of the king or his son, but the princess will do the kingdom some good, and . . . neither anarchy nor a puppet king appeal."

"So what? We quiver in fear and do nothing?" I don't want to endanger the royal family, but I'm not giving up either.

Bren grins. "I can't really imagine you quivering, to tell the truth."

"Oh, hush! It's a real question. I have to keep trying. I've seen what it does to a family to lose a child like that. And those boys—there are more like them out there. And girls." The idea of girls like my sisters—of Bean—being stolen and sold into a brothel—of Seri—I *can't*.

I look up at Bren. "I'm not going to stop when there's still so much that needs to be done."

"No, you're not," he agrees, a quiet statement of fact.

"Are you?" I ask uncertainly.

"No. But I don't know how much I can actually help you beyond this."

"I can't share the sash," I admit. "Not yet. But if what I think is true, then the Blessing doesn't do what it claims either."

"You think the Speakers are involved?" Bren asks dubiously.

"I don't know. But the cups they use are enchanted as well, aren't they? Not just blessed?"

He nods slowly. "They are. I always thought it was convenient how a child couldn't keep their memory of being snatched, no matter what."

A shiver runs through me.

Bren smiles tiredly. "I grew up knowing what was necessary for a thief to survive. It doesn't take very much: you must never be caught, and never leave behind either clues or a witness. The slavers have it down to an art." He raises a hand toward me, lets it fall. "If you wish, I should be able to get you the items from the Blessing. Do you have someone you trust who can look at them?"

I'd send them to Niya, but there's no way to discuss this with her without fear of being found out. Which leaves . . . Stonemane. I'd rather not owe him a favor—there are stories warning against owing the Fae anything at all—but I can't see a way around that.

"Yes," I say. "But don't steal them. If the Speaker you take them from doesn't know they're missing until they're needed . . ."

"I'll buy them off a Speaker for more than it will take them to get a new set," Bren says. "Probably the same Speaker you saw today. She's quiet, and trustworthy, and needs the money for her elderly father."

I nod, and glance about the streets. They're starting to look familiar again—there is the road we took to the brickmaker's yard. Which brings me back to the first thought that struck me when Artemian and I arrived tonight. "I thought you said you weren't going to help the boys."

Bren shrugs. "Turns out Kel Téran likes his drink. It was easy enough to have a man join him at the local tavern and hand him a bottle with a little something extra to make him sleep. He won't know what happened till sometime tomorrow, at which point the boys will be long gone."

"But you planned that, however easy you say it was. Why?"

Bren snorts. "You asked me to steal them, now you're asking why?"

"I didn't—"

"Didn't you?"

I wrap my arms across my chest. He's right, and I don't regret it one bit. "Maybe I did, but they were stolen from their families. And you said you wouldn't."

"Changed my mind," Bren says quietly.

Even though they were on the Scholar's territory. And I'm grateful for it. "Will you send them home?"

"Certainly. I think it a very good use of the money I lifted off of you when we first met."

"Are you—" I cut myself off as he outright laughs at me. I take another deep breath, not sure why I'm so infuriated, and say, "I would have given it freely had I known."

"Mmm. More's the pity, that."

"My ring you took—that was my grandmother's."

He raises his brows.

"I'll buy it back from you."

"Oh, Rae, no!" he cries with exaggerated horror. "That would be closer to blackmail, and I'm not such a criminal as all that. But I'll take good care of it, now I know how special it was to you."

Oh, the nerve of the man! "It wouldn't be a crime, you know, if you *didn't* steal once in a while."

"I don't know about that," he says, his voice light and cutting as a blade. "I'd say it was a crime for the brickmaker to buy each and every one of those boys, to keep them captive and engage his neighbors so that they wouldn't have even a hope of escape. What's more wrong, Rae? That he would do that, or that I stole those boys out from under his nose and left him to deal with the consequences?"

I shake my head. "I won't argue about the brickmaker, but—"

"Then you have no argument. What's the law but one man's decision of right versus wrong? I make my decisions how I see fit."

"Bren," I say, fighting frustration. Hurrying through darkened streets doesn't seem like the right time to discuss the value of rule of law, but I ought to give it a little effort at least. "If everyone makes their own decisions on that, we'll descend into anarchy. And then what we're trying to fight right now? The 'right' of men to steal others and sell them into slavery? That's what will gain power. Oppression gains power. Just because we disagree with the law doesn't mean we destroy it. You yourself told me that you don't want anarchy. That Alyrra should change the laws."

"That's because she is who she is. I, on the other hand, don't have that kind of power. So I'll make my own law around the edges of this one. And some of the wrongs will be righted."

"Because all you do is look out for the poor and oppressed? You, and Artemian, and Red Hawk?"

He laughs. "Not likely. Does the king not reward himself and his closest allies for their work ruling his realm? So, we all share in the bounty of Red Hawk's rule."

"You're not going to convince me," I say. "Because as much as you enjoy touting Red Hawk like he's some minor king, it's the most vulnerable of society who need protecting, and rule of law is what will help them. Not five different laws, not a thief on a throne, and not—"

"Not a king who doesn't care?"

Darkness take it! "You have no certainty he doesn't care."

"If he did, then you, country girl, would not be roaming the streets after dark in company with a thief, trying to uncover who is systematically conspiring to sell the common folk into slavery."

"The law can change," I cry, almost desperately. "That is what I'm trying to do."

Bren glances at me. "And, oddly enough, I'm helping you."

I let out my breath in a sigh, and find I have no arguments left. We're not going to see eye to eye. I don't want Bren to steal, not to help me, not to help himself. And certainly not to taunt me. "I'm grateful for what you've done tonight," I admit.

A beat, and then he says, "Didn't do it for your thanks." His voice is light enough to make it sound like a casual remark for all that it isn't. No, he didn't steal their freedom for me, or Alyrra; he did it for himself, for the boy he used to be.

"I know," I say.

We walk in silence for a few paces and then, as we turn a corner, he says tightly, "Rae."

"Yes?" I glance at him, surprised at his change in tone.

He's looking up the road toward a group of men gathered on the opposite side of the street, just outside an inn, the front of it lit by a great red lantern. "Keep your head down, would you? And if I tell you to run, you do it. No questions."

"Run?" I echo. I doubt I could outrun any of the men here.

"You know how to get back to West Road from here?"

I've been watching the streets, and at this point I recognize where we are. Only a block or two farther to the west side, and Red Hawk's domain. "I think so."

"Good."

"Shouldn't we maybe just turn around?"

"Too late," he murmurs. "That will just invite the chase."

As we draw even with the group, one of them steps forward,

his head tilted to see Bren's features past the shadow of his hood, the red lantern providing far too much light. "I've seen you before."

"Evening," Bren replies, his voice easy and carrying. If I hadn't just heard him cautioning me to run, I would never have believed him worried in the slightest.

The man shifts, and I catch the gleam of lamplight on metal. It's a knife of some sort. A long one. "You're in the wrong neighborhood," he says.

"Just passing through," Bren says. "I want no trouble."

He puts his hand at the small of my back, pushing gently, and I realize I've slowed. But Bren doesn't want us to stop for this conversation, and neither do I. This isn't the time for court manners.

The man starts after us. He is tall and wiry with a sparse goatee. "I'm talking to you. You unarmed?"

Bren half turns as he keeps walking. "Not particularly, but I've no interest in drawing blood."

The rest of the group is now focused on us. There are three of them, and they are all walking after us. "Who is he?" one of them asks the first.

"Seen him doing Red Hawk's work, I think." He raises his voice. "Am I right?"

Bren glances back at them, spreads his hands, palms up. "I'm just walking a friend home."

"You come here, walking through our territory like you own it, and we'll give you trouble," the man snarls. "I think he needs a lesson, boys."

He starts forward at a jog, his knife gleaming wickedly in the moonlight.

"Rae," Bren says, his voice no more than a puff of breath. "Run."

He aligns himself toward the man, a pair of daggers in his hands now, materializing as if from thin air.

"Bren," I say, suddenly terrified. There are *four* of them. How can he possibly get away safely?

"Run."

I turn tail and flee down the nearest alley, my uneven gait loud in my ears. I hear a shout behind me. Bren snarls in response, and then I can hear nothing but the uneven thud of my own feet on the packed earth. I reach the corner, my breath coming short and hard.

A hand closes on my tunic, yanking me back. I stumble as the man behind me wrenches me against him. He is tall and barrel-chested and stinks of sweat. I try to twist away, Matsin's lesson from this morning flashing through my mind, and then the man's other hand comes up to press a knife cold and sharp against my throat.

And then there's no running at all.

CHAPTER

27

Barrelchest marches me back down the alley, one arm twisted behind me and the dagger sharp and unforgiving at my neck.

"Got her," he announces as we near the fight.

Until that moment, Bren was doing well. Even against three men. One of them crouches on the ground to the side, his hand wrapped tight around his arm, dark liquid dribbling down to the cobblestones. The other two have Bren retreating toward us, blades flashing as they attempt to storm him, and yet he continually maneuvers one behind the other so that they cannot reach him together. He moves like a dancer—until he sees me in Barrelchest's grip.

Swearing a black streak, he steps back, raising his blades in a move that has the other two men stepping back as well. "What do you want with her?"

"Her?" the leader asks. "Nothing at all. Unless she's something to you. You're the one requiring a lesson."

Barrelchest shifts his hold on his knife, the point cutting into the tender skin below my jaw. I inhale sharply, pressing back against his bulk because there's nowhere else to go.

Bren eyes the men speculatively. "I think," he says slowly, as if pondering his words, "you had better take us to visit your master."

The man with the goatee laughs. "The Scholar doesn't take to trespassers. He'll be less kind than we will."

"Oh, I don't know about that," Bren says. "How exactly do you plan to teach your lesson?"

The leader shrugs. "I think we beat you till you can't stand, and then we take that girl of yours and escort *her*—"

"I think not," Bren says, his voice cutting through the man's. I swallow hard, wishing I could pull away from Barrelchest. I don't want to know how that sentence would have ended. "You had better take us in now."

The leader hesitates, staring. This isn't what he expected. "You go in to meet the Scholar, you're dead."

Bren shrugs, palming his daggers. They vanish without a trace. "That's up to the Scholar. Lead the way."

"I'll take those," the leader says, gesturing as if to point to the disappeared daggers.

"Off my dead body," Bren agrees. "Should you be so lucky. Lead the way."

"Not with your blades at my back."

"Oh no? And what of your blades?" Bren grins, to all

appearances perversely enjoying the situation. Eventually, one of the men goes ahead, followed by Bren and the leader side by side, and Barrelchest and I bring up the rear. He allows me to walk beside him, but he keeps his hand at my back, the dagger's point pressing into the fabric of my tunic. The wounded man, his arm temporarily bound, slips away, no doubt to seek out a healer.

Barrelchest doesn't have patience for my limp, shoving me along in front of him whenever he grows aggravated with my slowness. Bren keeps up a muted conversation with his companion, as if they were the best of enemies, and if it weren't for the one glance he darts my way as they turn a corner, his face going eerily hard and ungiving as his gaze skims Barrelchest, I'd think he didn't much care how I came along. No one we pass dares a glance at me—or Bren.

Surely this isn't how people disappear? Being walked down the street with a threat at their backs, and no one looking twice or speaking up? And yet there is no arguing with the fact that we walk unimpeded right to the Black Scholar's lair.

I don't know where I thought the Black Scholar would make his headquarters: a tumbledown old building, or perhaps private rooms in an inn. I am completely and utterly wrong. The Black Scholar's place of work is a library with soaring ceilings and wide windows. This late at night, heavy velvet curtains have been drawn across the windows. They reflect a red so deep it is nearly black. Shelves line the walls, or stand back to back, marching into the rear of the room, and, if they are not full, they are certainly well-populated with books. Here at the front, a large table sits surrounded by chairs. And by the window stands a single armchair accompanied by an ornate circular side table, two books at rest on its surface.

A slim hand reaches out and places a third book on the table. I start, not having seen the man sitting in the armchair. Given that he's dressed in a long black robe, I suppose it's no surprise I didn't notice him at first, even with the lamplight to brighten the room. He rises, his eyes barely registering me. They are focused, instead, on Bren.

"What have we here?"

"One of Red Hawk's men, sir. Found him trespassing—"

"Is that so?" The Black Scholar frowns, crossing the distance between us with the faint swish of fabric. Like his hands, he is long and slender, the robes draping elegantly over his figure. His eyebrows are dark, accenting well-shaped eyes. His carefully trimmed mustache and beard set him apart from the rougher looks of our captors. His manner is cultured, urbane.

The leader of our little escort hesitates and keeps quiet, aware that there is more going on here than he knows. Though what that is, I couldn't say either.

"Evening," Bren says, clearly amused.

The Black Scholar raises a hand to adjust his robes, sliding his fingers over the trim at the front. His clothes beneath the robes are black as well. I stifle a shudder—scholars may certainly wear clothes and robes like his, but their tunics and pants are typically light, and their robes range from the soft blue of winter sky to the earthen brown of rich farmland; I can think of only one time I ever saw a scholar wear anything close to this: an elderly man who elected to wear a muted gray. Black looks terribly harsh in contrast, as if there were no space for uncertainty here, no place for thoughtful debate. There is only the black of his robe, absolute.

"Indeed it is," he says, as if Bren had made a comment on the time of day. He gestures toward the men who brought us in. "You may go."

"But, kel . . ."

"I said, you may go," the Scholar snaps. Barrelchest releases his hold on me, retreating to the door.

"Kel," the leader tries again. "The man is armed."

"Of course he is. Even if you managed to take his daggers, I doubt you could have completely disarmed him. Not without killing him."

Bren offers the Scholar a slight bow. What, was that a compliment to him? I try to catch his eye, but he acts as if I'm not even there.

The Scholar's men make no further argument, though they glance at each other surreptitiously as they leave.

"Hold," the Scholar barks just as the leader reaches the door.

"Kel?"

"Double the guards at the doors and below the windows."

"Yes, kel."

Bren tuts softly as the door closes. "What of the roof?"

"It's sealed off," the Scholar says. "Though you may certainly attempt it."

I swallow hard. This is sounding much worse than it did a moment ago. Bren chuckles, waving away this offer as if it were a tray of sweets he has no interest in trying.

"And who, may I inquire, is this delightful young lady?" the Scholar asks, turning to me. I feel my stomach drop to my knees.

"I—um . . ." I glance toward Bren.

"Her name's Silaria, but she goes by Ria."

The Scholar holds up one long-fingered hand to silence Bren, watching me with eyes as hard as gemstones. "And what were you doing in this part of town, dear Ria, in such auspicious company as our friend's here, in the dark of the night?"

"I—I was trying to find someone," I stutter, trying not to think of how very many armed men the Black Scholar must have, considering the orders he just gave. I gesture toward Bren, wary of sharing the name he gave me. "He offered to help me."

"Did he?" the Scholar murmurs, his face inscrutable. "I see. And did you end up finding your someone?"

I risk another glance at Bren, but his expression offers me nothing. "Yes," I say, my hands wrapped into fists around my skirts.

"Do tell."

I take a slow breath. Bren is one of Red Hawk's men, and he's already told me how dangerous it is for him to be trespassing on the Scholar's territory. I know how to lie—I've always lied as necessary to protect Niya—and I'll do the same for Bren now. I make myself meet the Scholar's gaze and say steadily, "I live in the country, kel, but I've been visiting family in the city the last week or two. For the royal wedding. Just after I arrived, a good friend wrote, saying her cousin was snatched here. I started looking for the child's mother to offer my support. I was asking everyone I could, and someone introduced us"—I nod at Bren—"and he helped me find her. The mother, I mean."

It's not as gathered as I would have liked, but I haven't spent a lifetime thinking up these lies. All I can do is hope I don't trip myself up.

"All in the last week?" he asks mildly.

I nod, looking him in the eye as if I had nothing to hide.

"News certainly travels fast to and from the country."

"The royal couriers," Bren says easily, which is just as well, as my tongue is stuck to the roof of my mouth. "Ria's town is on one of their busier routes."

"Of course. And you"—he inclines his head toward Bren—"were only being helpful."

Bren grins. "You know me well enough to know I only get involved in things I have an interest in." The way he says *interest* sounds more like a stake in a profitable venture than a question of personal curiosity. And how would the Scholar know him that well?

The Scholar returns Bren's smile, his features suddenly wolfish as he bares his teeth. "Would this interest have anything to do with entering my neighborhoods?"

Bren spreads his hands. "I would not need such a paltry excuse as this to come here, if I wished—and if I meant to cause trouble, I would have brought a few friends along."

Which he did, but apparently, they are still safely hidden.

"Something else, then."

"It would seem so."

Bren and the Scholar face each other, their expressions slightly bemused, and for the space of a few breaths, no one says anything, as if a silent discussion were taking place between them. I eye Bren narrowly, wondering what I am missing.

Then the Scholar smiles, a cold twist of his lips. "Well, my boy, I don't much like finding you trespassing on my neighborhoods. I will have three things from you by sunrise tomorrow: what *Red Hawk's* interest is in this young lady's story; his word that his men will keep to his streets in future." The Scholar pauses, tilting his head to assess me. "And one hundred gold coins."

I gape at him. A hundred gold coins? That's a prince's ransom! Perhaps if we pooled all my jewelry with Melly's, and Filadon dipped into his own purse—but how would Bren even know to go to them? He'll go to the princess, or at least send a page to her. The thought brings intense relief. Alyrra will help.

"That may be more than his interest," Bren says softly, and brings all my newfound hopes crashing down. "At least be reasonable."

"I am," the Scholar replies, clasping his hands in a strange parody of an earnest student. "I have taken this whole situation very seriously. I suggest you find out your answer. You have, as I said, until sunrise. If that isn't reasonable, I don't know what is."

Bren nods and moves to the door, offering me a single apologetic glance. A feeling like lead in my veins fills me, deadening my nerves and slowing my thoughts. He is leaving. Without me. And he won't come back. Not after that look. I take one step to follow him, and find my wrist in the cool, long-fingered grasp of the Scholar. "Now, my dear, we must wait till morning."

"But—"

"Ah-ah," he tuts as if I were a naughty child. "You are my guest tonight."

"My family will worry, and . . ." I cut myself off only just in time. It would be strategically suicidal, at this point, to mention the princess.

"I'm sure your friend can get them a message," the Scholar says, sounding bored. His grasp tightens a little, exerting the slightest of pressure, but his point is clear enough. He has no intention of letting me go.

I turn to Bren, who is now carefully avoiding my glance as he opens the door. "You *will* send them a message?" I beg. If he will only get in touch with Alyrra, she'll pay the ransom. If nothing else, she'll know I will find a way to repay her, even if I must spend the rest of my life doing it. Only it's too late for a page to be allowed to disturb her, and she doesn't usually rise until well past sunrise. . . .

"I'll let them know," Bren says, nodding at the guards, who look in at us with interest.

"Conduct him out," the Scholar says, indicating Bren. "And one of you please tell Irayna to ready the guest room."

I stand stock-still, every sense screaming at me to follow Bren, to grab him and shake him and demand he take me with him. But I can't move. Even without the manacle of the Scholar's cool fingers wrapped about my wrist, my feet are rooted to the ground, as if I no longer had legs at all but stood upon a single immovable trunk. Bren has left me as surety against the Scholar's demands. Surety against one hundred gold pieces, with no way to pay them. He won't come back.

The Scholar releases me, returning to his armchair, where he settles himself comfortably, his robes smoothed out upon his lap, the book once more in his hands. I watch him, head turned.

"I don't suppose you country girls are taught to appreciate the finer arts," the Scholar says with biting contempt, "but you are welcome to browse my library while your room is being readied."

I stare at him.

He directs me toward the stacks with his eyes, then returns his attention to his book. There is no sound from outside, no boots passing along the hall, no voices drifting down stairways to us. Nothing. I wait, listening, as if by mere force of will I could make Bren come back and take me with him.

The Scholar turns a page, glancing my way as if amused. I close my eyes, gather my courage, and find myself thinking of Bean, who never sits still and never stops trying. She would have hollered at Bren, stamped her foot, and, if still finding herself captive, stomped over to the stacks to complain in a loud and carrying voice about the pathetic selection before her, regardless of its actual value.

My breath comes a little easier with that imagining. My feet drag themselves free, and while I don't stomp over to the stacks, neither do I stumble. I trace the spines of the books before me, pull one out. Poetry.

He smote the dragon high
Twixt the ear and the eye
The Sword returned to bite his neck
And so fell foolish Recknameck

I stifle a groan. Bean would have burst out laughing at this rubbish. I slide the book back and make my way down the shelf, hoping only to pass time, distract myself from what might happen tomorrow morning if Bren doesn't deliver up a hundred gold coins. But very soon I'm engrossed in what I find.

Recknameck is the worst of the books available, for the shelf holds also some of the great poets of old, ancient ballads, and—as I pass to the next shelf—histories, logbooks, and political treatises. I browse through the books, pulling out this red leather tome with gold leafing, then looking through that aged brown volume so worn the title stamped on the cover is nothing more than a series of ridges. As I pull out another history, a small book no larger than my own hand falls from the shelf. I stoop to retrieve it.

The cover is weather-stained, the pages so thin they crackle as I turn them. Intrigued, I sink down where I stand, sitting cross-legged with my skirts in a rumple around me, and begin to read.

It is an account of the so-called Fae Attack roughly one hundred years ago. Not to misrepresent—they attacked because our own fool of a king attacked their land some twenty years before that, looting and pillaging before returning home. As long-lived as Faeries seem to be, their memories are equally enduring. They repaid his visit in kind, and it was during those bloody years that much of our royal family was slaughtered. And, as some claim, a curse was laid upon the Family, so that their numbers have continued to dwindle, leaving us now with only the king, his son, and Verin Garrin.

Zaria's words about the real reason for the Fae delegation's presence come back to me—a curse, she had said. Perhaps I should not have dismissed her words out of hand. Filadon hinted that Kestrin had not been able to look at issues such as the slavers because of what he termed "more pressing concerns"—and that Alyrra had helped him when he most needed it. Somehow.

It seems an unlikely possibility that there might be dark magic at work here. . . . Yet, for the royal family to welcome a powerful Fae mage, unsworn to Menaiya? There must be some hidden trouble, with a very real possibility that the Fae are at the heart of it. Still, it seems unlikely at best that the journal in my hands might shed some light on just what has haunted our royal family. Yet I can't help being drawn into the account before me.

The journal is written in a light, elegant hand, the script flowing and perfectly formed. It takes me a few pages to discover the author's identity: a woman archer among the king's elite guard, part of a quad of archers who served in his bodyguard— unusual but not unheard of. What's curious are the doubts she holds concerning her king.

We march for Lirelei today, she writes. *The king remains adamant that a small show of force will drive back the marauders—that they are nothing more than pretty-faced pirates. I fear he underestimates them. Dare I suggest otherwise? Or will he think I criticize him? Fastu spoke out, albeit foolishly, and look where he ended: his bow broken along with his fingers and arms, left for a beggar in the street. Better not to speak. I will string my bow, and protect my people, and keep my tongue still.*

Behind me, I hear a knock on the door. At the Scholar's word, a maid steps in. I twist to peer at her from between the shelves; she is tall and gangly with a sharp chin and a crooked smile. "Room's ready, kel."

"Ria," the Scholar says, the name a command.

I scramble to my feet, slipping the journal into my pocket as

I turn to reshelve the history book I had taken down. If I'm to be imprisoned in my room, at least I can take some good reading with me.

The Scholar reaches the shelves just as I slide the book in beside its brothers. He looks pleasantly surprised. "Histories?"

"You have an unusual collection," I say, dropping my hand. The little journal feels like it's burning a hole through my skirts.

"And you have unusual taste for a peasant."

"I'm not a peasant," I say coldly. "My father owns a horse farm." And even if I were a peasant, why shouldn't I be interested in histories?

"Does he indeed?" The Scholar offers me a predatory smile, and I have the uncomfortable feeling that I may have just raised the ransom the Scholar wants of Red Hawk. I bite my tongue, calling myself five kinds of fool, but he only gestures toward the door and the waiting maid. I pass him, keeping my eyes on the maid. She inspects me, her hands on her hips, that crooked grin growing more impudent by the moment.

"Your father raise lame horses too?" she asks.

My head jerks back. I glare at her, trying to ignore the hurt of her words. I *know* this is how people see me, so why does it keep hurting? Her grin grows wide enough to bare her gums, and I finally find words to cut her with in return. "He *breeds* horses. Children are raised, though clearly your parents didn't bother with you."

"What! You—"

"That will be enough, Irayna. Show our guest to her room

and refrain from further insults, if you can. Maybe just try keeping your mouth shut."

"Yes, kel," she says, her face a mottled red beneath the brown. "Forgive me, kel."

"Kelari Ria?" the Scholar continues, a speculative glint in his eye.

"Yes?" I ask warily.

"I take a light refreshment before I retire for the evening. You will join me for it, in a half hour or so?"

It's not a request, not really. "As it pleases you."

"I look forward to it," he says, waving me on.

I can't say I feel the same.

CHAPTER

28

T he Scholar takes his evening refreshment in the library: a tray with tea, a plate of biscuits, and that is all. At his gesture, I sit down in an armchair newly placed opposite him, my hands tightly folded in my lap.

I have spent the last half hour alternately reading the journal and staring off into space as I try to imagine either an impossible escape attempt or what I might do when Red Hawk's response comes in the morning. At least Bren should eventually be able to get word to Alyrra regarding what we learned from the boys and the Blessing, even if . . . No, I will get away from here somehow. The other possibility is far too terrifying to consider.

A cursory inspection of my room revealed no easy opportunities to escape. It is on the third floor of a smooth-faced building, so I can hardly jump to the ground nor climb safely to the roof. Irayna locked my door from the outside, part and parcel, I suppose, of being placed in this particular "guest" room. While

I would like to think I'm capable of picking a lock, the reality is I have no idea how to proceed other than to stick things into the keyhole and jiggle them about. Which I will attempt, but not till later tonight, once everyone is asleep.

"I hope you have been made comfortable," the Scholar says now, reaching to pour the tea.

"Quite, thank you."

The Scholar smiles amiably and offers me a slender cup of tea, the scent of mint rising with the steam. To my surprise, he asks nothing further about my family, or Bren, or what we were doing in his territory. Instead, he asks me about books.

I blink back my astonishment, take a comforting sip of tea, and open myself up to the conversation. We debate the points made by Edhanburrah in his contentious *The Descent of Anarchy*, and I find myself enjoying the freedom with which I can voice my opinions—though I am careful not to speak too specifically about our own king. Baba and I brought a copy of the book back with us from the last Spring Fair, got from a local print shop there; my sisters and I read it together and debated its claims through half this past winter. Now the Scholar impresses me with his thoughtfulness, the way he pauses over his tea, considering his words, one hand caressing the cup. Watching him, I can almost forget the way that same hand held my wrist, offering the faintest of threats in the firmness of its grasp.

I rise to take my leave at the end of our conversation, the Scholar accompanying me to the door. "A delightful evening, Kelari Ria," he says with a warm smile, surprising me yet again.

"You are an exceptional host," I say, meaning it for the most part. If one overlooks his being my captor. "But, kel, may I ask one question?"

"You may ask," he replies, his expression reserved once more.

"In the morning, if Red Hawk does not meet your demands . . ." I trail off.

"Let us hope he does."

"But if he does not?"

His lips thin, his gaze dark, unbending. "I am afraid I shall have to kill you."

His words are a shock of cold water, washing away the pretenses of a shared conversation over a cup of tea, the false security I had been lulled into by thinking him an actual scholar, a man of education and manners. Which he is. But he is also a thief lord. And a killer.

With a gentle push, he propels me through the doorway. I turn back to him, strangely unsteady. I have grown up with the idea that one can reason with one's opponent, that manners and culture and civility lead to respect for each other's lives. But that is devastatingly wrong, and the man I have just spent an hour discussing politics and philosophy with will kill me as easily as he will let me go, and cares not what I think of either possibility.

"Good night, kelari," he says as a manservant steps forward to escort me away.

There is no word that will move him. I bow my head and retreat to my room.

I pace my room, considering my options. My mind jumps from the Scholar's demands to what the morning will bring, to the boys' stories, to the Darkness. And there is nothing I can do—no way to inform the princess, not about my own danger, not about what happened to the boys, or the clue we've uncovered.

My hands clench into fists, but even my anger is useless. I have never felt so helpless in my life. I raise my hands and press hard against my head, as if somehow I might order things, find a way forward when there is nowhere I can go and nothing I can do. Come sunrise, chances are I'll die. And leave all this behind, all the things I should have done, or could have helped fix.

I want my family desperately—I don't know what this will do to them, to Melly, and my parents, and my sisters—to Niya especially. It hits me like a wall of bricks. I stand stock-still, staring blindly across the room. Niya and I are a matched pair. We're supposed to be there for each other after Bean has married and our parents grow old and eventually pass on. If I die, Niya will spend those years alone. She can't even hope to stay with Bean's eventual family because the chances of someone else in her home discovering her secret is too high.

That's the one thing I've always promised her: that I would be there for her. That we'd have each other. It is only one thing more that I cannot help, but together with everything I have learned tonight, all that might be won or lost, it is one thing too much. I am *not* letting the Black Scholar destroy all these futures, all these hopes, even if I have to throw myself from the window.

Which I might.

I go back to it, running my hand over the smooth plaster finish, then turn to the room. I *am* getting out of here. There is a large bed to one side, a small table and chair by the window, supplied with a lamp, and that is all. I stalk over to the bed, pull back the woven blanket to assess the sheets. They're a fine, soft linen, and of course far too short to reach the ground, even tied together. But I carry Niya with me, and the gifts she gave me. I can use the bone knife hidden in her stitches to nick the edges of each sheet and rip it into strips. Braid those together, and I'll have a rope that should hold my weight comfortably enough.

I return to the window. The street lies relatively quiet, though I can hear the faint echoes of laughter and carousing from somewhere not too distant. But here I see only a young man passing by. I lean out the window, searching the shadows. There, by the corner, I spot a dark form leaning against the building. He might be waiting for someone, or he might be one of the Scholar's guards. I doubt I could safely descend with a makeshift rope and run away before such a guard caught me.

I step back from the window, moving to sit in the lone chair. Perhaps if I wait long enough, he will move on to another post. Or doze off. All I can do is hope. And wait. No matter what I try tonight, I must wait until the house has fallen asleep, the streets quiet.

So I hunch beside the lamp and read the spidery writing of the long-dead archer, following the army's march to the sea, their ill-conceived attack on the Faerie marauders, and, ultimately, their massacre.

They are an army, greater in number and skill than ours, and backed by a sorceress of terrifying talent. We were as the empty husks of wheat before them, chaff in the wind. Half our nmbers fell to Fae swords while their own were still sheathed, their eyes blinded by a fell darkness. The carnage—I cannot write of it. Death everywhere. The cries of the wounded in our ears, or at least, those whom we could save and bring with us. A rout, a complete rout. But a score of us left, and the king. At least we managed to protect him. He has sent to Tarinon for his remaining troops, and for every lord to raise troops of their own. The Circle of Mages will send their most adept mages to oppose the sorceress. We meet at Ajroon to rally once more against the Fae. Let us hope they do not harry our footsteps now, or we shall die long before we may hope for reinforcements.

It seems strange to me that, facing my own imminent demise, I find myself so compelled by the archer's words, reading feverishly of the survivors' flight to Ajroon, the raising of a second army while half the coast was laid to ruin—merchant ships commandeered, trading towns surrounded and their inhabitants marched out to the fields while their houses burned, leaving them with only the meager belongings they managed to gather in sheets and satchels before they were forced out.

Peculiar, is it not? wrote the archer. *They let those who do not fight live, and do not take what they carry from them. So we have half a country of refugees streaming in from the coasts seeking food and shelter, carrying their best silver, their favorite books, their jewelry. That is kindness itself compared to what Mendar says was the king's practice in the Fae lands. And while our people might curse the faeries, they curse our king equally. Few of these men and women join our forces to expel the Fae. Yet, if they do not, we shall fall soon enough. What sort of rulers would the Fae make over us? Is it treason to wonder?*

Over the following weeks, the army suffered loss upon loss. The mages fell in battle as well as the soldiers. But worse, far worse, were the deaths of the princes and princesses, and the king's brothers. *They do not die in battle. None of them. They simply disappear, as if they had never been, or as if they had sunk into their bed-clothes, or stepped from the trail to be swallowed by the earth.*

The king is mad with rage. I would that he feared the Fae more, but each loss just drives him harder against them. He will no longer speak to us, holding council with only Mendar from among our numbers, him and the mages, and the quad of captains over what remains of our second army. I should have spoken before, when I knew his first plan was flawed. I should have counseled him when we met in Ajroon, that a new strategy would be needed against the Fae. I should have argued that the sorceress must be stopped at all costs, let the Fae army do what it wishes. She is their true strength. But I have held my silence too long, and now when I speak he brushes me away.

We will die soon. I think often of my sister. I know she will be safe, for the Fae kill no children. I hope that our parents are safe with her. I hope my family will not hate me for having failed them.

I look up finally, consider the deep darkness through the window. Then I slip the book back into my pocket, untie my sash, and use my teeth to snap the knot of red thread showing through the back of the sash. I tug the thread out, and on the other side a tiny red diamond comes undone, delivering up to me my bone knife. It appears as a sudden weight upon my lap, the onyx and mother-of-pearl handle gleaming in the lamplight.

The blade is too wide by a hair to slip into the keyhole, nor do I suspect it would do much good regardless. There will be guards and more locked doors to contend with if I attempt to flee down the hallways and out through the building itself. No, my only hope is the window.

The rope takes barely a half hour to make, used as I am to braiding. I tie knots at intervals, to give my hands and legs purchase. I push the bed next to the window to serve as my anchor, positioning it so that even if my weight lifts it from the ground, it will remain firmly on this side of the window.

Then I blow out the lamp and wait. Once my eyes have adjusted to the dark, I peek from the window, searching for guards. The shadows lie deep and still, and it is impossible to determine what is darkness and what might be a man standing watch. In the end, I can only hope that the man I saw has left.

I wrap my knife in a final strip of fabric, just long enough to cover it properly, and then I lay it flat against my stomach, rolling the top of my skirt over it. I tug my sash down over its slight bulk to keep it in place. It is not ideal, but if I am caught, I do not want to lose my knife as well.

I wait a quarter of an hour longer, counting out the minutes with prayers, and then I lower the rope out the window. Far away, I can hear a dog barking, but here all lies quiet.

Taking hold of the sill in one hand and my rope in the other, I swing my feet over the windowsill, and freeze. It is so very far down, the road made of stone cobbles. If I slip, if I lose my grip on the rope, I will die. As certainly as I will die come morning, if Red Hawk cannot ransom me. Perhaps I should wait. Perhaps Bren will come through for me, and I don't need to attempt something as foolhardy as this . . .

And perhaps this is the only chance I will get. I wind my legs around the rope and carefully lower myself off the sill, gripping the rope in sweat-damp hands. *Don't look down*, I tell myself. *One hand at a time. That's all.*

I can't use my feet very well, so I keep the rope wound between my legs and use each knot as a resting spot, if only for a single breath. My whole body is shaking with tension by the time

I pass the set of windows below my own. As I near the street, my arms shudder with effort.

I drop to the ground, stumbling slightly, and turn.

A man stands just behind me, smiling. I neither saw nor heard him approach, and now the shock of it freezes me in place.

"Took you long enough," he says, reaching for me.

I try to run. I manage no more than two limping strides before a hand closes around my arm, yanking me back. I open my mouth to scream, but there is already an arm across my throat, as strong and unforgiving as an iron bar.

I manage a strained, gasping breath and am jerked backward as the man begins to walk. I scrabble to keep up, my feet backpedaling as he drags me effortlessly across the cobbles and around the corner to the Scholar's front door.

This time, I doubt there will be any windows for me to climb out.

CHAPTER
29

The cell I am locked in is the sort of thing I only ever expected to meet in tales of pure criminals. Here is the horror of a cold stone room, bars forming a barely visible cage across one wall, the taint of captivity and despair in the air itself. There is no hint of light here.

I huddle in the farthest corner, waiting for my eyes to adjust to the darkness as the sentry departs in company with a second guard who allowed us entry and brought us here, lamp in hand. But the darkness doesn't ease now, the inky blackness complete. I wedge myself tighter into the corner, as if there were safety in the stone against my back, my legs folding up to press against my chest—and a strange pressure against my stomach.

My knife.

I unfold myself, press my hand against the comforting line of the cloth-wrapped blade. It's something. And now that I am sitting forward, I notice the faint weight in my pocket: the archer's journal. The sentry had not bothered to search me, no doubt assuming that I had been searched upon arrival. I wrap my hand around the little book, fiercely grateful he did not find it. Else the Black Scholar would certainly kill me, ransom or not. One doesn't steal things from a thief lord.

Not that I can do much about that now. I should have left it in my room, but I forgot, and now is not the time to consider confessing and begging forgiveness. I push myself to my feet, put one hand out against the stone, and follow it around to the bars, working mostly by feel to find the lock.

Carefully extracting my knife, I slide it through the keyhole and wiggle it. But no matter how long I work at it, pinching my fingers and jiggling the knife in every angle I can find, the door remains locked. If I get out of this alive, I'm asking Bren to teach me how to pick locks. Just so I know.

I return to my corner, carefully rewrapping the knife and hiding it once more. It's a strange blade. For all that I've handled it enough to have sliced my fingers open repeatedly tonight, it hasn't cut me once. I know from experimentation that it is more than sharp enough to cut through flesh—chicken and goat, which is not all that different from human. Fae magic, I suppose. Too bad that magic doesn't extend to unlocking doors.

I pull away a little from the cold stone walls and close my eyes. I can't sleep, not properly, but the hour is late and I don't know what tomorrow will bring. I try to clear my mind, let myself drowse, but I jerk upright periodically, fear snapping through me. Each time, there is no one here; if I am to die, it is not quite yet.

Finally, I register the snick of a lock. Irayna shoves the door open at the end of the hall. I jump to my feet, moving forward to squint at her in the sudden light from the doorway. She surveys me with raised eyebrows. She holds a breakfast tray, a faint whiff of steam rising from the bowl of spiced oatmeal.

"I'm impressed," she says, sliding the tray beneath the bottom bars of the door. They are just high enough to allow the bowl to pass underneath. "I didn't think you had an escape like that in you."

"He said he'd kill me," I observe. "Why wouldn't I try?"

She shrugs. "Just didn't think you had it in you. Better hurry'n eat that."

I take another step forward. "Is there any news? Has Red Hawk sent word?"

"No. Had a messenger in just before dawn, but he wasn't from Red Hawk," she says. "The Scholar likes you, though. Can't say why." She looks me over, eyeing my rumpled clothes, her gaze lingering on my turned foot in its custom boot. "Anyway, he likes you, so he'll do it quick. Else he'd make you scream."

"Oh."

"He has the musicians play," she says, clearly relishing the look on my face. "Says it helps him enjoy the moment. And he uses small knives. But with the ones he doesn't mind, it's just a quick slash."

I had thought him cultured. His mind educated, enlightened. Not only does he kill, but he does so with pleasure, painfully. How is it possible to be both a gentleman and a monster?

"What happened to your face, anyway?" Irayna asks when I don't respond. "Got yourself a nice old bruise there."

"Accident," I say, and look down, waiting until Irayna loses interest. There is no way I want the Scholar to connect my bruise to that of the princess's attendant. Once Irayna departs, I force myself to eat. The oatmeal is freshly made, spiced with cinnamon and sweetened with honey, and on any other day would have made a welcome meal. Today, I can barely make myself swallow each bite. But if I meet with another chance to escape, I'll need my strength to take full advantage of it.

I am nearly finished when a pair of armed men enter. I set down the bowl and rise to watch them. They unlock the door and step back. "Go on, and no tricks, girl. We're right behind you."

I nod and step out. They flank me, escorting me up and through the hallways to a well-sized foyer where the Scholar waits. He is dressed in the same manner as the day before, though his clothes are clearly fresh and well-pressed. He inspects me, one quick glancing review, before saying, "There has been a change. We are going visiting."

"Visiting?"

He gestures to the door. "If you attempt to escape again, my men have orders to kill you without hesitation. You understand?"

I nod and follow him out the door.

A carriage has pulled up for us, gray in the faint light of dawn. The Scholar and I climb in, while his men take up their stations on posts behind the wheels and up beside the driver.

The curtains are drawn across the windows, leaving us in a shadowy underworld. The Scholar in his black robes seems to fade into the darkness of the cushions opposite me. We lurch forward, rattling on over the cobbles.

"Will you tell me where we are going?" I ask, trying to make out his expression. He seems distracted, detached.

"To see what I can get in trade for you."

"What!"

"I have received a proposition," he says slowly, as if he is still considering it himself. "We are going to learn more of it."

My hands clutch each other so tightly my nails dig into my skin. "What of Red Hawk?"

"What of him?"

I shake my head, not understanding this turn of events. "You said—"

"If we have not heard back yet, I doubt we will. This proposition, on the other hand, has merit. If I act on it before sunrise, you may still keep your neck intact. Or at least"—he smiles, a gleam of white in the near-dark—"I will not be the one to cut it."

"I see," I say, though I'm not sure I do.

"My honor," he explains, his voice patient in the darkness. "The only way you live is if Red Hawk ransoms you, which apparently he will not, or this proposition goes through. If the proposition is not to my advantage"—he shrugs—"you die. But if it is, then I have every reason to consider it."

"And the proposition?" I manage, my throat hoarse.

"That remains to be seen."

We ride the rest of the way in silence. The carriage pulls up to an old building, the door before us made of solid oak, plain but strong. Two armed men answer, watching the Scholar and his men with grim faces. I glance either way up the cobbled street, but it lies empty of any who might help me, the few people present studiously ignoring us, and the Scholar's hand is firm on my elbow. Not that I would attempt to run, surrounded as I am.

The guards escort us through a dark entryway, down a narrow corridor, and from there into a great atrium, the high walls open to the brightening sky, exquisite mosaics adorning the space. Halfway up one wall an iron railing abuts a closed door—an upper-room access to the light of the atrium. As we enter, a man rises from where he sits at a small table and chair, a pot of tea before him. His voice and bearing are equally hearty.

"Well, old man! It's been some time, hasn't it? How are your books keeping you? Not starting to molder among them, are you?" He laughs at his own jest.

The Scholar regards him icily. "It seems you are the same as always, Bardok."

I start, my eyes finding out the man's hands. His right hand lacks the final digit. I stare, unable to believe this. Why would we come here? What could Bardok Three-Fingers possibly want with me? And how did he hear about me?

"Nah, nah," Bardok says, crossing to us. He is even bigger than I thought, a good head taller than the Scholar, and built like a bear. He wears light armor even here, in what must be his home. Or at least, a safe house in his own territory. "I've put on a bit more." He pats his belly, which looks more muscle than fat from what I can tell. "It's the women, you know. Or"—he snorts with laughter—"you don't."

The Scholar, done with such inanities, cuts to the chase. "Your message was intriguing, but I have only so much patience. This is the girl. What would you offer in return?"

"That's her, eh?" Bardok looks me over. "Not much to her."

I clamp my mouth shut, seething. What does he know?

"Now what does Red Hawk see in her?" he continues on, musing. "See that jaw? She's no bed warmer."

I make a strangled sound. The Scholar's hand tightens into

a vise on my arm just in time to keep me from snarling at the man. Which would be foolish. Suicidal, even. But oh, to wipe that smile from his mouth, even for a moment.

"I expect not," the Scholar says, sounding bored. "What you would want with her is more to the question."

"You put a price on her head, I hear," Bardok says with a grin. "A bit too high to get your ransom. Me, I'm not so hard to please. I want something of Red Hawk, and he'll give."

"Will he?"

Bardok winks at me. "She might be able to charm her way into a quick death with you, old friend, but I won't offer her death. Red Hawk may be stubborn, but he's got his honor too. And like I said, I won't be demanding coin." He rubs his hands together. "I'm looking forward to a good game."

The Scholar's hold eases somewhat on my arm. "And why should I give up my game to yours?"

"I could tell you," Bardok says, his hands coming to rest on his hips, one hand unconsciously caressing the hilt of his short sword. "But I'd much rather show you. This way."

We follow Bardok out of the atrium and up a staircase to a second level lit by periodic luminae stones. Thief lords certainly don't lack for money, or the connections to get what they want.

"Here we are," he says, swinging open a door and stepping in. The Scholar pushes me in before him, as if I were a shield. I have a moment to take in the room before he steps through: an open window opposite, a guard seated on a stool halfway between door and window, his back to the wall, and across from him, two men. Chained. No mosaics here, just a small inset tile above the men's heads, a strange design of connected curves and crisscrossing lines painted onto it. It looks oddly familiar, but I can't place where I've seen it before.

I feel the Scholar start. Looking back, I see a fleeting emotion cross his features before his face ices over—disbelief? Or fury? "I see," he says.

"Good men," Bardok says cheerfully. "But they didn't just wander into my territory; they tried to spy on my own. Now, normally I would slit their throats and be done. But then I thought, sure you wouldn't want to exchange these two trespassers for your one. You can rough 'em up a bit, as you like, and so long as I've your word I won't see them again, I've no problem giving them over to you."

From the look of it, the men have already been "roughed up": both sport bruises, split lips, and black eyes. One man cradles his arm awkwardly in his lap, the other sits hunched, one hand at his temples. Their eyes, dark and glittering beneath the purple bruises, appear half-crazed with desperate hope as they look at the Scholar.

I avert my gaze, my stomach tight as a fist. The guard against the wall catches my eye. He tilts his head toward the window and mouths one word: *Jump.*

I stare at him, hardly registering the conversation continuing around me. The guard looks toward his charges as if I were not there at all, but I didn't imagine what he just told me. Why would he help me escape the thief lord he serves? It makes no sense. On the other hand, he can't truly have been serious. Jump? From the second story? With the Scholar holding me tight and Bardok Three-Fingers between me and the window?

But Scholar's grip has slackened somewhat, and Bardok has

moved forward to kick one of the prisoner's ankles. The man scrabbles away, pressing against the plain plaster wall.

"They're your men," Bardok says with disgust. "Why not trade for them?"

"I don't sanction trespassing," the Scholar replies. "You can kill them as well as I. Why should I give up the girl for that?"

I'm dead. I'm dead if I stay, and dead if I jump. I might as well jump. But I have to get away from the Scholar first. With my bone knife wrapped up tight at my waist, I have no weapon to turn on him, not without fumbling about for it and losing any element of surprise I might have had. I will have to find another way. My mind flashes over the single defensive lesson I've had, what way I might best break the Scholar's hold on me.

"She's useless to you," Bardok says. "The men you can make an example of."

"You're right," the Scholar says suddenly. With a vicious twist, he yanks me around, changing his grip from elbow to wrist, a dagger flashing out of his robes. "She's no use to me. But I don't give up bargaining pieces to anyone, Bardok."

The dagger presses against the pale brown of the inside of my wrist. The world goes quiet in my ears, though I am aware of Bardok speaking, the Scholar smiling as he looks up, past me.

I won't be able to pull my wrist away without slitting it. But oh, he won't expect me to move toward him.

With a shout, I piston my wrist in, landing a rather weak punch to his chest. The dagger slides up my arm, cutting sideways. I step in, snapping my knee up between his legs as he shifts his grip on his dagger. He shouts, hunching over in pain.

I twist my wrist free and use that same move Matsin taught

me, slamming my other palm into the Scholar's shoulder and sending him half falling backward. I dart around Bardok, who is doubled over with laughter, and throw myself at the window, tumbling over the sill and down, limbs knocking against the wall as I fall.

I land with a bone-jarring thump, then slide sideways a pace or two before hands grab me and ease me—down? I gasp for air, my vision spinning as I find my feet. A hay cart. I landed in a hay cart.

"Run," my helper says, shoving me forward. I can hear shouting above me. I sprint as best I can down the road, still struggling to breathe, knowing that any of the Scholar's men could catch me while going at a steady jog. Curse my stupid foot! My breath sobs in my chest as I reach a cross street.

"Here, Rae," a man says, standing a pace down the alley to my right. I stumble, staring at him. He whips back his hood, gesturing to me impatiently. Artemian. The moment I turn the corner, he is beside me, one arm wrapping around me to carry me forward. Two more paces and he pulls me through a doorway and down a connecting hall to another alley. Darkness swirls around me, but I think it must just be the running. And the fall.

"Get in," Artemian says, pushing me forward again as we exit the hall. In the alley, a small carriage waits, its door open. I scramble up, Artemian following and yanking the door shut behind him. The driver whips the horses into a gallop, jerking the carriage forward and sending me to my knees.

"Easy," Artemian says, catching my elbows and raising me to the bench. "What's this?" His hand is slick with something dark. He grabs my hands, bending closer to inspect me in the dim confines of the carriage. "You're bleeding."

"Oh," I say. Right. "The Scholar had a dagger." I take a shaky breath and find that I'm trembling all over. "Shock, probably," I add. I don't think the cut is deep.

"Hold on, Rae," Artemian says, his voice grim. "I'm going to wrap this up. We'll get you patched up in no time."

"Right," I say, holding my arm up as he directs. I can feel the wetness now, soaking my sleeve and dripping onto my skirts. I think of the Scholar, the darkness in his eyes, and of Bardok's laughter booming through the room.

"Gonna take a pretty big patch," I say, and try not to let out the half-hysterical laugh caught in my breast. I don't quite succeed.

CHAPTER

30

I t's her snoring that wakes me. The old woman sits on a woven cushion a few feet away, her back against the wall and her head tilted sideways, mouth gaping, giving all her breath and voice to a stream of snores that could wake the dead. Certainly worked on me.

I shift, inspecting the room, and a slicing line of pain runs up my wounded arm. My memories come tumbling back: the brickmaker's boys, the Black Scholar, the archer's journal, Bardok Three-Fingers, the dagger, jumping from the window. I squeeze my eyes shut for a breath. I'm safe now. Or at least, I should be.

But where am I? The room offers no clues. It looks to belong to a wealthy, though probably not noble, family. A small band of mosaic runs along the top of the walls, and beneath the woven rugs layered on the floor, I catch the occasional patch of bare mosaic, neither overly fine nor crude. I lie on a low bed; beside me, a carved table bears a tray with a cup of water. Then there is the snoring woman, a window I have no intention of jumping out of, and a door.

I consider the door. It is cracked open, which means I won't have to worry about locks. I could go out without waking the woman, and see if I can figure out where I am. Because if I need to escape, I suspect this is the best chance I'll get.

Artemian brought me here, I remind myself, though I don't remember much past the carriage. It must be a safe place, even if it is clearly not his own home. Still, I'm not sure I trust my assumptions enough not to check.

I sit up carefully, pushing back the blankets with my good hand. My temples ache, pounding loud enough to almost drown out the woman's snores. I stay sitting, one foot flat on the rugs, the other as flat as it gets, until the pounding in my head recedes to a dull thud. It takes me another moment to remember what I'm doing. Then I push myself to my feet, take one step as the room spins on its axis, and my knees fold. I land with a yelp, my wounded arm glancing off the carpets and bringing tears to my eyes.

The woman shrieks, jumping to her feet, her eyes wild. I hunch down and bite my lip to keep quiet against the waves of pain.

"Who's there?" she calls, still looking over my head.

"Me," I say. It is almost a question.

She glances down, sees me, and her whole body shudders with relief. "Ah."

The door swings open. I look up to see Bren poised in the doorway, a silver glint in his hand. I can't help the rush of relief I feel when I see him: I must be safe after all. He glances from me to the woman, and his face transforms from angles and hardness to amusement. He palms his dagger with a flick of his fingers. "Kelari Bakira, is all well?"

The woman flutters her fingers at her breast, the motion at odds with her large physique. "I woke with a start, kel. My apologies. The young lady is on the floor."

"So I see." Bren meets my gaze, his lips curving into a smile.

"Hello," I offer cheerily. His pants are rumpled, his hair unbound, and his tunic missing altogether, baring a lean, muscled chest. Kelari Bakira isn't the only one I woke up.

"Hello," he replies. He glances into the hallways, shakes his head and murmurs something, and I hear the faint sound of footsteps receding. He looks back in on us. "Kelari, would you fetch some food for our guest?"

"Yes, kel," Bakira says, bustling toward him. "At once."

He steps in, holding the door as she passes, and then closes it behind her. I take the time to readjust myself, making sure my skirts cover my legs and turned foot, trying not to giggle over the ridiculousness of looking proper in the company of a half-dressed man. Not that I haven't worked beside our own stable hands many a sunny afternoon and thought nothing of their taking off their shirts. But this is different. I think.

Bren crosses the room and sits down beside me. "Felt like going for a walk?"

"I like walks," I agree before I register what he's actually saying. Why can't I seem to think clearly tonight? Or is it still day? The shutters are closed, though, and no light leaks in through them.

Bren shakes his head. "Did you think you were still a prisoner?"

"I didn't know where I was," I admit, embarrassed. "I figured I would just check."

"We left the door open so you wouldn't worry."

"Oh."

"Oh," he agrees. We sit together in silence, Bren watching me from the corner of his eye. I should say something before he mocks me, but I can't think what, my thoughts heavy in coming. Then he says, "I'm rather surprised you didn't—though perhaps you did."

"Did what?"

Almost despite himself, he says, "Attempt to escape the Scholar."

"I did."

"What happened?"

I look down to the carpet underfoot, trace the interwoven flowers and stems with my eyes. "I cut a bedsheet into strips, braided a rope, and climbed out a window."

Beside me, I sense him tilt his head. There's something that catches in my throat at the feel of that, and I don't want to see the look in his eye. I don't want his pity.

"A sentry caught you."

"Yes," I agree. "I am learning to defend myself, but I didn't—I couldn't—"

"You were no match for him," Bren says. His words are soft, almost regretful.

"No." I shift, my gaze drifting from the carpet to his bare feet, the line of his legs, the daggers tucked into the sash at his waist. "Are you—?" No, I can't ask that. Only I want to know. I *need* to know.

"Am I?"

I make myself go on, voice unsteady. "Like that?"

He goes still, even his breath paused in his lungs. "Like what, exactly?"

"Do you take prisoners?" I ask, because I can't not. "Do you—or Red Hawk—have cells you keep them in, beneath your homes? Do you kill people?"

My words bleed into the room, and the silence enfolds them. It's a silence that holds far too many answers.

"I have killed," Bren says finally, his voice cool. "But I like to believe it was not unjustly."

Like to believe. There are so many things I would like to believe too. "You're a thief," I say.

"Yes."

I turn to him, as if he could somehow remake himself just for this one conversation. "But isn't that—it's inherently unjust," I plead. "It's taking what doesn't belong to you."

He meets my gaze unapologetically. "Yes."

I look away, unable to bear the steadiness of his gaze. *Yes.* Yes, he is unjust. Yes, he has killed. A sorrow wells up in me that I did not expect, that I do not know how to stop.

"Rae," Bren says, a faint note of disbelief in his voice. "You're crying."

I shrug. How does one dispute fact?

"You've known what I am since we first met."

"Of course I have," I say, keeping my face tilted away from him. At least I am not sobbing, though I cannot stop this: the steady fall of my tears.

"Then why do you grieve my words now?"

Grief. Is that what this is? This hurt that makes no sense, that I can neither swallow down nor dispel? "It must be because I am just a foolish country girl," I say, careful not to look at him.

"I never called you foolish," Bren says softly. "Rae." His fingers move uncertainly on his thigh, twitching toward me, then back to curl into a fist on his leg. It's the first uncertain movement I can remember him making.

I shake my head, swipe at my cheeks. "I'm just tired," I say, which is a lie and we both know it.

But there is a distinct relief in the way he turns to me. "Well, let's get you back in bed, then." He takes my elbow in one hand and slides his other arm around my back. "Up you get."

I stagger to my feet and thump down on the bed, thanks in large part to Bren pushing me in the right direction. I freeze as pain washes over me from my wounded arm.

"All right?" Bren asks softly, kneeling beside me.

I nod stiffly, aware that he must have seen my foot by now, though he knew about it already. He's been adjusting his pace for me all along, even if he misread my limp that first time. I just— didn't want him to see my foot bare. Well, there's no help for that now. I let my breath out in a sigh, and he must take that as a sign that I'm all right, for he lifts my legs onto the bed, levels a look on me that has me lying back at once, and pulls the blanket over me. I give silent thanks for that.

He takes a spare pillow and props my wounded arm on top of it, his touch surprisingly gentle. As he works, I find myself following his arm, the long curving scar that travels the outside of it from his wrist nearly to his elbow. It's healed but still slightly pink. And even though my cut begins on the inside of my arm, slicing up before curving out, I can't help thinking we match. I would laugh if I didn't hurt so much. Who would have thought a horse rancher and a thief would have matching scars?

"I suggest keeping your arm raised to reduce the risk of the bleeding restarting," he says. "You lost a lot of blood. We don't want you to lose any more."

"Is that why my legs aren't working?" With the pain receding, I find myself almost giddy.

He settles on the edge of the bed. "Nearly thirty stitches, Rae."

That sounds like a lot, but I see no reason to admit it. "Could have been more," I say. For some reason this strikes me as wonderfully absurd, and I find myself chuckling.

"It's not a laughing matter." Bren's face is stern.

"I think I'm drunk on relief," I tell him. "I've never been drunk before. It's actually quite pleasant." Although it feels hollow, coming on the heels of the grief of hearing from his own lips what he is, what he doesn't regret. I want so much to forget that conversation.

He tilts his head forward, his lips quirked down as if he were fighting a smile. "Not drunk, Rae. You had a rather bitter brew the healer made up for you. Do you remember? He said it would ease the pain and help you sleep, but also make you a bit woozy."

Now that Bren mentions it, I do recall a somber-faced man with a cup full of the bitterest drink I've ever swallowed. As for woozy ... "I'm having trouble thinking straight," I say. "I think." I can push it away, the knowledge of what he is, at least for now, while my thoughts can so easily and repeatedly shake loose of their path, spin away and latch onto new things. My gaze drops to his hair, hanging down to brush the blankets. I reach out to touch it. "Do you know, your hair is much finer than mine? Very pretty. Shorter, though."

"Pretty. Now I know you're not feeling yourself," he says, watching my fingers twirl his hair. "Or perhaps I should be worrying about my manliness."

I let out a shaky giggle. "That's absurd. I bet you have city girls coming after you in droves. You probably even have a sweetheart hidden away who thinks you're the light of her world."

Bren curls his hand around my fingers, stilling them. "No girls," he says, his voice so quiet I barely hear it. "No sweetheart."

"Surely city girls aren't that stupid," I say, smiling hazily. He doesn't answer. "Come to Sheltershorn, then. You'll be mobbed."

He scoffs. "I'm a thief, Rae. What country family would entrust their daughter to me?"

"We've got plenty of criminals," I assure him, trying to focus only on the fact that he's a thief. Nothing more than that, just someone who pinches purses and treasured gold rings. "Kelari Freshna lifts vegetables from the market stalls purely by force of habit. It would be a perfect match." I shift. I know I should answer him more seriously, but I don't want to, and my hand feels strangely comfortable in his. "Anyhow, Artemian said Red Hawk has girl thieves as well. You should get to know them."

"I already have," he says. He gives my hand a squeeze and gently sets it down on the blanket. "What about you? Will you be going home to some country lover of yours?"

I laugh. For the first time in a long time, this subject strikes me as funny. "Not likely," I tell Bren. "If you think country families don't want thieves, you should see what they think of cripples. Goats will sing before I marry."

Bren doesn't answer. I look up, focusing on his face. He is staring across the room, his jaw clenched. He's angry. I lift my hand, but I can't quite reach his cheek. He turns to look at me. I lower my hand at the hardness of his face, the cutting darkness of his eyes as he meets mine.

"It's all right," I tell him uncertainly. I'm not quite sure why he would be furious. It must be what I've said about him. Perhaps my tears have bothered him more than I realized; perhaps he despises me for them. Or maybe I've just said something else foolish. I swallow, meeting his gaze. "I didn't mean that about Kelari Freshna."

He lets his breath out in a bark of laughter that has none of the lightness of his other laughs. "Never mind Kelari Freshna. You'd better get some sleep. This will all look different to you in the morning."

It will? I shake my head. "Bren?"

He stiffens slightly, just a faint tightening of his shoulders, but I see it because there's no shirt to hide it.

"Your name isn't really Bren, is it?" I whisper. I don't know why I ever thought it was. No, I've known it wasn't, but I wanted to forget that, even as I wanted to believe a thief would only ever thieve small things, not kill or imprison or meet my gaze without apology while admitting his wrongs.

"No." He rises and moves to the door without looking at me. "I'll send Kelari Bakira in with food for you. You should try to eat before you sleep. It will help balance out the medicine."

I don't have any better name to call him by, so I use what he has given me. "Bren?"

He pauses, his hand on the doorknob. There is something terribly final in the way he stands.

"I'll see you again, won't I?" I don't know why it's so important to me, but I can't bear to part with him like this, a jumble of emotions and words that don't make sense, the possibility that I've wronged him after everything. Have I? He'd been upset, and then I used his name and that bothered him more. His not-name.

He turns toward me, his face shuttered, emotionless as a painting or a stone wall. "I'm not sure, Rae. It might be better if you didn't."

He steps out, holding open the door for Kelari Bakira to bring me a tray of food. And then he's gone.

I don't want to have lost Bren's regard, not because I've said or done something, or demanded truths of him I didn't really want to know. Whatever was in that brew is mixing me up, making me say and think things I would normally keep hidden. Even if he is—even if he has done things I can't understand, I don't want—I don't know *what* I want. I press my cheek into the pillow, and hope that the morning will bring some clarity.

Somehow, I doubt it will.

CHAPTER
31

I wake to a sense of surrealness, as if the room I find myself in is something I once saw in a dream. But it wasn't a dream, was it? This room, the low bed I lie on, the familiar shapes of the mosaics . . .

"A drink of water, kelari?"

I turn my head to the side, my neck stiff. Kelari Bakira—that was her name, wasn't it?—leans forward from her cushion. At my look, she rises and offers me the glass of water from the bedside table. I nod, and struggle to sit up while she hovers beside me. My arm *hurts*, a throbbing that immediately drives my worries from my mind.

Bakira holds the cup to my lips, and I take a few sips, the water cool and refreshing. I glance down at my arm, the white bandage wrapped around it covering the stitches. Twenty-some stitches. And a bitter brew that left me spouting nonsense to Bren in the middle of the night. *Had I actually suggested he marry Kelari Freshna?*

"Is he still here?" I ask, desperately hoping she'll tell me Bren has gone out, that I won't have to face him again with the absurd things I said last night between us. Won't have to face what he thinks of me now.

"The young master?" Bakira asks, setting the glass down. "He said to send for him when you were ready to leave."

"Oh," I manage. But I had told him I wanted to see him again, hadn't I? Because I couldn't possibly have left an avenue open for me to escape without facing the humiliation of my words. And actions. I distinctly remember my hand in his hair. Oh *God*.

"Let's get you up, then," Bakira says cheerfully. Despite her panicked performance of the night before, she proves herself quite competent, helping me to rise and change into fresh clothes. She sits me down on the edge of the bed and brushes and rebraids my hair as I stare at the floor, unfortunately rehearsing as much of our conversation as I can dredge up from the night before. I played with his hair. And grieved that he was only what he ever told me he was. And suggested he find a girl among Red Hawk's thieves or marry the village shoplifter. I clench my jaw and hope Bakira can't see the flush warming my cheeks.

When she is done, I thank her, forcing a smile.

"Of course, kelari. Here are your things." She gestures to a tray set beside the bed. It contains my sash, my bone knife, and the archer's journal.

"Ah," I say, and that's apparently all I need to say, for she fetches the items herself, laying the knife next to me, winding my sash about my waist and tying it there, and passing me the journal to slip into my pocket.

"The young master sent a sheath for your knife," she says, fetching what appears to be a leather strap from beside the cushion where she sat.

"That's a sheath?"

It actually *is* a bit more than a leather strap, it turns out, and Bakira shows herself to have a great deal more knowledge than I gave her credit for, expertly buckling the sheath to my calf and showing me how to reach my knife in its new home.

Once that is done, she bustles away. She returns with a tray of food and the information that the "young master" will meet me downstairs shortly, where he's arranged for a carriage to take me back to the palace. At Bakira's insistence, I choke down a slice of bread with olive oil and herbs, and a few chunks of cheese that stick in my throat as if they were stones. And then there is no more avoiding Bren.

Bakira leads me downstairs. I follow slowly, grateful to find my foot is only a little more tender than it has been the last day— and, indeed, I've managed to avoid any new blisters. A miracle, all things considered. Though I suppose my arm makes up for any shortfall there well enough.

Bakira gestures me into a small atrium, tiny in comparison to Bardok Three-Fingers'. Bren and Artemian chat together before what I take to be an exit to the street, though the door is closed.

"Hallo, Rae," Bren says, catching sight of me. "Sleep off the rest of that medicine?"

I stop short, and he in turn walks over to greet me, all smiles and laughing eyes.

"I'm feeling better, yes," I hedge, my cheeks warming yet again.

Artemian offers me a sympathetic smile.

"Glad to hear it," Bren says, his gaze flicking to my arm, the stitches hidden beneath my sleeves.

I shrug uncomfortably. "I'm sorry about last night."

"Nothing to apologize about," Bren says, his grin turning wicked. "I quite enjoyed our conversation. I take it I should visit your village at some point, meet the local thieving population."

Why did he have to say that? In front of Artemian too?

"I wasn't quite myself," I reply, voice tight. Can't he just let me be? I don't want this conversation—I have no idea why I so desperately wanted to see him again last night, because I cannot imagine a worse meeting than this.

"No," he agrees. "I imagine it wasn't that different from being drunk, though."

"I've never been drunk," I say, the words sharp with frustration and embarrassment.

"Then last night must have been very educational for you," he says, and laughs. "Though if you'd like to play with my hair again, I won't say no. What do you say?"

My cheeks burn with twin spots of humiliation, my hands curling into fists. Artemian turns his head away, but Bren is still chuckling softly and watching me, and I *hate* him, how stupid I've been, how stupid he must think me. I hate the sound of his laughter, laughter I've heard all my life, but coming from him now—*I hate it.* My fury sends me forward one sharp step, my fist pistoning out as if I could smash that laughter from him, undo him with my rage.

The painful *thunk* of my fist glancing off the bottom of his jaw brings me back to myself. Bren stumbles backward, one hand coming up to cradle his face, his eyes wide. We stare at each other.

Artemian makes a slight sound. I glance toward him, my fist still raised, my knuckles sending lines of fire up my arm. My other arm is curled against my torso, the wound protected. He stands a pace away, his mouth slightly ajar, his eyes darting between me and Bren. And then Bren starts laughing.

I pivot toward him, cradling my fist against my chest, furious and *hurt*. He massages his jaw with one hand and laughs as if I have told him the funniest joke he's heard in years.

"Clearly," he manages to gasp, "I've underestimated you country girls."

Pain flashes through me, cutting my breath from my lungs and burning my eyes. I don't have any words. None at all. Nothing that can undo this moment, or fix it, or save me from what I've done.

I turn and flee for the door, hobbling across the distance with my stupid limping gait. I yank it open, grateful to see a carriage waiting on the other side. At least I won't have the added shame of dealing with his laughter over not being able to find my way out. The driver opens the carriage door for me. Inside, I collapse onto the bench, dropping my head to my knees, my breath aching in my chest. Or is that my heart? What did I just *do*?

Someone else climbs into the carriage, sitting down opposite me in silence, and the carriage begins to rattle down the alley. I don't look up. I punched him. I punched Bren. So hard my whole hand aches with it. I *punched*—

"Are you all right?" Artemian asks.

I nod into the folds of my skirt, but I'm not. Tears have begun to leak out my eyes, God only knows why. I sniffle, try to blink my eyes clear. Why would I cry? That stupid boy-man, laughing at me. Baiting me.

"I don't think he meant to hurt you," Artemian offers, which only makes things worse.

"Well, I meant to punch him," I inform my skirts wetly.

"It was . . . impressive. I don't think he's been taken by surprise like that in a long time."

"He should have expected it," I say, voice shaky. I spouted all kinds of nonsense last night. And he thought it was funny. Only he'd been gentle then. I remember being surprised by his kindness.

And he saved my life.

So what if he baited me with my foolishness? How could I let my anger, all this resentment I've been harboring, come out at him like this? How could I attack the one man who has helped me against the snatchers, who made sure his men were there to pull me to safety when I leapt from that window?

I think of the foreign prince, of the violent wrath in his expression as he lunged for his sister. The way his hand hurtled toward me, fury and cruelty wrapped up together. I don't want to be him. I don't want to be anything like him. I don't want this anger inside me; I don't want to hurt those around me even if they hurt me. I don't want to be that kind of person.

Artemian says, "He was worried about you."

A sob lodges in my throat, choking me. I close my lips around it fiercely. I have no right to be weeping now, as if I am the one who has been wronged. I force a shaky breath, wipe my face on my skirts.

Artemian tries again. "He wasn't sure we'd be able to get you away from the Black Scholar so easily."

"Easily?" I echo. There hadn't been anything easy about jumping out of that window or running down the alley with my arm cut open.

"Red Hawk has been negotiating his relationship with Bardok Three-Fingers for some time."

I look up sharply, my face still damp. "Wait—you mean Bardok knew?" Artemian meets my gaze steadily. I remember Bardok's gleeful laughter as I kneed the Scholar, the way he bent over as if consumed by the hilarity of the situation, never attempting to reach for me. And it was his guard who told me to jump, though it was Red Hawk's men waiting in the street below. "Of course."

Bren did *so much* for me. And all I did was judge him and attack him.

"Neither Bardok nor Red Hawk like how strong the Black Scholar's grown," Artemian says slowly. "Now that you've gotten involved, you're going to have to be careful."

I make myself focus on him. He's right, of course. The Black Scholar is one man I don't want to meet again. Actually, I'd be perfectly happy to never meet either the Scholar or Bardok again. And I certainly don't want to meet Red Hawk. *That* would be five kinds of mortifying, after what I just did to Bren. Nope, definitely don't want to meet Bren again either.

"Also, you should be aware that Red Hawk sent word about you to the princess."

"He . . . did?"

"You spent one night as the Black Scholar's hostage, and a day and a night with us. She needed to know where you were."

"That long?" I ask, rubbing my face. "I didn't realize . . ."

"You were unconscious—or asleep—a long time. We were worried."

Maybe worry makes people say ridiculous things too. Maybe Bren drew out the stupidity of our conversation because he was glad I was awake—which is a stupid idea in its own right. Bren might not want me dead, but there's no reason to think he cares for me. Certainly not after I suggested he marry the village shoplifter. And not now. Never now.

I press my lips together and glare at my lap fiercely, in the hopes of driving away any more tears. Still, one useless, pointless tear drips over my eyelid and down my cheek. Perhaps Artemian won't say anything.

"Here," Artemian says, holding something out.

I expect it to be a kerchief, but when I look up, I realize it isn't that at all: it's a small, well-made bag. He's doing better than consoling me; he's changing the subject.

"What is it?" I ask, taking the bag.

"I believe you wanted the Blessing cup and stone? Bren sent out for them yesterday while you were recovering."

"Thank you," I manage, and set the bag on my lap, trying not to think of Bren being even more helpful while I recuperated, just before I punched him.

Artemian doesn't speak again until he leaves, offering me a kind farewell and stepping down from the carriage a block away from the palace so that I might enter the walls on my own.

CHAPTER
32

"You're back!" Mina exclaims as I step into our bedroom.

I offer her a weak smile.

"Is your friend all right?"

I blink at her, bewildered. She can't mean Bren. "Uh, just fine." I say.

Mina's eyes narrow as she turns to put away a folded tunic. Without looking at me, she says, "We heard a friend of yours needed help and the princess gave you leave to see to them."

It's almost accurate, if you consider the brickmaker's boys my friends. Maybe.

"Yes," I say after a moment, since this story must have come from the princess. Who else would have made it up? Bren, perhaps, what with his "friend of a friend" phrasing, but even that would have been routed through his letter to the princess. Or was it Red Hawk who wrote to her? I can't recall.

Mina says, "A letter came for you while you were gone. It's on your desk."

"Thanks." I consider the distance to my desk. It's not that much farther, considering how far I've already come. Still, I take a moment to gather my strength.

"You missed quite the musical evening last night."

"Mmm. The princess enjoy it?"

"Apparently her people don't have a tradition of insulting one's in-laws through song right before the wedding."

"Only time for it," I say. "Can't do it afterward."

"That's what Zayyid Kestrin told her. She was very amused. Two of our best musicians closed the evening with dueling insults that led into a love ballad—*Rae?*"

I am almost to the desk, but the room has started swaying strangely. I stumble trying to keep my balance.

"What's wrong?" Mina asks sharply, starting across the room to me.

"Dizzy," I manage, one hand reaching for the back of the chair. I grab it and steady myself. As Mina reaches me, I plop down into the chair, the cloth bag with its cup and opal falling to the floor beside me.

She crouches beside me and puts her hand on my wounded arm, hidden beneath my sleeve. I inhale sharply, stiffening with the unexpected pain.

She plucks her hand away as if burned. "What is it?"

I shake my head, waiting until I can breathe again. "Hurt my arm. I'm all right. I'll just sit here a bit."

"Let me see."

I let out a shaky breath in what is meant to pass for a laugh.

"Whatever for? There's nothing to worry about."

"Then you won't mind my seeing," Mina says firmly.

She waits, kneeling beside me as implacable as stone.

"You'd make a good mother," I grumble, and carefully tug up my sleeve. Without the bandage, there's nothing blocking Mina's view of my wound with its very many stitches. Her expression shifts from slightly annoyed to aghast, lips parted in horror as if I had placed the foreign prince's head on a tray before her. "It's just a cut," I say, and tug my sleeve down again.

She stands up, hands on her hips. "*How* many stitches are there?"

"Enough," I say with a certain amount of humor. "Going to read that letter."

She doesn't answer. I focus on turning to the desk and am grateful to find that the envelope, sealed with a blob of wax, is easy to open one-handed. By the time I glance over to Mina, she's gone.

The letter is from Mama, and I know at once she's received my letter and Filadon's about what happened with the foreign prince.

> *My dearest Rae,*
>
> *I have spent the night tossing and turning, thinking about your last letter and whether I should urge you to come home as soon as the wedding is past. I doubt you would be able to step away from your duties as attendant before the celebrations are finished, though I would rather I saw you here tomorrow. But I know you, Rae. I know that you did not agree to serve as a royal attendant for a lark. I know you did not choose such a post for yourself, even if you should*

have. And I know you will not walk away from such a duty lightly.

Whatever your reasons for choosing to serve our new princess as attendant, I trust you in them. I trust you to stand by the values and principles your father and I taught you, to do what is right— not just what is easy and desirable, but what is ethically right. I trust you to take care of those around you, to fight for those who need you, fiercely protective sister and friend that you are. But, Rae, I also urge you to take care of yourself. You may know how to care for princesses and horse farms, how to protect those you love, how to do what needs to be done. But I worry that you do not yet know how to truly care for yourself. So be careful, my heart. And come home as soon as you are ready. I will be waiting.

All my love,

Mama

I am *not* going to start crying again. I fold up the letter with shaking fingers, sniffing repeatedly as if that will help me keep my emotions in check. I miss Mama, suddenly and overwhelmingly. I want nothing more than to curl up on a cushion next to her, or let her hold me, or even just to walk into the comfort of our kitchen and help Mama make breakfast.

But the truth is I don't want to go home either, because then I would end up telling Mama that I punched the man who saved my life. That instead of protecting, I lashed out, and I feel broken inside now, turned into someone I don't want to be. She will be disappointed in me, even if she still loves me, because I *didn't* stand by what she taught me. I betrayed it in a moment of sheer pride and spite.

I look up numbly as Mina swings open the door, ushering in

both the princess and a second figure in flowing robes. I blink, but Mage Berrila ni Cairlin remains, looking as competent and businesslike as she did when she saw to my bruised face. With the princess beside her then as well.

I stumble to my feet, my good hand gripping the back of the chair to anchor me. "Zayyida?"

"Don't you dare curtsy," Alyrra says sharply. "I'm glad you've returned. Veria Mina informs me you are hurt, though. I've brought Mage Berrila to take a look."

"But"—I shoot Mina a hard look—"my arm's already been seen to."

"Not by a healer-mage," Berrila says with amusement, "if Mina's description is to be believed. Let's see your arm then, kelari."

She sets down a black bag beside the desk and takes charge of me at once, ordering me back into my chair with my arm propped on the desk. The princess, meanwhile, moves around so she can watch as Berrila eases up my sleeve.

I hear Alyrra's sharp inhale, but she doesn't speak.

Berrila's brow lowers as she inspects the cut, and then she transfers her glower to me. "Was this done by someone here, kelari?"

"Not in the palace, no."

"Hmph."

Alyrra quietly asks Mina to close the door. "I believe what is said in this room should stay here."

"It's better, I think, if no one knows about this," I say, nodding toward my arm. If I can keep word from getting out about my wound, the Black Scholar may not connect Alyrra's limping attendant with his clubfooted captive. That could only be a good thing.

"That will mostly be on you," Berrila says, "and the princess."

"Me?" I glance toward the princess, but she remains quiet, her expression neutral.

"Acting like you're unhurt when half your arm is patched together is a rather tall order. But I'll see what I can do to help you. You and your twenty-seven stitches. Quiet now." Berrila cradles my hand in hers, and a strange coolness spreads up my arm.

I don't realize I've been clenching my teeth until the constant low pain of the wound fades and I can feel my jaw aching. As I watch, the skin draws together perfectly beneath the stitches, a faint blue glimmer outlining the edges of the skin for only a moment before fading to the thinnest of threads.

Berrila remains still, her eyes focused on my arm, the coolness of her magic flowing through my body, easing the aches and bruises I've collected. I lean my head against the high back of my chair and let myself breathe.

"There," Berrila says finally. She gently tugs at the stitches in my arm. I tense, but not only does it not hurt, the stitches come away in her fingers like so much fluff. The magic has already separated them and pushed them out of my skin.

"Use your arm gently. You want your skin to stretch as it would for normal use; you do not"—she eyes me darkly—"want to tear through the magic holding your skin together. It is not actually healed. Be gentle."

I dip my head meekly. "I understand."

Berrila swivels to Mina, who has watched this all silently from a few paces away. "See that she gets plenty of rest and doesn't try to lift anything heavy. I'll leave a tea for her to drink, which should help with the blood loss, if you'll see it brewed for her."

I hope fervently it's altogether different from what Bren's healer gave me.

Berrila turns back to me, reasserting her glower. "And if Mina has to come fetch me again, everyone will hear about it."

It would be a threat, except that she seems to be seriously worried for me. I dip my head, grinning. "Yes, Mage Berrila."

With a snort of amusement, Berrila gathers up her bag. I cannot imagine that such a woman really knows about the snatchers, or would protect them while caring so much about her patients. Perhaps I'm wrong. Or perhaps she doesn't know. I blink away the thoughts. First, I have to ascertain that the Darkness really is an attack, then I can worry about who knows what.

Alyrra walks with Berrila into the hallway, and I can hear the faint sound of their conversation as they stand just outside.

"And thank you, Mama Mina," I say politely to Mina.

"Why didn't you say you were injured?"

Is that hurt in her voice? I look up, taken aback, but she's smoothed out her features. Perhaps she's just irritated.

"I was hoping not to draw too much attention to it. And I felt fine for the most part."

"Fine except that you were falling down."

"Just a little off balance."

"Because you've taken a serious injury, Rae!"

I blink at her, relatively certain I never gave her my nickname to use. Did she pick it up from Alyrra?

"I'm sorry," I say finally, since I don't know what else I can offer.

She lets out a sigh and turns away, shaking her head.

A moment later, Alyrra steps back into the room. "Mina, would you give us a few minutes?"

Mina dips her head and departs, shutting the door behind her.

Alyrra waits until the faint sound of Mina's slippers fades to quiet. Then she asks, "Rae, what happened?"

"Mina said you received a letter?"

"It didn't say much, other than that you were injured but safe, and would be returned to us once you were ready. What do I need to know?"

I tell her, as quickly and succinctly as I can, all I've learned from the brickmaker's boys, how they were enslaved and transported. I don't mention Niya's sash. I don't dare, because Alyrra *is* royalty, and she could demand it from me for study, and without a stronger story about where I got it from, I may not be able to protect Niya. Instead, I tell her that I'd been given the Blessing cup and stone on my way home.

"I want to see what they actually do. The cups are purportedly charmed to remove any trace of illness from the children."

"But you don't believe that."

"I . . . think there might be more than that at play."

Alyrra moves slowly to sit on the corner of the bed. "Why would you suspect that?"

"I can't say," I admit. "But I believe the enchantments don't need to remove memories."

Alyrra gazes unseeingly at the embroidered coverlet. "If that is true, this could get very difficult."

An understatement of epic proportions, if the Circle is involved. "I know."

"I hope you're wrong," Alyrra says. "But it's best not to make assumptions. We'll need a mage not affiliated with the Circle to look into it. Do you have someone in mind?"

I hesitate. "I thought I'd ask Verin Stonemane."

Alyrra raises her brows.

"You remember how he met me my first day? He visited our ranch once, to buy horses. I think he'll at least hear me out, and I can't think of anyone else to go to."

"He's an ambassador from a foreign government," Alyrra says. "He'll have to be very careful navigating any information that could affect politics here. But if you think he might assess them, it's worth a try."

I nod, not at all sure he'll help. I hadn't considered his role, or the politics at play, especially between the royal family and the Circle.

"Regardless, once you've spoken with him, I'd like to see the items myself."

"Of course, zayyida."

Alyrra's eyes drop to my sleeve, still pulled up to bare the cut. "I also would prefer it if you did not go into the city anymore."

I hesitate, considering this. I don't want to see Bren again, or risk meeting the Black Scholar, but I'm not sure I can do everything I need from within these walls. Then again, the Scholar will surely kill me if he catches me again. And this time, he won't wait to do it.

Alyrra, watching me, says, "I know you are committed to this work, Rae, but it's too dangerous for you to go back out. If there's any need to meet our contacts, I'll send Sage."

"As you wish." I'd almost forgotten meeting Sage at the

stables and going with her to that first meeting with Artemian and Bren. "I don't think I need to meet them again. But I do need to keep working on this."

Alyrra rubs her mouth, and in that movement I see the uncertainty she's been hiding. "We will keep working on it, I promise you that. But, Rae, I thought we lost you. When I realized you'd left and no one noticed until the following morning—we all just assumed you were with your cousin, and she thought you were with us—anything could have happened to you."

"I made it back here," I say, which isn't the most convincing argument.

Alyrra drops her gaze to my arm. "Twenty-seven stitches," she says. "Whoever cut you like that was trying to kill you."

"I know." Somewhat unwillingly, I add, "It was the Black Scholar."

She nods. "From the letter I received, I suspected it might be one of the rival thief lords. So it was unrelated to the snatchers?"

"Yes." Unless the thieving rings are involved—a possibility I'd entertained for a moment at the very beginning of my investigations. It seems quite possible that a man like the Black Scholar could be involved with the snatchers. And now I also know how easy it is to disappear.

"Even so," the princess goes on, "I won't forgive myself if you die—or disappear—because of me. Because of this work. Do you understand?"

"I won't disappear. I've never been at risk from the snatchers—they only take able-bodied young women."

Alyrra eyes me narrowly. "They may make exceptions for

those they think are dangerous to them. Are you asking to continue this work?"

I pause, and realize I don't want to risk my life any further. I don't want to be attacked, or cut, or held hostage, or treated like a gambling bit. But there is Mama's letter on my desk, her words still fresh on my mind, her trust in me to do the right thing. But also to be careful.

"I don't want to quit," I tell the princess. "I think we're so close to finding out information that might slip through our grasp if we stop now. I won't go into the city unless I need to. I wasn't dressed as a noble while I was gone, and there's no reason for the Scholar to realize my identity now. If he doesn't see me again, he can't possibly recognize me."

Alyrra is quiet a moment, her expression grim. "I spread about a story that you were unexpectedly called away to help a friend in need. If we can hide the fact that you're injured, he may not connect who you are. But such men did not get where they are without being clever. He may still figure you out, if word gets out about your wound."

"There no reason for it to get out." Even if the Scholar has placed pages and servants here who will carry him the odd tidbit of gossip, I should be able to hide the truth from them. After all, tunics are always long sleeved, warm in the winter, and wide and airy in the summer. Regardless of the weather, my arm will be hidden. No one should ever actually see my wound, as long as I avoid the baths from now on. Easy enough when there's a bathing room attached to our quarters.

"If you really want to hide your injury, you'll need to make an appearance tonight at the sweetening. Do you have the strength for that?"

It's a test, I think. Alyrra sits, poised and ready and a little too still. She's hoping I'll insist I need rest and that will mean rumors about my being unwell and more clues for the Scholar—so that I will step back from my work. But I'm not ready to make that decision yet, and I'm not going to let my injury get in the way. I've worked through pain before. I can do it again.

"I should be fine for this evening," I say easily. "I'll just take a little rest this afternoon."

Alyrra dips her head. "Very well. Stay safe, Rae."

"And you, zayyida."

Alyrra casts me a wry glance and lets herself out.

CHAPTER
33

I join my cousins for tea in the afternoon, as well as a conversation I've been dreading since I returned to the palace this morning.

"Where, exactly, did you go?" Melly asks as soon as the maid leaves. "We both know perfectly well you didn't hare off to help a city friend of yours."

"It's . . ." I glance between the two of them, Melly with her features glowing with health but her mouth pressed into a flat line, and Filadon straight and slim, brows heavy with frustration. ". . . complicated."

They exchange a glance. "Tell us about it," she encourages. "Whatever it is, we can help."

Ah, they think I'm in trouble with the princess. "It's not like that," I assure her. "The princess knows what happened better than anyone. She's the one who shared the story about a friend needing help. And it's at least true in spirit."

Filadon sets down his cup. "That was *Alyrra*? She doesn't make up stories lightly. What happened?"

I consider my tea, the faint wisp of steam rising from it, and sigh. I expect I can tell my cousins a part of it, given their loyalty to the royal family. But only a part. "The princess asked me to go into the city for her, to find out about a question she had. I ran into some trouble."

"What kind of trouble?" Melly asks. Her face has softened, and now her features hold only worry. I peel back my sleeve, exposing the still-healing line of the wound curving up my arm, sealed together by Berrila's magic. Melly and Filadon stare at it in silence. After a moment, I pull my sleeve down again.

Filadon rubs his eyes. "I don't understand," he says. "First the foreign prince, and now this. What is going on, Rae? Attendants don't get hurt. They—they—" He waves his hands back and forth helplessly. Is he actually flailing? "They *attend*."

"I know," I say consolingly. "The prince—that was Alyrra's own trouble with her family. You know that as well as I. It could have been any of her attendants; it just happened to be me." Although that's not strictly true, because I both failed to call for help and then baited him in order to provide a distraction.

I glance down at my arm. "I took a risk with what I was doing for her. I didn't imagine it would become as dangerous as it did. She certainly didn't mean to endanger me. And I won't be doing such work from now on." At least not for the time being.

"Who did that to you?" Melly asks, her voice shaking. I meet her gaze, and realize it is fury and not shock or worry that has unbalanced her.

I lick dry lips. "You've heard of the Black Scholar?"

"Himself or one of his cronies?" Filadon asks, his voice sharp.

"Himself," I admit.

Filadon leans back in his chair. "You ran into a thief lord on this errand?"

I ran into a couple, actually, in the company of the third one's man. But I don't say that; I just nod. "It was a bit of an accident."

"How did you get away?" Melly asks.

"I, ah . . ."

"Yes?"

"Kneed him," I admit. "And then I jumped out a window and ran for it."

"You're going home," Melly says flatly. "You should have left this morning."

"No, I'm not," I say with a little smile. "I'll be safe in the palace. But that's why I won't be leaving the palace as much. The princess doesn't want to take a chance on the Black Scholar finding me again."

"No, she doesn't," Filadon says, his tone curt. "Will he know where to look for you?"

"I don't think so. I didn't give him my real name or much else about me, other than that Baba is a horse rancher."

"And there are plenty of horse ranchers in Menaiya," Filadon agrees. "I can't imagine what the princess was thinking—the Black Scholar."

"She wasn't thinking of the Black Scholar at all. I just happened to get mixed up in things a bit."

Filadon looks unappeased. "I'll be asking the prince for his own explanation of what happened to you when we meet shortly."

"As you like," I tell him as he rises to leave. "But it might be better to just let it go."

"Oh no," Filadon says, with a dark grin. "I think it's about time Kestrin answered for some of this mess."

He drops a kiss on Melly's cheek before he departs.

I stay a little longer. I know I need another nap, but I don't want to leave the comfort of Melly's home. She steps out for a few minutes to speak with her maid, and I settle a little further into my sofa, glad I'm not on a cushion today. They may feel more like home, but they are harder to get up from.

I do miss home. I miss my family desperately. I miss Niya's clear gray gaze, and her touches of magic in our food, and the way her hair never quite stays in its braid. I miss Bean's energy and passion and tendency to pick up strays. I miss both my parents, so different in their ways and yet united in their love. And I miss silly little things: our kitchen table with its worn surface, and the shabby cushions we sit on to eat. That cracked bowl we should have gotten rid of years ago. Muddle with her bright coat and impudent manners.

I run a hand over my waist, over the beautifully embroidered sash I wear, and feel the slight bulk of my story sash tied just below it, hidden beneath my tunic, the ends tucked up. It might be one way to carry my family with me, and after my latest adventures, I'm not leaving it behind anywhere. Just as I have my bone knife strapped to my calf even now. After all, Bren may not be there to find a way to help me should I get into trouble again. It's wise to be prepared.

I take a deep, steadying breath, but now that I've thought of him, all the humiliation and sheer *awfulness* of our final encounter comes crashing back down on me. I bite my lip, but even that doesn't keep the tears from welling up.

I'm not going to cry again. I'm *not* going to cry.

"Rae?" Melly stands in the doorway, her brow creased with worry.

At the sight of her, my eyes start leaking tears again. I blink them away furiously. Haven't I cried *enough*?

She crosses to me. "Rae? Is it—has something else happened?"

"No, nothing else," I say, wiping my nose with my sleeve, which is decidedly not ladylike, and I don't even care. "It's nothing."

She eases down beside me, her gaze flicking from my wounded arm to me again. "If it was nothing, you wouldn't be crying."

"It's just I—I . . ." But how do I tell her when she doesn't even know Bren exists?

She takes my good hand in hers, her words practical as ever. "Start at the beginning, if you can."

I sniffle. "I punched someone." Tears spill down my cheeks. "In the face."

Melly's eyes widen, her jaw working but her lips pressed shut. Finally, she says, "Well, you've never done that before. I expect they deserved it."

"No, they didn't," I wail. "They—he—saved my life. It's just that he was laughing at me. And then he laughed more after I punched him."

"Aha," Melly says, features brightening. "Who is he?"

"Just a boy—man." No, he's far too infuriating to call a man. "Boy," I repeat.

"A boy-man." Melly nods, then pauses. "Is he mixed up with these thief lords who are hunting you?"

"Kind of."

"That's a yes."

"Yes," I echo, sniffing again. "It doesn't matter. What matters is I *punched* him, Melly. And he laughed at me. He just—he laughed. And I'll . . ." I'll carry that laughter with me the rest of my life. And I'll never be able to take back that punch. "I didn't really mean to hurt him. I mean, I did, but not really. I just wanted to stop him because . . ."

"Because laughter hurts," Melly says, finally understanding. "Oh, Rae."

Her gentleness breaks through what little strength I've managed to shore up, and I bend over, sobbing into my hands. Melly shifts, slipping her arms around me, and my head ends up on her shoulder.

"I don't want to be like that. To punch people."

"Rae, you'd just been attacked yourself, hadn't you? That's a lot to handle. That doesn't mean you're the kind of person who punches people. Especially not people you like."

Except that I *did*. Bren isn't a friend, not really, but as infuriating as I find him on occasion, I do like him as a person. I don't wish him harm. But I still punched him.

"It'll be all right," Melly says softly.

"No, it won't."

"Perhaps," she agrees. "But you will get through this."

That much is true. I let out a slow breath and rest against her, my tears slowing.

"Now, come. Have another cup of tea. And a biscuit. Life is always better after you've eaten a biscuit."

I let out a watery laugh and straighten up. It's the sort of thing Bean would say.

"That's better." Melly smiles and hands me the promised biscuit.

While it doesn't take away the past, at least it makes the present more bearable.

CHAPTER
34

Tonight is the sweetening, the last big celebration preceding the wedding procession in two days' time. Mina sends for her maid to help us both get ready. All the attendants have been provided with matching ensembles of pale blue silk embroidered with silver, a seamstress coming to ensure that any last adjustments are taken care of. Once we are dressed and our hair done up, we switch off with Jasmine and Zaria, keeping the princess company as she dresses along with half a dozen ladies of the court.

The ladies Havila and Dinari sit in a pair of armchairs set nearby the dressing table, a couple of young women hover nearby, chatting and telling jokes, and three more sit on the bed, joining in the conversation when they aren't giggling with each other. It gives the room a bright, festive atmosphere. No one reflects on the absence of the foreign queen, and Alyrra doesn't seem to note it herself. Perhaps she did not expect her mother to be present; it's hard to know what her own traditions might be.

Regardless, Alyrra seems cheerful and curious about the night's events. Havila provides a rundown of the evening's progression: the men and women will gather in different halls; there will be singing and dancing, and henna for the women; the men will play tricks on Kestrin, and the women will feed Alyrra more sweets than she could ever possibly want; and Kestrin will enter about halfway through the night. The women will present themselves as utterly demure while he offers Alyrra a set of gifts, at which point they will chase him out, saying he doesn't value her enough. He must then return with a second set of gifts.

"Really?" Alyrra asks, amazed. "You'll chase him out?"

They don't disappoint. When Kestrin arrives, kneeling before Alyrra where she sits on a sofa set up on the dais, he offers her an intricately designed gold set that easily weighs as much as all the gold my family owns. I stare at it in awe.

"You think that's a fit gift for a bride?" Havila demands, her cane thumping against the carpets of the raised dais to create a hollow boom. "Are you descended from prairie dogs? Have you the brains of a mud-dwelling fish?"

The whole hall immediately erupts into jeers and shouts. Alyrra's eyes widen, and Kestrin, looking up at her, grins impishly and runs out of the room, arms over his head as if fearing thrown vegetables, trailing an entourage of highly amused attendants.

"How very strange," the foreign queen remarks from her seat on the dais. "I should think you would have more respect than that."

Alyrra turns toward her mother. "I believe the point is he should have more respect for his bride. It seems an excellent custom. Perhaps it should be adopted in Adania as well."

"To call one's prince a rodent . . ."

"Oh, indeed," Havila says. "It is better, though, than having a viper as a prince, don't you think?"

The queen's expression shutters, her eyes glittering with fury for a bare moment before she gives a disdainful sniff. "You see, Alyrra? Even the old women here know nothing of respect."

Havila smiles, a smooth, pleasant look that says she has brought out for display exactly what she wished from the queen. And as the queen's eyes narrow, I can catch a terrifying glimpse of an evening ruined by this arrogant woman's pride and disrespect—an evening that Alyrra has every right to enjoy.

"Oh!" I cry, stumbling forward and bumping a tray of sweets set on a table beside me. I step on the edge of my skirt for good measure, and then my hand accidentally comes down on the edge of the tray, sending it flying. Jasmine shrieks.

I catch myself on my hands and knees and pain screams through my arm. I hold myself stone still, and then slowly ease the weight off my wounded arm. I take a shaky breath and try to school my features into something neutral.

"I told you not to allow the lame one here," the queen says, which is news to me.

Alyrra stands helplessly a few feet away, having leapt up from her seat, her hands still covered in half-dry henna. "Rae?"

"I'm sorry," I manage, and look up to find the dais littered with crumbling sweets.

"Someone pushed her," Zaria says from beside me, turning to scan the empty space behind the dais. What?

The nobles exclaim and shake their heads as Mina helps

me to my feet. A trio of servants swoop in to collect the fallen tray, scooping the destroyed sweets onto it and sweeping up the remaining crumbs.

"Are you all right?" Alyrra asks, her gaze flicking from me to where I stood, seeking the nonexistent perpetrator.

"Yes, only I'm so sorry to cause such a scene." My arm still hurts, but I can't check it now. It will just have to be all right.

"That hardly matters. At least the sweets didn't get on you!"

"Just my hands," I say ruefully, turning my palms over to show the sticky sweet crumbs attached to them.

"Nothing a bit of water won't fix," Mina says with impressive cheerfulness.

I agree with Mina's suggestion, and dip a quick curtsy before retreating from the dais. Havila throws me a considering glance as I step down, but she says nothing. I weave my way through the crowded hall to one of the food tables, where a servant offers me a napkin and a cup of water to clean my hands. A subtle check assures me that my wound has not begun to bleed again.

I look up as the prince makes his second entrance.

"Do you dare return?" Havila thunders from the dais.

"I come bearing gifts," he calls, "with my head bowed in repentance!" His head is, in fact, thrown back, chin lifted as he grins across the hall at Havila. I like this impudent, boyish prince more than I would have thought possible, especially given the laughter shining from Alyrra's eyes, all thought of her mother's anger banished.

"We shall see what your repentance is worth. Approach!"

He crosses the length of the hall to his bride. This time, each of his attendants carries a tray. I give a moment of thanks that brides don't have to give gifts in return; I'm relatively certain my arm couldn't bear that kind of weight for long.

"Can you see what they have?" one of the women near me asks of her friends.

"The last tray has a gold belt. The rest, I cannot tell."

"That will be for the wedding procession," the first says, beaming. "I cannot wait to see it!"

Havila continues to preside over the dais, playing the role of family matriarch as she considers each gift, likening them to cheap baubles, and then, in an act of charity, allowing that they might be enough. The outlander queen watches this all with raised eyebrows and faint bemusement, utterly unaware that she has failed to take up her own role in the festivities. Her whole demeanor suggests she comes from a land of finer customs. I doubt that very much. From what I've heard, their hall is strewn with rushes and bones, with dogs padding underfoot. One does not dare enter wearing anything but boots.

I wait till Havila dismisses a very merry Kestrin, his attendants passing off his gifts to Alyrra. I should be up there, but it doesn't occur to me that I've been missed till Kestrin turns to leave, his eyes sweeping over the hall and coming to a stop at me.

I dip my head. When I look up again, he's passed on. I hurry back to the dais. By the time I reach it, Havila has stepped down.

"You," she says, reaching out a hand to stop me, "are both foolish and very thoughtful. There might have been a better way to change the subject, you know."

"But it was so very effective."

"Reminding everyone of your purported clumsiness?" She

sighs. "I suppose the fact that you were pushed must be shared about a bit more."

"Well, but that's not really—"

"Don't you dare!"

I swallow and offer a tentative smile.

"Now go on up there and be helpful, you little fool." Havila gives me an affectionate pat and moves off, cane tapping with each step.

I wake early the following morning from liquid dreams, all darkness and shadow and bright blades. I sigh as I sit up. I never used to have such dreams.

It's early yet, the sun risen but everyone still abed after the late night we had. With no chance of sleeping again, I prop up my pillow and reach for the archer's journal.

Her words grow darker, more desperate as the days pass and the defeats continue. I come to the final entry, laboriously written, the letters pressed hard into the page, as if she were in pain.

I have betrayed my king. I meant only to leave—desertion is no small crime, but my heart is dead from all I have seen, and he refuses to speak with the Fae messengers, putting them to death. If we will not parley for peace, we will be slaughtered. Already so many lost: the swordsmen, the archers, captains, and whole troops of quads. I am the last of my quad. And while the invaders are kind in their conquests, leaving those who do not bear arms unharmed, still, many die who mean only to defend their homes. So I left to find my sister and our parents, and take them into the mountains until this evil time is past.

I rode out at dawn, the sentries letting me pass without a word, used to my coming and going. Not three hours later, the Fae caught me. They dragged me from my saddle, and there were too many to fight. I did not try. Perhaps they would have let me go had not one of them recognized me.

"The king's archer." Not anymore! But they would have thought less of a deserter. They argued then, about a punishment, a death that had been decreed for the king and those in the highest circle of command. As if he had left me anything to command, reassigning my men to Mendar! It was an empty position I held, for he knew I doubted him. The Fae argued, and I knelt among them stupid with weariness.

I did not understand until they pressed me up against a tree and, raising my right hand above my head, impaled it there with a dagger. I screamed then, screamed for their mercy, told them I had a sister and parents to care for. They were angry. It is easier to kill when you do not know such things about your enemy. They caught my left hand, meaning to do the same to it, and in desperation I demanded that they take me to the sorceress who leads them.

That stopped them. They argued while I hung there, blood trickling down my arm and over my chest. And then they took out the dagger, stanching the flow of blood with linen and magic, blindfolded me, and took me to their army's camp. Their general saw me first, demanding to know what my message was, thinking I was a courier from my king. He would have killed me as equal payment for the messengers my king has slain had I not asked for the sorceress.

She sent for me that evening. By then I was weak with pain, though a Fae healer had seen to my wounded hand. I am thankful that my best hand, my left, is still whole. I do not know that my right will ever hold a bow again. Nor do I care.

I saw the sorceress. All the rumors are true. All the stories of the darkness of her gaze, the coldness of her voice. To look upon her is to look upon one's own death. She looked upon me and knew me to be desperate, and she laughed. I felt like nothing, like scum, filth upon the earth. I hated her for it, and yet I thought—I am here. Let me ask what it is their messengers wished to say. This I can do. For my sister.

She wants our king in payment for the evils he committed in her own land. She wants him, and in return she has agreed to withdraw all her forces, to order a retreat to her lands. She offers no surety. But then, they are winning. She need offer nothing. She told me the death that I nearly suffered—my hands pinned above me and my belly slit open—was the death he visited upon the generals and captains he took hostage. All they have done, all they have brought to our land, is but a reflection of what he brought to them.

So I agreed. I took her message not only to the king, but also to his son, the prince; and to his advisors; and to the Circle of Mages. All know her demands. Someone of them will bend, will give him over, and in betraying him, save our land. Already the Circle discusses it.

I have done this, knowing that I brought treachery with me. But the king is mad with vengeance; he neither sees nor cares what becomes of his land. What am I writing? I am trying to ease my own guilt. In the end, if our king is betrayed, I can only say: I have done this. Right or wrong, or both, I have done this. Would that I were not a coward. Every morning and every night I will live and breathe this memory, this betrayal. Would that the Fae had slit my throat when they found me, that they had not given me the chance to sell my liege.

I have only one thing left to write. After this, I return to the remains of my home, to begin the search for my family. My wounded hand makes me unfit to hold a bow, and has earned me an honorable discharge rather than execution as a deserter. The irony almost makes me laugh. So I am leaving. And here is what I would record, that it not be forgotten. I learned *the sorceress's name, and as any mage will say, names have power. Should ever we need it, here is a record: Sarait Winterfrost.*

I sit a long time, staring down at the book. I'm not sure what I expected: some sort of heroic end, some great act of courage by the archer to set things right. As if things could be set right by a single person, when all her world appeared to be burning down around her. Instead, I have an account of failure and sorrow, of a single act that may have brought about the end of the Fae Attack, but only through betrayal.

I know the stories, have read the histories: when the king died unexpectedly—and, according to some, without leaving a body behind—his closest advisors and vassals sent messengers to the Fae generals begging their mercy. Within three days, there was peace. Within a week, the Fae departed altogether. It is precisely the retreat the sorceress promised.

What I hold in my hands is the explanation I never wanted to read. How is it that one can try so hard and yet fail so completely? Here is a woman whom I have come to respect, whose treatment by her liege outraged me, and whose decision at the end makes me ill. Not because she betrayed her king, or perhaps not only that, but because I understand it. And I do not know what I would have done differently.

CHAPTER
35

I take breakfast in the common room with the rest of the attendants, Alyrra having opted for her own private breakfast in her rooms. Our self-defense lessons, the second of which I spent escaping from the Scholar, will resume again after the wedding. Zaria nurses her cup of tea, and Jasmine and Mina keep up a comfortably slow conversation about what bits of gossip they gathered last night, and if there is anything the princess should know about.

Just as we are finishing up, a page arrives with a sealed envelope for me, bearing a note from Filadon.

The crown will, of course, cover those expenses incurred during your stay in Tarinon, he writes. *Prince Kestrin has also expressed interest in developing an ongoing business agreement with your father regarding stock that might be acquired for the royal stables. I assured him your father would be open to such a conversation.*

Short as the letter is, I have to read it twice before I find myself moving from disbelief to laughter. It might not be the stud I asked for, but becoming a supplier for the royal stables will have many benefits, and I suspect it won't be long before we can afford to purchase the services of a stud for our mares, if not buy the perfect stallion outright.

"What is it?" Mina asks curiously.

"My cousin—or rather, her husband," I explain, folding the note and slipping it away. "I'd be afraid to be his enemy."

Mina chuckles. "I've got family like that too."

Zaria raises her cup of tea in silent agreement.

"You've received a reward, I hope," Jasmine says. "After all you went through with the foreign prince."

It's the first truly nice thing she's said to me. "It will be good business for my family," I agree.

Jasmine nods. "Sounds about right. The reward ought to fit the recipient."

"What sorts of rewards would you expect?" I ask curiously.

Jasmine glances at the other two, and then Mina says, "Marriage proposals to choose from, and of course wedding gifts. That would be at the end of our tenure as attendants. In the meantime, though, just gifts of fine fabrics and jewelry, perhaps a riding horse or the like."

"Ah." It's just as well Filadon negotiated a business agreement. I'm certain I wouldn't want the royal family to pressure someone into marrying me to please them. Not only would such a man no doubt come to hate me if I agreed to it, but that would leave Niya alone, and then we'd both be miserable.

The other attendants carefully don't look at me, and I take the opportunity to rise and set aside my plate—though, technically, a servant will clear it for me. "I'm going for a walk, since the princess won't need us for lunch," I announce.

Mina nods. "We'll see you then."

In our room, I gather a bit of embroidery I begged off of Melly, stuff it into the bag with the Blessing cup and stone, and make my way to a small courtyard hidden away from the busier parts of the palace. About an hour ago, I sent off a short note by page. I am hoping that it won't go unanswered.

I take a seat on a stone bench alongside the arched galleries that line it, adjust my shawl, and take out my embroidery as if I've come out to sew in peace. It's ridiculous, but I am just country-bred enough that anyone who sees me will ascribe it to my peasant tendencies, and look no further.

Melly's embroidery project is a small handkerchief with a flowery border. As it turns out, my arm wound does not like to be tugged at continuously as I sew. I do it anyway, because the healer-mage said normal movement was important, but the wound takes a mundane task and elevates it to pricklingly uncomfortable. I'm also much slower than usual. By the time I finish outlining my first flower, I've begun to wonder if the letter will be answered at all. By the time I've finished the second, I'm only here because I can't bear to give up. Although I do set the sewing down on my lap.

So, when I hear a set of slippers approaching from the right, I look up with a sense of absolute relief to see Stonemane with his ebony hair and pale skin and infinite eyes. He wears Menaiyan clothes once more, quiet colors for the morning: a sky-blue tunic and beige pants, topped with a loose, open-fronted embroidered coat of darker blue to ward off the spring chill.

"Oh *good*." I wave for him to come sit beside me. "I'm so glad you were able to come."

He bows from the neck and seats himself at the other end of the bench, eyeing me with some bemusement. "How are you, kelari?"

"Well enough. Can you do that little trick of yours? I have a question for you."

Stonemane grins and the effect is devastating, his eyes bright and the unknowable years shrinking away until he looks halfway young. "And you're not even going to ask how I am. Very well."

He taps the bench with his finger, and that strange stillness rolls out from him again. I stretch my jaw, grateful to have this moment to gather myself and set aside Stonemane's beauty. By the time the stillness dissipates, I am ready.

"I wondered if you could look at some things for me. I believe they're enchanted, but I need to know how."

"I assume there is a particular reason why you are not going to the mages who are sworn to the royal family?"

"There is," I agree. "I'm finding there's only so many people I trust nowadays. I don't know any of the mages. I do know you."

He tilts his head, his gaze bent on me, assessing. "Are you asking a favor of me?"

I pause. Now *that's* dangerous ground. One doesn't deal in favors with the Fae, or so claims every tale I've heard of them. "No," I say with forced lightness. "It's a riddle. Aren't you curious?"

"A riddle," he echoes, a hint of self-derision in his voice. "Because we are all of us unnaturally curious about riddles."

"Well, it's a rather unnatural riddle. Look." I fish the opal from the bag. "This is used to bless children who have been stolen and then escaped."

He eyes me strangely. "You have a particular blessing for that?"

"We have a very important blessing for that. But I don't think it works the way we've been told." I hand him the stone. He takes it only because I'm shoving it into his hand.

"And I should involve myself in this because—?"

I really have no argument I can think of, so I appeal to the only thing I have left: his honor. "Because if Bean were stolen, you will have failed your obligations as a guest."

This startles a laugh from him. "I believe I've upheld my obligations as a guest quite admirably."

He means that he hasn't told a soul about Niya. And I'm grateful for that, but if he won't offer to look at the cup and stone of his own accord, I'll make whatever arguments I can. "You can always do more," I say reprovingly. "Tell me, what does that opal in your hand actually do?"

He sighs. "I suspect I might actually have been safer from you back when you feared me."

"That's what comes of giving girls knives," I observe. "And you don't really mean that. You are perfectly safe right now."

"One must consider the political context as well as the physical," Stonemane says almost gently. There's a hint of regret in his eyes, in the faint tightening of his features. He's not going to help me.

No. That's not acceptable. He *can* help. And I'm not paying any debts if I can avoid it. "I've considered both," I say firmly. "You have never been in any physical danger—"

"Not even from iron skillets?"

I gape at him. He grins again, darkly sly. "How did you—you couldn't have heard that!"

"I . . . may be able to hear conversations that pertain to me whether or not I am there. You spoke of it as you were planning to smuggle me out of your house. I was concerned for my safety at the time. And yours."

"Rude!" I cry, to cover my mortification. "And certainly not the behavior of an honorable guest." I point at the stone in his hands. "You may put things right now, both as our guest and the guest of the king, whose subjects are being stolen by slavers. Your words can't be overheard. I will tell no one your name in conjunction with what you tell me now. So tell me, what does that opal do?"

He considers it, brow creasing as he turns it over once, twice. "What do *you* think it does?"

I take a breath, let it out slowly. "An opal is usually used to strengthen memory. But the blessing this is used in removes memories."

"Does it."

"I'm not convinced that the memories need to be removed. I want to understand the spells themselves."

Stonemane dips his head. "You are right about the opal. It is typically used to strengthen memories. In some cases, it is used to draw forth particular memories. Based on the enchantment wrapping this stone, I would say it's used to draw forth all the most recent memories of the person it's used on. But there's nothing here that would destroy a memory."

"I see. And this?" I hand him the cup. "It's the second part of the Blessing. It's filled with thrice-blessed water and given to the child to drink. If the Darkness is taking a child, this is what protects them. I'd like to know how."

"The Darkness?"

"An illness that steals the light from a child's mind. It leaves them a husk of themselves. It only affects those who escape the snatchers—the slavers who have taken them."

"You realize how very strange all this is," Stonemane says.

"We . . . have known it to be a danger for decades."

"It is not a danger I've heard of before, in my various travels."

I'm beginning to think that it is one Menaiya alone faces. "Please." I gesture toward the cup. "That's why I need you to look at these."

For a long moment he hesitates, and then he sighs and sets the opal aside, focusing on the cup instead. When the Speaker used it, I'd barely registered it as more than a simple silver cup, without stem or base. As Stonemane studies it, I see that even the design upon it is simple: an embossed pattern of interwoven lines, at their center an inset stone—a topaz, semiprecious, and filled with the faint gleam and glitter of stored magic. The topaz must hold the fount of magic needed to power the spell embedded in the pattern around it. Without it, the cup would run out of magic after only a few uses.

Ever so carefully, Stonemane sets the cup down between us. "Where do these cups come from?"

"There's something very serious about them, isn't there?"

"Kelari."

"The Circle of Mages," I admit. "They're provided to the Speakers by the Circle."

"Ah. Then it is possible I have said too much already."

"You haven't said anything," I complain. "And you *are* the royal family's guest. If someone is preying on their people, it would be a service to share what you can tell. Maybe even a duty." I eye him hopefully, well aware that I have no argument whatsoever, but that he spoke so seriously of the duties of a guest when he stayed with us.

He lets out a soft, almost pained laugh. "Oh, very well, kelari. I want you to be careful with what I'm telling you. As a delegate of my people, it is not my purpose here to create trouble. What I tell you must not be traced back to me, or this conversation."

I meet his gaze. It contains the liquid ripple of the ocean, deep and unknowable, and so very much not human. "I give you my word."

He touches a finger to the engravings. "This is an enchantment. Whatever liquid is put in this cup will take on its properties: to destroy the uppermost memories in the person who swallows it, and to wipe out of the blood any remaining trace of the marker placed in the victim—the marker that would identify them to your so-called Darkness."

"You mean that those two things are separate—that the memories don't need to be lost?"

"Don't they?"

Of course they do; as Bren noted, if the memories aren't lost, how much easier would it be to hunt down the snatchers? I take a steadying breath. "The goblets prove the mages are removing our rescued children's memories, then."

"That, and nothing more."

"I don't understand."

"It's not a particularly nice thing to do, but it doesn't prove a wider involvement, if that's what you're looking for."

I nod. The mages could even argue that their intention had been one of mercy at the outset, to reduce the impact of the trauma of slavery upon those who escaped. And it would be my argument against theirs, what the truth is. I need more proof—either to exonerate the Circle or condemn them. But this, what I have now? It's not enough to do either.

Stonemane pushes himself up from the bench. "And now I really have said enough."

"Wait." I reach out a hand. "Can you tell how the children might be marked?"

"Because the method to mark them must also have a magical source?" Stonemane queries, one brow arching eloquently. "An excellent avenue of inquiry, kelari, but in this case I cannot tell you anything. The marker must be there. From the cup, I can tell only that the marker would be wiped out."

"But you're sure it's in their blood? How would it get there?"

Stonemane frowns. He's ready to leave, but still he answers. "I am certain. Possibly, as with the Blessing, the marker for the Darkness is ingested. I cannot say from what you have shown me."

"Is there anything else?" I ask.

"Only this: I cannot be a witness for you, and I do not recommend taking on the Circle of Mages without careful consideration. And irrefutable evidence. You are working with the princess, are you not?"

I nod.

"Make sure that the prince and king are aware as well.

"I understand."

Stonemane sighs. "I should not be surprised that, within a week or two of your arrival, you have set about trying to save someone. Be careful, kelari. The opposition you are up against in this is a great deal more dangerous than anything you would meet in your own town."

"I'm aware of that," I say, resting my wounded arm on my lap. I've already crossed a thief lord. I have no interest in inciting the fury of a mage. "I'll be careful."

Stonemane purses his lips and says, warily, "I have also discharged my obligations, kelari."

I grin up at him, well aware that I'll call on him again if I have no other option. "I thank you for your help today, verayn."

His lips twitch as if he cannot help being amused—but then he catches himself, his features sliding into a cool mask, and, with a slight bow, he departs.

CHAPTER

36

I remain on my bench for another hour, just sitting and thinking. The sun creeps over the edge of the roof and warms the courtyard, and a few pages hurry by, and, once, a young noblewoman passes through with her toddler in her arms. I watch them go by in silence, grateful that this child, born to a wealthy family, will likely never be snatched.

But mostly I am considering what I know: that the mages have enchanted the cups in unnecessary ways—suggesting the wish to hide something; that the Darkness is a magical attack, and something that the Circle might want to hide; and that they would not be involved with the snatchers if there were not some gain for them. People do not destroy others for no reason at all.

There is also the consideration that the Darkness doesn't take those children who are snatched—otherwise, they would be useless as slaves. So the snatchers must have a ward that keeps the children safe unless they venture past its boundaries. A ward that the Circle would never admit exists, that I wouldn't have believed could exist either, if it weren't for Niya's own wards, constructed following her own intuition to achieve the same end. It's not impossible, just different.

The snatchers are not politically powerful—at least, not openly so. So the gain must be something else. The simplest, most obvious answer is gold. I've seen what the Black Scholar would do to protect his territory, his power, and thus also his wealth. It should therefore come as no surprise that the mages, elite and educated as they are, would be equally ruthless in amassing and protecting their own sources of wealth.

But all I have is conjecture, and the belief that the Circle is directly involved with the snatchers.

With a sigh, I gather up my things and return to my room. I have just enough time to dress before attending Alyrra to lunch. In the brief moment before we depart, I mention I have news for her and Kestrin.

"I'll ask him to join us after the meal," she assures me.

Lunch is a quiet affair, with only a select few noble families in attendance—including Melly and Filadon, whom I am delighted to see—and no sign of the foreign prince. He has clearly been excluded from the royal family's inner circle.

Kestrin and Garrin return with us to the royal wing after the meal. I would have preferred only Kestrin, but I remember Alyrra saying that the prince trusts this cousin of his implicitly. I fetch the bag with the cup and opal, and return to the princess's suite just as a servant sets out tea. Kestrin has already dismissed his attendants, and Alyrra gives Jasmine leave to go.

Once we are alone, Alyrra turns her attention to the men.

"Verayn, you will remember that when I appointed Kelari Amraeya, it was with the specific hope of having her look into some questions I had regarding the disappearance of children in the city."

Garrin frowns, glancing toward Kestrin, who nods soberly.

"I expected it would take some time to learn anything of substance, but Kelari Amraeya has been exceptionally effective." She turns to me. "Will you tell us what you learned from your visit to the brickyard, and the children?"

It's a hard story to tell without implicating anyone—specifically, Bren. I name him only as a contact who took me first to the brickyard, and who then managed to help the children escape. I relay their stories of being transported by water, all but the one, who was sold into slavery upon arrival in the city.

"After they were blessed, I was given the items used in the Blessing. I have had someone with magical abilities assess them."

"Who would that be?" Garrin asks. He sits forward, elbows on his knees, listening intently.

"I cannot say, verin. I promised to keep their identity hidden."

"And we are to believe someone whose name we don't know?"

"There is no concern there," Kestrin says, touching Garrin's shoulder. "I'm sure we can have them assessed again by someone we trust. What did you learn, kelari?"

"That the cup serves two functions, separately. To remove the marker in the blood that draws the Darkness to it, and to wash away those memories brought forward by the opal."

"One does not entail the other, then," Alyrra surmises.

"No," I agree.

Kestrin shakes his head. "What did you mean by 'a marker that draws the Darkness to it'? What I have heard is this Darkness is already within the children. Or"—he shrugs—"that it isn't even real."

"It's real. And it's sent. It seeks out the marker in their blood."

Kestrin rocks back, his expression shuttering.

Beside him, Garrin remains perfectly still, eyes narrowed. "You are suggesting that it is a magical attack?"

"That is what the evidence suggests, yes." I take the opal and cup from the bag and offer them to Alyrra. "It would be best to have someone you trust look at these to confirm what I've learned."

Kestrin rubs a hand across his mouth. "Let us assume, for a moment, that this is true. That there is a magical attack, which the common people have come to call the Darkness, that obliterates the minds of children who escape the slavers."

Garrin shakes his head. "You are effectively arguing that there's a kingdom-wide conspiracy to rid the streets of unwanted children. That seems unlikely at best, and very dangerous ground if you attempt to then implicate the Circle."

"I'm aware it's dangerous ground," Kestrin says. "But if the Circle is involved with slavers—"

"Cousin, the Circle just tried to have a spare heir declared after myself, not even a month ago, when you were absent for a few days. They could try to have you and your wife declared unfit if this gets out, on the grounds that you are attempting to undermine them. They could succeed."

"But if they are involved with the slavers, wouldn't that undermine *them*?" Alyrra demands, echoing my confusion. She holds the cup loosely in her hand, forgotten.

Garrin smiles derisively. "No. You haven't any mages in Adania, have you?"

She shakes her head.

"Your country is too small for such a rare talent to arise, and even if one did, such a child would leave to study beneath a trained master. But we have the Circle."

Kestrin sighs. "What my cousin is trying to say, veriana, is that the Circle is strong here."

"How strong?" Alyrra demands.

Kestrin exchanges a glance with Garrin. Then he says, "Imagine the power of a single mage, veriana. Grant him a pair of amulets within which to store his power, and he becomes a formidable force. We've all heard of lands taken over and ruled by a sorcerer until their power—their amulets—could be broken. The Circle is nearly forty mages strong. What could my father do if the Circle turned upon him? What could he do if they decided to name themselves rulers in his stead?"

Nothing. That's what. I swallow hard. I had never thought of it from this perspective. The Circle swears loyalty to the crown, they've upheld the true king for generations . . . but I see now it's a choice. One they can change at any time. And with forty mages united, the violence they could do Menaiya if they so choose would be devastating.

"You mean," Alyrra hazards, "that your family are essentially prisoners to the Circle?"

Kestrin winces. "We do what is necessary to pacify the Circle. Grant them what lands and avenues of income they require. Ensure their access to the gems they need to create amulets.

Ignore whatever kickbacks they might receive from those to whom they grant their favor. In return, they help secure our borders, perform services to the crown, and ..."

"And allow us to continue to rule," Garrin says. "However much that rule may be worth."

I never imagined the royal family's position or power to be so precarious. It's stunning.

"Why don't they take the throne for themselves?" Alyrra asks.

"They don't need to," Kestrin says darkly. "They hold the power of coercion over my family, and gain legitimacy by paying us lip service. But it's no small threat that they are lining up their own choice of heirs after Garrin. Until this past month, we had every expectation that the Circle's heir would eventually reach the throne."

And now he doesn't believe so? I glance between the royals but don't dare interrupt. Alyrra nods, as if this makes perfect sense. Something happened during those days that Kestrin was absent, when Alyrra gave up her post as goose girl and returned to the palace. Something that has changed the balance of power even just a little, in favor of the royal family.

"So, there's hope our line might yet persist," Garrin says dryly. "But only if we do not upset the Circle. Whether you truly believe the Circle is involved with these slavers or not, you *cannot* pursue this angle. Anything that could be construed as a direct attack on the Circle will destroy us."

Alyrra glances from the men to me, as if I might have some idea what to do, when it never even occurred to me the Circle might be the true power behind the throne.

"It doesn't mean you have to give up this work," Kestrin

offers. "It just means that we aren't in a position to challenge the Circle yet. We will get there."

Garrin snorts. "So you hope, cousin. Allow me to point out that none of the kings that have come before have managed to bring the Circle to heel."

"Even so, if the slavers are, in fact, stealing children from across our land, then we can work to stop them. But we must focus on them directly, and leave out the Circle."

"You can't leave out the Circle," Garrin observes. "You said yourself that we ignore kickbacks the Circles receive for services rendered. They're not going to be pleased when you declare war on the people who—if the Darkness is what you say, kelari—have been lining their pockets for decades."

"We are hardly fit rulers if we sell our people's children for our own security," Alyrra says. "If the Circle requires some replacement in income to satisfy them, then perhaps we can look to that in a way that doesn't risk our people."

Kestrin smiles. "Well said, veriana."

Garrin considers his cousin and then turns his gaze to Alyrra. "I am not convinced the problem of these snatchers is as wide as you believe, veria, but if you are both set on this, then let me serve as your shield. You are new here, and if you begin your tenure by undermining the alliances the Circle has established, they will do their best to remove you and Kestrin from power."

"What do you propose?" Alyrra asks.

"That I take on this effort. Your attendant can still report to you, but let me be the one to order any initiative against the slavers."

"Cousin, you are as vulnerable as we are," Kestrin argues. "Possibly more so."

Garrin shrugs, a gesture both rueful and resigned. "Exactly. So preserve yourselves, and let me worry about myself."

The conversation has shifted, and I know Garrin is speaking about something else now. Whatever danger the family faced, Garrin hasn't cleared it. I remember Zaria's words about a curse, and about the Fae mage being here to offer his aid. Even if a curse can't last generations by definition, there's some trouble here, and I would bet our horse farm there's magic at its root.

Garrin turns to me. "If you have another way to identify your slavers, kelari, another way to stop them, then we can take that approach."

I glance at Alyrra, and she dips her head, her expression grim. So I nod once to Garrin.

When I began this work, the snatchers seemed a ruthless and dangerous enemy. I've a feeling there's a great deal worse I have no idea about, and the Circle is just the tip of it.

CHAPTER

37

When I return to my room, I find a letter waiting from Ani: her first. It is short, slightly disjointed, and utterly heartbreaking.

I hope you are well, dear friend, she writes. *I hope you are finding out the things you intended to learn, though I realize now that there is little hope. Not for us, at least. Each day that passes, I feel like I lose a little more of my sister. I want to hold on to every memory of her. I don't remember what the last thing was that I said to Seri. I forgot what we did together the night before she disappeared, but Mama reminded me, and I'm holding on to that, but, Rae, she's fading. I'm afraid one day I'll forget what Seri looks like. I'm terrified I'll wake up one morning and won't think of her, won't miss her, because that's all I have left. I am trying to hold on to her, and it hurts so much, and I do not know what you are doing, but please, whatever it is you can do there, do it.*

I love you, my friend. Come home when you've done what you can. I know you can't fix or solve everything. I know you'll try for what you can do. I wish I could be there with you, doing something. Be safe and know I miss you.

I sit at my desk, the letter before me, and wish I could hug my friend, just sit with her and hold her through her grief. I know she has other friends, and loving parents, but I want to be there as well.

Because everything I've done and learned so far hasn't uncovered anything but a possible conspiracy the royals dare not touch. That may be a great deal to have learned, but it does the snatched children and their families little good.

I sit for a long time, stewing over the conversation between the royals and thinking about the archer whose journal I stole from the Black Scholar. The archer who betrayed her liege in order to save her people.

This is different, of course. It's not the king whose sacrifice is needed because he did some great wrong in the past. It's the Circle, and the wrong they have done is ongoing. Betraying them would potentially destroy the king and leave at least a faction of the mages still in power, if not all of them. It would put the people even more at their mercy, without the king there to buffer their decisions. Though he cannot know what they are doing. Can he?

No. If he knew, then Kestrin would surely have known, and my words this afternoon would not have shocked him. Nor would he have aided Alyrra in finding someone to help investigate the snatchers if he already knew of a possible connection.

I take a deep breath, exhale slowly. I am not giving up on the snatchers. I cannot bring back Seri, or undo Ani's grief, but I can fight with all I have to stop the snatchers themselves.

The fact that the mages are lending their aid to protect the snatchers means they must also be gaining something from the arrangement. If I can figure out that piece—especially if it is something more significant than gold or coin—I might be able to discover who is delivering it to them. And then I would have a better idea who the snatchers themselves are.

I look at Ani's letter, and know that I have an ally in almost anyone who has lost a family member to the snatchers. I might not know how to track the movement of resources, or what wealth the Circle is accumulating, but I know someone I can ask.

I leave my room, taking the back stairs down with just a cursory nod to Captain Matsin, who watches me pass through the guard room with lifted brows. By the time I reach the far side of the palace complex, my foot has begun to ache from keeping up such a brisk pace over the tiled floors.

I reach the bench-lined path across from the administrative buildings just as a group of workers step out.

Taking in the richness of my clothing, one of them says, "Apologies, veria. I'm afraid we're closed."

"I'm looking for Kelari Kirrana," I say, glancing past him in hopes of spotting her.

"Oh, Kirrana already left, veria," one of the girls says. "She's going home to stay with her parents for the festivities—we all have tomorrow off. But she might still be packing up. You could check the women's residence."

I ask directions, and a moment later set off for the residence, moving as fast as I can, hoping I don't end up with more blisters.

The building lies on the other side of the tax office, a two-story structure of adobe and plaster, just like home, if a great deal bigger. Its humble appearance is hidden behind the other buildings, making it invisible from the palace proper.

An elderly woman sits on a cushion in the large welcoming room, spindle in hand. She glances toward me inquiringly as I enter. "Can I help you, kelari?"

"I'm looking for Kirrana."

"I believe she's still upstairs. Follow the hall back, take the stairs up—you'll be all right on those? Good then; hers is the third door on the left."

I thank her and hurry on, reaching the top of the stairs just as Kirrana steps out of her room, a satchel over her shoulder.

She looks at me in surprise. "Rae! Are you coming to see me?"

"Yes. Is there somewhere we could chat for a few minutes?"

"Of course. Come in," she says, and ushers me into her room.

It's a small space, and clearly shared. Her side has only two cushions set out, a stack of blankets, a midsized trunk for belongings, and a wardrobe. No doubt her sleeping mat is rolled up within it, along with the rest of her belongings. The other side of the room is its opposite in every way, the sleeping mat out and only barely visible beneath a tangle of blankets, clothes spewing from the open wardrobe, and the floor littered with bottles and containers of what can only be makeup.

Kirrana offers me a cushion. "What did you want to talk about?"

Hidden away in the women's residence with the door closed, I feel as safe talking to Kirrana as I did in the princess's rooms, warded from listening ears. "Do you remember our conversation about the snatchers?"

She stills, focusing on me. "Yes."

"Can you swear to me you won't speak of this to anyone?"

"I swear it."

"All right. I've found out that the children who are snatched are transported by boat downriver. It's possible they're also taken by other routes, but of a half dozen children who were snatched, five reported boats."

"You think these children are being taken out of the country, or just taken downriver?" Kirrana asks. "I assume out, but . . ."

"Out of the country," I agree. "Too many have been lost for them to all be here. My contact in the city thinks so as well." It's so little, without the connection to the Circle. I don't dare mention that to Kirrana, not after promising Alyrra my discretion. This one detail of how the boys were transported hardly seems enough to launch an investigation from. It is hope alone that has brought me here.

Kirrana nods slowly. "That means the snatchers are leaving through Lirelei . . . and probably coming back in that way as well. In any transaction, something is always received for something given. They'll be bringing whatever it is they are trading for the children as they come in."

"Can that—would that be reflected in their taxes?"

Kirrana twists her mouth to the side, thinking, and then says, "I doubt there's a trail through any tax filings. We're talking about the black market. For that, you have to look for anomalies. Things coming into the country that we're not sending out exports to equal."

"So how do I search for that?" I ask, hope making my words come a little too fast. *Anomalies* has the sound of something that can be traced.

Kirrana grins. "First, I'm sending a page to my family to tell them I'm coming tomorrow. Then I'm collaring a friend who works in the administrative archives who can lend me her key. And *then* I'll show you how to search the reports from the port wardens in Lirelei, and we'll look for anomalies."

"You're sure you want to do this?" I ask as she hops to her feet. "If anyone discovers what you're actually researching, it will put you at risk."

"I know. But it still needs to be done, and I'm not sending you off to muddle through this on your own. I'll be right back."

Kirrana, as it turns out, makes a habit of doing people good turns, and so the particular friend in question only asks her to be sure to put back whatever she's researching when she's done and lock up behind herself.

We make our way to the administrative archives, a building I didn't know existed till this moment. It is lit by luminae lamps, which is stunning until you consider that the building is *filled* with paper and would go up like a bonfire if real lamps were used and a stray spark fell in the wrong place.

We pass room after room of shelves, and then tour a number of additional rooms, Kirrana murmuring softly to herself as she inspects the ledgers and bound stacks of papers carefully stored on the shelves.

"Here," she says finally, at a door with a plaque that reads, quite helpfully, "Lirelei, Five-Year Port Records."

I turn slowly, considering the floor-to-ceiling shelves filled with records, from incident reports to ledgers containing logs of every ship that docked or weighed anchor there. "That's . . . a lot of information."

Kirrana grins. "We'll start with the incident reports. You take this year's, I'll take last's. We're looking for something showing up that shouldn't have—something valuable. Here."

She hands me a stack of papers bound together between two thin boards—a precursor to the actual bound set of papers with a proper cover that she lifts down for herself. We settle ourselves at a table in the larger central workspace, and start reading.

There are incidents of cargo being accidentally destroyed, a ship piloted by a drunken captain that rammed into one of the docks, and various other occurrences. A great deal of damaged property, but not much else.

"What would constitute an anomaly?" I ask as I turn another page to find a report of a ship that accidentally ran aground a league up the coast and required a rescue ship to unload its cargo before its hull could be repaired.

"We're looking for an import that was unexpectedly found and should have been declared. Something the snatchers were conveying to pay for the children. Or, failing that, perhaps a boat that was transporting children as part of their cargo."

"Wouldn't we have heard about that?"

"You're right. An error that egregious would have been covered up very quickly. So yes, something smaller than that."

"Right," I say, but the current report about a herd of goats wreaking havoc on the docks and butting sailors into the waters makes me wonder if even that is a realistic goal.

An hour later, I've found nothing. Kirrana is still working on her file, and sends me to the room to return my papers, bound back up again in order, and pull the reports for two years ago.

Around midnight, I lay my head on the table beside my file. "I had no idea so many things could go wrong at a port."

Kirrana laughs and turns a page. She's now five years back, and we're reaching the end of what's stored here. Older files get moved to a storage facility somewhere off site, and I don't think anyone would lend us that key, no questions asked.

"Amraeya."

"Mmm?" I tilt my head slightly, my cheek still pressed against the tabletop.

"Look at this."

I straighten and go to her side to see the report she's holding. It details a shipment that had been processed, and how the port warden stepped into the captain's room at the end and noticed a slight gap in the planks composing the back wall of the room. Upon investigating, he located a small compartment containing a box with two large gemstones. The captain claimed they were not meant for import, and were being held in trust. The warden confiscated them for processing and filed the report.

"Gemstones," I whisper. I can hear Kestrin saying quietly, *grant him a pair of amulets.* Small gems are easily come by, but large gemstones? Those are prized by the Circle. They would give a great deal for a steady supply of amulets, especially given that an amulet, once drained, cannot be reused. Arguably, they *need* those gemstones in order to maintain their power.

"I get the feeling this makes a lot of sense to you," Kirrana says. "Something you're not telling me?"

I nod. "Yes. I can't tell you everything, but the gemstones would make particularly good sense."

"All right," Kirrana says. She whips out a set of wax tablets she had brought with her from her room, opens them up, and carves the date of the report into the wax with her stylus, alongside the captain's name and the ship's name. I've used wax tablets before as well—they are much more economical—it's just jarring to see them here, alongside the veritable mountain of papers.

"Now, if you were a snatcher and your payment was intercepted, what would you do?"

I shrug. "Make sure it didn't happen again?"

"Right. I'm just about at the end of this file. Did you read any reports in the next one with any of these names? The warden, perhaps? Or the captain?"

I shake my head.

Kirrana considers this. "Nothing violent happened on the job, then. Well, let's pull the wage reports and see how long the warden stayed on."

We tromp back to the same room and this time, Kirrana hands me another stack of bound papers: monthly reports on wages paid to all the port wardens of Lirelei.

I page quickly through the year, noting the name of the warden in question in each month before moving on to the next month. There he is again, the month of the incident report. But he isn't listed at all the following month. Instead, there's a note that a junior warden had been elevated to take his place due to his unexpected passing. I stare at the page for a long moment, but there's nothing else here. No mention of cause of death, or possible foul play, or anything.

"He's dead," I say.

Kirrana nods. "That would suggest that what happened could have been related to the snatchers."

"It could just be a coincidence," I argue, not quite believing myself.

"Right. But look here," she says, and passes me the ledger recording incoming shipments. "The ship had a new captain the next time it came in."

A shiver runs through me as I stare at the ship name, and beside it, a new name. Beneath that is a seal stamped in black ink, followed by the name of the owners of the ship. "Berenworth Trading Company. Who are they?"

Kirrana looks at me disbelievingly. "You haven't heard of them? They're huge in the import/export business."

"I think our town is too small for them." All our imports are brought by wagon, and our exports are primarily horses.

She nods. "Makes sense. My father's a merchant. He doesn't like to do business with them. Says once folks start, it's hard to back out. That's not completely unusual," she adds, at my look. "But it fits, doesn't it?"

I rub my hands over my face. "How do we prove anything? *Can* we prove anything?"

Kirrana sits a long moment, staring at the ledgers set out before us. "In taxes, one coincidence is just that: a coincidence. But when you start noticing a pattern of anomalies, of coincidences, that's when you know something's going on. Maybe this particular find of ours doesn't have anything to do with the snatchers, but something surely happened. Now we have to investigate it."

"How? If it isn't a coincidence, and Berenworth is involved

with the snatchers, it could be dangerous."

Kirrana grins. "I'm a paper kind of girl. I won't be asking anyone any questions. And I think we've done enough tonight. I'll see what more I can learn about Berenworth tomorrow."

Tomorrow? "But what about your family? Aren't you supposed to visit them?"

"I will—during the day. I'll just come back in the evening and see what else I can find."

That's right, she has the day off for the wedding. Which I decidedly don't. "I don't think I can come then."

"You do what you have to. I think we've found all the big breaks we're going to. From now, it's going to be slow work trying to uncover whatever other evidence there is." Kirrana smiles, then yawns. "Starting with taxes," she adds when she can speak again.

"I thought taxes wouldn't show us anything."

"They might not. But now that I have an idea of who to focus on, there might be some interesting details to consider. We should also go over all the records of their shipments. But not tonight."

"Definitely not tonight," I agree. It's getting harder and harder to keep my eyes open. "You'll be safe? No one can know what you're doing."

"Safe and careful," she assures me. "Let's put these away and both of us get to bed."

I can't argue with that, and a few minutes later I am on my way back to the royal wing.

My legs are tired, my turned foot aching, by the time I reach the top of the back stairway and find Captain Matsin leaning against the table, waiting. The remaining guards are arrayed about him in their usual activities—some sitting at the table, one at a bench polishing his sword. It's Matsin's face, hard and cold, that brings me up short.

"Kelari."

"Captain," I say, stepping through the threshold.

"I'll walk you," he says, and falls into step with me, his hands clasped behind his back. It's a conscious pose, one that says: I am not reaching for you, do you see? But I am certainly coming with you.

Out in the hallway, he says quietly, "I was ten minutes away from alerting the princess to your absence."

"What?"

"You disappeared, kelari. Again."

My jaw tightens. How much does he know about the Black Scholar? The princess must have told him something. I'm not sure how else he would have known. Still: "I am not missing now, Captain."

"You left before dinner without a word to anyone, and don't return until past midnight. How are we to know you're safe?"

"It's not your concern."

He comes to a stop before the door to the attendants' suite, and for a half breath I think he's going to reach for it, hold it closed. But he just looks at it, then raises his gaze to me. "If you are going somewhere at night, please make sure at least another attendant knows. If you need to leave the palace, take someone with you."

It's the sort of advice my mother would give me, which is just infuriating. Because it's good advice. Further, I really don't want to worry the princess. Refusing to be sensible will probably result in Matsin reporting my comments to the princess. I sigh. "I'll be sure to inform someone in future."

He dips me a bow and steps back. "Thank you."

I nod, and head through the doorway. I really only want to go to sleep. But as I reach the common room, a figure straightens up on the couches. It's a boy, a page. The same one who explained what a friend of a friend was to me a few nights ago.

"Kelari," he says, and shoves himself to his feet. He holds out an envelope. "I'm to carry back your answer."

"I'm sorry for your wait," I say as I open the envelope. The boy grimaces but doesn't respond. For all I know, he could have been waiting hours. I scan the note within quickly. It says nothing more than to meet an hour before dawn at a particular building out past the women's residence. It is signed "Bren."

I stare at the signature long enough that the boy says, "Well?"

I look up blankly. I don't want to see Bren again. Perhaps that's just the coward in me, because I know I need to apologize and I don't know how. But he wouldn't arrange to meet me without good reason; avoiding him isn't an option. I take a shaky breath. "My answer is yes."

The boy bows and departs, leaving me alone with Bren's note and a tangle of shame and anxiety I want nothing more than to forget.

CHAPTER

38

I surface to the stillest part of the night, glad that I'd drunk two extra glasses of water to make sure I'd wake. Any later, and I might miss Bren altogether.

I collect my skirt from the chair by my bed, pulling it up over my sleep pants. My nightshirt is long enough to pass as a tunic; I have no wish to attempt to get it up over my head one-handed just now. Instead, I drape a nice shawl over it, strap on my bone knife in its sheath—because that only seems wise—and head out.

The guard room quads eye me with interest but allow me to pass without question. Captain Matsin appears to be off duty, for which I give a silent moment of thanks. I have, as promised, left a short note for Mina on my desk. Should something go wrong, she'll spot it easily. Hopefully, though, I'll get back in plenty of time to remove it before she wakes.

Out past the women's residence I pause, shrugging deeper into my shawl. It's dark here, and my instincts say not to wander farther into the shadows. I probably shouldn't be out here at all, a woman going to meet a man alone in the dark of the night. It reeks of impropriety. But that's not really how things stand. As long as no one takes note, and I don't run into trouble, it should be fine. So I stay near the main path and scan the darkness for Bren.

"Rae."

I pivot, peering into the dark. There's a man-shaped shadow leaning against the far building. He shifts forward and a fall of moonlight brings into sharp relief the contours of his face, the inky blackness of his hair.

"Bren," I whisper.

He turns, a liquid darkness in the gray of the night, and moves silently down the side path. I follow after him, settling my shawl over my shoulders more firmly as I go, as if the chill I feel has anything to do with the cool spring night. I am seeing more of Bren in his element now, somehow having infiltrated the palace walls. And while he hasn't entered the palace proper, his ability to come this far tells me that the Scholar might do so as well, or send his men.

"Over here." Bren's voice, pitched low, only just reaches me through the night air. I follow the sound of it to an open-air stairway. He leads me up and up, patient with my slow progress, and then along a hallway to a second, smaller service stair up to the roof.

In the moonlight, all I can make out of our surroundings are the small platform we've come out on, cluttered with broken furniture, and across from us, the palace proper with its own roofs, most rising higher but some below us, spreading out in a multilayered weaving of floors and courtyards.

Bren hops up onto the shingles that spread out past the platform and holds out a hand to me. At least the roof he stands on is relatively flat and wide. Even if I trip, I'm not likely to come to any harm before I manage to catch myself. Still, I slide my feet out of my slippers before clambering up, knowing I'll have a better grip barefoot.

"Where are we going?"

"We're almost there. Don't stop now."

His hand still waits for me. I grimace and take it, knowing I'll likely need the help to keep my balance. He laces his fingers between mine, leading me along the roof to where it butts up against an adjacent building and then curls around the corner of it and under an overhanging balcony, protecting us from sight.

I hadn't realized how intimate a handhold can be. Here, with the sky stretching above us, and the roofs wide and silent around us, and Bren's hand warm around mine, it feels as though we are alone together while the whole world sleeps. That his hand is there when I inevitably wobble only makes the moment more real.

I'm almost grateful when we reach our destination. Bren releases me to remove a small pack from beneath his cloak. He spreads a thin blanket on the tiles where we stand, hidden from view by the slightly higher roof running beside it, and gestures grandly. "Won't you sit, veriana?"

"I'm not a lady. Remember that whole country thing?" I say, easing myself down onto the blanket. I rearrange my skirts over my feet. I know he saw my foot that night after I escaped Bardok, when I fell out of bed and he helped me back in, but it's easier to cover it. Even if my skirts still lie flat over one foot and curve over the bump of the other.

"True enough." He takes out a packet and passes me something. I accept it without thinking, then stare in confusion at what I hold: flaky, light dough baked to perfection, stuffed no doubt with spiced chicken. I sniff it. Definitely chicken.

"What is this?" I ask.

"A chicken tasty."

"I mean all of this." I gesture with the tasty to the blanket beneath us, the rooftop with its hidden spot.

"A trysting place."

"What?"

Bren's shoulders shake. "Well-known among the servants, and therefore not policed by the guards and safe for us to use. But this isn't a tryst."

"I should *hope not.*"

He laughs out loud at that.

I take a calming breath. I don't know why his words have discombobulated me. "What is this really, Bren?"

A pause, and he says lightly, "A peace offering. For the country girl who knows how to punch."

I feel myself flushing and am grateful for the dark. "Why?"

He doesn't need to bring me a peace offering. If anyone should apologize, it should be me. And why would he care, anyway? I wasn't supposed to see him again.

Bren looks down at his chicken tasty. "You're as prickly as a burr," he says ruefully.

It isn't an answer, and he knows it. Even if it's true.

Finally, he mutters, "I've done enough things wrong that I know when I need to set things right, and I know that if I don't do it sooner, later most likely won't come. So, peace offering."

"Oh." I look down at my own tasty, thinking of his life. How each day is uncertain as the last, how he's had to fight to survive in ways I can't imagine. How he's likely watched friends die, and lived with regrets he can't put to rest. That he doesn't want me to be one of those regrets leaves me strangely unable to answer him.

"Oh," he agrees, his voice laughing at me. He takes a bite of his tasty, and I make myself follow suit. It's delicious, the bread flaky and tasting of butter, the chicken bursting with spices and tender enough to nearly melt on my tongue.

"These," I say, "are incredible. Peace offering accepted."

"They're the best in the city," Bren agrees. He produces a flask and two small cups, offering one to me. It's mint tea, still hot.

I take it, cradling the warmth of the cup in my hand.

"Also . . . ," he says, and looks at me, mischief in his eyes.

"Yes?" I ask warily.

"What's that on your finger?"

I blink, looking down, and find my grandmother's ring glinting back at me from my pinky. I set the tea down and touch it disbelievingly. "How did you—?"

Bren chuckles. "Thief, remember?"

I look up at him. "I thought thieves didn't un-thieve things."

"Let's say that being taken hostage and nearly killed because you were in my company probably entitles you to another punch or two. I figured returning the ring might save my face."

"I shouldn't have punched you," I say, my cheeks burning.

Bren seems to have a unique ability to put me in a constant state of deep mortification. "You did get me out alive. I just—" Just what? Couldn't stand his laughing at me when I've been laughed at by others all my life? Why should it have mattered so much? "I'm sorry," I whisper. As apologies go, it has nothing on Bren's returned-ring, chicken-tasty, predawn-picnic extravaganza.

"It's fine, Rae. I believe Artemian has wanted to punch me for quite a while. He rather enjoyed watching you do it. Unfortunately for him, no one believes his story, at least not in my hearing."

I scrub the smile from my lips, because I can't just laugh this off. "Bren. Would it have been all right if I angered you and you punched me instead?"

"No." His voice is suddenly hard, brooking no argument.

"Then why is it fine if I punch you?"

He looks at me, and the silence spreads out between us until I feel like I'm drowning.

"You see," I say, my voice hoarse in my throat.

"No," he says again. "Rae, there are certainly times when a woman punching a man is an irredeemable act of violence. When she is stronger, or more vicious, and she uses her actions to abuse him. But that wasn't what happened."

"I *wanted* to hurt you." There it is, the truth I can't hide from.

Bren rubs a hand over his hair, grasping the back of his head for a moment, and then says, "I like to push people. I especially like to push you, Rae. Because you're clever and you push back. And I was glad to see you that morning, looking your usual prickly self, and so I pushed you more than I should have. Artemian told me you wept half the way back to the palace."

I look away, toward a dawn that seems like it will never arrive. Is this why Bren came? Because he found out how I fell apart? "He shouldn't have told you that." My voice is small, shaky.

"In a fight between you and me," Bren says with inexorable calm, "I would always win. We both know that. So your hitting me—it's a sign of trust, in its way, that you could lash out and know that I wouldn't hurt you back. It wasn't abuse."

"You're right. I knew you wouldn't hurt me back." It hadn't even occurred to me. "That doesn't change the fact that I wanted to hurt you."

"And you'd do it again?"

"*No.*"

"Then it is not all that you are, and it doesn't have to define you. It's something you did, which you regret. It is not actually *you*."

I look at him, his words clicking together in my mind: that this is the difference between me and the foreign prince, for his is a practiced violence, and mine was a single act, regretted. That I am not the same as him, for all that I was willing to let my anger ride me as it does him. I am and can and *will* be different; I do not have to let this break me. I nod, a jerky, stiff motion. It is all I can manage.

Bren exhales softly. He leans forward, reaching across the blanket to pick up my half-eaten chicken tasty and offer it to me. "Here. Please eat."

I take it, looking down at it, then back up at him. It is a peace offering in every sense, and I want this so much, the forgiveness, the calm, the quiet between us. "Thank you."

He nods and leans back against the wall, his eyes turning to the brightening horizon. With one leg stretched out, the other bent at the knee and his arm draped over it, he seems completely at rest. Always before, there was a readiness to his stance; now, even though he likely could leap to his feet if need be, he seems at ease.

I eat slowly, sip my mint tea as the details of the night world slowly gain clarity. It's a gentle quiet that surrounds us, the world coming awake with the sounds of birdsong and city bustle, still somewhat distant from the palace. There's something wonderful in the simplicity of the moment. I wish I could hold on to it forever.

Eventually, though, the dawn grows brighter and the details of the world come into focus. "How are the boys?" I ask softly. "Are they all on their way home now?"

He nods, his body shifting into that loose readiness I've come to recognize. "All but one, the eldest. He says he's an orphan and won't go to what family he has left. They were particularly unkind, it seems."

"Then . . . what will he do?"

Bren shrugs casually. "I've found him a place. He'll be fine."

That does not sound half as comforting as Bren may want me to think. "What sort of place?" I ask suspiciously.

"He'll be a servant, that's all. What did you think?"

"A servant like the page who works here?" I ask. "You mean he's one of Red Hawk's boys now?"

"And if he is?" Bren demands. "He's safe, and fed, and free to leave. Can you do better?"

I grimace. I can't, especially not now that he's already in Red Hawk's fold—having Melly hire him would only put my cousins at risk. "Being allied with thieves is hardly safe," I say finally.

"It's the best I could manage," Bren says.

I look away. He's a thief; why would I expect him to keep this boy from the life he himself has chosen? I can't, and it's my own fault for not questioning him more thoroughly to begin with. I clear my throat. "You said you needed to talk to me about something."

A pause and then Bren says, "What are the princess's plans for handling what you've learned?"

"She has involved Zayyid Kestrin and Verin Garrin. They're unsure about the Circle's involvement in the Darkness."

"They are involved though, aren't they?"

"It's hard to say." I let out a slow breath. I can't tell Bren everything, even if he knows most of it.

"Because you need a mage to tell you, and they're all part of the Circle." Bren smirks. "Also, because the royals want to keep the Circle happy."

I glance askance at him.

"Politics," Bren says with a hint of contempt.

He doesn't know the half of it. "I was able to use the stories the boys told us and the possible connection to the Circle to do some research," I tell him, and explain what Kirrana and I learned. "It's not evidence of anything, really," I admit. "Just an indication that something is going on that needs to be investigated further. Have you heard of Berenworth before?"

"They've an office on the east side, run a lot of ships down to Lirelei, and upriver as well. That's all I really know. Are they your only lead?"

"So far. I'm not sure what else we'll be able to learn. It's possible Berenworth is not actually involved. We don't yet have proof."

"I see," Bren says, his gaze moving to the horizon. Out over the rooftops and past the line of the palace wall, the sky has begun to lighten, from darkest blue to gray-blue, the distant stars losing their brightness. "The princess is keeping you out of the city from now on, though, correct?"

"She'll send Sage to Artemian if we need to contact you."

Bren grunts and pushes himself to his feet. "Good. If you need to get in touch with me more directly, use the page I've been sending you. Now come; it's getting close to sunrise. We need to get you back."

I rise, brushing out my skirts as he packs up the evidence of our picnic. He escorts me back to the service stairs, and then continues on down the hall just a step ahead. I follow him down the second set of stairs, pause on the last step.

"There's something else," I say.

Bren turns, brows lifted. When I don't go on, he takes a step back to lean against the wall, arms crossed, as if to assure me I have all the time I need.

"I accidentally took one of the Black Scholar's books," I admit. "I'm not sure if he'll notice, but there probably isn't a way to return it, is there?"

"You *what*?" Bren breathes.

"It was an old journal he had in his library," I say, trying to sound casual, reasonable, as if I've done nothing wrong. "I was reading it, and I stuck it in my pocket without thinking, and I ended up taking it with me."

"The journal," Bren says.

Of course he would have seen it among my belongings when I'd stayed in his safe house. After a moment he lets out a low chuckle. My eyes dart to him, and I'm relieved to see he truly is amused—because how bad can it be if he's laughing?

"Stealing from a thief lord, Rae. I should be recruiting you instead of trying to get you off the streets. If for no other reason than to see what you do next."

"I didn't *mean* to steal it," I fret.

"No," Bren agrees. He rubs his mouth. "We'll have to hope he doesn't realize the book is gone until you've returned to your family. How much longer are you planning to stay here?"

"Through the summer."

Bren looks at me as if I've lost all reason.

"My cousin invited me!" I say defensively.

"Try not to leave the palace, ever. He'll be looking for you anyway; if he realizes you stole something from him in addition to humiliating him in front of Bardok, he will be looking for you with everything he has."

"I know," I admit. "Do you think it's possible the Black Scholar—or Bardok—is involved with the snatchers?"

"It seems unlikely."

"Artemian said the Scholar's been gaining in power."

"He has, but it's more likely to do with other things than with this."

"Why?"

"Thieves' honor," Bren says slowly. "That would be encroaching on others' territory, at a minimum."

What he doesn't say is "wrong." I shake my head. "Do they use networks of street children too? Would they even care if the street children in their territories disappeared?"

Bren shakes his head. "That's mostly Red Hawk."

"So how do we find who's working on the streets? Even if Berenworth—or some other organization—is transporting the children, they might not be the ones doing the actual snatching."

"I already told you," Bren says quietly. "Get a quad and catch someone."

It's a dead end for inquiry, in other words. At least for me.

"Any other questions?" Bren asks. "I feel like you must have a dozen more you're not asking."

"You want them all?" I ask, irrationally irritated. "Fine. Why did the Black Scholar let you go but keep me?"

"I'm Red Hawk's right-hand man. I'm a little too dangerous to take hostage unless he wants a bloodbath on the streets. Or his doorstep. That ransom was really for me, not you."

Red Hawk's right-hand man. I exhale softly. It does make sense, the danger of reprisal. The Scholar letting him go—all the power Bren clearly has—doesn't have to mean that he is secretly Red Hawk. It wouldn't make sense for a thief lord to spend so much time on me anyhow, taking me about the city and meeting me on rooftops. Bren is just what he's said, even if he hasn't given me his name. There's a relief in that.

He straightens from the wall and lifts something up over his head. "It's time to go. Take this, will you?"

I reach out my hand even as I ask, "What?"

His fingers close around mine, pressing a warm metal disk into my palm. "Wear it until you leave the city."

"What is it?"

"Protection, or an attempt at it."

I glance down at my palm to find I hold a thin gold pendant, a circle encompassing a cutout of a hawk in flight. It hangs from a worn leather cord. "This is yours?" I ask, that uncertainty creeping in again.

"It's his sign, Rae. Keep it on you always."

I nod.

With a faint smile that seems as regretful as it is amused, Bren dips his head to me and slips away, disappearing down the paths in a matter of moments.

CHAPTER
39

The wedding procession goes smoothly that afternoon, almost unbelievably so. By midmorning—after I've managed a short but direly needed nap—half the noblewomen of the palace depart along with the princess's party in a mass exodus to a great tent village that has sprung up past the city gates. Traditionally, the groom's party comes to fetch the bride from her home. In this case, a symbolic procession from the lands to the west of the city has been planned.

We spend the day with the princess, resting, eating, and singing celebratory songs. In the afternoon, we move outside to watch a horse race and I very nearly embarrass myself by cheering aloud when the little mare I'm rooting for noses ahead at the last moment. Then we retire to the tents again to relax. The men arrive in the early evening, bringing with them the great bridal amaria. The wooden palanquin is swathed in silks, the supports of the arched roof carved and overlaid with gold, and the inside appointed with velvet. It is carried by no fewer than twenty men, ten to a side, with an equal number who walk to either side to relieve the bearers as needed.

Alyrra ascends to sit wide-eyed and bright-cheeked, looking younger than I've ever seen her. Or perhaps just happier. Kestrin calls out to her from his mount on a richly caparisoned white horse, and she blushes and dips her head to him. I feel a faint twinge of envy, watching how their eyes meet, the pleasure in Kestrin's face, and the shy sort of joy radiating from Alyrra.

No, I tell myself fiercely. I am happy for them, and that's all there is to it. What may come to me—or not—is irrelevant.

With a high fluting note and a resonating *boom* of the drums, the procession starts forward: first a set of guards, then the musicians, then Kestrin and the three other men from either family on their horses, and then the amaria carrying Alyrra. Behind her come all the rest of us, women first and then the men. Most of us walk, though a few of the men ride, and a few of the women are borne along on litters. I spot Havila, riding in a smaller though indisputably elegant litter carried by two pairs of men, her cane laid across her knees.

Melly slips through the throngs and joins me as we reach the city gates. She looks tired, her skin beneath her makeup slightly peaked. She slips her arm through mine, shakes her head at my questions, and keeps pace with me as I slowly but inevitably fall toward the back of the procession. At least I manage to keep up with the last of the women, and don't suffer the embarrassment of being overtaken by the men.

The drumbeats resonate through the streets and the very walls of the surrounding buildings. The edges of West Road are packed with spectators, as are all the cross streets, every window and rooftop, and every person in the gathered throng sways to the sound of the drums, singing together. This song has few words; it is mostly a call, one that brings each person to the tips of their toes, brings them closer to those beside them. It is as deep as our bones and as wide as the land upon which we stand.

At last we arrive at the palace, my turned foot aching with the promise of new blisters. My slippers may be well enough made this time, but such a long walk in new shoes is never a good idea. The royal party pauses before the doors, turning so that all gathered in the plaza can see them. Then the king raises his hand, and a breathtaking display of fireworks breaks into the evening sky, bursts of white and red and orange and green. I've never seen even a single firework before, and find myself awestruck by both the beauty of these streaks of fire painted across the sky and the resounding explosions as each new firework bursts forth.

I would have stood and gawked the whole time, but Melly points out this is the perfect time to catch up to the princess, and so we gently nudge our way through the crowd toward the amaria.

After the last of the fireworks, the procession floods into the great courtyard and Alyrra descends from her amaria to her new home. I manage to rejoin my fellow attendants as they converge to walk behind her, as Kestrin escorts her into the great receiving hall. And the wedding is over—all but the feasting.

Once Alyrra has been settled on her sofa on the dais alongside Kestrin, we make way for the nobles lining up to approach and congratulate the couple. I slip away from my fellow attendants to rejoin Melly, who is now about a third of the way down the line.

"Thanks for staying with me," I tell her.

She shakes her head. "I was glad for the company. Even if it was too loud to speak."

I smile, but I feel a rush of guilt. The whole point of my invitation to come here was to keep Melly company, and I've done everything but that. And she's still looking out for me. "I'm sorry I haven't been able to spend more time with you."

"Don't be absurd. It's good to see you doing something new and different, Rae. Something you wouldn't have imagined back home."

Being taken hostage by a thief lord certainly qualifies. "You're looking a little pale," I say just as Filadon joins us.

He grimaces and speaks right over Melly's assurance that she's fine. "*That* is because she insisted on acting as if everything were normal."

"I'll rest when I'm ready," Melly says archly.

I glance from one to the other, and realize what they aren't saying. "Morning sickness?"

Melly shoots Filadon a displeased look. "Just a little nausea and tiredness, Rae. Nothing to worry about."

I really have done a terrible job looking out for Melly. "Why didn't you tell me? You shouldn't have walked! You could have met the princess just as well right here, with the other half of the court."

"I wanted to walk with you," Melly says gently. "And I'll go up and rest once I've given them my greetings."

She didn't want me to fall behind alone, as she knew I probably would. I feel my cheeks burning and look away. "Have you tried ginger tea for the nausea? Or even just extra ginger in your food?"

"No."

"Mama always recommends it. And walking, but I think you've done enough of that."

Melly laughs as she turns to Filadon. "See, my love? It's perfectly normal to feel like this. You worry too much."

"Yes, but if you had felt weak out there—"

"Which I haven't yet, not once," Melly says bluntly. "And *if* I had, then Rae would have gotten me help."

I'm not sure how, but I certainly would have.

"Ah, there's the foreign prince," Melly says in a complete change of topic.

I turn my gaze to watch as he descends from the dais, having given his own words of congratulations. Today, he wears several thick golden chains over a close-fitting velvet jacket, cream sleeves puffing out from the shoulders, and his legs encased in the usual shockingly tight fabric that passes as pants among his people. Does he think he must prove his royalty by flaunting his gold? It seems in poor taste, especially in comparison to the much more muted display of wealth by our king and prince.

"Do you think we're free of trouble from him now?" Melly asks as he moves across the room, coming to a stop beside a red-haired man. Daerilin, the impostor's father.

Filadon sighs. "I'd like to think so, but I don't trust him. And that Daerilin has been keeping far too low a profile."

"What could they do?" I ask, looking from the two men to Filadon. His brow is lined with concern. Isn't it a good thing if Daerilin has stepped back?

"I don't know. That's the trouble."

From what I've seen of the prince, anything he planned would be personal and violent. I look up to where a noblewoman bends over to embrace Alyrra.

"There are still soldiers posted throughout the royal wing, right?" I ask.

Filadon pats my arm. "There are. They won't reach her alone, Rae. It will be all right."

If he believed that, he wouldn't have looked so worried. And the prince didn't reach her alone last time either; not really.

"You see," Melly says lightly, "there's more than enough to concern us without bringing in how much ginger I've eaten today."

"We are eating ginger for every meal," Filadon says solemnly. "Starting with breakfast."

"I'm the one in charge of the menu, so you had better ask nicely," Melly says with a grin, and tugs me another step forward in the line. "Although I suppose a little ginger might be called for."

"A little," Filadon echoes, shaking his head. "I shall have it grated into your oatmeal if you don't watch out."

Melly just laughs.

CHAPTER

40

I wake up late the next morning, having stayed at the banquet until the princess was ready to retire. Along with a few chosen elder noblewomen, including the foreign queen, we escorted Alyrra to her new rooms at the end of the evening. The suite, located right across the hall from her old one, is not all that different but for the bedchamber—a shared room between Kestrin's suite and Alyrra's new one. It was enough to bring another blush to Alyrra's face.

I smile at the memory as I slowly work through a few morning stretches, grateful that I didn't wake with foot cramps. I do have a new crop of blisters, though. It's almost enough to make a girl give up attending once and for all. I shake my head at myself and change quietly, slipping out the door a few minutes later in search of breakfast.

Like Mina, it seems the other attendants are all still abed. I make a small pot of mint tea and sit down with a plate of cheese and bread, a few black olives on the side. There, on the table, are three letters that must have been delivered this morning. The top two are for Jasmine and Zaria respectively; the third is for me.

I open it up with some curiosity, as I don't recognize the hand that addressed it, and scan the note.

> *Dear Rae,*
>
> *I have been thinking about our conversation, and have done some more reading, and have thoughts and possibilities to discuss. If you are free at all today, come meet me where we last saw each other. I have today off as well and we can chat easily.*
>
> *Your friend,*
>
> *Kirrana*

I brighten up at once. It doesn't take me long to get ready to go—a quick, careful bandaging of my foot to protect the blisters, an outfit from home that won't stand out on that side of the palace complex, my hair braided down my back, and I'm on my way.

I knock at the closed door of the administrative archive. Sure enough, Kirrana's voice calls through to me, and a moment later I'm ushered in.

Kirrana is as cheerful as ever, though her eye is faintly shadowed, as is the skin beneath her left eye patch.

"Tell me you haven't been here all night," I demand.

She laughs. "Not at all. I was at the tax office last night, and came back here again this morning. There's no need to stare! I love challenges and riddles, and this is both. And . . . well, you know why I care. I'm surprised you made it here at all this morning, though."

"The princess will spend the day with her husband and his family," I explain. "She won't need us till dinner."

"That's good. I have to say, I was relieved to know your family is staying in the palace, after the news this morning."

"What news?" I follow Kirrana over to her worktable. It's covered with stacks of ledgers and log books.

"It hasn't spread yet to the royal wing, then? The king must have heard, at least."

"Heard *what?*"

Kirrana laughs. "Yesterday evening during the wedding procession at least a half dozen noble households on the north side were all robbed. Probably more."

I stop short, recalling Bren joking about his plans for the wedding the first time we met—his words had been perfectly honest. My hand creeps to the pendant hidden beneath my tunic. I accepted it as a protection, but in anyone else's eyes it will mean I've aligned myself with Red Hawk, that I support his actions, accept them. Maybe I do, partly—but not completely.

"Don't worry," Kirrana says, misreading my stillness. "No one was hurt. They took a great deal of jewelry, and quite a bit of food too."

"Food," I repeat, bewildered. Bren hadn't struck me as hungry, and the house I'd sheltered in had been well-appointed.

"From the sound of it, bags of grains and lentils and beans. Anything dry that could be stored."

I frown, eyes narrowed. "Surely the nobles didn't report all that? Would they even have noticed?"

Kirrana snorts. "I doubt it. But we get the news from the servants and pages passing through, and when I stepped out to get breakfast from the dining hall, that was all the talk."

"But why food?"

"Because people get hungry," Kirrana says, as if it were the most obvious thing. And perhaps it is. Red Hawk keeps a network of street children, and the ones I've seen are all on the scrawny side. Paying them in coin might be a great deal more trouble than paying them in grain; it saves them having to answer where their wealth came from.

"What is it?" Kirrana asks.

I shake my head. "I know people get hungry. It's just, back home, everyone takes care of each other. If one family has a bad harvest, or loses too much livestock, we all help out. I knew the city is different, I just . . ." I can't comprehend a community that allows their own to go hungry. And I don't want to see Red Hawk's thievery as partly a good thing.

"There's a lot of need here," Kirrana says. "And neighbors care, but if the whole neighborhood is hungry, you can only do so much."

She takes a seat at the table and gestures for me to do the same. "Anyway, I'm more concerned with this other kind of thief."

I sit down, relieved to rest both the topic and my foot. "I understand you have 'thoughts and possibilities' to discuss."

Kirrana grins, the corner of her eye crinkling. "That I do."

As it turns out, Berenworth Trading Company established an office in Menaiya some thirty-five years ago, filing a very modest tax report in their first year. They've been growing their presence steadily since then. "That aligns nicely with the growth of the snatchers," she observes. "Though again, it could be coincidental."

I nod.

"They provide a general description of their company for tax purposes, with a brief listing of other ventures they're engaged in through their holdings in other countries. In the first three years, they mentioned their overseas mines, and they still maintain a brisk business in imported gems."

"They don't report their mines anymore?"

"It's an optional description," Kirrana says. "They've opted to describe other things since those early years, but there's no questioning the fact that they engage in a very legitimate gem and jewelry import business. A good percentage of the gems the noblewomen wear are funneled through them."

"The mines would explain the larger gemstones," I say. "Menaiya has mines as well, though, right? In the mountains?"

"Yes, but the gems are not quite as high quality, and certainly not as large as the descriptions of the ones that poor warden discovered." Kirrana taps her wax tablets once, absentmindedly. "I can't help thinking that mines are the sort of place that would happily use small children whom no one would ask questions about—children who could fit into tighter spots than an adult."

I shudder. It never even occurred to me to ask where the jewels I'd ordered came from. "But we don't have proof, do we?"

"None at all. Just coincidences, like the port warden's death and the captain's replacement, following the discovery of those two gems. And the fact that the snatchers showed up around when Berenworth did, and their presence has grown in tandem."

"And we have potential motives," I agree. There are the children as both salable goods and useful workers, and the gems as a valuable trade to the Circle. What we're striving for is a preponderance of coincidences, enough to warrant an actual investigation into Berenworth, with soldiers to search ships for children and apprehend what slavers they can find.

"You're brilliant," I say, eyeing her with admiration. We started with almost nothing, and in the space of days, she's brought us so far. "You know that, right?"

"No," she says, dropping her gaze humbly. "I'm just a damn good tax clerk."

I laugh.

Not to be distracted, Kirrana says, "If you have time, you can look at loading records while I check more incident reports."

"Loading records?"

"Just look for anything strange—maybe loadings that happened at unusual times, or some other detail that doesn't sit quite right. We're looking for people who were in the know making an unconscious mistake in their reporting, accidentally recording a truth instead of a lie."

"Sounds good," I say, and set to work on the ledger Kirrana pushes over to me. This time, I'm working forward from the last available records five years ago to the first, each in their own ledger. The records, though, come from the river dock here in Tarinon, instead of the port wardens in Lirelei.

"I've already gone through all the Lirelei records," Kirrana assures me. "I didn't find anything else that stood out."

It's a bit like looking for a glass bead in a horse pasture, when you haven't any idea what the bead even looks like. At some point, Kirrana produces a small stash of snacks and we break to eat, then go back to reading.

"Where are last year's records?" I ask when I finish with the final book in my stack.

"Still at the river wardens' office, I expect," Kirrana says. She sits back and stretches. "Incident logs are sent up semiannually unless there's a big enough incident to warrant an investigation. Loading ledgers . . . there's only a rush on those when it's a five-year tax assessment to adjust rates. We had one two years back, so no rush this year."

I rest my chin on my stack of ledgers. "We've found enough to raise interest. It might be enough to get the princess and . . . her allies to launch an investigation."

I wish, though, that there was some way to take down those at the top—the mages who are betraying our people. I don't want to hurt our royal family, or bring about the anarchy Bren spoke of. I don't want to spend the rest of my life with the regrets the archer gave voice to in her journal. But when I consider that the Circle is actively enslaving our people, and will walk away untouched, my anger hardens into a fist in my belly.

"You want another anomaly," Kirrana says. I blink at her, and she adds, "To fully convince the royals to investigate Berenworth. The company is powerful enough that a single anomaly and a coincidence or two won't be enough. Right?"

I nod, even though that wasn't what I was thinking. But she is right.

"Well," Kirrana says, springing up and industriously stacking ledgers. "I say we go for a walk. It's a lovely spring day. Let's get this put away and go visit the river wardens."

"Is that a good idea?" I ask, taken aback. "Will they even be open?"

"Yes and yes. Palace offices are closed an extra day; everything else is back to business as usual. But I've been to the wardens' office before, and they know me. They won't be surprised to see me. Come on," she urges me.

Laughing, I push myself to my feet and help her clear off the table, carefully returning each ledger to its place. The docks are on the east side of the city, nowhere near the Scholar's territory. In full day, in Kirrana's company, it should be fine. I do, as I promised Captain Matsin, write a short note to Mina advising her that I am going for a walk with a friend but will be back by early evening, and we collar a page out on the paths to deliver it for me.

Then we continue past the practice fields, where guards are drilling, and on to the side exit. Out on the street, Kirrana hails a passing wagon for us, in an effort to save my foot the walk. The middle-aged woman who drives it won't even take a coin in exchange for a ride on her crates to the other side of the river. Her brow furrows as she notes the faded yellow bruises on my cheek, but she says only, "I'll take you across the bridge to River Road, but you'll have to walk down to the docks yourselves."

We rattle along in the spring sunshine, Kirrana pointing out various historic buildings and points of interest. The bridge we take is humbler than the one the princess's carriage crossed over for the wedding ceremony. While I can just see the thin towers of the temple to the north of us, most of the view is taken up by a dock. More than a dozen boats are moored there, at least half of them actively loading or unloading.

Kirrana points. "See the galleys with the green-and-white pennants? Those are Berenworth's."

I run my gaze over the boats, searching. All but one are merchant galleys, with space for at least one set of rowers, though the oars are pulled in right now. They aren't the deepest vessels—they can't be, on the river—but there's space for a single-level hold beneath the rowers, and a small cabin on deck for the kitchen and the captain's quarters. Looking over them now, I spot three different galleys flying Berenworth's colors.

"Here we are," our driver announces as we reach the end of the bridge. She pulls off to the side, where the bridge intersects with the road to the dock. "You two enjoy your day!"

We thank her and clamber out of the wagon. It's a short walk down the road to the multiroom building that serves as the main office for the river wardens.

Any anxieties I'd entertained about our showing up unannounced are eased the moment we walk in the door.

"Kelari," the head warden says with a smile and bow to Kirrana. He's a tall, lanky man with the longest mustache I have ever seen. "It's always a pleasure. Do you have another project to check on?"

"Always something new," Kirrana agrees pleasantly. "Today I need the loading ledgers from last year. A discrepancy has been noticed, and they want me to make sure it didn't get carried over."

"Of course," he says, and takes us to the records room in back. The room is relatively bare but for a central table—low, with cushions around it, just like at home! And a wide window, unshuttered to allow in the sunshine. The monthly ledgers are lined up on a shelf, with other shelves reserved for additional reports.

He waves toward the ledgers. "You're in luck. We were

planning to send these up next week, and then you'd have had to fight the administrative building for them."

"I'm glad you've been slow," Kirrana says with a grin.

He laughs. "Let me know if you need anything."

Kirrana assures him she will, and with a quick bow, he departs, closing the door behind him. Kirrana hands me the first set of ledgers and quietly lifts down the incident reports for her own review.

About halfway through my second ledger, I pause. "This is odd," I say. I flip back a page, then forward.

"What is it?"

I turn back to the loading bill. "This was the only ship loaded on this date. It's one of Berenworth's."

Kirrana gets up and comes to look over my shoulder. "About a year ago, hmm? That is odd. There's always more movement than that on a particular day. What about the next one?"

"Very busy," I say. In fact, there were no fewer than ten ships loaded the next day—more than usual. "Were the offices closed for some reason?"

I flip back again.

Kirrana frowns. "Look, there's nothing recorded for the two days before that."

"The queen's death," I say, staring at the date. "The city was shut down for the three days of mourning, wasn't it? This ship should never have been loaded."

"It's possible the warden wrote down the wrong date on the first log after reopening," Kirrana says in a voice that clearly suggests she doesn't believe herselfit.

"It's also possible they forgot to change the date when they wrote up the log." I squeeze my eyes shut. "When I first started asking questions, I heard a rumor that nearly two dozen children disappeared over those days."

"I've . . . heard that too."

I look up at Kirrana. "That would be the sort of cargo that would need to be loaded as soon as possible."

"Exactly the sort of thing a corrupt warden would come out to approve so no one would ask questions later," Kirrana agrees softly. "He was probably well paid for his troubles too."

It's only a date, one day off from the rest. The cargo itself is all innocuous—sacks of grain, crates of carpets. Kirrana goes back to her wax tablet and makes a note of the log date. There are precious few words on her tablet, just cryptic references to the logs and ledgers that bear each anomaly we've identified. Enough for us to find them again, but not enough for anyone else to know what they're reading.

I look again at the page before me, trace the black stamp at the bottom. It's the Berenworth seal, used by each captain alongside their initials to prove their relation to the overarching company. Two thin circles frame a center with calligraphic writing decorated with three small star-shaped flowers. A variant of asphodel, I think. The writing says, *From the earth, the wealth of man.* I suppose it sounds like a perfectly valid motto considering Berenworth's investment in mines, and that the wealth of the asphodel is in its roots, which have a number of medicinal uses. But it still rubs me the wrong way. Perhaps it's the implication that one can just take what one wants.

"Do you think it's enough?" Kirrana asks.

"It might be. Do you think we'll find anything else?"

"I doubt it," she admits. "To find out more, you'd need an informant on the inside, or a contingent of guards who can inspect the ships for—well, for children."

We don't have any informants, and I wouldn't know how to go about cultivating one. But the royal family certainly has soldiers, if they're willing to use them. That will be up to the princess, and Kestrin, and his cousin Garrin, who offered to shield them both from the impact of this investigation. Garrin wanted an angle that wasn't the Circle, and now I have one.

"I'll talk to the princess," I say. "I think we have enough to warrant their attention."

"I'm glad," Kirrana says. "I'll keep my tablets with me for now. Let me know if you need anything from them."

"I will," I promise.

CHAPTER

41

Kirrana sets off directly from the docks to spend the rest of the day with her family. Emboldened by our earlier ride together, I keep an eye out for carts and wagons driven by women, and manage to buy a ride back to the wide plaza before the palace for the price of the spare coin in my pocket. It's certainly the best way to cross the city without drawing notice or further blistering my foot.

As the cart rolls away, I become aware of a man approaching. I glance sideways to find myself looking at Captain Matsin, wearing an older set of leather-and-velvet armor.

"Kelari," he says, his expression grim. "May I walk you into the palace?"

I have the distinct feeling he wants to chastise me more than he wants to walk, but I dip my head and start forward.

We pass through the gates in silence. Just when I'm beginning to wonder if he means to speak at all, he says, "I saw you leaving the palace earlier today with another young woman."

He must have been in the practice fields, then. "Yes," I say.

"I followed you."

"What?" I turn toward him, shocked. He's been following us *all afternoon?*

He meets my gaze. "It only took me a few minutes to realize there was someone else following you, closer behind you than I was. I continued after you to make sure you remained safe. Were you any more aware of them than you were of me?"

My mind goes blank. I shake myself, try to rattle a few thoughts free.

"I thought not. They followed you back, and I decided it best that I come forward and walk you in."

"Did you recognize them?"

"No. They weren't dressed as a soldier, but they moved as if trained."

I take a shaky breath. Who would be following me? If it were the Scholar's men, they could have easily apprehended me on my way back, or at least made the attempt.

"You don't know why you were being followed?" Matsin queries.

There's definitely more than one possible reason.

"The man was a Menaiyan, so it likely doesn't have anything to do with the princess's brother. Are you involved in anything else that might incite interest?"

I eye him warily. He isn't trying to trick information out of me, is he?

Matsin sighs. "Don't tell me. Tell the princess. And I suggest you send word to your friend to be careful as well."

An excellent idea. Since I don't know where Kirrana lives, Matsin escorts me to the women's residence, where the elderly caretaker gives me the appropriate directions. Then I return, finally, to the royal wing, my limp distinctly more pronounced.

I write a quick note to Kirrana, advising her that we were followed and counseling her to be careful until we can find out who it was.

Write me back, I say at the end. *Just let me know you got home safely.*

The note entrusted into the hands of a page for immediate delivery, I go in search of Alyrra. Matsin's news has disturbed me enough that I know I need to share everything we've learned— before anything else might happen.

Thankfully, Alyrra is in, and within half an hour she manages to arrange for Kestrin and Garrin to join us in her new interior sitting room to hear my news. Kestrin wears the same faintly glowing expression as Alyrra; it's endearing and makes him seem boyish again, as he did the night of the sweetening. Theirs might be an arranged match, but they are certainly happy in it.

Garrin is more somber, though he stretches out his legs and looks at me from deep brown eyes with their frame of lashes as if he were a court beauty in his own right. He probably is.

"We spoke just a few days ago," he says amiably. "Is there really news again so soon, kelari?" He pauses, his brow furrowing. "I hope you have not delved further into your questions regarding the Circle."

"No, I have left them out of it completely, as you counseled, verin." As much as it irked me to do so.

"Then please," Alyrra says. "Tell us what you learned."

It takes a surprisingly short amount of time to explain the

research Kirrana and I completed, outlining the anomalies related to Berenworth: the gemstones that would be prized as amulets, the port warden's death and captain's removal, the overseas mines, the loading of cargo on a day when the docks should have been closed, and the coinciding disappearance of a great number of children.

"You've been busy," Garrin says quietly. "I am impressed, kelari."

"My friend did much of the research, and knows the records well. I couldn't have done it on my own."

Alyrra nods. "It's a great deal to consider." She turns to the men. "How much do we know about this company?"

Kestrin shrugs. "They're well known and seem legitimate. There's no need for them to be involved in something as unsavory as this, given the level of business they are engaged in. But it's also quite possible they are. It is easy enough for a man to take advantage of another in order to grow just a little richer; I wouldn't be surprised if it were even easier for a company to take advantage of the most vulnerable at their fingertips."

Garrin shifts, crossing his arms. "I have to say, I find it hard to believe that Berenworth is involved in chasing down children in back alleys. That is how it is done, is it not? I think it more likely that some of their captains are illegally transporting a few children and bringing back payment with them than that the whole of the company is engaged in the widespread disappearances we have heard about."

I take a deep breath and hold it, trying not to say anything too insulting of Garrin's intelligence. Sheltered as he is by living in the palace, he still doesn't believe the issue is as big or as real as it is. This isn't just a couple ships taking a dozen children out of the country every month. It's much bigger and more devastating than that, and it must, by necessity, be organized.

Thankfully, Kestrin saves me from the words at the tip of my tongue. "It's possible, cousin, but I disagree. The involvement of the Circle, which appears irrefutable at this point, implies that they have an ally they would trust not to betray them. They wouldn't deal with individual slavers, or captains. Not directly, even if such exist. There must be someone organizing it all." He nods to me. "There's enough oddity to what you've uncovered, kelari, that I do think it should be looked into. Quietly."

Garrin sits forward, his expression grim. "Agreed. If these *are* just coincidences, we don't want to raise concern among the merchants and their companies that we're investigating them needlessly. If Berenworth is truly involved, we'll need ironclad evidence to back up our claims before word gets out."

"You'll take this on, then?" Kestrin asks him.

"Of course, cousin. Did I not say I would?" Garrin turns to me. "Have a copy of the evidence you have gathered delivered to me. I will start with that. I have a few men who can begin looking into Berenworth, both from the records side of things and from the outside."

"My friend has the notes we took with her. I'm sure I can get a copy." I hesitate, knowing I need to share this as well. "Captain Matsin informed me, on my return from our research this afternoon, that I was followed from the palace. It's possible someone has already found out what I am working on. Though I don't know how they could, as I haven't spoken of it to anyone but my friend, and you."

And Bren. The thought occurs as the words leave my mouth. Would *he* have me followed?

Kestrin and Alyrra exchange a look. Garrin frowns. "That's concerning. If you need to leave the palace again, I'd prefer you take a guard with you."

I nod.

"Your friend returned safely?"

"She's with her family right now. I've written to tell her to be careful."

Kestrin nods and says, "See that she has an escort on her return. Like you, she should be careful for the next few weeks, till we've uncovered what's happening and who is involved. If she prefers to remain with her family, that can be arranged."

"Thank you."

"I'll speak with my father about all this as well," Kestrin says. "He may wish us to involve Melkior."

That would be the lord high marshal of Menaiya. Arguably, he would be the person to head up such an investigation, rather than Garrin, but perhaps that's only once it becomes official.

Garrin nods. "I'll wait till I've heard from you. There's no immediate rush."

No rush? There are children being stolen *every day*. But perhaps, if you've never seen it, never held your friend while she wept for her stolen sister, then taking your time seems of little consequence.

"What about me?" I ask. "Is there anything more I can do?"

Alyrra shakes her head. "Not at this point, Rae, unless you can see another method to uncover more information."

"In which case," Garrin says quickly, "let me know. I'll be

happy for your insight, but, given that you're being followed, it may be best if you step back as much as possible."

I nod, only because I don't have another angle to investigate. But I'll keep thinking about it. And it's quite possible Kirrana will come up with something as well.

I wouldn't be surprised if she did.

CHAPTER
42

A page arrives with two notes for me as I am getting ready to attend Alyrra to dinner. I very nearly snatch them from his hand, gasping my thanks. It is the same page who brought Bren's notes, but an initial glance tells me the topmost one, at least, is not from him.

It's from Kirrana. I sit down in my desk chair and read it with relief. She is perfectly fine, enjoying her time with her family, and her father will bring her back this evening. She'll be sure to be careful and stay in the palace complex until she hears further from me. Therefore, I am not to worry.

I grin and send up a word of thanks before opening the second note. This one is, indeed, from Bren. It says only:

*I thought you said you wouldn't leave the palace. My man
tells me he followed you all the way to the docks and back without*

your noticing a thing. Would you please take a guard with you next time?—Bren

I lean against the chair back, the letter dangling from my fingertips. It was just Bren being overprotective. There is no other danger; no one has discovered what Kirrana and I have been working on. All is well.

It is almost too good to be true. Silly Bren, watching over me like a mother hen and scaring me half to death. I will have to let Alyrra know when I can catch her alone.

"Ready to go?" Mina asks from across the room, focused on putting the last touches on her makeup.

"Yes," I say, and hide the letters away.

The evening party goes well enough. The others manage most of what needs to be done, and I just smile and chat amiably with whoever addresses me, generally aware that, in fact, the court still seems given to thinking rather partially of me. The women offer me condescending smiles, the men nod to me from around the room, and no one lets the foreign prince come anywhere near me. It's all rather wonderful.

I watch Alyrra's brother closely, and he seems brighter today than he did before the wedding, his pale eyes alight. I cannot imagine why, though. He spends most of his time standing aloof, rarely speaking to anyone other than his mother, the queen. Our nobles, while they greet him politely, do not even attempt to engage him. If they have rallied around me, they have positively flocked around the princess, according her every courtesy of her station and acknowledging her place before them. It must grate on him, the realization that he has ensured her their support where she had to work for it before.

By the end of the evening, my foot is hurting once again, my ankle aching and at least a few blisters burst. I'm grateful when the royals retire early, Kestrin and the king walking together with Alyrra to the royal wing, all of us attendants trailing behind them.

Alyrra moves to the door to her suite, and Kestrin winks at her, promising to meet her soon, before moving farther down the hall with his father, toward his own door. It's quite sweet how he ensures she has her own space, and is comfortable in the space they share. He will no doubt wait in his own sitting room until she has made herself comfortable in their bedroom.

We pass through the empty rooms and into the bedchamber. Zaria goes to pour Alyrra a cup of almond milk. I shift; we don't usually walk Alyrra all the way in and I wonder if she simply forgot to dismiss us this time.

"A lovely evening, but oh! I am tired," Alyrra says, moving toward the bed. The blankets do not lie quite flat, a few larger wrinkles disturbing the surface. Odd, that. Shouldn't they have been pulled taut by the maids?

I blink at the bed as Mina says something and the princess laughs in return. "I know," she says, sitting on the edge of the bed, near one of the wrinkles. "I'll just sit for a moment, and then you can—"

"Get *away*!" I cry, leaping forward. I catch Alyrra's elbow and yank her off the bed as the wrinkle contracts in on itself. My wound shrieks with pain—I should not have used that arm. But I can hear a faint rasping sound, a warning I've heard twice out on the plains, one that anyone would be a fool to ignore, wounded or not.

"What?" Alyrra asks, stumbling.

"Back, back," I gasp through the pain.

"You're acting like a madwoman, Amraeya," Jasmine says, rounding on me. "There's nothing wrong with the bed. See?"

"No—don't," I manage, stepping forward, good hand out, as Jasmine yanks off the bedclothes.

She screams.

An orange-and-white saw-scaled viper balances precariously on the edge of the bed, its body easily as thick around as my wrist. Startled, it throws back its head and then slides off the bed in a heap, right onto my feet.

I freeze. It writhes once, righting itself and disappearing completely beneath the hem of my skirt. I can feel it rasping its scales against each other, its weight heavy over my feet, cool snakeskin wrapped around one ankle. Its warning *rsss-rsss* sounds beneath the ongoing, gasping shrieks issuing from Jasmine's mouth.

"Rae?" Alyrra says softly.

I don't move, except to speak. "Get out. All the rest of you get out. *Jasmine.* Listen to me."

She takes a gasping breath, and while her mouth remains open, the screams stop.

"If you move quickly, the viper will attack you. You have to move slowly, slide your feet backward. Don't lift them. You must not scare it."

"Scare *it?*" Zaria demands from somewhere behind me. "You're—"

"Out," Alyrra says, brooking no argument. "Now. Mina, you too."

"You too, zayyida," I say. My hands are beginning to shake. I curl my wounded arm against my chest, wrap my other over it to still my body. I cannot afford to frighten the snake lying over my feet.

"Alyrra!" Kestrin's voice breaks through the room. I can't see what Alyrra does, don't dare look back, but he says nothing more. I hear the thud of footsteps slow as they near. They're coming from a little farther away—the door to Kestrin's suite.

"A snake," Alyrra says softly. "It's on Rae's feet right now. Jasmine, move back."

"Gather everyone in the outer room," the king orders an unseen attendant, voice cool and sure. He must have still been with Kestrin in the hallway when Jasmine started screaming. No wonder it took them a few moments to reach us. "Send a quad in to me."

Kestrin eases into view, moving slowly toward Jasmine. "Veria, step back."

"Slowly," I breathe, but she doesn't hear me, or perhaps she simply can't manage it. She takes a fast step back, jerky with fear. The snake's coils tighten.

"No—" I raise an arm toward Jasmine.

She shrieks and throws herself tumbling back. Her foot arcs through the air before my skirt. The snake rears into view and darts at it, fangs bared. It's going to bite her, and with venom like that—

Kestrin's hand comes up, fingers outstretched at the edge of my vision—and the snake *bounces* off the air.

As I stare, it pulls itself back beneath the hem of my skirts, scales sawing against each other, and wraps itself even more firmly around my ankles, rough against my skin. Faintly, I can hear the king murmuring something, but I can't make sense of it, of anything really.

What just happened? I glance toward the prince and find him looking at me in return, eyes dark as the viper's. Then he reaches out, hooks an arm around Jasmine, who is lying on her back and sobbing, utterly unaware of what just happened, and pulls her slowly away. By the time he's gotten her to the door, a quad has arrived and they get her the rest of the way out.

"You too, veriana," the king says to Alyrra. "We'll need Mage Hedhrawy, I think. I don't believe we have any snake tamers here."

Captain Matsin's voice sounds from the doorway. "I'll send for him."

Alyrra slowly shifts back, and then it is just the prince and me in the room.

"Kestrin?" the king asks from the doorway.

"I'll stay here. Send in Hedhrawy when he arrives."

A silence, and then the king says, "Kelari, you're doing well. Hold on a little longer and we'll have you free."

And then the door shuts behind him.

Kestrin moves slowly, staying against the wall until I can see him from the corner of my eye again without turning my head. I can feel his gaze on my face, studying me.

What I saw just now, that was magic. Kestrin's magic. He isn't supposed to have a talent any more than my sister is. Except she's a horse rancher's daughter who helps with local births and takes care of broken animals. *He* is the crown prince, in line to be king one day. A sorcerer king. That's one big secret right there, and I'm pretty sure he doesn't want me to know it.

Kestrin takes one final step to the side. I turn my head to meet his gaze. He says nothing, his expression inscrutable. Gone is the mischievous young man of the wedding, the laughing prince of the sweetening. For just a moment, I think of the Black Scholar with his ebony robes and shining intellect and cool, calculating approach to murder. But Kestrin is nothing like him. No, he can't be. I've seen how he protects Alyrra, seen his kindness and joy, and I don't believe he'll hurt me for this. At least, I don't want to believe it.

I'll just have to be smart about how I navigate this. Which means I need to say something, make it clear I'm not a threat, that I can be trusted. But what?

Kestrin eases down until he's squatting against the wall, his eyes trained on the bottom of my skirt. "You're very calm," he says. He glances up and catches the look of disbelief on my face. "You are, at least compared to Jasmine."

"It was—very lucky the snake pulled back. I thought for sure it would bite her." For how low I keep my voice, it's still too bright and not at all convincing. Kestrin considers me in silence.

"Don't you think, zayyid?" I ask hopefully. If he will just play along with the idea that I didn't see anything, then it will all be all right. Won't it?

"Are you afraid it will bite you now?" he asks quietly.

I flash back to the Scholar again, smiling over our conversation on political philosophy, and then pressing a dagger to my wrist. *No.* The Scholar might have had manners and intelligence, but he didn't have morals. The prince does. He *must*. I shake my head to clear it. "I'm not in any danger from it."

"You've seen this type of snake before?"

"It's a saw-scaled viper. Their venom is extremely potent, but he's comfortable right now. He won't attack." Not unless he's incited to, which Jasmine has already illustrated for us. I should maybe not have said any of that.

Kestrin smiles humorlessly. "You are perfectly safe regardless, don't you think? I would venture to say Alyrra would never have left you here if she didn't believe it."

No, she wouldn't have. Oh, thank *God*. She must have known Kestrin's secret as well, known that he could and would keep me safe regardless of my knowing his secret. *That* is a great deal more comforting than having to convince myself of Kestrin's moral strength. And apparently, he was perfectly aware of my uncertainty on that score.

"You see. You are perfectly safe, kelari." He glances to the snake, which now rests silently about my feet, then back up to me. "I should like to rely on your confidence, much as the princess does."

I'm not sure it can really be this easy, but I'm not about to argue. "You have it, zayyid."

"I thank you." He smiles again, and this time there is warmth to it. "I hear someone coming. We'll have this snake off you in no time, and all will be well. I would do it myself, but"—he shrugs—"I have certain appearances to keep up, and you said yourself you are in no danger."

"Thanks a lot," I grumble, surprising a huff of laughter from him.

A voice calls through the door, and a moment later a man in mage's robes steps through—Hedhrawy, no doubt. He looks vaguely familiar. I must have seen him once or twice during the wedding festivities. He is tall and broad shouldered, with a slight belly nudging at the front of his robes.

He nods to me and takes a moment to confer with the prince, bending down to inspect the snake as they speak. Then he tells me, "I am going to persuade the snake to fall asleep. Once it is more lethargic, you can step away and we will remove it to a basket."

"Do you have a stick?" I ask. "Preferably with a forked end?"

He tilts his head. "You have experience with snakes?"

"Enough that I'd like to pin its head down once it's sleepy, just in case." Even sleepy snakes can wake up. And they're not always in a good mood when they do.

"We'll call for something of the sort," Kestrin says. "If you will start, Master Hedhrawy, I'll see to that."

It doesn't take long. Hedhrawy doesn't even reach for the large ruby amulet hanging from a chain about his neck, so small is the magic needed to nudge the flow of blood and breath through the snake toward sleep. Its coils relax about my ankles. Kestrin reappears with another guard and what appears to be roasting fork from the kitchens. The guard carries a colorfully woven covered basket, no doubt to house the snake.

"Don't hurt it," I say fretfully. "It didn't ask to be put here."

The mage and the guard stare at me, but Kestrin doesn't seem to mind my rudeness. "We'll take care, kelari. Here." He approaches another step before the guard comes to his senses, stops the prince, and gently presses the fork against the base of the snake's neck himself.

I slip one foot free, take a half step back, and slip the other one free. The snake remains still, proving my roasting fork precautions unnecessary. The last I see of it is the mass of coils resting loosely on the floor as the prince ushers me from the room.

CHAPTER

43

I sleep the sleep of the dead, for which I am grateful: no echoing memories of the brickmaker's boys, or the Black Scholar's cold voice and colder blades, or the foreign prince's violence, or the *rsss-rsss* of a saw-scaled viper. I wake to a faint but persistent knock on the door.

"Go away," Mina groans from her bed.

I push myself out of bed and hobble to the door, my turned foot aching each time it comes down on the cold tiles. I have just enough presence of mind to grab a shawl and pull it around my shoulders before cracking open the door.

A page waits on the other side—a girl, which is unusual but not unheard of. It also explains why she was allowed in at such an hour, while a male page would have been told to wait at the hall door, or come back when we were awake.

"A letter for you, kelari," she says. "I was told it was urgent."

"Thank you."

She dips a curtsy and departs. I go to sit at my desk and unshutter a single pane from the luminae lamp. Mina rolls over and hides her head under the blankets.

I frown, looking at the envelope. I don't recognize the name at all. I open the envelope as quietly as possible, scan the contents, and then find I do not know what I have read. I squeeze my eyes shut a moment, my heart thudding, and start over.

> *Kelari Amraeya,*
>
> *I am writing to you with regard to our daughter, Kirrana. Upon your advice, my husband decided to accompany her back to the palace yesterday evening. On their way, they were set upon by a group of assailants. My daughter is gone. My husband was left unconscious, and he has only just now awakened and been brought home, and told me his story.*
>
> *Please, if you have any idea who it was that posed our daughter the danger you feared, tell me. We are searching for her, but we have no idea who has taken her, where she could be. If you have any information at all, we would be forever in your debt.*
>
> *Siyela*

Gone. My stomach turns to stone. Kirrana is gone. I turn the letter over in my hand, fold it and refold it. Try to think.

I need to speak to Alyrra. She'll be able to order an investigation, get the right people involved looking for Kirrana. Who is gone. Like Seri. Only worse—only violently, her father beaten unconscious. Targeted.

I lurch from my seat. Out in the main hallway, I see quads posted before both Alyrra's door and Kestrin's. I clutch the letter tighter in my hand. The princess is asleep, of course she is, with Kestrin, and I don't have the right to go barging in there. But Kirrana is in danger. I have to do something.

"Kelari?" Captain Matsin detaches himself from the quad by Alyrra's door and moves toward me. "The royal family is having a private conversation right now and cannot be disturbed."

I understand. I do. An assassination attempt, or something close to it, was made on her life last night. Perhaps they've learned who placed the snake in her bed and they're deciding what to do. But Kirrana's life is at risk *now*. I look up at Matsin. If I can't get in to see Alyrra, then he is my next best choice. He's loyal to the prince and princess, and honorable in his way. Even if I can't trust that he won't carry out an order against me, I can trust him up to that point. It will have to be enough.

"Could I have a word with you?"

It doesn't occur to me that there's really nowhere to actually *have* a word with him until he pauses where he is. Then he gestures me on, and as I reach him he falls into step with me. We stop at a door just before the great sweeping staircase that the royals use. It leads to a small, windowless guard room I never even noticed; the guards within immediately step out at Matsin's request.

He leaves the door partially open, for propriety's sake, and turns to me. "Something has happened?" he hazards. The bright yellow glow from a luminae stone lights his features and gleams on the oiled leather and polished bronze of his armor. I'm still in my nightshirt and pants, my shawl doing very little for propriety, but it hardly matters in this moment.

"A woman I've been working with—a tax clerk—she's

disappeared. The same one I went out with yesterday, when you followed us." I hand him the letter and let him read it himself.

His expression, serious before, grows increasingly grim as he peruses the letter. "What, precisely, were you researching?"

"The princess can tell you that."

He raises his gaze to me, then nods. "You're sure it's related?"

"There would be no other reason to target her." And her family has no idea that the snatchers might be involved. "I need to visit her family, tell them what I know," I say with sudden decision.

"You're not leaving the palace."

What? "Kirrana is *missing* and you're worried about me going to see her family?"

"You were wounded, were you not? By someone who might prefer to finish the deed he started? And then you were followed by an unknown man? You can't go to this family as if there is no danger to you at all."

"How do you know all that?"

"Because the princess swore me to silence and told me to keep a watch on your safety. I understand you're not exactly safe outside these walls."

Fair enough, though I wish she'd told me. "I'm not going to *walk* there. I'll take a carriage." He opens his mouth to protest. "And you can come with me, if you're that worried."

He closes his mouth. Takes a breath. "All right."

I stare at him in astonishment. Did he just agree to go with me?

"But not now. I can't leave my post here. I'm off duty in an hour; we'll go then."

"I should go sooner—"

"Not alone. I swear I'll take you to find your friend's family, along with a quad as escort. And I'll report her as missing at once. She works at the tax office; the palace guard will help investigate. You write back to her mother with what you know and send it ahead of us. Agreed?"

There's a sharp look about him, a heightened awareness that tells me he's taking this very seriously. And that I should not underplay the threat the Scholar still poses to me. There's likely not much I can accomplish alone that Matsin isn't about to order. "Agreed."

I set up in the common room where I won't disturb the other attendants, and send off a flurry of letters, my mind jumping from possibility to possibility. First, a letter to Kirrana's mother, telling her that I will be bringing Captain Matsin in the next hour or so, as I'm able, and that he will have the palace guard informed and set to work immediately. Then a letter for Alyrra to be delivered when she will accept it, and another for Garrin, because he has taken on the responsibility of the existing investigation.

I get up and pace back and forth when I finish, then sit down to rest my foot. I will no doubt walk plenty today; it's better not to start out hard. But I cannot sit still, tapping my hands nervously against the table as I think of Kirrana followed and attacked. My hands still. It was Bren's man who followed us yesterday to make sure we were safe. And Sage told me, that first time we went to meet the thieves, that Red Hawk's men helped search for a girl who disappeared.

I write a brief note to Bren describing Kirrana's disappearance and explaining that I'm going to her home. I don't know that he can do anything, but I'd rather ask than miss a chance to help her. Bren told me how to contact his trusted page—not that I had expected to need to do so. I'm glad for it now.

While I'm waiting for him to arrive, I return to my room to change into one of my simpler new skirt and tunic sets, wrap Niya's story sash about my waist. I pause a moment in the room, trying to think.

This is my fault. For involving Kirrana, for drawing attention to her. I should have known she was more vulnerable than I. It's my fault she's been taken.

But that's not right—in the end, it is the snatchers' fault. Berenworth Trading Company. The thrice-cursed Circle of Mages, who are too powerful to take on, too dangerous to face. Darkness take them!

I take a shaky breath, check my pockets. I should have my bone knife. I cross to my desk, slide the drawer open quietly so as not to wake Mina. There is the knife, and beside it the archer's journal. The archer, who destroyed her king to save her people. And the Fae sorceress with her seemingly incredible magical ability. I stare a long moment at the book, then slip it into my pocket, bind my knife in its sheath to my calf, and write one final letter.

Bren's page arrives just as I'm finishing, his hair sleep mussed but his eyes alert. He accepts my note to Bren, promises to pass off the other note to another page at once, and departs.

I set out after him. There's still a half hour before Matsin will be able to take me to see Kirrana's family. I don't intend to waste it.

CHAPTER

44

The women's residence lies quiet and mostly empty. Most of the palace nobles may still be asleep, but it's morning and the work of the world has already begun. Inside, the elderly caretaker has rolled up her sleeping mat and is puttering about the front room. I tell her that I want to leave a note for Kirrana and she waves me up, apparently unaware of Kirrana's abduction.

Upstairs, I find the room unoccupied, as I'd hoped. Kirrana is organized, but thankfully not so much so that she cleans out her hairbrush daily. I harvest one of the hairs left on its bristles and head out once more. My final note should have been delivered by now; I can only hope it will be answered.

The courtyard is just as quiet as it was the first time I came here, the mosaic tiles familiar. Only this time, the favor I have to ask is a great deal more personal, and I'm not sure Stonemane will grant it without some form of payment. I don't have much to give him, for I doubt he would want jewelry or coin. But perhaps he'll humor me, as he did last time.

I try to distract myself by revisiting the last passages of the archer's journal. Her desperation and regret are clear on the page, but so is her sense of betrayal by her own liege. Before she ever betrayed him, he turned his back on her, until her service to him became an empty thing. How that must have hurt; it's as if I can see her pain in the shape of each letter she penned. It's a deeper betrayal in some sense than what the Circle has done, but only because I don't know those mages. Their betrayal is impersonal, but equally as devastating. Berenworth, at least, never presented itself as an organization in service to the people. Not that I won't do my best to see Berenworth destroyed, if I can prove the truth of their involvement. Or if Garrin can. But that still leaves the Circle.

"Kelari, I am glad to see you well."

I look up with a start, then hastily get to my feet and offer Verin Stonemane a curtsy. He is dressed simply this morning, tunic and pants bearing just a touch of embroidery at cuffs and sash. His hair falls over his shoulders with its usual inhuman sheen, setting off the darkness of his eyes against his pale skin.

"Thank you, verayn, for coming to speak with me on such short notice, so early."

"It is no trouble," he says, seating himself at the other end of the bench. As I sink back down, he rests a hand on the bench, taps it once. That same strange dimming rolls out from him, the world momentarily muffled, and then my ears pop and sound resumes.

"You have more questions, I presume," he says.

I shake my head. "No. It is something different. A favor to ask."

"Indeed." His voice is neutral in its coolness, but that is a warning in itself.

I straighten my back. "A friend of mine has gone missing, verayn. We are investigating her disappearance, but I wondered if you might be able to trace her. I am concerned she's come to harm."

Stonemane lifts his brows. "If you are yet again not going to one of the mages of the Circle, I must assume it's because you do not trust them to find her. Was she investigating the Blessing the Speakers give? Or perhaps the snatchers themselves?"

"The snatchers," I admit. "But only through the various records available to us—shipping logs and tax records. Nothing direct."

"Taxes?" He gives a soft laugh. "I would not have thought of that. But I am afraid I cannot help you. It is not my place as ambassador to come between the royal family and the Circle."

"But that's not—Kirrana's work points to the snatchers directly, not the Circle."

"And still, it is not my place." I take a breath to argue, but he raises a hand, stalling me. "Not all of us are heroes, kelari. I cannot save every person in this kingdom."

"I'm only asking you to save one person. My friend."

"Whom you cannot trust the Circle to find. This is not apolitical. Even if the king himself asked this of me, I would defer him to his own mages. I already granted you more than I should have in our last meeting."

I swallow hard, shake my head.

"I am sorry, kelari," he begins.

I can't sit any longer. I rise to face him, palms upturned as if begging. I *am* begging. "Help me, verin. I will pay whatever debt you ask."

He laughs, but it's a sad sound. "I find I do not actually want such a debt from you."

"I know," I say softly. "You didn't mean it the first time either. You were testing me. But I'm offering it now. The only other thing I can offer you is a certain bone knife I own; it is Fae made. You might know it."

He recoils. "I will not take back what I gave you."

"Why not?" I demand. "You gave it in payment of a debt. It is an equal return."

His lips thin. "I have no use for it."

Then what does he have a use for? I have nothing of unusual value beyond the knife. But perhaps what Stonemane needs is not a *thing.* He is here, after all, as the first permanent delegate since the Fae Attack. He and the Cormorant came for a particular reason . . .

"I am sorry, kelari," he says again, rising to face me. "I require neither debt nor payment because this battle is not mine. I cannot join it for you."

"What is your battle, then? Is it—whatever the curse is that dogs our royal family?"

He raises a brow. "A curse doesn't seem likely, don't you think?"

I meet his gaze with its hidden currents and decide I have nothing left to lose. If I end up looking a fool, well, it's worth the risk. "More like a sorceress," I say quietly.

That stops him.

I go on: "Does the name Sarait Win—"

He closes the distance between, his hand pressing hard over my mouth. *"Quiet."*

Fear sends me jerking back a half step. I come up sharply against a wall that isn't there, the air blocking me, Stonemane's fingers, long and cool, still pressed against my lips.

We remain frozen like that, my heart thundering in my breast as I remind myself he is *not* the Scholar, never mind if he's caught me, or if they both have slim, long-fingered hands.

Then he drops his hand and says, "Don't ever speak that name out loud."

I focus on this: his fear. "Is she listening?"

"Always." He turns his gaze on me, and I finally understand the stories told of those who lose themselves in the eyes of the Fae. They swallow me whole, darkness flooding my senses until there is nothing but the fathomless depths, the faintest of glimmers like starlight lighting the abyss within which I float. I hear his voice from far away, from within the beat of my heart. "Tell me, how did you know it?"

The words slide up my throat, called forth whether I will them or not. "The Black Scholar—" I grit my teeth—become aware that I can do that—but the words are still pressing against my tongue, crowding into my mouth. And the darkness of his eyes holds me. I cannot see past it, cannot find my way out. "Stop," I croak, the word heavy on my tongue, shoving past smaller, sharper words that I will not allow out. "Stop. *Please.*"

Reality snaps back into place around me with an almost audible *crack*: the courtyard, the morning sunlight streaming down on my shoulders, Stonemane standing a pace away, pale and grim and unhappy. Well, he can be as unhappy as he likes, I'm the one who was trapped.

He waits, and I keep my gaze on the mosaic underfoot, until

my breathing slows to normal. "I read it in a book," I tell him, my voice rough. "You could have asked."

He gestures once, a twist of his hand before it drops back to his side.

"Find my friend," I say, raising my gaze to his chin, "and you can have the book."

Silence.

I slip my hand into my pocket and draw forth the journal, holding it up. My hand is not quite steady, but there's nothing I can do about that. "Do we have a deal?"

"No one can know I helped you."

"I understand."

"Very well." He gestures toward the abandoned bench, asks, "You have something of hers for me to use?"

I take four steps to the bench and sink down, immeasurably grateful for its support. I pass the kerchief with the hair I took from Kirrana's brush to him. Stonemane seats himself silently. I watch as he snaps off a short length of hair, placing it on the bench. He marks the four cardinal points around it, each touch of his fingers leaving behind a faint glow. Then he holds his hand above it, palm flat and fingers spread. A faint rush of cool air fans my face.

I wait, watching as Stonemane remains focused on the bench. It seems no different in essence from what Niya attempted in Ani's kitchen a month ago. And, like then, nothing changes. No . . . the hair glitters, and then in the blink of an eye, it flares to red-yellow and falls to ash.

"Warded," Stonemane says, sitting back. "And powerfully so. I would guess the wards are not tied to her but to the place where she is."

I close my eyes. I had hoped—foolishly, perhaps—that Fae magic would be able to reach Kirrana where our own mages might fail. But the snatchers have warded her too well. No, not her, but where she is. And I have been where slaves were held before. I cast my mind back to the brickmaker's yard. If there were a ward protecting the boys from the Darkness, it would have been there too. I remember the prison cell of their room, and the kiln room, and the plaque above the door there. With a faint quickening of hope, I ask, "If you knew the shape of the ward, could you counter it?"

"Perhaps."

"A moment," I say and rise to move forward before remembering the invisible wall that had hemmed me in before. "Can I reach the fountain?" I ask, not looking at him.

"Of course."

Of course, meaning he will expand the magic surrounding us to allow me? Or of course meaning that the wall at my back was there only for those moments, just as Kestrin blocked the viper from reaching Jasmine? I start forward again in silence, reach the water unimpeded, and return to draw the ward I recall upon the bench between us with wet fingers. "Like this?" I ask. It is not quite right, but it is as close as I can get.

Stonemane studies my work. "I don't recognize such a sigil. I can put the question to the Cormorant. He has been making a study of the local forms of magic."

"Thank you." I sit a moment, then hold the journal out to Stonemane.

He takes it, and the exchange feels wrong, somehow. Ugly. Which it is—but I didn't ask him to use his magic on me, try to force my answers when I would have simply told him. He must fear that sorceress very much. *Sarait Winterfrost.*

I look up as Stonemane gets to his feet.

"Does Alyrra know?" I demand. "About the sorceress?"

"She knows better than I do," Stonemane says.

Good. I will worry about Kirrana and leave the sorceress to Alyrra and Stonemane. I turn my gaze to the fountain, waiting, but he doesn't move on. He only stands there, hovering.

Finally, he says, "Forgive me, Rae. I . . . the one you named has been known to use others as her pawns. I had to be sure of you."

Why do people who use force seem to think they are being reasonable? Matsin cornering me, and Alyrra ordering it; her brother asserting his power; the Scholar protecting his territory and his reputation? There was nothing reasonable about my punching Bren, and there's nothing reasonable about any of the rest of these choices. I raise my eyes to glare at him. "Don't you do it again."

He grimaces. "No."

"And I never gave you that name to use, either."

He flashes me a pained smile. "No."

"Stop looking so beautiful about it, then," I snap. He blinks at me and grins—which is that much worse. I shouldn't have said that; I must be more frazzled than I realized. "Find my friend and I'll see about forgiving you," I say, so we're clear.

"As long as you don't fear me," he says, stars glimmering in his eyes again. Gah!

"I don't trust you," I say, and give up waiting for him to leave. I need to get back to the royal wing to meet Matsin and go see Kirrana's family. All the rest of this mess can wait till later. I stand up, nod to him, and stump off without another word.

CHAPTER
45

Matsin is waiting for me in the guard room at the top of the back stairs, but not for the reason I expect. "The princess wishes to see you," he says. "At once. The other attendants have already been called in. I'll wait till you're done."

I nod and hurry on to her suite. Whatever this is about, at least she must have received my note by now. I open the door to find the king poised to leave, and Kestrin sitting beside Alyrra on the sofas opposite him, their expressions hard. Arrayed to the right, standing against the wall, are Mina, Zaria, and Jasmine. To the left stand Kestrin's own attendants.

"I will leave you to this, then," the king says to the royal couple. "Should you require my presence, you have only to send for me."

Alyrra dips her head. "I am grateful for your support, verayn."

I step hastily to the side and curtsy deeply as the king strides toward the door, his gaze sliding past me and then snapping back. "Kelari Amraeya?"

"Tarin."

He pauses a moment longer, then nods once and continues. There was something he wanted, though I can't say what, and he clearly decided not to pursue it for the time being. I straighten from my curtsy as the door closes.

"Rae, please stand to the side here," Alyrra says, indicating the wall where her remaining attendants stand. "My mother should be in shortly. We will be discussing last night's events. You are all here merely as witnesses. Even if she speaks to you, don't answer. Just look to me."

"I understand," I say, glancing once toward the small hexagonal table set next to the sofa where Alyrra sits. My note lies there, unopened. She doesn't know. "Zayyida—"

A knock sounds behind me, at the door.

"Quickly, Rae."

I hurry to take up a position beside Mina. Alyrra waits until I am in place, then calls out in a carrying voice.

The foreign queen sweeps into the room, followed by the noblewoman who attended her from Adania. With a curious glance about the room, she says in almost perfect Menay, "It is rather early for morning visits, don't you think, child?"

Alyrra gestures to the couch. "Won't you sit? We have much to discuss."

The queen makes no move to seat herself. "I have not even had breakfast, child. Tell me what it is and let's be done."

Seated by Alyrra, Kestrin goes utterly still, his eyes glittering with fury. But it's Alyrra's reaction that makes my blood run cold: she laughs, a gentle chuckle that puts her visitors on edge. The queen may pretend affection for her daughter, but it's clear she does not truly understand her.

I glance to Mina beside me, but she remains still, expression neutral. What is it that's happening here? Attendants by and large aren't expected to *stand* attendance, lining the walls like sentinels. Eight of us together provide a gauntlet of witnesses for whatever Alyrra has planned.

"As you wish," Alyrra says, the ring of steel in her voice. "I require two things of you. First, my brother shall be removed from the succession and sent into exile. Second, Lord Daerilin shall be stripped of his rank, title, and lands, and also exiled, though not with my brother. As I imagine you will not have the least argument with these demands, you are welcome to go eat your breakfast."

The queen stares. "Whatever do you mean by this, child? I am hardly going to exile my own son or my most trusted vassal."

Beside her, the Adanian noblewoman's face has paled almost to gray.

"You know," Alyrra says quietly, "that my brother has never respected either my person or my life."

The queen sends a poisonous look toward me. I didn't even realize she'd noticed me. "If this has anything to do with that lamentable incident with that attendant of yours—"

"It seems my relationship with each of you has been characterized by one lamentable incident after another," Alyrra interrupts, her voice light and cutting. "Do you know how traitors are punished, Mother?"

The queen narrows her eyes. "Certainly. You made that clear with what you did to Daerilin's daughter. Who do you think has betrayed you now?"

Kestrin's hand slowly curls into a fist. Just as slowly, he flattens it out once more, but the fury does not leave his eyes. Now that I know he carries a magical talent, I am both frightened by his anger and amazed at his control.

"Last night, an attempt was made on my life. I will spare you the details, since it is still before breakfast." There is no mistaking the edge of sarcasm to Alyrra's voice. "However, we have traced the chain of those involved back to Daerilin, who bribed one of my maids to betray me. Daerilin would not have acted without the explicit approval of my brother, if not yourself. I wonder, do you know anything of what I speak?"

"Certainly not, child. It sounds like some strange conspiracy you have concocted. You have not even said what was done!"

"Last night, a venomous snake was placed in my bed while we were at an evening gathering. The snake would have bit me had it not been for the quick thinking of my attendants."

"A snake?" the queen demands. "That is hardly an attempt on your life!"

Alyrra does not turn her head away from her mother as she says, "Kelari Amraeya."

I take one limping step forward, my stomach clenched tight.

Alyrra gestures toward a basket tucked back between two sofas. "Show my mother what that contains."

I look to the basket, recognizing its colorful weave, the thick cover strapped down over it.

As I cross to it, Alyrra says, "This is a saw-scaled viper, Mother. It is the single most deadly snake of the plains."

I lift the basket as steadily as I can, my wounded arm aching. The viper within rasps its scales together, the distinctive *rsss-rsss* clearly audible. I turn and set it a few paces from where the queen stands.

"The cover, Amraeya," the princess says.

I kneel beside it to undo the leather ties, my heart thudding. Last night, Mage Hedhrawy set a ward to keep the snake within the basket, but I don't exactly want to test his work. Still, an order is an order, and clearly Alyrra chose me because I've already proven steady around snakes. I take hold of the edges and slowly lift away the cover, careful that it shields my hands.

The snake hisses, scales rasping and tongue flicking. The queen leans away, only her pride keeping her from a hasty retreat. It lifts its head to keep her in view, and perhaps it is only I who notices how its head stops at a level with the top of the basket, pressed against an invisible barrier there.

"Would you like to pick it up, Mother? Do you truly trust that it won't bite you, that its venom can be counteracted in time by the mages who live in their own building separate from the palace?"

"This is all very dramatic, Alyrra, but there's no need for it. Come, let us call your brother here and sort things out as family. There is no need for any of this." She waves a hand to encompass both the snake and the row of attendants beyond it.

"I think not," Alyrra says. "That has only ever worked for you, not for me. I am no longer that same daughter you abused, Mother."

The queen's eyes widen. "I never abused you, Alyrra! Every-thing I have done has been for your best interest."

"Was it in my best interest when my brother first pushed me

down the stairs of our hall and you laughed? Or was it in my best interest to allow him to beat me when he wished, year upon year? Or perhaps you think it was in my best interest when you sent the one woman most certain to betray me as my companion on my journey here?"

What sort of monster is this woman, to have allowed all that—to have turned her face from such violence, to have *known* the impostor was not to be trusted, and still sent her with Alyrra? I glance around and see a range of controlled emotions upon my fellow attendants' faces, from the disbelief in the widening eyes of the man across from me to the hardening of Jasmine's jaw in what can only be anger.

"Alyrra," the queen says, her voice deepening with warning. She casts a single concerned glance toward Kestrin.

"Let us not bother with such lies right now, Mother. We both know whom you have protected. Make no mistake, this attempt on my life was an act of war, and this meeting is our parley. You have a choice now: you may exile Daerilin and my brother, or you may refuse. If you refuse, I will request the king's support in raising what soldiers I require to march on Adania and take the hall from you. Of course, we will insist you remain here in safety until the matter is resolved."

I press my hands against my thighs. I have always known that Alyrra is a princess, that she has an immense amount of power at her disposal. But somehow I managed to let that knowledge slip away from me. The reality of the princess's words shock me. She will change the succession of her homeland's throne, and she will go to war to do so, if she must.

"And," Kestrin says, breaking his silence for the first time, "I guarantee that we will provide everything Zayyida Alyrra requires."

Alyrra raises a hand. "To be clear, Adania's crown will go to cousin Derin, as is his right. I have no interest in ruling over Adania, nor adding it to Menaiya's lands."

"You cannot do this," the queen says, her voice tight with outrage.

"It is your decision how Derin comes to rule," Alyrra says implacably. "Though it might be best not to involve the Menaiyan armies. What will you choose?"

A chill crawls up my spine. Alyrra is all princess right now, nothing like the girl who reminded me of my little sisters, the girl whom I thought might need my support.

The queen lifts her chin haughtily. "You cannot take away your brother's throne over such a prank as this. The Council of Lords—"

"I am not concerned with how you deal with your Council of Lords. That is your worry. Let us be clear, Mother. I cannot trust my brother, the crown prince of Adania, to treat servants justly, to respect and protect high-ranked women, to prevent an attempt on my life—I, who am both his sister and a princess in my own right. Nor can I trust him to uphold and honor an alliance to which I have committed my life, and upon which Adania will be greatly dependent. If he cannot be trusted in any of these things, why should he be entrusted with the keeping of all of Adania?"

"You are overblowing—"

"He will *not* be king," Alyrra snarls. "This snake may seem like a small thing, but it is the final act in the making of his downfall. He will not rise again after this. Do you understand? You have failed as queen dowager and regent, and I will not allow your failure to endanger Adania any longer."

"I have only ever *protected* our land!"

Alyrra's face pales with fury, the skin of her cheeks blotchy. She takes a slow breath and says coldly, "It seems there is no point in our continuing this conversation. Prince Kestrin has dispatched a pair of quads to take Daerilin and your son into custody. They will each be exiled as I choose. Should you require me to ride to Adania before you to assure Derin of his right to rule, I will do so."

The queen goes still, as if she has only just realized she cannot win. "You cannot do this."

"It is already done."

The queen shoots an uncertain glance toward Kestrin. "The king—"

Kestrin shakes his head, dismissing this. "My father is not here only at Zayyida Alyrra's request. Rest assured his support of her is guaranteed. Your companion is present as your witness. You see our royal attendants are present as ours. I am sure you appreciate the delicacy of the situation."

The Adanian noblewoman remains silent, her eyes wide. No doubt she will have plenty to say to their Council of Lords, but here, in this moment, she reserves her silence.

"Alyrra, will you not hear reason?" the queen pleads, and in her voice I hear the first true emotion she has let slip this morning: a rising panic.

"You had no place for reason when I begged for it, Mother. I've heard your reasons half my life. I am done with them. I have no doubt Cousin Derin will make an excellent king, and a kinder ruler than you or my brother could ever be. There will be no further arguing this."

The queen closes her eyes, her face ashen. She is only a regent; with the prince exiled, she has lost her throne as well.

Alyrra rises to offer her mother a small curtsy, hardly that of one peer to another. "I look forward to the coronation."

The queen dips her head and departs in a haze, her companion in her wake.

With shaking fingers, I slip the cover back over the basket and fasten it. Around the room, the attendants shift slightly, as if they had held themselves taut as a wire and only now dare breathe.

"He isn't going to go away because you exiled him," Kestrin says. I glance toward him. He is focused completely on Alyrra. "He will come back, and he will bring trouble with him."

She shakes her head. "I have taken his power, his title, and his wealth from him. I will not take his life as well."

"And if he returns?"

"Then we will do what we must," she says tiredly.

Kestrin nods and waves his hand once, dismissing all of us attendants. I hesitate as the others file to the door. My letter still sits untouched on the small table. Alyrra needs to know—

"Go," Kestrin says, his voice flat. He meets my gaze with all the authority of his position. It is not an order I would dare countermand.

I dip my head and go.

CHAPTER

46

Filadon waits in the hall outside the royal suite. I entertain a momentary hope that he is here for Kestrin, that I will be able to escape to the guard room and go with Matsin to Kirrana's home, but from the way Filadon looks at me, I know he's here for me.

"Hallo, Rae," he says. I have the distinct feeling he is sorry to be here.

"Verin," I say slowly, and his eyes flicker shut for a half moment. Yes, whatever his reason, it's political and not something he's pleased about.

"Come," he says, offering me his arm. "We're going for a walk."

"I can't just now," I say, glancing down the hall to where Matsin waits, filling the doorway of the guard room. I should have left with him some time ago; I'm not sure how much longer he'll wait. "I realize there's something you need to say to me, but there is something I must do. It's urgent."

"Walking clears the mind," Filadon says, taking my arm and turning me to the staircase. Matsin nods once to me and steps back. "There's something we need to discuss. I'm sorry, Rae, but your errand will have to wait."

I stop at the top of the stairs and look up at Filadon, catching his gaze. Even if Matsin will wait, Kirrana needs my help. "And if I refuse to come with you just now? Because my *errand* involves someone's life?"

I have never seen him look so grim. "This one involves yours. And it shouldn't take long."

"Filadon—"

"Yours and your family's."

I go still staring at him, thinking of Kestrin's secret that I discovered just last night. Filadon looks away, then tugs me forward. I let him lead me down the stairs, descending gingerly as each step with my left foot presses into burst blisters. We proceed into a small salon with wide windows that look out onto a mosaic-tiled courtyard, the fountains at its center familiar. I must have been past it before.

"This particular room," he says as he shuts the door, "is protected from listening ears. Much like the royal suites."

"So what is it we need to discuss that requires such privacy?"

"I think you know."

I'm not admitting anything, just in case this is a test. "I think you need to say it out loud."

Filadon nods. "The prince has a secret that only a select few know: his father, his wife, me, the captain of his bodyguard, and one of his attendants."

"And now me."

"And now you."

I consider Filadon silently. Kestrin may have thanked me for keeping his secret in confidence . . . but he's no fool. The secret I carry could easily be turned against him, and in such a way that I could both reap the benefit and escape the repercussions. Perhaps Filadon is Kestrin's closest friend precisely because he can be trusted with such a secret. But I'm *not* Kestrin's friend, and I've only served Alyrra a short time now. What will Kestrin demand of me to ensure his secret?

There is only one thing I can think of that would ease his concern, and there is *no* way I am telling him of Niya's talent. It might be a secret of equal weight, one that will assure mutual silence, but it will also put Niya in the prince's power. And princes use the tools at their disposal. Maybe not immediately, but no doubt eventually, Niya would get pulled in to do his bidding.

I'm not giving Niya up, and I won't let Filadon do so either. Because this is what he meant—not my family's lives, but Niya's. Unless it's already too late. "You haven't told him about Niya, have you?" I demand abruptly.

"I have been trying to come up with some leverage to give the prince. I can think of nothing else."

"*No.*"

Filadon sighs. "Rae, he will not move against your sister because then you would move against him. It's a perfect balance."

"I said, *no.* What hold does he have on you? Why does he trust you?"

"We've known each other since childhood. When I promised my silence, he believed it. And he needed me. I was useful to him." Filadon shrugs philosophically. "Still am. Also, it helps, I think, that I look for neither reward nor an increase in rank from him."

"I don't want those things either," I say sharply. "I'm useful to Alyrra, and I'm your kin. Surely he can trust in that?"

"You're Ramella's kin."

"I see. You mean for everything else, that's enough. But for this, it isn't."

"Rae, this is—perhaps you don't realize what could happen if it were known."

"Oh, I realize," I say, looking out at the fountains again: three pools, each nested within the other, so that they overflow from the smallest to the next to the largest, a small movement leading to greater and greater repercussions. I have the sudden nearly uncontrollable urge to dash past Filadon, gather my things, and leave all of this behind. Only some things can't be left behind. And I cannot leave while Kirrana is missing.

"There's no need to look so hunted, Rae. We'll find a way to keep the balance."

I stare at him. "Do you know what I watched transpire this morning? I saw a man be removed from a royal succession and his throne given to a spare heir in a quiet conversation that played out before breakfast, without him even being present. Do you have *any idea* what our prince and princess are capable of?"

"You're afraid of them."

"Only a fool wouldn't be! I respect Alyrra—and Kestrin. I will be loyal to them, but for God's sake, Filadon, that whole family is terrifying."

And then there are the mages, who are meant to stand for our protection, and yet are connected to the snatchers. And I've been so busy between them and Berenworth, I haven't even looked to see if the Speakers might be involved. There is literally no one left to trust except myself and a thief. At this rate, Bren likely has some terrible secret he's hiding, since everyone else seems to.

"This morning was not exactly palace life as usual, Rae. But it's been a long time coming. I understand the princess has a number of scars. You must have seen them while attending her."

"Yes," I say, the word short and hard.

Filadon nods. "Those were by and large inflicted by her brother. What you witnessed was both necessary and long over-due."

"I'm not saying what Alyrra did wasn't necessary. But that wasn't some private family dispute. A crown changed hands."

"I know," Filadon says.

"And now you're saying you're going to put my sister's life in Kestrin's hands, because you don't know what else to do." The thought terrifies me.

"Rae—"

"The answer is no. You may tell Kestrin you have one hold on me, and if you give it to him I will not only despise you the rest of your days, but I will hate him, and I will not rest until I have made sure that he cannot use that hold against Niya. Or, *or*, he can accept that I am deeply loyal to the princess and the royal family as a whole, that I respect him and value your counsel, and I have pledged to keep his secret. It's his choice, and yours. He can send me home tomorrow and never allow me near the king's city again, and I won't care. But he can't have Niya."

Filadon makes to speak, but I cut him off.

"So help me, Filadon, if you betray Niya to him, I will get all my family away, and I will make sure Melly knows exactly why we had to flee our own home."

Filadon's jaw tenses. Melly is the one thing he could truly lose through betraying Niya, and he knows it as well as I.

"I was wrong, Rae. You have learned to politick."

"No. I've always known how to protect Niya. It's what I've grown up doing. I may not be able to manage any of the rest of this, but Niya I will keep safe. And I will do the same for the prince." I meet Filadon's eyes, knowing he needs this from me. "His secret is the same; he will be equally destroyed if he is found out. I would no more do that to him than I would to Niya. I will keep his secret, Filadon. All you have to do is convince him of it without risking Niya. *You* know politics. Surely you can find a way."

Filadon looks away, his gaze absently moving over the furniture: a maroon-and-gold sofa set, maroon-and-black carpets underfoot highlighted with cream. I've almost gotten used to the absurd wealth on display in every room of the palace.

"I will try," he says finally. "Perhaps just the knowledge that there is a hold that can be had on you, one that you would fight so desperately to protect, will be enough for him. He doesn't want your enmity, Rae. If I'm not mistaken, he's grateful indeed that Alyrra has taken to you. We'll see if just the promise of a hold, and the already proven fact of your loyalty, will be enough."

If it isn't, I'd rather Kestrin destroy me than ever learn about Niya.

I dip Filadon a curtsy. My foot gives a twinge, but it's worth it, for it brings Filadon up short. "Verayn," I say. "I put my trust in you."

He doesn't speak as I let myself out. Nor does he follow me.

This time, I make it back to the guard room successfully. Matsin waits, fingers drumming impatiently on the center table where he sits. He looks up at the sound of my step, and is rising from his seat before I pass through the door.

"There's a carriage waiting below, kelari," he says. "Let's go."

CHAPTER

47

The sun has just cleared the palace walls when I finally clamber into the waiting carriage. Matsin swings up to sit beside the driver, the quad he has brought with him mounted and ready to escort us. We pull out of the palace gates, turning to rumble east toward the river. We cross over the soaring bridge that passes Speakers' Hall, and continue into the merchants' quarter, eventually leaving the main road for smaller streets.

The carriage draws to a stop before the wide steps to a carved and painted door. The home within will be well-appointed but not rich, just as the door is—it lacks the bronze inlay that characterizes wealthy homes, but is a step above most of what I've seen in the city.

As I alight, a figure detaches itself from the wall farther down and saunters over to meet us. Matsin swings down from his seat, glancing from me to—

"Bren?"

His eyes laugh at me. "Rae, glad to see you've brought a guard with you this time."

I've never seen him so well dressed: his clothes are pristine, the muted green of his tunic and sand brown of his pants lending him an almost somber air. He's forgone tying back his hair, as many of the nobility do, and I have a momentary flashback of him sitting on the edge of my bed, my hand in his hair.

Oh *no*. That won't do at all. "Captain Matsin," I say sharply. "Allow me to introduce a friend of mine, Bren. Bren, Captain Matsin of the royal guard."

Matsin dips his head. "Matsin en Korto," he says, naming his lineage. It's a formal introduction that demands a response in kind.

Bren grins and bows with a flourish, that of a bow to one's peer. "Bren," he says, and lifts his brow in challenge.

"Do you have some information?" I ask abruptly. Bren was right: I am prickly as a burr. But Kirrana's in danger, and there's no time to waste on games.

"Not yet. I wanted to hear what I could from the family. That may help my men in their search."

"You have men searching?" Matsin asks.

Bren spreads his hands, the picture of innocence. "Of course. Don't you?"

I turn my back on them both and knock on the door.

"Kelari, you know and trust this fellow?" Matsin says as footsteps approach from the other side.

"Yes," I say, which is mostly true. "It was his man following us to the docks, to make sure we were safe."

"Ah, good, then the soldier *was* trustworthy?" Bren asks.

"The soldier was me," Matsin says.

"That's a yes?"

The door swings open, saving both Matsin and me from replying. We are welcomed in by Kirrana's mother. Kelari Siyela takes my hands, pressing them firmly in hers. Her skin is dry and cool. Her face is pale beneath its natural brown, her eyes so shadowed they look bruised.

"I am so sorry," I whisper. Until this moment, Kirrana having gone missing was real but not. Faced with her mother's fear and grief, the reality slaps me in the face as hard as the foreign prince's palm. Kirrana is *gone*, and it is almost certainly my fault.

"There is nothing to apologize for," she says, because she does not know. "Please, come in. Have you any news of Kirrana?"

"I'm afraid not," Matsin says as we file into the entry hall. "We've launched an investigation within the palace complex. Her friends and roommate are being questioned, as are her colleagues and superior at the tax office. If there's a clue there, we'll find it. What I need to know now is what you can tell me. Or your husband, if he can speak to us."

"He's resting upstairs," Siyela says, pausing at the door to the sitting room. "Do you wish to speak with him?"

"With your permission, that would be very helpful," Bren says without a glance at Matsin. So we follow her up the stairs, past a room where two young women sit on cushions, sewing baskets untouched on the carpet beside them. They turn to watch us pass, their expressions tight with worry. Kirrana's elder sisters. I had forgotten about them. In their eyes, I catch a glimpse of Ani's grief, dark and terrified.

I follow behind the two men to linger in the doorway of the

bedchamber where Kirrana's father lies, the blankets resting over his slim figure. He turns his head toward us, and my lungs stutter. His face is a mass of bruises, dark and shiny and puffed up, his lips split and his eyes barely visible. Whoever did this meant to punish him, not just knock him out. And those men now have Kirrana.

I clutch the doorframe unsteadily.

He speaks in a low, rough voice, the words clumsy behind puffy lips. "There were five of them," he tells us at Matsin's urging. "We weren't far, only two or three blocks from here. We were passing an alley, and they came up on the other side of us. They were armed—told us to walk into the alley or they'd kill us where we stood. We should have—" His voice breaks on a sob. He shakes his head.

"They would have killed you if you'd shouted or tried to run," Bren says. "You did the right thing, doing as they said. Then what happened?"

"I offered them my purse, my boots, whatever they wanted. They laughed and took it all. I thought—but then they said they wanted her too. My *daughter*. My Kirrana!"

"Did they hurt her?" Bren asks. "Or just you?"

The man shakes his head, tears leaking down his swollen cheeks. "They—they leapt on me, beat me—I couldn't fight them off. One of them grabbed her, got his arm around her neck. They just dragged her away, laughing. She couldn't even get breath to scream."

I sag against the doorframe, my hands shaking. I *know* how easy it is to be taken hostage, to be forced to walk where you don't want to go. To be dragged by the throat to a hopeless fate.

Kirrana might be more able to run, but she had as little chance as I when the Scholar's men caught me.

"I am sorry," Bren says. "It's a good sign, at least, that they didn't assault her in the alley, or cut her."

Siyela gives a soft, muffled sob, turning her face away.

"Have you attempted to trace her?" Matsin asks. "Using the services of a mage, I mean. They might be able to locate her. We've sent what we found in her room to the Circle, but I haven't had word back yet."

Siyela shakes her head, makes herself look back at us. "We tried. He said she's warded. That's all we know about her now."

"Kel," Bren says, turning back to Kirrana's father. "How well could you see the men in the dark? Did you notice anything unusual about them? Any inkings, perhaps? Unusual scars?"

"The—the one who spoke, he had an inking on his neck. Near the start of his tunic. It looked—I couldn't tell. Like a boat, perhaps."

Bren frowns. "And the others? Perhaps a weapon that stood out? Or a bit of jewelry?"

"The leader wore a silver ring. The other men—I didn't see them well. They all had their hoods up."

Bren slides a look to Matsin, who shakes his head. But I have the distinct feeling the look was an act—it was too smooth, too open. Although if these descriptions meant something to Bren, surely he would say something? Unless he's waiting until we leave Kirrana's family.

Matsin asks another question. I stare down at the floor, then look up again as Kirrana's father finishes speaking. "Kel," I say hesitantly. "Did Kirrana have anything with her?"

"Just an old set of wax tablets in her bag, nothing important."

I nod woodenly. Would the snatchers have known she had it with her? Would they have even known it existed? It seems impossible, and yet her disappearance shouldn't have happened at all. The real question is *how* they could have known.

I've made a mistake somewhere, I just don't know where. And Kirrana is paying the price of it.

CHAPTER
48

We depart less than an hour later, our questions largely unanswered, and with even less to give in return. I take my leave of Siyela with a gentle embrace, and clamber up into the carriage. A moment later, Bren climbs up behind me, settling on the opposite bench with a smirk—not for me, but for Matsin, who steps in behind him with a fearsome glower. Because of course it's inappropriate for a young man to ride alone with a woman, never mind that I've been alone quite a bit with Bren.

While Matsin certainly doesn't qualify as chaperone material, he can't leave me alone with Bren either. He seats himself on the opposite bench as well, the seat long enough to allow some space between them. Judging from Matsin's black look, that's a good thing.

"Did that description mean anything to you?" I ask Bren as the carriage starts forward. "The man with the inking?"

"You'd be surprised how many men have inkings on their necks," Bren says dryly. His expression is easy, but there's a warning in his eyes. He doesn't want me to ask, which means the description *does* mean something to him. Whatever his secrets, I want Kirrana safe.

"Does the silver ring help narrow it?" I push.

"That's what I intend to find out." He turns to Matsin. "Do you have any leads? I've already had my men comb the area of the attack. We haven't located any witnesses."

"You expect me to tell you if *we* did?" Matsin says, raising a brow. "Correct me if I'm wrong, but you're not with any guard. You're a street boy, and with all your talk of having men, you're part of one of the thieving rings. What makes you think I'll even let you off this carriage?"

"Captain—" I begin, equal parts infuriated and worried. He *can't* arrest Bren.

"You don't trust me?" Bren interrupts, amused. "Come now, if the princess herself approves of me—"

"Why would I believe that?"

"Because I am the one our dear Rae has been working with these past couple of weeks. If you want to keep her safe now, you had better share what you know. Or has it not occurred to you that she may be next?"

Our dear Rae? Was that calculated to infuriate Matsin, or is Bren not thinking clearly?

Matsin says, "*Kelari Amraeya* will be safe enough in the palace."

"I have my doubts regarding that. However, *assuming* you can keep her safe, that doesn't help the girl who's already been taken.

Let's say my men turn up some evidence I think you could use. How shall I let you know?"

"Afraid to walk into the palace?"

Bren grins, all sharp teeth. "Not at all. Are you sure you want me walking in?"

Gah! These—these *children*. "You can route your information through me," I tell Bren sharply. "And you"—I glare at Matsin—"can stop baiting the man who is helping us. Whoever he is, he is trustworthy in this, and I expect you to treat him as your ally."

"Do you."

"As the princess does," I grate. "You can worry about his vocation once we've recovered Kirrana."

"Excellent advice," Bren chirps.

"And *you* can be quiet," I snap.

Matsin's lips twitch. He glances sideways at Bren, who shakes his head slightly. Are they *commiserating* over me?

"Better to leave than to accept silence," Bren says with an air of beleaguered heroism. He rises, feet spread to take his weight as the carriage rattles along.

Matsin glances out the window. We are just past the river. "I don't believe we'll be stopping until we reach the palace."

"No need to stop," Bren says, as if this were the most foolish thing he's heard in a while. He turns and smiles at me. "I doubt we'll meet again, Rae. Safe travels."

"Prosperous arrivals," I respond automatically, before I even realize he is moving, the door flying open as the horses trot along. He bounds away—not out, but sideways, catching an outer railing on the side of the carriage perilously close to the wheel before disappearing from view altogether, the door swinging back.

Swearing a black stream, Matsin shoves his head out the door, but wherever Bren is, he's no longer hanging off the carriage. One of the soldiers riding at the rear shouts a question, turning his horse, but Matsin calls back, "No, let him go," and then swears again.

After a long moment he returns to the bench, sitting down heavily. "Which ring is he associated with? I'm aware the princess had contact with thieves on the west side. Is this—"

"Did you know I had tea with the Black Scholar the night I went missing?" I ask cheerfully.

He stares. "*That's* who's looking for you?"

"And visited Bardok Three-Fingers," I muse, pleased my distraction technique has worked. "But you're right, it's the Scholar who wants me."

Matsin's eyes narrow. "How would you have met those two?"

This is the man who has taught the princess and the rest of us self-defense—or at least, begun our lessons. If I'm going to distract him, I might as well get something useful out of it.

I smile tightly and say, "Taken prisoner by one, nearly bartered to the other. Do you know what else? I attempted to escape by climbing out a window. But a man came up behind me as I reached the street and put his arm across my throat, and dragged me back to the house. Same as what those other men did to Kirrana."

"Did you pass out?"

"No, but I couldn't get my feet under me, and if he'd pressed any harder I might have."

"Probably a chokehold."

Sounds about right. "What, precisely, does one do to break such a hold?"

Matsin studies me and then nods. He knows exactly what I'm doing in changing the conversation. We spend the rest of the ride going over how to reach back to one's attacker's hands, catch hold of a finger, and pull it until it breaks. Although Matsin does not attempt to make me practice in the carriage.

"The pain will usually cause an attacker to release their hold, even if only momentarily," he tells me.

"And then?"

"Then turn around, put your thumbs in their eyes, and dig them in and across," Matsin says, holding up his hands toward an imaginary attacker's face and demonstrating. Brutal but doubtlessly effective.

"And then run," Matsin finishes.

"Always run," I agree, because in the end, I can't argue with escape. At whatever pace one is able to manage.

We alight in the palace courtyard. Matsin moves aside to speak with his quad. I glance around as I start toward the doors, and jerk to a stop. There is one other carriage pulled up in the courtyard. It is heavily guarded, and there, coming through a side door with a fully armed escort, strides the foreign prince, his features pale and skin pulled tight, like a living skull, his straw-colored hair falling unkempt over his forehead.

I back up until I am all but covered from sight by the bulk of the carriage beside me. But the foreign prince doesn't notice. He barely looks about the courtyard. They reach the second carriage and his lips shape a snarl as he says something hard and sharp to the soldiers around him. I creep forward, keeping in the shadow of the carriage, to watch as he waits and then realizes he will have to open the door for himself. He does so, his eyes bright with fury, and climbs into the dim confines of a carriage that would be beneath the lowest of our nobles.

A soldier slams the door shut and locks it. The windows are small—too small to allow a full-grown man egress. Now that the prince is closed into the carriage, a dozen hostlers lead up horses for the guards. A quad climbs up to ride on the carriage, while the rest mount up on the horses.

Matsin has paused, watching as the captain leading the escort calls a command. The guards start forward, the carriage rattling over the pavers and through the wide gates, carrying the foreign prince with it. There's a deep relief in seeing the carriage disappear beyond the gates. I don't doubt Kestrin has arranged for the prince to be taken far beyond our borders.

"Still here, kelari?" Matsin asks, having turned back to me.

"Yes." I nod, gather myself. My foot is hurting no more than it usually does when blistered, and my wounded arm only twinges slightly when I move it. No need to delay any longer.

I take a step forward and something twirls past my face, pale as a rosebud, and then flits sideways to land on my shoulder. I blink, turning my head to see a tiny white-breasted bird, its wings pink and its beak decidedly laughing. Not a rosebud at all.

There's something strange about it though, its eyes dark but not bright. I'm used to birds eyeing things with a sort of liveliness about them, shrewd and aware. This bird is *not*. Even the slight opening of its beak—what I had initially taken as avian good humor—seems hollow and somewhat unnerving.

It's not alive. My stomach gives a sickening lurch and I reach to flick the thing from my shoulder before my mind registers that I might not want to touch it. The dead-eyed bird takes flight before I can, though, whirling around and landing on my other shoulder.

I freeze, staring. My thoughts fly to the dead horse's head speaking from the grave. Is this the same or different? What sort of spell would do this? And what does it want with me? The thing hops once and lets out a single-toned chirp, like a bell.

"What is that?" Matsin asks, staring at the not-bird. "It's not natural, is it?"

"No." I flap a hand at it. If it takes off again, I can attempt to make a run for it. Instead of flying, it tilts its head and then spreads its wings, leaping from my shoulder to land on the back of my hand. "Oh!" I jerk my hand back and the bird *flattens*, its feathers smoothing and its limbs going stiff. It tumbles past the backs of my fingers to the ground, and there it remains, a folded bit of paper, pale against the stone pavers.

Paper.

I rub the back of my hand as if to wipe away the feel of the not-creature on my skin. Matsin reaches down and picks up the paper. It faintly resembles a bird even now, folds for beak and wings apparent. He turns it over, and there on one corner are written the words *open here*.

"I think," he says, raising his eyes to mine, "you had better read this."

It's mage-sent, that much is clear. I take the paper, grateful that it doesn't revert to feathers and beak and dead eyes again. I touch the unfamiliar script, and then follow its directions to unfold the paper bird into a single thin square bearing a message.

Kelari Amraeya,

I have attempted to trace your friend. I'm afraid I cannot pinpoint her precise location, even with what you provided me. I can tell you this: she is still here, in this city. If my estimates are correct, and I believe they are, she is right now near the river docks. Unfortunately, I cannot work past the wards that guard her enough to tell you where exactly she shelters, whether within a boat or a building.

I hope that this information is of some use to you.

When you have finished with this note, fold it over once and order it to "Fly away home."

Adept Midael, the Cormorant

I stare at the words. Kirrana's in the city. At the docks.

"Kelari?" Matsin glances from the paper to me.

I hold the letter tight in my hand, my heart stuttering with hope. "We have a lead."

CHAPTER

49

The moment I walk into the attendants' suite, Jasmine looks up and says, "The princess wants you. She said to send you in whenever you returned."

I thank her and turn around to head straight to Alyrra's rooms. She must have read my letter at last.

Alyrra is getting ready for lunch, but she sends a page for Kestrin at once. While a maid puts the finishing touches on Alyrra's hair, I pour myself a cup of tea from the pot sitting on a side table and snag a pair of biscuits. I never had breakfast and I don't know if I'll manage lunch, so I'll take what I can find now.

As soon as the maid departs, Alyrra turns to me. "Any news about your friend?"

I swallow the last of my biscuit. "We have a lead. I need your help, zayyida. We believe she's being held on a boat at the docks. We need to be able to search for her."

"I'll see it done. Tell me everything."

By the time Kestrin and Garrin arrive a quarter of an hour later, Alyrra has heard my story and briefed me on how to retell it once everyone has gathered. At her request, Kestrin dispatches a page for Verin Melkior, the lord high marshal of Menaiya, and sends for Captain Matsin as well, who has already requested permission to report in.

Melkior bears the power of his authority in his very person, tall and broad shouldered, his hair just starting to gray. When he enters the room, his bow to the royals seems almost a favor granted them rather than their due. Matsin enters just behind him.

I wait as everyone settles into place, trying not to fidget. I cannot push this meeting to move any faster than the royals wish. The royal guard doesn't have the authority to stop a merchant ship—for that, we need the river guard, which falls under Melkior's jurisdiction. Thankfully, the disappearance of a tax office employee falls under him as well, which means Matsin has already made him aware of Kirrana's case.

Finally, Kestrin asks Matsin for his report. He provides a concise summary of Kirrana's disappearance and what has been learned in the intervening hours.

"I fail to see why this concerns all of us," Melkior says heavily. "It's a worry, of course, but the girl and her father were out at night and clearly set upon by some shady characters. We will try to locate her, but I don't see any reason to believe she was taken because of whatever special case you had her working on."

"She was investigating the snatchers, as they are called," Alyrra says steadily. "Slavers."

Melkior raises his brows. "Yes, I understand that you are

concerned about them, zayyida, however small their actual presence might be. But how would they have known of this girl's involvement? There is no reason to believe they are at work here."

However *small*? No reason? Does he mean to imply that her abduction was a chance coincidence? That the men who took her meant only to—to assault her? Even if that were true, how is that any less concerning?

Kestrin frowns. "The girl was warded against traces within hours of her abduction. That would imply more than a random attack. Wards that can stand against a trace are carefully controlled by the Circle, are they not?"

Melkior nods grudgingly. "Too much opportunity for misuse. The Circle rarely issues them. Very well, then, there's a chance there's more at play. We have no leads on where the girl might be, though, unless you, Captain, have uncovered anything further."

"Not me, verin," Matsin says, nodding toward me. "Kelari Amraeya requested aid from . . . a mage of her acquaintance."

My fingers itch at the thought of the paper bird. I've already sent it back to the Cormorant. If I want to be able to call on him or Stonemane again, I must protect their identities now. Which means not having anything to hand over should I be so ordered.

"What did you learn, then, kelari?" Melkior demands.

I take a breath. "In confidence, I asked a mage known to me to try to bypass the wards blocking Kirrana from being traced. They were not altogether successful, but they sent word that she is somewhere near the docks."

"Somewhere?" Melkior shakes his head. "That hardly

narrows down her location."

"I suspect she would be on a galley operated by Berenworth Trading Company, based on the research she completed. It's possible we are wrong; we didn't manage to find conclusive evidence. But the fact that the trace succeeding in narrowing down her location to the docks leads me to believe that a search of the ships would be worthwhile."

Melkior huffs. "A fine idea, kelari. But every decision has its ramifications. We can certainly search all of Berenworth's ships, but that will undoubtedly cause significant loss for the company, and it's unclear that it's necessary. This girl could be *anywhere* at the docks, and there's no certainty that she's on a ship at all. To punish the whole company"—Melkior shrugs—"that could be construed as excessive."

Excessive? *Unnecessary?* I open my mouth to argue. Matsin clears his throat, shaking his head at me once. Melkior looks inquiringly toward him, then back to the royals. I take Matsin's cue and wait for Alyrra to respond. But she doesn't; instead she flicks a single glance at Garrin, then looks back at Melkior as if in thought.

Kestrin sighs, and it is finally enough to prod Garrin to sit forward. "I believe that in this case we might consider it a necessary investigation. We've been focused on the thieves in the city, but if the rumors of children being snatched are actually true, then this warrants an equal focus. If the girl can't be found—if there is nothing at all being hidden—then let it fall to me to manage the merchants' displeasure."

Melkior considers Garrin. "You may have less to lose, verin, but a single note of concern from an unnamed mage hardly constitutes the sort of evidence one should accept to close down our docks." Melkior turns to Kestrin. "Zayyid, we endanger our merchant class by impounding boats over rumors and a single girl gone missing."

Alyrra tilts her head. "One would think we might also be endangering the common folk by ignoring their pleas and what evidence we do come across that such rumors are not grounded in falsehood. You forget, verin, but I lived among the people, and I asked you about the snatchers before I ever returned to the palace. I have no doubt that the problem is an epidemic where you see only a few incidents. We have this chance to investigate. It must not be squandered."

"No," Kestrin agrees. "Garrin has the right of it. Melkior, if you will send your men with Captain Matsin, together they can inspect the boats at the docks at once. If we find no further evidence, then the boats will be released, and the captains and crew will have lost no more than an afternoon. If, however, we find that at least one of them carries a shipment of children, then the crew must be brought in for questioning."

"I should like to go alone," Garrin says. "I'll take my own men to see to my safety, but I think it best that I be there to assuage any of the galley captains' concerns."

"And I as well," I say, before the moment can slip away.

"What?" Garrin says blankly as the others stare. "You?"

"Yes, verin. Kirrana may answer to my voice where she might not to those of unknown men."

"A merchant galley's hold is hardly a place for a lady," Garrin says. "Nor are the docks."

"Then it is just as well I am a horse rancher's daughter. I would help search for my friend, verin. I will stay out of your way; I will not hinder your men. But I must be there."

He considers me, his eyes narrowed, and I cannot tell what he is thinking. Alyrra doesn't speak, and Melkior just shakes his head. Finally, Garrin says, "As you wish, kelari. Let us only hope we do not meet with any trouble."

CHAPTER
50

It takes more time than I would like for Melkior to send out orders, and for Garrin's men to assemble alongside Matsin and his quad in the front courtyard. I wait inside the first of a pair of carriages: one for Garrin, and one for me, given that I shouldn't ride alone with him. I shouldn't have been alone with a handful of fighting men either, but that's somehow less noteworthy. Palace folk have an interesting way of assessing propriety. I suppose all the noblewomen go places alone with their guards now and then.

Finally, Garrin arrives and we set off. I check my calf sheath as we leave the palace, but my bone knife is still safely in place. I take a moment to assess the magic-sealed cut in my arm as well: it's healing well, the glimmer of magic nearly gone, the scar tissue showing through where the scabs have fallen away. It's still tender, but it hasn't leaked even a drop of blood in days. My turned foot is tender but the last of the blisters from the wedding procession have either burst or drained. They aren't infected, at least, and should heal up well enough. And the bruise on my cheek has faded to a mottled yellow, barely visible, in large part thanks to the healer-mage's aid. I may be a bit roughed up around the edges, but I'm holding together.

When we arrive at the docks, the head warden with his resplendent mustache comes out to meet Garrin. I step down to join the conversation, glancing around once for any sign of Bren. I sent his page with a second message for him, letting him know we were going to the docks. Given his last interaction with Matsin, I told him not to join us, that I was only informing him of my movement because I didn't want a lecture. Although, truthfully, I want him to know where to search for Kirrana as well, in case he can do something the guards cannot.

Thankfully, though, there's no sign of Bren just now. The head warden bows to me, recognition flashing in his eyes, but he focuses his conversation on Garrin. Within a few minutes, we know which of the three Berenworth galleys docked will leave next.

"Verin," Matsin calls. We turn to find him approaching in company with nearly a dozen river guards. "Allow me to introduce Captain Diara. She has received Verin Melkior's orders and will lead the soldiers performing the search."

The captain at his side proffers us a bow, a polite smile on her lips and the gleam of intelligence in her eyes. "We are honored to be of service."

"Very good," Garrin says, his expression warming.

I smile, delighted to find a woman in command. I've seen only a few among the guards.

"I understand you wish to search *The Silver Star*. We'll make quick work of it."

"Excellent." Garrin nods to me. "Kelari, if you'll wait on the docks, I'll rejoin you once we've gained access to the holds."

I dip my head. I promised not to interfere, and I'll adhere to that for the time being.

Diara has brought a pair of quads with her. They follow behind as she and Garrin walk up the dock to where *The Silver Star* is moored. Matsin orders his quad to stay with me, and continues on after the others.

I station myself a few paces from the gangplank, aware of the quad arrayed silently around me, as if I were at immediate risk of attack. Their weapons are sheathed, but there's no way anyone would think of bothering me regardless.

I turn my attention to the ship. It's a wide-bottomed river galley. From the boys Bren stole free from the brickmaker, I know the single-level hold is where the snatched will be hidden. Will Kirrana be there? Or am I wrong, every coincidence of proof I've attempted to gather lined up incorrectly, so that we will be searching the wrong boat? There are a dozen here; if we search the wrong one, then the true criminals will have the chance to escape, taking Kirrana with them. But I don't have anything else to go on.

I stare at the slim mast with its sails tied up, the green-and-white pennants flapping in the light spring breeze. There are a few men on deck, busy with whatever work it is a boat such as this needs. It hardly seems possible that people might be held captive beneath their feet.

As I watch, Garrin strides forward to meet the captain of

the galley, nodding to the man's bow. They speak for a few minutes, the captain frowning and then nodding and gesturing to the lower level where the rowers would sit. No doubt the hatch to the hold is there.

They move forward together, the soldiers first and then the captains and lord, disappearing from view. I wait what feels like an eternity, my eyes going from *The Silver Star* to the other galleys, the warehouses behind the docks, the houses built out along the edge of the opposite bank.

One of the soldiers beside me clears his throat. I glance back quickly to see that the party has emerged from the hold. My breath catches as I scan them, but Kirrana isn't among their number. There's no one new there at all.

No.

I step forward without realizing I'm moving.

"Kelari?" one of the soldiers asks.

"We're going on deck," I say tightly. "I intend to look as well."

The soldiers don't argue, though I sense the look they exchange among themselves. It's not their place to stop me, though.

I pause before the gangplank, remembering how easily Diara traversed it, how Matsin stepped right across it. The boat bobs at its moorings. It's steady enough for someone who is used to such things, but I'm not—either steady myself, or used to these things.

But if Kirrana is hidden on that boat, I'm not going to let this stop me. I step onto it, limping my way across. I have only one moment, when the boat dips just as I take another step with my turned foot, and the plank isn't where I expect it. I throw out my arms, wavering, and then my feet take my weight again and

I continue on, aware of the guards tensed behind me, watching.

By the time I step on deck, Garrin and the captains have all come up to it, as if waiting patiently for me to finish crossing. I raise my chin, aware of the faint warmth of my cheeks.

"Kelari," Diara says as they shift toward me. "Allow me to introduce Captain Grefan."

The captain of *The Silver Star* is tall and graying with a sinewy, ropy look to him, all lean strength and hard living. I murmur a greeting and, because my ankle is still not quite steady after that dip, attempt a bow in the manner of Diara herself. It feels a hundred times more graceful than the best of my curtsies. Why did I never think of this myself?

Grefan inclines himself slightly in return, the movement almost an insult. "I am sorry, kelari, to hear of your friend's disappearance."

I don't think him sorry in the least. I turn to Garrin. "Verin, did you find any sign of her?"

"I'm afraid not, kelari. I'm sorry."

"I would like to take a look below myself, as we discussed."

"I don't think you can," Grefan interrupts with amusement. "Not with that foot of yours."

Oh, the gall of the man! I'm *not* letting this go without a fight. Until I've seen that hold and made sure for myself that Kirrana isn't here, I'm not leaving. I may not be a noble lady, but I know how to act like one. Jasmine has given me plenty of tutelage there.

I eye Grefan with contempt. "I assure you I am well aware of what I am capable of, however little you may know of the subject."

I stride off toward the hatch, and if I stumble slightly as I go, well, there's not a thing I can do about that but grit my teeth and keep going, cursing the captain each step of the way. Matsin and his quad fall into step with me as I near the hatch, the men walking tall, with squared shoulders, as if they were my honor guard. A glance shows me Garrin watching with an amused curl of his lip, Diara beside him, and Grefan hurrying after me.

"Are you quite sure about the ladder, kelari? Perhaps take a look at that first."

If I can make it down a rope of braided linens, I can certainly make it down whatever the boat offers—in this case, a wooden ladder bolted to the opening. Matsin casts me a glance that conveys a grim approval and precedes me down. I sit on the edge of the hatch, put my toes on the rungs, and start down. My wounded arm *hurts* with each step I lower myself down, but I'm careful to keep my expression easy. I'm not about to grant Captain Grefan the smallest iota of satisfaction.

The hold runs the length of the ship and is filled with crates stacked nearly to the ceiling, strapped down to keep from shifting. It's dark and faintly damp, the sound of water loud against its sides. There's clearly no space in this hold for a hidden room, the walls curving with the hull of the ship.

"Where did they search?" I ask Matsin.

"They walked along, tapping on crates and calling."

I purse my lips. "What do you think? We've one last chance to search this hold. If you were keeping a young woman hostage, where would you put her?"

"In a crate," he admits. "But short of opening each of these, if she's unconscious or even just bound and gagged, we won't know she's here."

"Then we open them," I say shortly.

Matsin nods. "I'll speak with Diara. But Garrin will have to approve your request."

"If he doesn't, I'll go back up and speak to him."

He nods and scales the ladder, disappearing into the bright sunlight above in a matter of moments. His quad waits below with me. I nod to them and slowly walk the aisle, listening. There isn't even the scuffle of a rat to be heard.

"Kirrana!" I call. "Kirrana?"

I pause, listening, but there's no answer. Diara starts down the hold ladder as I call again, "Kirrana, can you hear me?"

"Don't think she's here," Diara says conversationally. "You really want every last crate opened?"

"Yes."

"That'll take a while. And we'll have to close them up again when we're done."

"That's fine," I say. I'm pretty sure she's asking for a bribe for herself and her men, but I don't have much to offer in my pocket, and this is her duty anyhow.

Diara sighs and sends one of her men back up to collect the necessary tools. I move back to the ladder, and there is Garrin looking down into the hold, a frown settled low over his brow, Matsin speaking quietly beside him.

"Kelari," Garrin calls down to me. "I understand you are checking all the crates?"

"Yes, verin. If Kirrana cannot answer, we won't know if she's hidden within or not."

He nods. "I'll remain above, if you don't mind."

"Of course."

I head to the back of the hold, scanning the crates as Diara's man returns with a set of bars to use as levers. Matsin descends, and he and his men each take a bar. The other soldiers move to the prow to begin their search.

"Here," I say, pointing. There're rows of crates against the stern that haven't yet had additional crates piled on top of them. "Let's start with these. We can shift crates over as we go to reach the ones underneath."

It doesn't seem likely that they'd hide a person beneath other crates, but I'm not going to risk missing Kirrana on a faulty assumption either.

Matsin pauses beside me to look. "Unusual, don't you think, that these crates against the wall are only one deep, and the rest are stacked high?"

That *is* strange.

"We'll see. Keep an eye out, kelari."

"For what?"

"For what Diara and her men are doing while we're working here."

I nod and move back to lean against the flat boards of the stern to watch, crates stacked to either side of me. Between my wounded arm and my clumsiness as the galley occasionally bobs, I'll do the most good staying out of the way. Across the hold, Diara and her men work systematically through the far crates, opening the tops, peering in, then fitting them back down and hammering them shut. But if Matsin doesn't actually trust them, then they could just as easily look in on Kirrana and cover her back up again.

I glance toward Matsin, then back at Diara.

"Stay," Matsin says, looking sideways at me.

Is he always so perceptive?

"If what you're thinking is accurate, there's no point looking on that side anyway."

Because Diara would attempt to start us on a part of the ship where there was nothing to be found? Or is Matsin just trying to keep me safe and out of the way? I bite my lip and stay where I am.

The men work through the first set of crates to the left, then start on the next row, shifting over the topmost crates as they're opened and resealed. I watch them with a growing sense of helplessness. Maybe I'm wrong. Maybe every bit of evidence we gathered was so circumstantial, so indirect, that I'm on the wrong ship now, and Kirrana is somewhere else entirely. *Wrong, wrong, wrong.*

I stare across the hold at Diara's men. They are nearly a third of the way through the crates. A pair of Matsin's men cross the aisle to start on the crates to the right of me, but it seems less and less likely Kirrana will be found.

I've failed her, and now I will go back to the palace and the snatchers will continue, because all I've learned is that those behind them are too big, too dangerous for even the princess to take on. This corruption is so deep, so vast, that all I've managed is to ensure that nothing will be done. I've handled this all wrong and now Kirrana is paying the price, and nothing will change. The royals will apologize for inconveniencing Grefan, and Berenworth will go on, as will the Circle, and whoever is on the street doing the actual snatchings.

I shove away from the wall. If I can't stand still, at least I can pace. But as I step forward, the boat dips again. I take a quick step sideways to regain my balance and my turned foot bangs painfully into a crate. Clenching my jaw to keep from cursing, I boost myself up onto the crate to take the weight of my foot—and promptly freeze as my arm protests. Because I'm still a clumsy cripple who can't seem to go three days in service to the princess without gaining a new wound. I lay my throbbing arm across my lap and lean back, rest my cheek against the rough wood.

It takes me a moment to realize what's wrong. I straighten with a jerk.

"Kelari?" Matsin says softly from where he squats atop a crate.

"Come here," I whisper.

He does, crossing the crates to crouch beside me.

"Listen," I say. "Tell me what you hear."

He leans his ear against the wood, his brow furrowing.

"There's no water," I say for him. "The sound of it is too distant."

He looks at me, his teeth bared in a sharp, pleased smile. "Well done, kelari. We've a secret room to find."

CHAPTER
51

Together with his men, Matsin pulls away the crates, one by one, shoving them farther down the hold.

"Haven't you searched all those crates already?" Diara asks, walking over to us.

"We heard something," Matsin says. "Just checking."

Diara grunts, and then goes back up the ladder.

"Do we need to worry?" I ask softly as Matsin watches her climb up.

"Perhaps," he says. "But we've got our own quad and Garrin's up above as well. It's unlikely they'll attack while we have backup and a lord watching over us."

"What's this?" one of his men says in surprise, pulling away a crate to reveal a low door, and over it, a thin piece of wood mounted to the wall. My heart jumps as I recognize the inked ward painted there.

"The door we're looking for," I say. "Can you open it?"

It's barred from the outside, and takes only the work of a moment for the soldier to lift the bar and push the door open. Matsin warns me back with a raised hand, and together he and the first soldier duck into the darkened room.

I glance back through the hold to see that the remaining soldiers of the river guard are walking toward us. The sound of Matsin's voice rumbles faintly in my hearing. The soldiers keep coming. They look grim, but no one has reached for a weapon yet.

I glance back toward the secret room. Please, let Kirrana be there. And let us all get out safely.

I hear a faint whisper and turn back to the soldiers just as one of Matsin's men gives a shout. The soldiers race toward us, swords drawn. I scramble up on a crate and back away alongside the wall, the hem of my skirt catching under my feet. I don't know how to fight, don't have the first idea of how to defend myself against *swords*. I fumble my bone knife from its sheath, even if it will do little good against a weapon with longer reach.

The hatch bangs shut, plunging the hold into half-darkness, lit only by a single lantern hung from a peg. And then the soldiers meet in a flurry of blades. A scream lodges in my throat. I can't quite make out what's happening, only that the fight is swift and brutal, the clash of swords and the thunk of bodies against wood, the sickening sound of metal plunging into flesh. Matsin appears as if from nowhere, slamming into the fight, and within another breath, it is over, the floorboards slick and dark.

"Report," Matsin barks. His men answer equally shortly, but for one man who reports a cut on his arm.

"Bind it," Matsin tells him. Turning to the others, he points his sword toward the little door. "There are five children in there. Get them out while I check the hatch. We'll have to fight our way out."

I slide down from my perch, aware that I'm shaking. It's an absurd reaction—the soldiers never got close enough to endanger me, but I can't wipe the horror of the fight from my mind.

One of Matsin's men moves to the door, entering silently. I wait, clenching my bone knife in my grasp as if that might still my trembling. He emerges again a moment later, herding a pair of young boys before him. They are both no more than nine years old, their eyes huge.

"Is . . . ," I begin, and stop, knowing that Kirrana isn't here. Matsin would have said so by now.

"Can you take them?" the soldier asks, nudging the boys toward me. "There's three more."

I nod shakily, gesture the boys forward. We've found five children—this, *this* is proof. And at least these children can be returned to their homes, or given shelter.

At the top of the ladder, Matsin swears softly.

"Come," I say to the boys. "Hold hands and follow me."

I reach the ladder as Matsin jumps down, skipping the last two rungs. "We'll have to try to ram it open."

I look up at the square of daylight showing around the edges of the hatch. "How?"

"However we can," Matsin says grimly.

"It's barred?" I ask, shifting my grip on my knife. My bone knife, that won't cut my skin, but will slice through meat and bone as easily as butter.

Matsin nods.

"You help with the children. Let me try something."

"What is it?" he asks, glancing from me to the hatch.

"I think my knife can slip between the wood up there."

"It's not going to cut through a wooden bar, kelari."

"It might," I say. "It's Fae-made."

His eyes widen, and he casts a glance upward again. "Can you brace yourself up there well enough to try?"

I look up and know he's right. Maybe if it were just my foot I had to take into account, I could manage it. But my arm still throbs from my clumsiness earlier, and I know I won't be able to hang on with one hand and saw with the other.

"Take it," I say shortly, and turn back to the children.

Matsin scales the ladder again, moving silently. He pauses, listening. One of the soldiers gestures to me, and I move the children a few feet back and crouch down with them. The faint creak of footsteps sounds off toward the stern, perhaps near the stairs to the rear deck.

Matsin reaches up, slides the bone knife into the gap between hatch and floorboards, and works it silently up and down. We wait what feels like a lifetime, the children gathered beside me, the first two plus a third little boy and two young girls behind him, eleven or twelve years of age.

Matsin's men gather at the foot of the ladder, waiting. One with his arm bound by a strip of cloth; the others unharmed. And Diara's men all dead. These men, the most elite of all the guard, are terrifying.

Matsin leans back, studying what he can see through the crack, then descends once more. "That's all it can reach, but you were right. It cut through the wood like butter. We might be able to break through what's left of it now."

"Shall I try?" one of the soldiers asks. If Matsin is tall, this man is built like a bull, huge and burly and made of muscle.

Matsin nods. He hands me back my knife as he tells the man, "Expect an immediate attack. Bring them down with you. I'll go up when you go down. We fight our way out from here."

"And the children?" I ask, because clearly these words aren't meant for us.

"You stay," Matsin says tersely. "My men and I go up first. When I give you the all clear, you bring the children up and send them straight to the docks—to your carriage. You stay with them, and if I give you an order, you follow it." He turns his gaze on the children. "All of you do what the lady says."

I nod and say, "Yes, kel," and a small, wavering chorus of voices rises up to echo me.

Matsin looks back at me, and it's as if he can see right past my facade of calm to the roiling horror beneath. "If we end up fighting, don't watch. Make yourself move. Get these children to safety. That is *your* fight."

I nod again. "I understand."

The burly soldier climbs up, and Matsin follows after him, scaling the back of the ladder so that he's ready to swing around and up as soon as the way is clear.

It takes three massive thumps for the hatch to give. The burly guard hurls it away, to the sound of shouting above. He draws his dagger and takes the final step up, his head clearing the hatch, and then he ducks back down, the dagger swinging up. It smacks against something flashing silver. The guard's other hand swings out, grabbing his attacker's wrist as he drops off the ladder, twisting to send his attacker flying down past him to slam into the planks underfoot.

Diara shouts as she hits the ground, but she's already moving, rolling and shoving herself up, one hand reaching for her dagger—and then a sword cuts straight across her neck, held by one of Matsin's men.

I scream, twisting away, my arms going around the two boys beside me, hands reaching to cover their eyes. The burly soldier spares us half a glance as the other man shoves Diara's flailing body backward, blood pouring from her throat. *Oh God.* I look up only to see that Matsin has already made it out, and another guard is on his way through the hatch, dagger in hand. There is shouting above now, the clang of weapons, and a moment later a ragged scream.

I force myself to look to the children. My responsibility. I gesture the girls closer, ring all the children around me. "Listen carefully," I say, and tell them what to expect above deck, what our carriage looks like, that they're to get in it and stay in it. "We will get you back to your families," I promise. "But we need your help."

I pair them up, an older girl for each of the boys, the youngest boy for me.

"Now," I hear Matsin shout. "Amraeya, *now*!"

"*Up!*" I push the first boy forward. He climbs quickly, the girl he is partnered with clambering up nimbly behind him. "You next," I say, and the next boy and girl go up.

"I'll be right behind you," I promise the last boy, but it's a lie. He'll be faster than me. "You keep going, stay with the others," I tell him, and climb as fast as I can after him, grasping the hilt of my knife tightly.

Matsin stands with a scarlet-rimmed sword just before the

hatch. "Go," he says before I can even take in the bloodshed before me. There are two sailors facing him, but one is wounded, and the other glances around desperately, as if seeking an escape.

"Amraeya, *move.*"

I do, past a fallen body, this one a river guard. I catch up to the little boy who is mine to watch over as he stares at another corpse, the eyes wide and unseeing. It's Matsin's man—the one who went into the hidden room to bring out the children.

"Go," I rasp, shoving the boy along, but he barely moves. "*Go,*" I cry.

He can't seem to move. I grasp his hand and hobble as fast as my aching ankle can take me, watching as the two girls hurry across the gangplank, each with their hands tight around the boy who is their ward.

I skid on a puddle of wet—not blood. *Not* blood, I tell myself as I recover my balance, even if it's a lie.

The boy shrieks in fear.

I twist as a sailor grabs him by the arm. I don't think, don't register the sailor's short sword. Instead, my hand swings around and the bone knife glances off his neck, sliding sideways and cutting through flesh and muscle. He screams, shoving the boy away, his sword flashing through the air. *I'm going to die.* I scramble back, slippers sliding, and my bad foot turns, sending me sprawling on my back as someone shouts behind me.

The next moment, there's someone over me, blades flashing, and then the sailor cries out again, a gargling, horrible sound that rattles through his throat. He falls back, his sword dropping from his fingers.

"Can you get up?" the man above me says, stepping sideways, his eyes scanning the deck.

"Bren?" My voice is light and shaky. I cannot quite believe he is here.

He nods once, never looking at me. "See if you can stand."

He sheaths his dagger, his sword still in his other hand, and reaches out to help the boy to his feet. The boy. I push myself up, my ankle throbbing.

"Keep moving," Bren says, as if blood weren't dripping from my knife, as if the sailor weren't collapsed on the deck beside us, blood spreading out around him. But then there's blood dripping from Bren's sword too.

Don't think about it.

"How are you here?" I pant out, staggering forward, Bren pacing me with the boy in hand.

"I got your message," he says grimly. "Figured I'd watch to see if you needed backup. Good thing I did."

He turns suddenly, shoving the boy into my hands, and then his blade flashes up to block another blow. The metal gleams crimson in the sunlight. The attacking sailor snarls, shoving forward, but Bren presses back. How many sailors are there? And where are Garrin's men?

"Rae, go!"

I grasp the boy's shoulder and push him onto the gangplank. He's shaking and unsteady, but I can't carry him with my ankle hurt. "Go," I tell him. "To the carriage—as fast as you can!"

"Kelari!" Garrin calls. His men sprint across the dock toward us. He runs behind them. I wave and urge the boy on. He makes his halting way across, weeping as I hold his hand and try not to stumble.

There is not a thing I can do to help Bren except get to safety. It seems an impossibility when my feet touch firm ground. I glance over my shoulder to see Bren do something—I'm not sure what—and the sailor pitches sideways, losing his footing and toppling over the railing. Bren spares me a sparkling grin—how wrong that looks, amid all the bloodshed—and turns back to the fight.

It is almost over now, and I am grateful to see Matsin still standing, his voice carrying as he shouts an order. Captain Grefan is no longer visible, cut down or wounded or fled, I cannot say. The remaining sailors and single river guard seem to be backing away. They drop their weapons, one by one.

"What happened?" Garrin demands as his men come to a stop beside me, looking up.

"Where *were* you?" I demand.

"I went back to the warden's office to see what other galleys—" Garrin shakes his head, his gaze flicking from the blood saturating the bottom of my skirts to the crimson-streaked decks. "What *happened*?" he repeats.

I transfer my blood-streaked knife to my left hand and wrap my good arm around the shoulders of the little boy, aware he is shaking as badly as I am. "We found some children. And then Diara and the crew attacked."

Garrin closes his eyes, gives himself a little shake, and then looks toward the ship with renewed determination. "Take the children to your carriage. I'll handle the rest of this."

"Thank you," I say, because I don't think I can turn around

and look at the remains of the bloodbath. I continue to the carriage, the bone knife still in my hand. The children have gathered by its side, though not a one has set foot in it. I lead my charge over to join them.

"Up we go," I say, my voice unnervingly cheerful, and the children allow me to herd them into the carriage box. I stay outside a moment longer, wipe the blood from my knife with trembling fingers using a fold of my skirt. The hem is heavy with the stuff, dripping. So much blood. I shove the knife into its sheath halfway clean, scrub at the spatter of blood on my hand. Blood from a dead man. One whom I wounded, and Bren killed.

I stumble one foot to the side and empty the contents of my stomach upon the stone wharf. I'm shaking still. Shock, I decide, latching onto what I've learned from Mama.

"Kelari?" a voice asks. It's one of the older girls, watching me from the door of the carriage.

"Coming," I rasp, and spit to clear my mouth.

When I look up, I spot Bren standing by the railing of the galley, Matsin a few paces away, talking to him. The fighting is over, and both of them are spattered with blood but appear relatively unharmed. Matsin gestures toward the dock once, the gesture half invitation and half order. Does he mean to detain Bren or only offer him safe passage off the ship? Or question him first?

I step forward, one hand on the side of the carriage, as if there were anything I could do from here. Bren glances across to me, grins, and tosses his sword to Matsin, hilt first. Matsin just manages to catch it, talking a half step back in surprise. It is all the distraction Bren requires. He jumps the railing, diving straight down into the narrow space between ship and dock.

I swallow a cry. He's already gone. Matsin, swearing, drops the sword and leans over the railing, then straightens to look over at me. He shakes his head and turns away, frustration in every line of his body.

Serves him right.

I turn back to the carriage and climb up to join the children. Inside, we sit silently together. I can't seem to find any words, nor do they ask any questions. They're still terrified, their instincts numbed. I look down and find myself staring at the creases of my fingers, dark with blood, and beyond that, the hem of my skirts, equally dark, my slippers wet with it.

I clench my hands together.

"One of your friends died," the girl across from me says. "A soldier."

I nod, but she's wrong. I don't know him at all, not his name, or if he leaves behind a wife, or children, or a grieving mother. I was only thinking of Kirrana, but now someone else has been lost, and there is no bringing him back.

I force myself to take another deep, gulping breath, and look around, and realize I'm only partly right. For there are five children around me, wide-eyed and terrified, but alive and free as well. Even if I have failed Kirrana, and lost the soldier's life, and failed Seri, I have done this much.

It's something.

CHAPTER
52

We wait in our carriage, watching through the windows as three more quads arrive from the palace. A new captain from among the river guard shows up with his own quad to help impound the ship. Whether or not he is in the slavers' pockets, he apparently knows when to keep his sword in its sheath. The dock as a whole has been shut down, not a single boat allowed to load or unload cargo, or depart.

Bren would have had to swim past the docks altogether to leave the water safely. My fingers go to my chest, to where the pendant he gave me lies hidden beneath my tunic, strung on a thin gold chain so it won't stand out. He could have drowned. The thought leaves me as empty as it found me, my mind still frozen in that moment when my knife cut into the sailor's throat, as easily as cutting through goat meat.

No. I shove all such thoughts away and force my focus back to the carriage. I cannot do anything about Bren, or the dead.

But I can help these children. I share my name with them, and then check each for injuries, having them stand and turn in a circle to look for anything that they might have missed in the fear and frenzy of their escape. Other than a number of bruises and scrapes, some of which are older than others, they seem unharmed.

Matsin has a street vendor deliver freshly made flatbreads stuffed with spiced potato. The children devour them down to the very last crumb, and then curl up on the benches and on the ground between them, and rest against each other. A little boy puts his head in my lap, and an older girl sits beside me, leaning against my shoulder. I put my arm around her, not sure if I am comforting her or she, me.

Garrin finally looks in on us. "We're headed back to the palace, kelari."

"We'll need a Speaker for the children," I say, having managed to think this far ahead. "As soon as possible. And . . . they should be asked about what's happened to them before they're given the Blessing."

He nods. "I'll have a rider go ahead to arrange it."

Sure enough, when we roll into the palace courtyard, a Speaker hurries through a side door toward us, a guard by her side.

I help the children down from the carriage as the Speaker introduces herself. "I've everything ready just inside here," she says. "Come, my little ones, and we'll have you taken care of."

"Kelari," Garrin says as I make to go with them. "You'll be needed above. Matsin will report, I'm sure, but the family will want to hear your story as well."

"But the children . . ."

"They'll be fine now," he says firmly. "The Speaker will see to them. You can come check on them after if you wish."

I nod and turn back to them. "I'll see you shortly. You'll be safe now. Nothing can hurt you here, not once you've had the Blessing."

The eldest girl nods. "Thank you, kelari."

"Ready?" Garrin says. "They're waiting for us."

I nod to the children, and then wave quickly before turning back to him. "Yes."

It seems a long way to the royal wing. Garrin has to repeatedly slow himself to allow me to catch up, but at least that grants Matsin the extra minutes he needs to catch up with us himself.

At the entrance to Kestrin's suite, Garrin pauses and looks back at me. "You had better change, kelari. It won't do for an attendant to come in covered in blood."

No, I don't suppose it would. And I don't want to wear these clothes any longer than I must.

"Be quick," Garrin says, and turns his back on me, letting himself in.

"Kelari," Matsin says hesitantly.

I look up, nod. "I'll be right back."

In my room, I grab a change of clothes and hurry to the washroom. I leave my bloodied slippers and soiled clothing in a corner, the hems stiffening and the spots darkening to black, and pour water to lather and scrub my hands and feet, the scent of lavender rising from the soap. I don't have time to actually bathe, but I want the blood off me now. My ankle is slightly tender from the fall I took while trying to flee the boat. Beyond that, I am unharmed. It seems an impossible thing.

I dress quickly, pausing only to clean my bone knife before strapping it back onto my calf. I do not want it on me, do not want to remember what I have done with it, but I would be a fool to pretend it didn't save my life—all of our lives. At least in its calf sheath, I do not have to look at it. That done, I wrap Niya's sash around my waist again, pretending that the scattered brown spots on it are anything but blood. I almost take it off again, but Niya gave it to me as a protection, and I don't dare leave it behind. I make myself let it go, and ease on my new riding boots. They may not be quite appropriate for the occasion, but they will give my ankle the support it needs, and that's all I care about right now.

Ready, I hurry back to the royal apartments. The royals have gathered in Kestrin's apartments, and this time the king has joined us as well as Melkior. Kestrin gestures me to a sofa, and I ease myself down gratefully as Matsin launches into his report. I listen, but as he progresses to the attacks, I find I don't want to hear this at all. I hunch my shoulders and stare at the carpets underfoot, looking up only occasionally to track the reactions of the royals. Mostly, I am grateful for the way Matsin brushes over the violence.

Melkior listens with an expression that morphs from disbelief to outrage. Alyrra and Kestrin grow progressively more grim as they listen, and the king . . . it's hard to say what the king thinks. He maintains a steady calm, but his expression hardens slightly over the course of Matsin's recitation. I can only hope that means he too is infuriated by the betrayal of the river guard and their attempt to kill us, or keep us captive in the hold.

"We lost one man," Matsin finishes. "Selej en Tharo. I'll inform his widow tonight, and request permission to offer her three years' pay compensation."

"You may," the king says, and Matsin nods his thanks.

I repeat the man's name to myself, a mantra of what was risked and lost. *Selej en Tharo. Selej en Tharo.*

"I don't understand how they expected to get away with it," Kestrin says, sitting back. "Garrin was there—were you not, cousin? They must have known you would notice that Matsin, Kelari Amraeya, and their quad had not left. They could not have expected to kill you too. It makes no sense to me."

I look up, taken aback. He's right, it doesn't make sense.

But Garrin shakes his head. "All Grefan would have had to tell me was that Kelari Amraeya and her escort had already departed. If Diara commandeered the carriage and had it driven away, I wouldn't have thought to ask. I was at the river warden's office, and didn't realize what was happening until it was already over, and Matsin and his men had fought their way free."

"A desperate move by them, though," Kestrin says slowly.

"That, or an overconfident one," the king says. "Did you notice anything on board the galley that would have marked it as one used regularly for transporting slaves? If we are to investigate Berenworth, it would be useful to know if there are any markers of a slave boat."

Matsin hesitates, glancing toward me. "The room we discovered was hidden behind a false wall in the stern of the cargo hold, tarin. Beyond that . . ."

"There was a ward above the door, as well, tarin," I say. "I believe it is what hides the children from being traced. Perhaps, knowing what it is, a mage might be able to trace those who have been snatched past such a protection." The king will know that the Circle isn't to be trusted—Kestrin and Alyrra will make sure of it. Perhaps Kestrin can inspect the ward himself.

The king nods. "Garrin, see that the ward is removed from the boat and brought here for assessment."

"Tarin," Garrin agrees.

I look down, relief flooding through me. If the king himself is involved now, surely the snatchers will be stopped. This work will continue, and Berenworth will be properly investigated, and even if the thrice-cursed Circle isn't brought down, the snatchers themselves will be stopped.

"Melkior, I'll want an investigation into how the river guards could be so corrupted that they would attack our own palace guards," the king adds. "A full review of the river guard should be conducted."

Melkior agrees, and then asks a few more questions of Matsin, and one or two of me, and the nobles discuss the need to impound the rest of Berenworth's ships at the dock and search each one.

"I'll use my own men," Garrin says. "If I am still to be involved? I'll make sure each hold is fully searched, and I trust my men to do a good job of it. I am only grateful that Kelari Amraeya insisted on such a careful search this first time."

"It is between you and Melkior," the king says. "Though it might be easier for you if you step back."

"Easier, yes," Garrin says, rubbing a hand over his head. "But I've seen those children now, and I—I should like to be involved."

He hadn't seemed particularly caring of the children, but

then, he may not have many children in his life. It is not as if children are a part of the court. Perhaps Garrin simply doesn't know how to interact with them, even if he cares. And there were certainly other concerns pressing on him.

"As you wish," Melkior says now. "I should be grateful to have you at the helm of such an investigation. It will ease the way considerably."

Garrin dips his head. "It is my honor."

And as simply as that, I am no longer needed. Everything I have been pushing myself toward these last few weeks has been achieved in this: the establishment of a formal investigation into the snatchers, led by one of the highest nobles of the realm, with the support of the whole royal family.

It's out of my hands now. I'm grateful—I never again want to set foot on another ship with a room full of slaves, or find myself unable to run fast enough again, or spill blood upon my hands.

Except that Kirrana is still missing. I press my lips together. But the other galleys will be searched now, and surely, surely she will be on one of them.

As the meeting is adjourned, I push myself to my feet. I feel unsteady and strangely heavy; it's the shock wearing off, I expect. Alyrra gestures to me, and in a quiet voice asks if I am well. I nod, pause, try to nod again and realize I can't.

"You should rest," she says, watching me, a hint of sorrow in her eyes. "You've been through a great deal today, and it might not all seem real yet. I'll send for Mage Berrila to check on you. Please don't worry about attending me the next few days. And if you wish to stay with your cousins—or go home—I will of course understand."

"Thank you, zayyida," I say, and push myself forward. I'm not leaving yet, not before Kirrana is found, but I don't have the energy to discuss that now.

In the hallway, Melkior and Garrin converse in lowered voices. As I pass them on my way to the attendants' suite, Garrin turns toward me. "A few words with you, kelari?"

Melkior nods to us both and strides away.

"Verin?" I ask, unsure what more Garrin could want.

"Like you, I hope your friend might still be recovered. Do you have any ideas, any possible leads?"

I take a shaky breath, gather my thoughts. "I believe she might be on one of the other galleys, which you already intend to search. Beyond that, I know little."

He nods. "The research that you did, were the details lost entirely?"

"It can be done again," I assure him. "Kirrana was excellent, but, given both motivation and time, I suspect another clerk could find what she did. Especially now that we know what we are looking for. If I work directly with a clerk, I think we could re-create it relatively easily."

He smiles. "You are a wonder, kelari. I am sorry you must leave us."

I don't have to, and I don't intend to quite yet, but I have no interest in discussing it either. Instead, I dip my head in acknowledgment and make my excuses, retreating to my room.

CHAPTER

53

S itting at my dressing table, I let my hair down and brush it slowly, the action strangely soothing. Once it's smooth again, I plait it into a pair of braids. Country style, and wonderfully comforting at that.

And then my hands are still, and I can't escape the memories of this afternoon. I open my dressing table drawers, as if that might distract, as if something as stupid and mundane as brushes and jewelry could drive away the thought of screams and bloodshed on the boat, the sound of the sailor dying. The sight of my knife cutting him. My hands start shaking and my stomach heaves. It was self-defense. It was to save the boy, I remind myself, but I cannot breathe through the horror of it. I push myself to my feet, gulping great breaths of air, but it's not enough.

Stop thinking. Just stop.

Eventually, my panic subsides, my shaking with it. I stand a few moments, and then I start for the door. If I cannot rest, at least I can check on the children.

As I step into the main hallway, Alyrra lets herself out of her suite. She looks toward me in surprise. "Rae?"

I nod. "Do you require attendance?" I ask, almost hopefully. At least it will take my mind away from what I saw on the boat.

"No. I am only going to the palace temple. Unless you would like to come with me?"

I shrug and then find myself moving to accompany her. I rarely went to our temple in Sheltershorn, but perhaps it will do me some good. I can go to check on the children from there; they won't remember me at this point, and will hardly be waiting for me. And I don't doubt they're all right now. A few minutes longer won't signify.

Alyrra says nothing as we pass down the halls, and in a short time we enter the temple with its plush carpets and great arches. There are shelves against the wall containing holy books and scholarly writings, but other than that, and the richness of the room itself, it is very much like the temple at home. We leave our shoes by the door and find different spots to sit quietly on the carpets. Alyrra rises after a time and prays, bowing and prostrating herself, but I only sit, letting the peace of the room seep into me. I repeat soft words of praise, letting the rhythm soothe my nerves, remind me that there is something to believe in above and beyond the violence of this world.

Eventually, Alyrra finishes and moves toward the door. I follow her out, grateful that she does not break the silence until we part ways in the royal wing. It is only as I let myself into the attendants' suite that I realize I've forgotten to seek out the children.

I hesitate, turning back to the door, and a voice calls out from the common room. "Kelari?"

I look back to find a page hastening toward me. "The king requests your presence."

"The king? Now?" I ask before I can help myself. Of course now. When else?

"Yes, kelari. At once."

I touch my hand to one of my braids, but there isn't time to put up my hair, not with the page waiting. Never mind. They are only country braids after all. But what does the king want from me? Is it something to do with the slave ship? Or something else entirely?

"Do you know what this relates to?" I ask.

"No, kelari," he says, and gestures me down the hall. "We should go."

I follow him to a part of the palace I haven't seen before. As he reaches a carved wooden door, he says helpfully, "This is the royal library."

At least that allows me to prepare myself for the sight of a great many books. Or it should have, only I had no concept there were this many in the world. The walls of the great room within are not only lined with shelves, but there are shelves standing back-to-back to create aisles—and not just one or two, but at least two score, if not double that number. The Black Scholar has nothing on this library.

"How are there so many?" I ask as we cross the room.

"Any book brought to the city has to be turned over to the palace scribes to be copied before being returned. They've the same policy in all of the port cities as well for any book brought in by a traveler."

Ah. I remember being asked at the city gates if Veria Sanlyn or I were bringing in any books. It had been an odd question, but easily answered in the negative, and I'd thought no more of it in my excitement to see the city.

"This way," the page says, and I follow him down a back aisle to a hall where there is a series of private rooms. The room we enter is lined with books—there must be easily a thousand here, possibly more—and armchairs, and in one, the king sits, a book by his side, looking everything and nothing like the Scholar. A second, empty armchair faces him.

I curtsy and immediately wish I hadn't, my ankle throbbing. But there's no standing up now, without the king's permission. I hold my curtsy as the page makes his own bow and departs. And still I wait as the king looks me over. Finally, he says, "Kelari Amraeya."

I push myself up, half stumbling as my foot informs me that I cannot learn to bow fast enough. But that thought brings back memories of Diara, her throat gaping open, blood spurting through the half-light of the hold. My stomach turns and I make myself focus on the carpet underfoot instead, try to regain that tranquility I found in the temple.

"There is something we need to discuss," the king says, gesturing to the armchair set at an angle to his.

I limp across to it, perch on the edge.

"You have put me in quite the quandary."

Surely he isn't referring to the snatchers? I look up, dread curling in my stomach. If the king is involved—

"My son tells me that you saw something he did not intend last night."

"Last night?" I echo, bewildered.

"With the snake."

Oh, that. It feels like a hundred years ago. "Tarin," I agree.

"So," the king says.

I once thought Kestrin capable of holding back every emotion, of appearing to harbor no more feeling than stone, but his father may as well be sculpted of ice. There is not even a memory of warmth in his eyes as he looks at me.

I wait, my shoulders tense. Kestrin wanted a hold on me, but Filadon promised me this morning that he would try to sort it out. I did not expect the king himself to take up the conversation, at least not so quickly, though perhaps I should have. Kestrin is his only son and heir.

"I understand," the king says finally, "that you are loyal to Zayyida Alyrra, and to our family generally. But the secret you carry could unbalance the monarchy and quite possibly lead to shifts in power that would result in war. Simply put," he says, turning one hand over, palm up, "your knowledge concerns me."

I take a slow breath. It's going to be a great deal harder arguing with a king than with Filadon. "Is my word not enough, tarin?"

"It is something," the king says, and there is a regret in his voice that I don't quite trust. "But it is not enough. There is little choice here, kelari."

I wait. I know I could make this easier for him, ask him what he wants of me, but there is no reason I can imagine to politely aid someone in causing me damage to save themselves—even if I understand the wider reasons.

"Filadon promised Kestrin he has a hold on you that would even the balance," the king says softly, watching me. "If you will give me that hold, then I need nothing further."

I don't even hesitate. "I cannot, tarin."

He nods, as if he expected no different of me. "I have one other option. You have seen the Blessing to stave off the Darkness."

I go still, my insides clenching. I shake my head at him, a denial that has nothing to do with his words.

"One of our court mages, a man whom I trust implicitly, can perform the task," he explains. "If you wish, you may submit yourself to him. He will remove just those memories related to what you saw that night. You see the items there, on the table."

I glance to the table, noting for the first time a silver tray bearing a pitcher and a familiar silver goblet, a low round bump beside them that must be an opal.

Submit myself. Have my memories destroyed, and hope that this mage only takes what he must. Or give up Niya. I shake my head again, but now I'm trembling, my hands gripping the fabric of my skirts.

"It is your choice, kelari," the king goes on. "I will hold your secret in trust. There is no reason to resort to such measures."

"No. Tarin." As if there were any other answer to give. I could not put Niya in such a man's power. "The hold Filadon has—I will take it to my grave with me. I would do the same with your son's secret, if you would allow me to keep it. That is all I can offer you."

It isn't enough. I can see it in the slight crease of his eyes, a faint indication of regret that he will not voice. "Perhaps you require some time to consider your predicament. I will leave you here, and return within the hour."

He departs quietly, his footsteps muffled by the carpet. I hear the far-off click of a door, and then all is quiet. I curl into my armchair, arms wrapped around myself. It is loud, deafening, this silence that folds me up. I've seen the Blessing, and while I know it doesn't destroy the mind, it robs one of all recent memory. What will be left when this mage finishes? Will he take everything that has happened in the last few weeks—the whole of my visit to Tarinon, and even before that? Or can he truly only take those memories relating to the prince? How can he know which they are?

He can't. I don't believe it. And the king has given me this time to realize that. To understand the gravity of what might be done to me. Even if I were willing to give up everything I've learned—the whole investigation, everything we need to research Berenworth's anomalies—I cannot give up Kirrana while she is still lost.

Nor can I betray Niya in her place.

Surely there has to be some other way.

The king wants a hold on me. Something real, something he can use. I wipe clammy hands over my skirts. His son is a mage. And he has access to a whole host of other mages. There's no need for me to betray Niya when I can give him a closer hold on myself.

I rise, limp to the table with its double burden of silver goblet and opal. But this is a library, and on the shelf behind it waits paper and ink. I gather these and seat myself at the table, and draw out my bone knife.

When the king returns a half hour later, I am curled up on the armchair, absently playing with the end of a braid. I blink up at him as he pauses in the doorway and find him looking somewhat taken aback.

"Tarin," I say, dropping my braid and rising to my feet, my ankle aching.

He raises a hand, stopping me before I can curtsy. "You have decided?"

"Yes." I gesture to the folded paper on the table.

He crosses to it, unfolding it carefully, and then pauses. I watch as his eyes skim the paper, his fingers carefully remaining at the edges. When he turns to look at me, there's a certain humorous gleam to his eyes. "Kelari."

"You weren't going to take my memories, were you, tarin?" I say, having reasoned this out in the calm after my decision. "Filadon would surely notice, and that would destroy his loyalty to you and to your son as well. I suspect the sort of loyalty he has toward your family is hard to come by. He wouldn't betray you, of course, but you would have betrayed him, and he would likely depart to live in the country after that, unable to serve you so closely after such an injury to him and his family. Don't you think?"

A faint curve of the lips. "It was a risk, yes."

"Not one you would have taken," I agree, encouraged by his reaction. "Your plan was always to frighten me into giving you a hold on me. There is your hold, tarin."

"Your hair and blood are an interesting sort of hold."

"Not at all. Hair and blood, given willingly? Zayyid Kestrin could easily find me with that, or it could be used by a mage in your service cast a curse on me. That should be incentive enough for me not to anger you."

"True," he agrees. "I'm impressed you considered all this, especially given the threat hanging over you."

"You're not getting any other hold on me," I say firmly.

"There is no need. Your actions have convinced me he is quite safe."

I blink at him, taken aback. He watches me, amused, and I find myself asking, "What would you have done if I'd given you my hold?"

"Used it."

His words chill me to the bone. He is still very much a king, even if I'm being chatty with him. Still someone who uses power easily and dangerously. No doubt he can see the effect of his words.

I swallow and say lightly, "But this suffices, tarin?"

"Almost. Consider that even a trace based on blood or hair can be warded against."

Light and shadow! I knew that, was only just reminded of it today. This hold I've offered the king won't serve at all if a ward can block it.

He tilts his head. "To ensure that what you have given me will actually hold, you will need to allow a mage to, ah, create a connection, shall we say. One that can be drawn upon regardless of how well warded you may one day be. It requires a good deal of magic and a willingness on your part, but it can be done."

I look up hopefully. I've never heard of such a thing, but considering the need for a mage to accomplish such a feat and the fact that there isn't one within a day and a half's ride of our town, that's not altogether surprising. Niya wouldn't have come up with it on her own. Still: "This connection—that's all it is? It does not grant control over me?"

He is definitely amused, the skin at the corners of his eyes crinkling. "No, that I promise it won't. We'll see to it tomorrow."

"Because you never intended to take my memories."

A smile now, clear as day. "As you say." He sets the paper with its burden of hair and blood down. "I am glad you've proven your trustworthiness, kelari. The service you have performed my daughter-by-law, in protecting her from her brother's intentions two times over, and the work you have done regarding these slavers?" He dips his head in an approximation of a bow. "I am grateful to you. I hoped you would make the right choice here."

"Thank you, tarin," I say uncertainly. This unexpected honesty and forthrightness is almost as unnerving as his usual cool demeanor.

His look is far too perceptive, but he says only, "It is unfortunate, I think, that you do not plan to make the court your home."

I curtsy and murmur my thanks, since agreement seems like it might be a dangerous commitment.

With a soft hiss of laughter, the king finally dismisses me.

CHAPTER

54

I leave the king's library in hope of finding the children. From there, I promise myself I'll go check on Melly. I am bone tired and want so much to see my cousin—to make sure she is well, despite her morning sickness, and just to sit with her, even if I cannot speak of what has happened. But making my way to where the children are being kept through unfamiliar hallways proves impossible, and it is not long before I'm thoroughly lost.

I close my eyes a moment, turn around, and try to find my way back, but even that does not work. Eventually I find myself facing a gallery of paintings. I remember this hall vaguely from a short tour Mina gave me on one of my first days: these are the portraits of the royal family and those closest to the crown.

I almost turn back, but then I realize the nearest portrait is that of the king, ten years younger, with a surprisingly plain-faced woman sitting beside him, and between them a boy who would one day grow into the prince I know. The queen died a year ago, her death so sudden many considered it a mystery, or the workings of a curse I never took seriously. A curse that bears a name, and whom Stonemane and the Cormorant are working to oppose.

This palace is so full of secrets it beggars the mind. I walk a few steps farther down, and here is a portrait with another family of three, sharing some of the same physical traits as the royal family, but different in the details. The plaque beneath identifies them as the lord and lady of Cenatil, the boy their son, Garrin. Like Kestrin's family, they are posed upon a sofa, this one red with a floral pattern rendered in gold leaf.

I tilt my head, studying the shape of the flowers, the starlike petals. Where have I seen those before? Somewhere recently . . .

The truth comes to me so suddenly, I stumble back, my stomach dropping. No. No, it can't be. I turn away from the portrait, then back again, staring at the flowers. Asphodel. And now that I look, they are engraved in the frame as well.

It's a coincidence. Nothing more. It *must* be. But every sideways clue, every oddity Kirrana and I uncovered, has brought us closer and closer to the wider truths we are fighting for. I reach out to touch the wooden frame, trace the curve of a flower there, cool against my fingertips. Asphodel. The same flower that graces Berenworth's seal.

This is a palace filled to the hilt with deadly games and twisted betrayals. For this is a portrait of Garrin, who volunteered to protect Alyrra and Kestrin from the ramifications of the investigation by taking it on himself, who consistently tried to downplay the threat the snatchers pose to the common people, who left Matsin and me to be locked in a hold and cut down rather than find one more piece of evidence.

What fools Kirrana and I were, assuming that the Circle would be the top of it. No, Berenworth is backed by one of the most powerful lords after the royal family, a man in line for the throne himself, who benefits from every child sold into slavery. A man whom Alyrra and Kestrin trust to investigate the snatchers and assess Berenworth's role in the disappearances. And a man to whom I have explained nearly all the details of what I know, and how we learned it. I've armed him with everything he needs to hide the truth ... except for the very final details of what Kirrana and I found.

I start forward, my foot aching with each step. I need to find the princess, tell her all this at once. But if I tell her about Garrin, then ... then what? There are the mages involved, and who is to say the crown itself is not involved? I don't believe Kestrin knows, but what if the king does? I can't wrap my mind around the rami- fications of what I've learned, but I need to tell someone. I need to make sure I'm not the only one who knows. And the only person I can trust right now with this is Alyrra.

I'll tell her, and if she cannot do anything, then I'll tell Bren as well. Perhaps there *is* a place for thieves—at least honorable thieves—when the government has betrayed their people so deeply.

The next servant I see, I ask for directions back to the royal wing. He directs me to familiar halls, and from there I head toward the back hall with its stairway up to the guard room. I pass a few servants, a young noble on his way somewhere, and then, as I round the corner to the stairway, I see a young page crouched on the ground. He looks up as I pause, his face set in hard lines and furrows.

"Are you all right?" I ask, moving toward him.

"F-forgive me, kelari," he says, ducking his head. "I've just turned my ankle."

I know that pain well enough. "Let's have a look," I say, coming to a stop beside him, my mind running through how I can tell Alyrra. Will the asphodel be enough of a connection to convince her?

The boy proffers me the injured ankle. It isn't swollen yet, but when I ask him to rotate his foot, he winces and freezes up. I can't tell if it's only a strain, or something worse. My usual patients are horses.

"Can you stand?" I ask, glancing toward the back stairway, then the other direction. There's no one to hand him off to, though.

"I'll try," he says.

I offer him a hand up. Between that and the wall, he's able to stand, but the first step he takes leaves him gasping and clinging to me. My ankle throbs as I take his weight.

"Looks like we'd better get you to a healer," I say as cheerfully as I can. "I'll walk you there. Come."

The going is slow, for I must support the boy without putting too much strain on my own ankle. We stay close to the wall, and I periodically pause to let him lean against it so that we can both rest. My mind spins around and around what I've learned, trying to ferret out the best way to phrase my explanation to the princess.

As we reach the next courtyard, the boy gestures with his chin. "There's a shortcut that way, kelari. Servants' passages, if you don't mind."

Anything to deliver him to the healers quicker, get this additional weight off my ankle, and go on to Alyrra. We turn down an empty hall, the sound of our passage echoing slightly. I don't *see* any servants, but the hall is certainly nowhere near as ornate as the usual palace halls, or as wide. Most of the doors opening onto the hall are closed, but here and there one stands open. I glance through the first to see an empty storage room.

"Not much farther," the boy says, as if comforting me.

"No," I agree. I'll start with Garrin's absence during the fight on the boat—

An arm snakes around my throat and yanks me back, pulling me off my feet. My mouth gapes open, but I cannot get any breath, my feet scrabbling beneath me as I am hauled backward.

"Got her," a voice says.

I claw at the arm as it clamps tighter—chokehold. A vision of Matsin in the carriage flashes before my eyes, his gaze steady as he talks me through this. I reach up, following the line of my attacker's arm to his hand, grasp his finger, and *yank*.

I feel bone crack and my attacker swallows a cry, shoving me away from him. I land on all fours, my mouth open as I gulp great lungfuls of air. Vaguely, I can hear someone laughing. *I need to get up.*

I push myself up and then a hand grabs my arm and twists it behind me. I give a gasping cry, trying to pull away, but my arm is pinned behind me, and then another hand shoves a gag into my mouth. The force of it pushes me against my captor, the muscles of my arm crying out in a protest I can't voice.

I cast about wildly—and catch sight of the page. He watches me, perfectly balanced on his feet, a line between his brows as if he were slightly perturbed. He makes no move to call for help, no move to do anything at all.

My captor turns and propels me into the empty room we passed only a moment ago. The second man follows after us, shutting the door behind him.

CHAPTER
55

The guards—for guards they are—leave me gagged and bound on the floor of the storeroom and depart without a backward glance. The door closes on the sound of the second guard mocking the first for his broken finger.

I lie in the dark, my cheek pressed against a fine layer of grit, the tiles cold against my skin. My arms are tied behind me, my ankles bound together. They did not bother searching me, and so did not discover my calf sheath with my bone knife, but no matter how I try, I cannot reach my fingers around to where it is hidden beneath my skirts.

I swallow, my breath coming hard through my nose. I cannot seem to breathe properly, for all that it is only my mouth that is blocked. Is this what happened to Kirrana? Was she left bound and gagged and forgotten? Do they intend to come back for me, or will they leave me here, unable to cry for help in a room no one may enter for weeks?

No. I squeeze my eyes shut, force them open again. I'm going to escape. My family will hear this story from my lips, no one else's. I won't be a sad disappearance, an inescapable casualty.

I twist, trying again to reach my calf, my fingers barely managing to catch on the fabric of my skirts.

A door opens in the wall. I start, staring, for there was no door there before, was there? A golden glow falls through the new doorway, and then a figure steps out, luminae lamp in hand.

I tense, every instinct screaming at me to run, but I've never been able to do that before, and even less so now, bound as I am. So instead I lift my chin and look straight at Garrin.

"A shame, kelari," he says softly, and strangely, he looks far more regretful·than the page who tricked me here. "Every chance you had to save yourself, you kept putting yourself forward. Why would you do that? Have you no sense of self-preservation?"

Is he actually blaming me? Him? This despicable excuse for a noble who sells children into slavery?

He sighs. "I am going to cut your legs free. I suggest you come quietly. If you do not, I will have to bind you again, and bring others to carry you. I would prefer not to take such drastic measures."

He doesn't mean to kill me. The thought sends a flash of relief through me even as I realize I should have known that. If he wished me dead, the guards could have done that easily enough. There was no need for him to come here himself.

He kneels beside me, head tilted as he studies me. I glare up at him, the gag filling my mouth.

He winces. "I'm not a murderer, kelari. I'll see you out of this alive and well, if you will only comply. I simply can't have you here anymore."

He sounds so reasonable, so very civilized. He and the Black Scholar would no doubt get along very, very well. Garrin isn't about to send me off to the country and set me free. I'm not sure what "alive and well" constitutes, but I doubt we'd agree on our definitions.

"Will you come quietly, kelari?" he asks.

I consider my options, but they aren't many. Better to allow him to cut my ankles free and follow quietly, watching for an opportunity to escape, than refuse that chance altogether. I dip my head.

"Very good."

Once I'm on my feet again, he sets a hand on my arm and lifts the luminae lamp. I let him guide me to the doorway, stepping into a narrow stone hallway.

"A moment," he says, turning back to the door. I lean against the wall beside me, resting my foot. My throat aches, and my wounded arm throbs. I wriggle my wrists in their bindings, but they are too tight to work a hand free.

Garrin swings the door shut, then pulls a lever that seems to retract the door until it lines up perfectly with the wall. Alyrra once mentioned that the palace contained secret passages, and so did Melly. I would have much preferred never to see them at all.

Garrin looks at me, shakes his head. "You're so predictable," he says, almost as an apology. "I knew if I put a wounded child in front of you, I'd have you. There's not a noble lady in the palace who would have seen to the boy herself. But you? Of course you would."

I grumble a curse at him through the gag. He must have set the page to waylay me after our report to Alyrra and Kestrin. It was only the worst coincidence of timing that he caught me on the way back from the portrait gallery.

"I should have preferred it, really, if you were a bit more selfish," Garrin says, and taking my arm, guides me along.

What? Does he actually feel bad for what he's doing? Not bad enough, or I wouldn't be here, shuffling through dark stone passages. I keep an eye out for doors, for any sign of life. If I can just alert someone to my passing, perhaps I can be rescued.

But there's no chance of that, for Garrin keeps me pressed against the opposite wall of the two doors we pass, and the third is the one he wants. We step out into another storage room, this one stacked with crates.

"In you go," he says, nodding to the nearest crate, its lid beside it.

I pull back, horror getting the better of me.

Garrin very carefully sets down the lamp and meets my gaze. "You may get in on your own," he says, "or I will force you in. Either way, you will go. Again, you will not be harmed. What do you choose?"

I hold still, listening, but there's no sound from beyond this room, no indication that anyone is out there and might take note of a disturbance. With a terrible sort of resignation, I dip my head and move to the crate. With my hands bound behind me, it is almost impossible to climb in without tipping over—until Garrin catches my arm and steadies me, helping me in. The gentleness of it rankles, as if his manners could offset the evil he is committing.

I only just fit in the crate, my knees bent to my chin, and my back curled forward to fit my arms behind me. Garrin lifts the lid and sets it down, shoving my head between my knees. I cry out, but it's a faint, muffled sound, easily lost beneath the pounding of nails into the lid of the crate.

By the time he is done, I can barely breathe, even though there are air holes drilled into the sides. I feel like the gag is choking me, and I'm trembling now, the sides of the box closing in on me. It's dark without even the faint glow of the luminae lamp through the air holes. I'm alone, my senses reeling. I feel I might be sick all over myself—only I can't, because then I will choke on my own vomit, and I *can't* die like that. And there's no getting out of here, no escape, no one who cares.

Not true. I inhale hard through my nose and hold that breath, then slowly let it out and inhale again. I'm going to get out, I tell myself on the next inhale. There are people who care. With each breath I remind myself of who: Mama and Baba. Niya, whom I promised I'd grow old with. Bean. Melly. Filadon. Alyrra. I will get out—of this crate, of this future Garrin has consigned me to—and once I do, I will not rest until I've brought his actions into the light.

Eventually, a pair of workers enter the room, lift the crate, and carry it out. I scratch my fingers against the wood at my back, try calling to them through my gag. If they hear me at all, they ignore me. The crate is set down, then shoved back, the side air holes blocked by things on either side of me—other crates?

I catch my breath speeding up again and it is all I can do to slow it, focus on the fact that they will not keep me in this crate forever, whoever they are. Whoever Garrin is sending me to.

Eventually the crate rattles forward, and I deduce I'm riding in a wagon. The air is slowly growing more and more stale, but there's a faint fall of light from a single air hole somewhere above my head. There's air. It will have to be enough.

The ride does not last long. I'm unloaded and transported some distance and then taken down a set of stairs. As before, whoever carries me seems not to care about the faint sounds emanating from my crate. Of course they don't. These are Garrin's men, or the snatchers themselves.

"We supposed to let her out?" a man's voice asks as the crate is set down.

"Aye. Put her in the first cell."

I wait a painfully long time as the man locates a bar to pry the lid off with. Then I look up into the faces of two men, half-lit by a grimy lantern. We're in a small, dank bricked hallway, smelling of must and the acrid stink of urine. At the other end, a darkened stairway leads upward.

"This one's old," the first says to the other.

"Same as the last," his friend responds.

Kirrana. Surely that's who he means. Whatever happened to her, at least now I'll have some idea.

The first man hunkers down to meet my gaze. "We're going to get you out, girl. You try anything, and you'll go right back in. Got it?"

I nod.

They cut my wrists free and lift me out by my arms, which has me crying out in pain around my gag. Then I'm dragged forward, my legs too numb to hold me, and deposited inside a cell.

"Here," says one, and grasps the gag, working it out of my

mouth as I lie on my side, my hands too numb to use. I want to thank him, but all I can do is swallow down great gulps of air, my mouth aching. But no, I remind myself, I don't want to thank him. His removing my gag doesn't change the fact that he's holding me captive and sending me on, most likely to enslavement.

"What's this?" the man says, tilting his head.

He's found my knife, the only thing I have left—

But instead of reaching for my leg, his fingers snag at the chain around my neck, tug. "Got yourself a pretty gold necklace, do you? Don't think you'll miss it if we—" He breaks off with a curse and drops the chain as if burned, the hawk pendant sliding down to fall upon the stone with a soft clink.

The other man lets out a low whistle. "Wouldn't take anything off of her, if I were you. It'll be your death, you try to sell that."

"Not about to," says the first man, wiping his fingers and backing away from me. "Best tell him upstairs as well."

"He's not going to like it," the second says. "You found it; I think you get to do the talking."

"You're the one who accepted the delivery. Don't see why I should have to report on it."

They leave still bickering, shoving the heavy wooden door shut behind them. I hear the faint creak and snick of a bolt being slid into place.

The air is dank in my cell, moisture and decay filling my lungs. I look around slowly, forcing myself to take note of where I am. Light filters in through the gap beneath the door. The cell I'm in is no bigger than a closet, hardly large enough to sit in with my legs stretched out, should I manage to sit up. Instead, I'm curled up at the center, my legs barely able to unbend. There's a scattering of moldy hay beneath me, and a bucket in the corner that adds a faintly putrid scent to the room, and that is all.

They knew the hawk pendant, at least. Whoever the man in charge is, he cares enough about Red Hawk that his men were concerned by my pendant. Which would suggest he's a thief himself, or closely involved with them.

Not Red Hawk, not with how much he's done, how dedicated Bren has been to helping me. Bren's own history. But the Black Scholar, or Bardok? I could easily believe it of the Scholar, at least, remembering both his intelligence and his cool detachment. He's been growing in power. Perhaps he's funding his growth through the sale of children to the snatchers. And if he has me now—if he comes downstairs and discovers me—there's no way I'll live to see the inside of a slave ship. I stare across the room as the possibilities run through my mind, the stones damp and gritty against my cheek.

That's curious. There hasn't been much rain the last week; not since the day at the brickmaker's yard. Where else would the water come from? The Black Scholar's prison was dry as a bone: it would be, given his prized book collection. The Scholar's prison also didn't look like this. I force myself up to a sitting position, staring down at the damp gleam of wetness across the floor. Either it's not the Scholar upstairs, or this is a separate prison he keeps.

I half crawl, half drag myself to the wooden door with its small, barred opening at face height. I force my feet under me and stagger upright, my good hand grabbing at one of the bars to keep myself standing. I look between them, out into the hallway, where a faint fall of light illuminates the opposite wall. On that wall hangs a plaque with a familiar ward. A ward I have seen not twice but three times, I now realize, though I didn't recognize it that second time. I was too frightened, too distracted, and it was made differently then as it is now: a painted tile rather than carved wood.

I'm still standing there when a man descends the stairs, his tread heavy, the light from the lamp he bears gaining strength as he approaches. I back up a pace from the door and lift my chin. "I would speak with Bardok Three-Fingers," I say, my voice strangely calm and collected.

"Would you?" A familiar chuckle rumbles in the hallway, and the door swings open. He wears the same light armor as before, his thick hair pulled back in a warrior's knot, one hand lifting the lamp to light my face. "Well, who would have thought?" A grin stretches across his broad face. "If it isn't the Scholar's little runaway."

CHAPTER
56

Bardok sets his lamp down just inside the doorway and steps forward, a smile on his wide face. "This just gets more and more interesting. So you're a royal attendant, are you? Ha! Poor Scholar never knew what he had in his hand, did he?"

I shake my head. It takes all my courage not to back away from him.

"But how is it Red Hawk gave you his sign? He doesn't share those easily." He raises a brow. "Can't imagine he cares for a girl like you."

Like me? What is *that* supposed to mean? "You may have abducted me, thrown me in a vile little cell, and have my life in your hands," I snarl, "but you can keep your insults to yourself. You don't know the first *thing* about me."

Bardok leans against the doorjamb and laughs, a great big belly laugh that rumbles through the room. "You've fire, at least. But you're stupid, girl. Stupid to think you could poke your nose in where it doesn't belong and not lose your head for it. Stupid to think that little pendant could protect you. Stupid"—he dips his head and smiles—"to think you were ever safe."

I wait. I'm not sure that his words require an answer, and in any case, I don't have one. I've most certainly been stupid. There's no argument I can make regarding that.

"Wasn't expecting you, though," Bardok admits. "Thought you'd be some arrogant little chit I could ship off downriver without a thought. But this, now, this I can use."

"Use?" I echo, even as my mind repeats *ship off downriver.*

"Mm-hmm. See, I don't like sharing this city with other thieves. It's uncomfortable. Never know when you're going to rub elbows with another's man. And here you are now, prettiest little present I've received in a while, even with that plain face of yours."

"How do you mean?" I ask, my voice not quite steady. He nods, that wide smile back on his face, and I'm terrified of what he might say next.

"Red Hawk wants you alive, doesn't he? That's what that little pendant means. And we all know how the Black Scholar feels about you. So if I want to finish them both? Nothing easier! I send Red Hawk something of yours, make it look like it's from the Scholar, and within a day I'm betting we'll have a nice, bloody street war on our hands."

And then Bardok will no doubt sweep in and kill whoever he can, once they're weakened.

"He won't," I say. "Red Hawk's not killing anyone over me. I've never even met him."

Bardok hesitates, brow furrowed, and then he grins. "Ah well, you would say that! But you carry his sign, and there's a promise in that. I see no reason not to make the attempt. So, what shall we send him?"

He steps forward again. I back up until I'm pressed against the wall. There's nowhere else to go.

"Thought you weren't supposed to harm me," I cry desperately.

"Ah, orders. Who's going to report back, tell me that?" Bardok shakes his head and takes another step forward, crowding me into the corner. He's head and shoulders taller than me, and broad enough to fill the room. He grins, tilting his head, and catches one of my braids in a great meaty hand. I hold still, aware that I'm shaking, but there's nothing I can do here, no way to fight him. At least I can hold on to my dignity.

"Every girl in the city has black hair but the princess," he says conversationally, "so there's no use in taking a bit of hair." He drops his gaze to my ears, pauses over my earrings, and then tugs hard on my braid, forcing me to turn as he inspects the rest of me. "Ah, but how about this ring? Would Red Hawk know it?"

My stomach drops. My ruby ring. "N-no. I don't think so."

"Ha! Yes, he would, or one of his men would. The ring it is! Though if we want blood, I think we'll have to send it attached, don't you?"

"Attached?"

He rumbles with laughter. Turning, he hauls me out of the cell to the hallway. There's not much here: just a bench shoved back against the wall, but that's what Bardok wants. He whips me around, sending me crashing to my knees beside the bench. I try to push myself back up, but he shoves me down. Desperately,

I try to twist away. If I can only reach my knife, I can cut him, stop him—but Bardok knows what he is doing, one hand closing on the wrist of my wounded arm and yanking it forward, around him as he turns his shoulder into my back, pinning my arm to the bench. I flail with my other hand, trying to get past my skirts, get to my knife, but my fingers are stiff and I can't see what I'm doing, and pain ricochets through me as he leans into my arm.

He pulls his dagger from his belt, and with his other hand flattens my fingers against the bench.

"Wait," I cry, trying to pull back, my free hand grasping wads of my skirt. "No—*please!*"

"Only take a moment," he says kindly. "I suggest you don't move, or you might lose more than you have to."

His dagger slices down through my flesh. I scream, scream as blood spurts from my hand, scream as Bardok scrapes the dagger hard, cutting through the remaining muscle and tendon. Pain shrieks through me, flying up my arm, my voice separate from me now, a sound without control. Bardok releases me and turns. I stare as he lifts my little finger, the ruby ring gleaming wetly in the lamplight, a bit of bone protruding above it.

"That'll do nicely," he says in the ragged space between my screams. "Do be quiet, girl. It's not that bad." He raises a brow. "Nothing I haven't lived through."

He pulls me up by my elbow, shoves me back into the cell, and goes upstairs still holding my finger.

In the dark, I think of Mama. I hear her voice, calm and soothing, discussing the treatment of injuries and wounds. Keep open wounds elevated above the heart. Bind them to slow the blood flow. A calm patient will bleed less, so try to help them regulate their breathing.

I do what I can, tearing off a strip from my skirt and pressing it against my wound. I'm shaking continuously now, but what does that matter? *Hold it up*, I tell myself, as if I didn't mean a part of my own body. Breathe slowly, make sure it clots over. There's no way to know if the wound is clean or if I'm rubbing dirt into it, so I try not to think about it. Try not to think about the fact that I've lost a finger now. That I could lose my hand, my arm, my life to infection. Or to the slavers who own me now.

Try not to think.

A pair of men come for me some hours later. They shove a sack over my head and tell me if I make a sound, they will kill me. They hold my arms, and I am grateful beyond words that they do not bind my hands together again. My left hand throbs, the pain of my severed finger the only thing I can focus on, far greater than the old, familiar pain of my knife cut.

I go numbly where the men take me, down a hall and then through a door to the outside, where I can hear the faint splash of water. I stumble down a set of stairs with them, and then I'm shoved roughly into what must be a boat. It rocks crazily and I give a little gasping cry and then clamp down on my lips, pressing my hands to my breast as if I could protect myself from the men.

"Shut up," one of the men says tiredly.

I sit silently, waiting as they row us across the river and on to our destination: a ship, I would guess, judging from the slap of water against its sides and the rope ladder shoved into my hands to climb aboard. They send me up, calling once to the men at the top who answer them. I go slowly, feeling for each rung with my good hand, hooking my wounded hand around the ropes, terrified that I will start bleeding again, that I will fall. With the sack over my head, each step is an exercise of trust in a fractured world.

Then a hand closes on my arm, yanking me up and over a railing. I huddle there, listening as one of my escorts finishes climbing up behind me. My wounded hand is wet again.

"She's bleeding," a man says, his voice just above my head. "He cut her up. You might need to stitch it or the like."

"We don't keep healers on board for this sort," a second voice answers, a few feet away. "What do you think we are? Agents of mercy?"

"Well, cauterize it then. Orders are she's to be sold alive and unharmed."

"Unharmed, and you all cut off her finger?"

"I don't give the orders," the first man snaps. "Just keep her alive."

"We'll get her below for now. The captain can decide what he wants to do about it later."

My teeth are chattering again, and I want desperately to see where I am, but I don't dare pull off the sack. The second man grabs my left wrist, jarring my wounded hand and sending shafts of pain up my arm. He swears as I choke on a scream, trying desperately to swallow it down. Don't let them hurt me more. *Please.* He transfers his grip to my right arm, his hand wet and slick against my skin, no doubt with my own blood.

Somehow, I make it down to the hold, stumbling forward to be shoved against a wall.

"Head down," the man says, his hand pushing on the top of my head. I thump to my knees, shuffle forward as he half shoves, half guides me through a low doorway.

"This one's special, you hear that, brats?" he says from behind me, his voice no higher than my own head. He must be bending down, speaking through the doorway. "Touch her, and the captain will have your skins."

A faint rustle from straight ahead, and that is all.

"Good," the sailor says, and the door creaks shut.

I reach up and take off the sack, but with the door closed, the darkness is absolute. I sway where I crouch, then sit down hard. "Who's there?" My voice comes out rough and low, hoarse from screaming.

No one answers.

I wait until it's clear no one will. Then I pull myself to the side, moving slowly, until I reach a wall. There's no one here, though the faint rustles suggest someone shifted out of my way. I can't find the energy to think about it through the pain. Instead, I lean against the wall and let the darkness take me.

Sometimes, when you think things are finished, they are only just beginning.

I sit with my hands cradled in my lap: one still relatively whole, the other with a half-healed cut curved around my arm and my little finger shorn away.

I can hear a child whimpering, somewhere near me in the

darkness, but I do not know how to reach for them without crying out in pain. I do not know that they want to be held. So I sit, listening to the rhythmic splash of oars cutting through the water, propelling the boat downriver, and feel all that I have done wrong bear down on me.

I am well and truly caught. And Red Hawk will be delivered my ring, and Bren will see it, and believe it from the Scholar, and I cannot tell him otherwise. Will there be more deaths because of me? A street war? I can't imagine it, can't see a thief lord I've never met deciding to launch a killing spree because of a bloodied ring. Even if I had met him, there's no reason. Red Hawk is strategic, that much I know. But he likely also has his honor, and if the pendant I bear means that much . . .

I shudder and hunch in on myself. There is nothing I can do, not about Red Hawk, not about Bardok or Garrin, not about the snatchers, not even really about myself. Stupid of me to think—

My thoughts jolt to a halt. I stare into the dark, and all I can think is *no*. I am *not* stupid. I've made mistakes, but I've been up against men whose utter lack of morals is almost inconceivable. They abducted me, hammered me into a crate and transported me like so much fabric, cut away pieces of me, took from me my safety and dignity and *body*.

My breath feels like fire in my lungs. I am suddenly and deeply furious, enraged that my body should have been violated so. I have never loved it enough; I realize that now, in the face of having it so abused. My plain features and strong build are *mine*, just as my turned foot is, born with me and part of who I am. And only now, as I cradle my mangled hand in my lap, do I understand this.

Damn Bardok for his laughter, and his blades, and his easy violence and uncaring selfishness, chopping off my finger as if he had the right to take what he wished and could throw away the rest. As if such violence was nothing, was only to be expected, because I am a woman and his captive, and there is no law here, not in the prison of his home nor in the underbelly of this ship.

But I will not go willingly into this nightmare of his making. I will not accept the darkness and violence of the thieves and sailors, the slavers who surround me. I will learn every aspect of what they do, and then I will undo them, destroy them, whether the law aids me or not.

This I promise myself, in the darkness of the hold.

I feel a grin touch my lips. It is like no smile I have ever worn before, violent and dangerous and hopeful, as sharp as the knife I carry with me. Just as I still wear Niya's sash. I am not alone, even here, and I will not be broken, cut to pieces, and sold to the highest bidder.

Something rustles close beside me. I turn toward the sound. No, I am not alone at all.

"Who is here?" I ask.

I hear the faint sound of children shifting, listening.

"My name is Rae, and I intend to escape." It is a promise as dark and deep as the river we travel, and as unstoppable. "Tell me who you are."

ACKNOWLEDGMENTS

I have been trying to write this book for almost ten years. I know this because, when my eldest daughter was six months old and we traveled to Morocco to visit my brother, I began my first draft in a composition book. I wrote while pumping milk in a dark room beside her crib while she napped. It was NaNoWriMo, and if I couldn't handwrite fifty thousand words, at least I could make a strong effort. My daughter's now ten, and Rae's story has stayed with me over the years as I've drafted it and set it aside and then drafted it again. I am so grateful to be able to share it with you now, dear reader, even if it has morphed into a duology and forced me to do the one thing I promised myself I would never do: write a cliffhanger. Sorry about that! ;)

Many thanks to my agent, Emmanuelle Morgen, for continuing to champion me and my stories, for helping me to take a breath and not worry about what's beyond me, and for always, always having my back. You are wonderful, and I am so grateful to be working with you and have your friendship.

I am deeply grateful to my wonderful editor at HarperTeen, Alice Jerman, for your ongoing awesomeness, for fighting for those extra days to edit when I most need them, for your keen eye and exceptional insight. This story would not be what it is without you. I am so thankful to be working with you! Thanks also to the HarperTeen team for all your work to polish and promote this story, including Jessica Berg, Clare Vaughn, Gillian Wise, and my publicist Lauren Levite. Many thanks to my wonderful UK editor, Fliss Alexander, as well as Maurice Lyon for all your help through Fliss's absence, and the entire marketing team at Hot Key Books, especially Isobel Taylor and Molly Holt. You are all so much appreciated! And of course, to Jenny Zemanek, graphic designer extraordinaire: I cannot imagine a more perfect cover. Thank you.

I owe a debt of gratitude to my many, many beta readers who waded through drafts in various stages of disrepair. My thanks to Shy Eager, W. R. Gingell, Nam Heui Kim, Tia Michaud, and Charlotte Michel for reading that relatively early draft that I didn't know what to do with. Thanks to Anela Deen, Anne Hillman, A. C. Spahn, and Janelle White for working through a subsequent still-somewhat-disastrous draft, and to my husband, Anas, Shy Eager (again!), Eli Hinze, A. C. Spahn (also again!), and Stacy Crawford, for providing detailed feedback at the eleventh hour. Many thanks to Laurel Garver for her incredible eye to detail to help give this story an additional shine.

At its heart, this story is both about Rae and about slavery. Rather than depicting historic experiences of slavery, I've modeled the slavery you see in this book around modern-day human trafficking. I am grateful to the Underground Railroad Freedom

Center's Modern-Day Slavery exhibit for opening my eyes to what this looks like. The examples of slavery you've read here were all taken from cases of modern-day slavery still happening in the world now. For more information on human trafficking, you can visit the Polaris Project online.

My family has, of course, continued to be my most important support crew. Thanks to my parents, my husband, my two wonderful girls, and my brother and sister-in-law, for their kindness, support, and provision of hot meals when I don't manage to make them myself. You are the best.

In mentioning support crews, I would be remiss if I didn't acknowledge the amazing supporters of *Thorn*, *The Sunbolt Chronicles*, and now *The Theft of Sunlight*. Readers, reviewers, bloggers, bookstagrammers, and more—thank you all. I am so grateful to you for helping to share my stories with your circles, and giving them wings to fly. You rock.

As those who follow me may know, I am extremely challenged by naming characters, and often resort to asking for help on my Facebook author page. Many thanks to Anela Deen for naming Seri, and Marisa Stroud for Siyela, as well as all the brainstorming that helped me to get to Ramella's name. I'm frankly rather shocked I didn't need more help, but that's possibly because most of my characters were taken care of in *Thorn*. Phew.

And finally, I am grateful to God, for all that He has given me, in my writing and in my life.